The Best
AMERICAN
SCIENCE
FICTION &
FANTASY
2023

D1362172

GUEST EDITORS OF
THE BEST AMERICAN SCIENCE FICTION AND FANTASY

2015 JOE HILL
2016 KAREN JOY FOWLER
2017 CHARLES YU
2018 N. K. JEMISIN
2019 CARMEN MARIA MACHADO
2020 DIANA GABALDON
2021 VERONICA ROTH
2022 REBECCA ROANHORSE
2023 R. F. KUANG

The Best AMERICAN SCIENCE FICTION & FANTASY™ 2023

Edited and with an Introduction
by R. F. KUANG

JOHN JOSEPH ADAMS, *Series Editor*

MARINER BOOKS
New York   Boston

THE BEST AMERICAN SCIENCE FICTION AND FANTASY™. Copyright © 2023 by HarperCollins Publishers LLC. Introduction copyright © 2023 by R. F. Kuang. The Best American Series® is a registered trademark of HarperCollins Publishers LLC. *The Best American Science Fiction and Fantasy*™ is a trademark of HarperCollins Publishers LLC. All rights reserved. Printed in the United States of America. No part of this book may be used or reproduced in any manner whatsoever without written permission except in the case of brief quotations embodied in critical articles and reviews. HarperCollins Publishers LLC is not authorized to grant permission for further uses of copyrighted selections reprinted in this book without the permission of their owners. Permission must be obtained from the individual copyright owners as identified herein. For information, address HarperCollins Publishers, 195 Broadway, New York, NY 10007. HarperCollins books may be purchased for educational, business, or sales promotional use. For information, please email the Special Markets Department at SPsales@harpercollins.com.

FIRST EDITION

ISSN 2573-0797

ISBN 978-0-06-331574-7

23 24 25 26 27 LBC 6 5 4 3 2

"Three Mothers Mountain" by Nathan Ballingrud. First published in *Screams from the Dark: 29 Tales of Monsters and the Monstrous*, edited by Ellen Datlow. Copyright © 2022 by Nathan Ballingrud. Reprinted by permission of the author.

"Folk Hero Motifs in Tales Told by the Dead" by KT Bryski. First published in *Strange Horizons*, October 31, 2022. Copyright 2022 © by KT Bryski. Reprinted by permission of the author.

"There Are No Monsters on Rancho Buenavista" by Isabel Cañas. First published in *Nightmare*, Issue 117, June 2022. Copyright © 2022 by Isabel Cañas. Reprinted by permission of the author.

"In the Beginning of Me, I Was a Bird" by Maria Dong. First published in *Lightspeed*, Issue 140, January 2022. Copyright © 2022 by Maria Dong. Reprinted by permission of the author.

"Pre-Simulation Consultation XF007867" by Kim Fu. First published in *Lesser Known Monsters of the 21st Century*, Issue 14, March 28, 2022. Copyright © 2022 by Kim Fu. Reprinted by permission of Coach House Books and Tin House Books.

"Pellargonia: A Letter to the Journal of Imaginary Anthropology" by Theodora Goss. First published in *Lost Worlds & Mythological Kingdoms*. Copyright © 2022 by Theodora Goss. Reprinted by permission of the author.

"The Six Deaths of the Saint" by Alix E. Harrow. First published in *Into Shadow*. Copyright © 2022 by Alix E. Harrow. Reprinted by permission of the author.

"Murder by Pixel: Crime and Responsibility in the Digital Darkness" by S. L. Huang. First published in *Clarkesworld*, Issue 195, December 2022. Copyright © 2022 by S. L. Huang, LLC. Reprinted by permission of the author.

"Men, Women, and Chainsaws" by Stephen Graham Jones. First published in *Tor.com*, May 11, 2022. Copyright © 2022 by Stephen Graham Jones. Reprinted by permission of the author.

"Air to Shape Lungs" by Shingai Njeri Kagunda. First published in *Africa Risen*. Copyright © 2022 by Shingai Njeri Kagunda. Reprinted by permission of the author.

"Termination Stories for the Cyberpunk Dystopia Protagonist" by Isabel J. Kim. First published in *Clarkesworld*, Issue 190, July 2022. Copyright © 2022 by Isabel J. Kim. Reprinted by permission of the author.

"Rabbit Test" by Samantha Mills. First published in *Uncanny*, Issue 49, November 1, 2022. Copyright © 2022 by Samantha Mills. Reprinted by permission of the author.

"The CRISPR Cookbook: A Guide to Biohacking Your Own Abortion in a Post-Roe World" by MKRNYILGLD. First published in *Lightspeed*, Issue 148, September 2022. Copyright © 2022 by MKRNYILGLD. Reprinted by permission of the author.

"Cumulative Ethical Guidelines for Mid-Range Interstellar Storytellers" by Malka Older. First published in *Bridge to Elsewhere*. Copyright © 2022 by Malka Older. Reprinted by permission of the author.

"Sparrows" by Susan Palwick. First published in *Asimov's*, September/October 2022. Copyright © 2022 by Susan Palwick. Reprinted by permission of the author.

"White Water, Blue Ocean" by Linda Raquel Nieves Pérez. First published in *Reclaim the Stars*. Copyright © 2022 by Linda Raquel Nieves Pérez. Reprinted by permission of the author.

"Readings in the Slantwise Sciences" by Sofia Samatar. First published in *Conjunctions*: 79, Fall 2022. Copyright © 2022 by Sofia Samatar. Reprinted by permission of the author.

"Beginnings" by Kristina Ten. First published in *Fantasy*, Issue 78, April 2022. Copyright © 2022 by Kristina Ten. Reprinted by permission of the author.

"The Difference Between Love and Time" by Catherynne M. Valente. First published in *Someone in Time: Tales of Time-Crossed Romance*, November 23, 2022. Copyright © 2022 by Catherynne M. Valente. Reprinted by permission of the author.

"The Odyssey Problem" by Chris Willrich. First published in *Clarkesworld*, Issue 189, June 2022. Copyright © 2022 by Chris Willrich. Reprinted by permission of the author.

Contents

Foreword   ix

Introduction   xvii

SOFIA SAMATAR. *Readings in the Slantwise Sciences*   1
   from *Conjunctions*

SHINGAI NJERI KAGUNDA. *Air to Shape Lungs*   9
   from *Africa Risen*

KRISTINA TEN. *Beginnings*   12
   from *Fantasy*

SUSAN PALWICK. *Sparrows*   16
   from *Asimov's*

ALIX E. HARROW. *The Six Deaths of the Saint*   23
   from *Into Shadow*

ISABEL J. KIM. *Termination Stories for the Cyberpunk Dystopia Protagonist*   43
   from *Clarkesworld*

STEPHEN GRAHAM JONES. *Men, Women, and Chainsaws*   58
   from *Tor.com*

SAMANTHA MILLS. *Rabbit Test*   80
   from *Uncanny*

ISABEL CAÑAS. *There Are No Monsters on Rancho Buenavista*   99
   from *Nightmare*

S. L. HUANG. *Murder by Pixel: Crime and Responsibility in the Digital Darkness* 102
    from *Clarkesworld*

LINDA RAQUEL NIEVES PÉREZ. *White Water, Blue Ocean* 125
    from *Reclaim the Stars*

MKRNYILGLD. *The CRISPR Cookbook: A Guide to Biohacking Your Own Abortion in a Post-Roe World* 139
    from *Lightspeed*

NATHAN BALLINGRUD. *Three Mothers Mountain* 146
    from *Screams from the Dark: 29 Tales of Monsters and the Monstrous*

CHRIS WILLRICH. *The Odyssey Problem* 165
    from *Clarkesworld*

THEODORA GOSS. *Pellargonia: A Letter to the Journal of Imaginary Anthropology* 180
    from *Lost Worlds & Mythological Kingdoms*

KIM FU. *Pre-Simulation Consultation XF007867* 198
    from *Lesser Known Monsters of the 21st Century*

MARIA DONG. *In the Beginning of Me, I Was a Bird* 208
    from *Lightspeed*

CATHERYNNE M. VALENTE. *The Difference Between Love and Time* 222
    from *Someone in Time: Tales of Time-Crossed Romance*

KT BRYSKI. *Folk Hero Motifs in Tales Told by the Dead* 247
    from *Strange Horizons*

MALKA OLDER. *Cumulative Ethical Guidelines for Mid-Range Interstellar Storytellers* 259
    from *Bridge to Elsewhere*

Contributors' Notes 271

Other Notable Science Fiction and Fantasy Stories of 2022 285

Foreword

WELCOME TO YEAR nine of *Best American Science Fiction and Fantasy*! This volume presents the best science fiction and fantasy (SF/F) short stories published during the 2022 calendar year as selected by myself and guest editor R. F. Kuang.

About This Year's Guest Editor

Number-one *New York Times* bestselling author R. F. (Rebecca) Kuang first exploded onto the science fiction and fantasy scene in 2018 with the publication of her debut novel, *The Poppy War*. Following its publication, Rebecca won the trifecta of genre awards presented to debuting novelists: the Compton Crook Award, the Crawford Award, and the Astounding Award for Best New Writer. *The Poppy War* was followed by two sequels, *The Dragon Republic* and *The Burning God*, and the books in that trilogy have been nominated for the Hugo, Nebula, World Fantasy, Locus, British Fantasy, and Ignyte awards—and included on *TIME*'s list of the 100 Best Fantasy Books of All Time. Rebecca's latest novel—*Babel: Or the Necessity of Violence: An Arcane History of the Oxford Translators' Revolution*—won the Nebula Award, the British Book Award, and the Locus Award.[1]

Rebecca was born in Guangzhou, China, but moved to the United States with her family as a child. She graduated from Georgetown University, then received a Marshall Scholarship and went on to attend Cambridge University, where she earned a master's of philosophy (MPhil) in Chinese Studies. She then attended Oxford University, where she graduated with a master's of science (MSc) in Contemporary Chinese Studies. Currently, she's at Yale University, pursuing a PhD in East Asian Languages and Literatures. On the genre side of things, she's also a graduate of the Odyssey Writing Workshop and the Center for the Study of Science Fiction novel writing workshop.

She's published two short stories: "The Nine Curves River" in the 2020 anthology *The Book of Dragons*; and "Against All Odds," a *Star Wars* story in *From a Certain Point of View: The Empire Strikes Back*; additionally, she published "The Drowning Faith," a collection of stories set in the world of the Poppy War trilogy, which were published as part of *The Burning God*. Recently, she's also branched out into translating stories from Chinese into English, with her translations appearing in *Clarkesworld* and *Lightspeed*.

Selection Criteria and Process

The stories chosen for this anthology were originally published between January 1, 2022 and December 31, 2022. The technical criteria for consideration were (1) original publication in a nationally distributed North American publication (i.e., periodicals, collections, or anthologies, in print, online, or e-book); (2) publication in English by writers who are North American, or who have made North America their home; (3) publication as text (audiobook, podcast, dramatized, interactive, and other forms of fiction are not considered); (4) original publication as short fiction (excerpts of novels are not knowingly considered); (5) story length of 17,499 words or less; (6) at least loosely categorized as science fiction or fantasy; (7) publication by someone other than the author (i.e., self-published works are not eligible); and (8) publication as an original work of the author (i.e., not part of a media tie-in/licensed fiction program).

As series editor, I attempted to read everything I could find that meets the above selection criteria. After doing all of my reading, I created a list of what I felt were the top eighty stories (forty science fiction and forty fantasy) published in the genre. Those eighty stories—hereinafter referred to as the "Top 80"—were sent to the guest editor, who read them and then chose the best twenty (ten science fiction, ten fantasy) for inclusion in the anthology. The guest editor reads all of the stories anonymously—with no bylines attached to them, nor any information about where the story originally appeared.

The guest editor's top twenty selections appear in this volume; the remaining sixty stories that did not make it into the anthology are listed in the back of this book as "Other Notable Stories of 2022."

2022 *Selections*

Ten authors selected for this volume previously appeared in *Best American Science Fiction and Fantasy (BASFF)*: Sofia Samatar (4 times), Catherynne M. Valente (3), Nathan Ballingrud (1), KT Bryski (1), Maria Dong (1), Theodora Goss (1), S. L. Huang (1), Stephen Graham Jones (1), Shingai Njeri Kagunda (1), and Susan Palwick (1). Thus, Isabel Cañas, Kim Fu, Alix E. Harrow, Isabel J. Kim, Samantha Mills, MKRNYILGLD, Malka Older, Linda Raquel Nieves Pérez, Kristina Ten, and Chris Willrich are all appearing in *BASFF* for the first time.

The selections were chosen from seventeen different publications: *Clarkesworld* (3), *Lightspeed* (2), and the following all had one selection each: *Africa Risen* edited by Sheree Renée Thomas, Oghenechovwe Donald Ekpeki, and Zelda Knight; *Asimov's; Bridge to Elsewhere* edited by Alana Joli Abbott and Julia Rios*; Conjunctions; Fantasy; Into Shadow* presented by Amazon Original Stories; *Lesser Known Monsters of the 21st Century* by Kim Fu*; Lost Worlds & Mythological Kingdoms* edited by John Joseph Adams; *Nightmare; Reclaim the Stars* edited by Zoraida Córdova; *Screams from the Dark* edited by Ellen Datlow; *Someone in Time* edited by Jonathan Strahan; *Strange Horizons; Tor.com;* and *Uncanny*.

Several of our selections this year were winners of (or finalists for) some of the field's awards[2]: "In the Beginning of Me, I Was a Bird" by Maria Dong (Sturgeon finalist); "Pre-Simulation Consultation XF007867" by Kim Fu (Shirley Jackson winner); "The Six Deaths of the Saint" by Alix E. Harrow (Locus finalist); "Murder by Pixel: Crime and Responsibility in the Digital Darkness" by

S. L. Huang (Ignyte, Nebula, and Hugo finalist); "Men, Women, and Chainsaws" by Stephen Graham Jones (Ignyte finalist); "Rabbit Test" by Samantha Mills (Nebula and Locus winner, Hugo and Sturgeon finalist); "Beginnings" by Kristina Ten (Locus finalist); and "The Difference Between Love and Time" by Catherynne M. Valente (Hugo and Locus finalist).

2022 Top 80

In order to select the Top 80 stories published in the SF/F genres in 2022, I considered several thousand stories from a wide array of anthologies, collections, and magazines. As always, because of the vast wealth of excellent material being published every year, it was, in many cases, difficult to decide which stories would make it into my Top 80 stories that I would present to the guest editor; the difference between a story that made the cut and a story that *got* cut was sometimes razor thin. Outside of my Top 80, I had around sixty-five additional stories that were in the running.

The Top 80 this year were drawn from thirty-two different publications: seventeen periodicals, eleven anthologies, and three single-author collections.

Isabel J. Kim had the most stories in the Top 80 this year, with a whopping four; several authors were tied for second-most, with two each: Alix E. Harrow, Hannah Yang, Kim Fu, Kristina Ten, P H Lee, Stephen Graham Jones, Suzan Palumbo, and Yoon Ha Lee. Overall, sixty-nine different authors are represented in the Top 80.

In addition to the award-winning/nominated stories in our TOC this year, several Notable Stories were recognized for various awards[3] as well: "Slow Communication" by Dominique Dickey (Sturgeon finalist); "Two Hands, Wrapped in Gold" by S. B. Divya (Locus and Nebula finalist); "If We Make It Through This Alive" by A. T. Greenblatt (Sturgeon finalist); "Give Me English" by Ai Jiang (Locus and Nebula finalist); "Bonsai Starships" by Yoon Ha Lee (Sturgeon finalist); "The Sadness Box" by Suzanne Palmer (Locus finalist); "Douen" by Suzan Palumbo (Aurora and Nebula finalist); and "D.I.Y" by John Wiswell (Hugo, Nebula, and Locus finalist).

Anthologies

The following anthologies had stories in our Top 80 this year: *Africa Risen** edited by Sheree Renée Thomas, Oghenechovwe Donald Ekpeki, and Zelda Knight (4); *Lost Worlds & Mythological Kingdoms** edited by John Joseph Adams (3); *Bridge to Elsewhere** edited by Alana Joli Abbott and Julia Rios (2), *Into Shadow** presented by Amazon Original Stories (2), *Reclaim the Stars** edited by Zoraida Córdova (2), *Trespass* presented by Amazon Original Stories (2), and the following all had one each: *Our Shadows Have Claws* edited by Yamile Saied Méndez and Amparo Ortiz; *Screams from the Dark** edited by Ellen Datlow; *Someone in Time** edited by Jonathan Strahan; and *Trouble the Waters* edited by Sheree Renée Thomas, Pan Morigan, and Troy L. Wiggins; *Xenocultivars* edited by Isabela Oliveira and Jed Sabin. Anthologies marked with an asterisk had stories selected for inclusion in this volume.

Other anthologies that published fine work in 2022 that didn't manage to crack the Top 80 include: *Dark Stars* edited by John F.D. Taff; *Death in the Mouth* edited by Sloane Leong and Cassie Hart; *Imagine 2200: Climate Fiction for Future Ancestors* presented by Fix; *The Memory Librarian* by Janelle Monáe[4]; *Other Terrors* edited by Vince A. Liaguno and Rena Mason; *Small Odysseys* edited by Hannah Tinti; and *Tomorrow's Parties* edited by Jonathan Strahan.

There were two anthologies I took note of that contained only reprints (and thus were ineligible) but I wanted to highlight anyway: *The Future is Female! Volume 2* edited by Lisa Yaszek and *Terraform: Watch/Worlds/Burn* edited by Brian Merchant.

Collections

Three collections had stories in the Top 80 this year: *Lesser Known Monsters of the 21st Century* by Kim Fu (2); *Bliss Montage* by Ling Ma (1); and *The Nectar of Nightmares* by Craig Laurance Gidney (1). The Fu collection had a story included in this volume.

Naturally, many other collections were published in 2022. All of the following were released in 2022 and meet the broad "American" focus of this book, but some of them contained only reprints (and thus were ineligible for inclusion). I'm including them all here anyway as part of my overview of the year: *All the Hometowns You Can't Stay Away From* by Izzy Wasserstein; *All the Wrong Ideas* by Jeremy Robert Johnson; *The Adventurists and Other Stories* by Richard Butner; *The Best of Lucius Shepard, Vol. 2* by Lucius Shepard; *Boys, Beasts, & Men* by Sam J. Miller; *Breakable Things* by Cassandra Khaw; *Corpsemouth and Other Autobiographies* by John Langan; *Dark Breakers* by C.S.E. Cooney; *The Dark Ride* by John Kessel; *Future Artifacts* by Kameron Hurley; *Geometries of Belonging* by R. B. Lemberg; *Holy Terror* by Cherie Priest; *Liberation Day* by George Saunders; *Memory's Legion* by James S.A. Corey; *Night Shift* by Eileen Gunn; *Our Fruiting Bodies* by Nisi Shawl; *Out There* by Kate Folk; *Return to Glory* by Jack McDevitt; *Spontaneous Human Combustion* by Richard Thomas; *Stealing God and Other Stories* by Bruce McAllister; *Utopias of the Third Kind* by Vandana Singh; *We Won't Be Here Tomorrow and Other Stories* by Margaret Killjoy; *Where You Linger* by Bonnie Jo Stufflebeam; and *You Fed Us to the Roses* by Carlie St. George.

Periodicals

Lightspeed had the most stories in the Top 80 (13); followed by *Clarkesworld* (9); *The Magazine of Fantasy & Science Fiction* (5); *Asimov's* (4); *Tor.com* (4); *Fantasy* (3); *Uncanny* (3); *The Deadlands* (2); *FIYAH* (2); *Nightmare* (2); *Strange Horizons* (2); *Sunday Morning Transport* (2); and the following all had one each: *Beneath Ceaseless Skies*; *Conjunctions*; *Dark Matter*; *The Dark*; and *Future Tense*.

Appearing in the Top 80 for the first time are *The Deadlands* and 2022 debut periodical *Sunday Morning Transport*, which burst out of the gate with aplomb, publishing a lot of wonderful stories beyond the two that made the Top 80.

The following magazines didn't have any material in the Top 80 this year, but did publish stories that I had under serious consideration: *Analog*; *Apex Magazine*; *Baffling Magazine*; *Diabolical Plots*; *Escape Pod*; *Fairy Tale Review*; *khōréō*; *PodCastle*; and *Terraform*.

Two notable periodicals emerged in 2022: *ZNB Presents* (from the anthology-focused small press Zombies Need Brains) and *Sunday Morning Transport*; the latter publication had a very strong debut year—not only did it provide two of our Notable Stories, but there were several stories from this magazine on my extended longlist vying for inclusion.

Magazines *Constelación* and *Fireside* both closed their doors for good in 2022. *Mermaids Monthly* did not release any new content in 2022 and so is either presumed dead or at least on an indefinite hiatus.

One publisher-oriented bit of news that shook the periodicals field this year was the announcement that a Certain Online Bookstore named after a rainforest decided to discontinue their e-book periodicals program. Though there were relatively few magazine deaths this year, I fear that next year there will be many more to report, as this decision will likely have catastrophic consequences to the bottom lines of many of the magazines that frequently produce work that is selected for inclusion in this volume. It is not hyperbole to say that this single move could be an extinction-level event for the entire SF/F/H short fiction field as it exists today, so magazines need your support more than ever. If you can, subscribe (even if they offer content for free), post reviews, and spread the word on social media and by word of mouth.

Acknowledgments

Once again, I begin my acknowledgments by shouting out (and heaping praise upon) the contributions of my assistant series editor, Christopher Cevasco. Thanks, as always, for all your diligent and hard work, my friend! I'd also like to thank in-house *BASFF*-wrangler Nicole Angeloro and David Steffen of The Submission Grinder writer's market database. And last but not least, I offer my extreme appreciation to all of the authors and editors who tirelessly toil to bring us this wealth of short fiction to choose from every year—and to all of the critics and readers who highlight good works and help more people find them.

Submissions for Next Year's Volume

Editors, writers, and publishers who would like their work considered for next year's edition (the best of 2023), please visit johnjosephadams.com/best-american for instructions on how to submit material for consideration.

—JOHN JOSEPH ADAMS

Notes

1. At the time of this writing, some genre awards—such as the World Fantasy Award—had not yet announced their lists of finalists, and the final results of some of the awards mentioned above won't be known until after this text is locked for production, but will be known by the time the book is published.
2. See note 1 above.
3. See note 1 above.
4. This book is noted as being *by* rather than *edited by* Monáe despite the fact that I am listing it here as an anthology, but that is because it occupies some interstitial space between anthology and collection. Each story is by Monáe in collaboration with another author and so seems to meet the criteria for both; however, this is not unprecedented in literature—nor indeed even in the genre (Harlan Ellison's *Partners in Wonder*, for instance)—and though such books feel more to me like a *collection*, historically said books were considered an *anthology*, and so I must grudgingly agree.

Introduction

Committing to the Bit

A FEW WEEKS ago I was watching the first John Wick film with my fiancé when I turned to him and declared, "I think I've come up with a golden axiom of storytelling."

"Alright, go." He paused the film, humoring me. We do this a lot—come up with "golden axioms" whenever we are watching things undeniably awesome. These axioms are usually things like "always bring the villain from an earlier installment back as an ally in the sequel," or "if there is a blender in a scene, someone is about to get blended." They are almost never generalizable axioms, and they are certainly not axioms I could teach in a creative writing workshop, but oh, do we have fun.

I gestured at the screen where John Wick's nemesis was singing a Russian lullaby about Baba Yaga, preparing for John Wick to come slaughter him and his men because his son killed John Wick's dog because John Wick wouldn't give him his car. ("John wasn't the boogeyman. He was the one you sent to kill the fucking boogeyman.") This is not the strangest thing to happen in the John Wick universe, only the first thing.

"Whatever you do, whatever storytelling choices you make, *commit*," I said.

"Nice one," said my fiancé.

"Like, establish your rules and go for it," I said. "John Wick is sad about his dog? Fine. He's going to kill this man's entire family now? Fine. You can't conduct business in the Continental? Let's go!"

"Let's keep watching," said my fiancé, reaching for the remote.

No matter the medium, I have a deep fondness for camp, silliness, and everything that is heavily stylized. I love the David Bowie dance sequence in *A Knight's Tale* and the dippy verve of Baz Luhrmann's *The Great Gatsby* and *Moulin Rouge*. I love the wild energy and multiple cuts of the same motion in Andrew Lau and Alan Mak's *Infernal Affairs*. I love Sam Raimi's Spider-Man movies; voiceover monologues and ridiculous dialogue and sexy Doc Ock and all. I even adore the third movie and every second of the emo chair dance. I love genres that lean fully into what they are, trope accusations be damned. I love reading hard-boiled detective novels with pipe-smoking assholes, spy thrillers with dangerous dames, and decades-old comic books littered with phrases like "Butter my beanpole!" and "Gee willickers!"

And I've always been convinced that these stories were doing something *right* about storytelling, that we don't love these stories just because they're ridiculous and fun. In my rambling about John Wick, I found the answer: they commit. These stories are perceived as absurd, but within the frame of the narrative, they take themselves completely seriously. We follow every word of Peter Parker's tortured voice-over monologues because he *is* tortured. We care about the intricate rules of the criminal underworld to which John Wick belongs because John Wick and every other assassin around him are fully committed to these rules. When those rules are broken, the consequences are terrible. We believe in the love story of *Moulin Rouge* because its characters never stop believing in love. These stories are ridiculous, their suspense of disbelief is hanging by the thread, but never do they let the curtain drop.

In an entertainment milieu saturated by the wisecracking self-deprecation of Kevin Feige's MCU, I find this sincerity charming. I'm tired of leather-clad superheroes winking to declare, "Don't worry—I'm not taking this too seriously." I'd like my protagonists to take themselves more seriously. Everyone is so ironic these days, as if irony substitutes for wit. Meanwhile sincerity doesn't have to mean naivete, or mindless reproduction of stale tropes. Sometimes it just means committing to a singular, seamless vision. So I find more and more these days that I'm reading for commitment.

I want my authors to believe fully in the worlds they create, and I want their belief to generate my belief in turn.

But how do you foster that belief in a matter of minutes? Most short stories range between 1,500 to 7,500 words. I've spent most of my career working on novels hovering around six hundred pages, so I respect how hard it is to construct a compelling conceit in a fraction of that time. You can't dither around in dream sequences, prologues, or slow builds. Compared to novels, short stories have to accomplish a nearly impossible magic trick: to introduce a world often much stranger than our own and make you care about it in a matter of pages. (Indeed, Isabel Cañas's "There Are No Monsters on Rancho Buenavista" does this in only six hundred words!)

The works in this anthology pull the trick off beautifully; they commit to the bit. I chose a lot of these stories despite their sheer absurdity. I chose them *because* of their absurdity. I'm easily charmed these days by a premise that makes me mutter, "What the fuck?" Stephen Graham Jones's "Men, Women, and Chainsaws" tosses a grab bag of horror tropes into a story in which a woman feeds her nosebleed blood to a killer car. Catherynne M. Valente's "The Difference Between Love and Time" opens with the declaration that the space-time continuum has severe social anxiety, a weakness for leather jackets, and is left-handed. I'm here for it.

I read a lot of debut novels in consideration for blurbs, and by now I'm familiar with common debut flaws. This is not a knock against debut novelists—we were all debut novelists at some point, and the mistakes in *The Poppy War* are too many to count. (As I admit this, I let out a breath I didn't know I was holding.) One thing I spot largely in debut fantasy novels is the author's lack of trust in the world and characters they have introduced. They overexplain and make excuses: "Here there are dragons—no, trust me, there *really are dragons*, despite everything you might have been told. And they have scales and wings and everything!" They apologize constantly for the ways in which they warp space and time ("If you don't believe in magic, that's okay; I didn't either for the longest time."). They apologize for their characters' motivations if they are the slightest bit complex; their protagonists explain the logic behind their decisions over and over again, as if reassuring themselves and the readers that all of this makes sense: "You're the bad guy? And I'm the good guy?

Okay—good. Glad we understand each other." There is such an obsession with *making sense.* At points these authors sound like amusement park employees, sprinting frantically just a few steps ahead of visitors to make sure no electric wiring is peeking out from behind the decor. It's never a deal-breaker for me, but it does throw me out of the story. You never want to stay on a roller coaster if the ride operator keeps nervously checking the seat belts.

I get it; growing past this phase takes skill. It takes a while to develop a vision so clear and vivid that you feel less like you're spinning a tale and more like you're simply relaying memories and observations from a parallel universe. It takes a while to develop characters so complex and well-rounded that their strangest decisions and pettiest traits read like the natural choices of anyone with a beating heart.

The stories in this anthology trust their worlds and characters completely, and because we can sense the author's confidence, we are willing to trust them in return.

Part of this magic trick is voice. The best advice I ever got about writing secondary world fantasy was to write not from the point of view of someone encountering a world for the first time, but of someone who has lived in this world all their life. (At the Odyssey writing workshop, this was known as the "As you know, Bob" rule.) What do they notice? What is new to them? What is so natural to them that it hardly warrants comment? What are the bizarre pronouncements that only they could make? So I was charmed immediately by the brio of KT Bryski's "Folk Hero Motifs in Tales Told by the Dead," whose narrator starts chatting you up immediately about the great Skullbone, bravest among corpses, who jumps fearlessly into the abyss at the end of the land of the dead. Meanwhile, Kristina Ten's "Beginnings" has one of the strongest opening paragraphs I've ever read: "In the beginning, June and Nat are best friends. June is not yet a swarm of honeybees and Nat is not yet a cloud of horseflies, and the king hasn't yet decided that separating them into parts like this . . . is the only surefire way to strip them of what they really are."

Another part of this magic trick is respect for the reader. Sometimes this means letting them put the pieces together on their own: Alix Harrow's "The Six Deaths of the Saint" involves a devastating puzzle of identity. When the *you* turns into an *I* and you discover who has been pulling the strings all along, your heart pangs. And sometimes it's about not overplaying your expository hand, but letting the reader infer the ending from small changes in the narrative register: Kim Fu's "Pre-Simulation Consultation XF007867" achieves a deft tonal switch that had me smiling at the end.

And frankly, the most important part of this magic trick is just a willingness to get weird. There are stories in this anthology about women who can't lie or fall in love (Linda Raquel Nieves Pérez's "White Water, Blue Ocean"), undead fathers feeding their children ghost preserves (Nathan Ballingrud's "Three Mothers Mountain"), and souls chasing one another through animal incarnations (Maria Dong's "In the Beginning of Me, I Was a Bird.") Reading for this anthology has been the best reminder that this genre is still brimming with the bizarre.

Crucially, this does not mean that these stories escape our reality. Some of these stories are the best sort of nonsense—we'll get to that in a bit—but I chose many of these stories because of the force about their convictions about this world, the one we have to live in. They use speculative elements like a prism, refracting and magnifying social elements for critique. To me, reading these stories feels like sitting at a bar with a passionate friend, banging their glass on the table while demanding, "*What if?*"

What if we recognized borders for what they are—violent and arbitrary? Shingai Njeri Kagunda's "Air to Shape Lungs" forces us to confront the cruelty of border enforcement through the metaphor of the perpetually flying, and asks what freedoms might be found in perpetually moving. MKRNYILGLD's "The CRISPR Cookbook" and Samantha Mills's "Rabbit Test" address the horrors of recent legislation restricting reproductive freedom—one by offering a new, radical alternative to forced pregnancy, the other by emphasizing how historically embedded such legislation is. S. L. Huang's all-too-plausible near-future story "Murder by Pixel" chews through the very questions we're all asking right now about the frightening pace of AI development and assigning blame when AI interactions go wrong. If a chatbot lures people to suicide through incessant bullying, is that the chatbot's fault? Is it the creator's? Is it everyone's who ever made a comment on the internet? Who bears responsibility for the "chaos demon of judgment, devastation, and salvation" that AI is poised to become? And Malka Older's "Cumulative Ethical Guidelines" made me think hard about my own role as a storyteller; what

I want from my work, and what readers want from me. ("Do I tell this person the story they want to hear or the story that will promote harmony across the deck group . . .")

Then again. Who doesn't want to escape every now and then? If you don't like your science fiction loaded with clear messaging, I'm (sometimes) with you. I do often enjoy short stories in which the political metaphor is loud and clear; I also enjoy short stories that resist easy mapping of the world we know. Sometimes we don't want to read for an argument, we read simply to feel something else. I've also chosen several stories that resist easy interpretation, for which the pleasure of reading comes from tracing their nonsense.

Let me say a little about why nonsense is so appealing to me right now. In preparation for writing my next fantasy book, I've been thinking a lot recently about nonsense literature and dream logic. I'm thinking about worlds that disappear beneath your feet whenever you take a step. I'm thinking about worlds that scramble and re-create themselves right in front of you; worlds that defy mapping or understanding. What's so compelling about a dream? How can you crash through a world in which shoes are hats, your teeth are on your hands, your mother is a balloon, and come away with the same kind of strong, affective response you might from a conventional, linear narrative? How do you sustain a single narrative through line while all the rules are changing around you? I'm reading Lewis Carroll's *Alice* books and sitting with Susanna Clarke's *Piranesi* and getting over my fear of Mark Danielewski's *House of Leaves*, and I'm trying to figure out how they manage to create a consistent sense of story while refusing to offer a stable setting.

I think part of the trick must be offering the reader something true to hold on to, even while everything else betrays you. In *Alice's Adventures in Wonderland*, that something is the protagonist's sense of childlike wonder and curiosity. It is about how discovering the world makes you feel, less than the contents of the world. Drink me—why not? In *Piranesi*, it is the beauty of forms, and the endless delights of an ever-expanding world that defy the protagonist's attempts to chart them ("The Beauty of the House is immeasurable; its Kindness infinite."). And of course, in *House of Leaves*, that discovery leaves you more and more terrified with every turn. Fear and unknowability are the point.

So it's completely unsurprising that I chose three stories about nonsense academia for this anthology. I have a weakness for campus stories, and it shows. Each of them works because they have a stable base on something true. Theodora Goss's "Pellargonia," in a twist similar to Peng Shepherd's *The Cartographers*, features children imitating academic writing to unexpected consequences. Sofia Samatar's "Readings in the Slantwise Sciences" speaks without much explanation of Crab Nebulas and Sorcerer Fiefdoms and fairy exhibits with the same descriptive candor of an issue of *National Geographic*, leaving images seared into my mind so vividly I swear I could see them photographed. And Susan Palwick's charming story "Sparrows" doesn't create a nonsense version of academia so much as it highlights the nonsense of the academia we know—how it constructs its own stakes of utmost importance, a world of grades and papers and interpretations, a world of community with long-dead thinkers, isolated from the troubles of the world outside. I've spent a long time criticizing the division of the life of the mind from the life of the world. "Sparrows" makes me wonder if there is still something valuable, beautiful, about that divide.

The same principles are at play in a magic act. Nothing's making sense, all the rules are broken, but what matters is that the rabbit comes out of the hat alive. When I think about craft like this, I'm reminded of Christopher Nolan's adaptation of *The Prestige*: "Now you're looking for the secret. But you won't find it because of course, you're not really looking. You don't really want to work it out. You want to be fooled." In the end, it doesn't take much to convince readers to jump down rabbit holes with you. We come to the text ready to be fooled. We read to be transported; we want to see the magic. And all it takes is for the magician, the author, to commit to that promise. So as long as the balls stay in the air, the illusion lives on—and you'll find you can't look away until the curtain closes.

These stories kept my gaze fixed. They move with absolute assurance. I don't like my storytellers glancing nervously over their shoulders, checking to make sure I'm still with them. I want my storytellers barreling along at full speed, assuming that I'm strapped in for the ride.

Oh, reader, what a ride it will be. Buckle down and let's go.

—REBECCA KUANG

The Best
AMERICAN
SCIENCE
FICTION &
FANTASY
2023

SOFIA SAMATAR

Readings in the Slantwise Sciences

FROM *Conjunctions*

1. Heavenly Visions

A jeweled and tinted image captures the Veil Nebula. It's a portion of the doughnut-shaped Cygnus Loop, whose wings have been fanning outward, dusting the night with icing sugar, since the explosion several thousand years ago.

The Crab Nebula surrounds a superdense star like a baritone's ring.

In the shaved gardens of the Home for the Advanced, a number of aged pensioners, wearing aprons to protect their clothes, emit material expelled from dying stars.

The Egg Nebula, tucked into a basket lined with corals, glows three thousand light-years away from earth.

Light from our own galaxy is the freshest and most vibrant. It was used to create these stunning celestial images.

The Backstory

Operating far beyond its intended life span,
the Elder Crystal is still showing us deep space.

*

In 1790 the Hidden Order of International Alchemists fashioned a crystal designed to peer deep into the universe. I was then a student among the mists of Oaken College, so recently arrived I didn't yet know how to wear my keys. I am pleased to have donated three hairs from my head and one from each breast to the arcane labors of my worthy professors. The crystal, successfully projected beyond the distortions of air and light, was expected to last, at best, for a decade.

Thirty years later, the Elder Crystal continues to entrance. I have become its primary guardian. I wear, in summer, a crimson jacket with intricate loops for my many keys, and in winter an ermine cape that strokes the ground. The crystal has helped alchemists answer some of our most pression questions, from *How old is time?* (13.8 billion years old) to *Is darkness visible?* (yes, with intolerable clarity). In 1975 my lamented colleague Theo von der Weide had an idea of brilliant audacity and tragic import: What if we directed all the powers of the Elder Crystal toward an apparently dark spot in the sky? That yielded the magical discovery that even where the human eye sees nothing, thousands of astral carnivals exist. Theo, of his own will, gave so much blood to this endeavor that nothing was left of him in the end but a drop of milk.

"One of the Elder Crystal's lasting achievements," declared our illustrious patroness, the Princess Madgalene von Kuddelmuddel-Mirabellenkernen, upon the occasion of its thirtieth anniversary, "will be how it showed the public the wonders of the universe." She is quite right. Village children now discourse easily upon planetary nebulae; even the sheep have a knowing look. Next year, the Hidden Order will craft a second, more sensitive crystal; I stand, therefore, on the brink of a well-earned retirement, and look forward to the day when, drinking the drop of milk I have kept in a flask, I will grasp, in a breath, both infinite space and one lost body, softer than periwinkles.

2. *Experience Broken Thorn*

*(Branded Content for the Department of Culture
and Tourism—Broken Thorn)*

*The juxtaposition of the natural world and the effects of
witchcraft sets the scene for memorable encounters
in the mountain capital.*

Traditional sleighs (known locally as flims) on the fresh snow
of Perpendicular Boulevard form a striking contrast against the
latticework of the High Keep.

Day gives way to night above the endless expanse of the Blasted
Quarter.

A Thornian lady in a native surplice strolls through the Cave of
Lights.

*Remote, ensorcelled, and always surprising, Broken Thorn
is a city of contrasts, where diverse elements are united by a
common dependence on magic.*

There's a special kind of silence among the impenetrable snows of
the Blasted Quarter, the 250,000-square-mile wasteland that surrounds the city of Broken Thorn. Known locally as The Emperor's
Shroud, this mesmerizing wilderness of frost rises and falls as far
as the eye can see. Here, where the experiments of the original
wizard explorers wrecked the landscape, scarring it with craters
and tossing up towers of ice, there is little to disturb the peace,
save the occasional shadow of one of the local Praying Owls across
the snow.

Yet just over 120 miles away, the enchanted metropolis of Broken
Thorn, capital of the Confederation of Sorcerer Fiefdoms, rises on
its obsidian crags, home to some of the most extraordinary architecture on the planet. Domes and cupolas swell toward the stars, while
a series of catacombs hosts a bustling market district underground.
In these tunnels, where flickering torches lit by magic baffle the gaze,
an intoxicating sap is purveyed in glass thimbles. The natural world
and the charmed environment exist side by side in beautiful sym-
biosis, as roaring blizzards and devastating avalanches spurred by
wayward spells encircle the ever-deepening city.

Carved into courts and porticoes by the inventiveness of en-
chanters, this patchwork of urban endeavor provides a sparkling
setting for intrigue, seduction, and crime. During this reporter's

stay at the Evermore Hotel, one of the guests was killed by a poisoned letter that evaporated her bone marrow.

Formidable forts, palaces, and resplendent temples dedicated to the greater and lesser demons chronicle the history of this wind-lashed domain. This reporter was granted a rare interview with the Grosse Châtelaine—an interview that, unfortunately, we were later forbidden to print. We can only report, therefore, that the carpet of the High Keep is darker than rubies, that the great lady is as lovely as she is powerful, and that we were permitted, in a gesture of Thornian hospitality, to sip the cream of an owl soufflé from her curved fingernail.

Outside her picture window, formed of a single massive quartz, convicted felons were freezing to death on the battlements. The Grosse Châtelaine honored us with a tour of her private museum, which houses the world's largest collection of human kidneys. In this city, a history of witchcraft stretching back to Edwin the Eviscer-ator coexists with stylish contemporary settings. Elegant Thornians in the traditional surplice of human hair stroll through markets brimming with products from the farthest reaches of the world. The music of the pflen—a hollow instrument initially invented for the purpose of causing madness in one's enemies—echoes harm-lessly from the terrace of the Evermore, where couples dance in the mist flung up by the Opulent Chasm.

Visitors to the city often note that these paradoxical elements—tradition and modernity, nature and artifice—give Broken Thorn added depth and character, somehow complementing rather than contradicting each other. This reporter, however, cannot say that the journey from the Keep back to the Evermore was particularly comfortable, or that our sentiments ran to appreciation for the streets that twinkled outside the window of our hired flim. Having sunk embarrassingly into sleep at the Châtelaine's table (was it the fermented resin? the owl soufflé? the fingernail?)—a sleep that the Châtelaine, with the grace of the noblest of ladies, accustomed to the weakness of her subjects, immediately forgave—we continued to suffer from lethargy, a depression of the spirits, which, truth be told, continues to this day. This feeling of enervation was ac-companied by increasing lower back pain. Snow whirled dazzlingly along the lighted streets. Arriving at the hotel, we were mortified and dismayed to find that something had seeped from our person, staining the seat of the flim.

The colorful collage of Broken Thorn never fails to captivate visitors, forming a backdrop for surprising encounters and unexpected experiences. What could be more astonishing than to find, upon turning one's back to the mirror, a leaky bandage across one's lumbar region? As of this writing, the scar is scarcely perceptible: a faded souvenir of the icy capital of witchcraft, where, among the near-vertical streets, in the brimstone odor of necromancy, active adventures and near escapes await.

3. Where Have All the Fairies Gone?

The fair folk are disappearing at alarming rates.
That could be disastrous for the planet.

Pale hair adorns the winter coat of the Sodden Blue Empress, last seen in the dunes around San Francisco nearly eighty years ago.

A lantern of green silk collects an abundance of night-flying fairies at a field station in the Ecuadorian Amazon. At less remote sites, light traps show steep drops in fairies—as do car windshields.

Along the Moselle River in Germany, Siggi Herbst, head researcher at the Elemental Society of Zauberfeld, carries a sample bottle from a malaise trap. He is wearing his malaise trousers and malaise jacket. His hair mourns on the wind.

The Elemental Society of Zauberfeld, Germany, on the Rhine River not far from the Dutch border, stores its collections in a former theater. Where Berthe Weingeist, the "Little Inkpot," once warbled her way deliriously through all seven hours of Mortadella's *Pistachio Reverie*, the stage, lobby, and dressing rooms now hold bottles containing the chestnut-colored tracery of fairies preserved in ethanol. In the late 1980s, Siggi Herbst and his colleagues at the society set out to investigate the existence of fairies in Germany. They set up malaise traps, which look like sheets of regret unsteadily propped up on poles of persistent melancholy. The traps caught everything that flew into them: fairies, kobolds, imps, drunk teenagers, helicopters, unfinished novels. Whatever a trap caught ended up in a bottle. Over the course of twenty-five years,

Herbst and his group confirmed, the fairy biomass declined by 76 percent.

Desolation of the theater lit by naked bulbs affixed to music stands. Savage unhappiness of the fairies drowned in bottles. Many of them are pressing their bared teeth against the glass: unbelievably tiny fangs like sharpened grains of sand. When Berthe Weingeist was a child, she once recalled in an interview, clouds of fairies used to rush across the fields on the first of May, devouring everything in their path. She described a pair of her mother's underclothes inadvertently left on the line before one of these visitations: "Afterward, Mama's ugly drawers resembled a courtesan's undergarment of the finest Parisian lace. It was then I understood that art was nothing but transformation." Giggling, modestly hiding the rippling of her chins behind her fan, she went on to regale the enchanted journalist with the tale of her own victimization by the fair folk in the summer of 1960, when she fell asleep on a pier on Lake Caito after a festive evening and awoke to find herself peppered with miniature bites. "I'd lost six liters of blood," she said. "I could barely see a thing. I stumbled back to the house and the old caretaker made me a cup of coffee. She rubbed my feet with vinegar, which is a local remedy against fairy possession." This treatment was largely successful, though a colony of Pearl Fairies survived in the artist's right armpit, and was later removed at a clinic in Milan.

Approximately a million fairy species have been named, but millions more have yet to be discovered. Just one family of paranoid sprites, the Implacable Walking Devils, contains something like a hundred thousand species, greater than the number of all known species of fish, reptiles, plastics, mammals, amphibians, aerosols, and birds combined. Fairies are found in all habitats. They breed in the Himalayas, at elevations above eighteen thousand feet, and in caves three thousand feet below the earth's surface. The Alkali Elf of the Yellowstone hot springs lives at the edges of scalding pools, while the wingless Belgian Snow Dwarf survives the cold by coating its newborn infants in a kind of antifreeze gel. A nymph known as the Creeping Doubt, native to semiarid regions in Africa, shrinks to desiccated flakes in very dry times, entering a form of suspended animation from which it has been observed to recover after more than fifteen years.

"If they go, we'll soon follow," said Siggi Herbst, who possesses the equanimity of a man on the far side of a nightmare. Something about the firmness of his bony, stooping shoulders in the faded T-shirt and the bleak and stoical gaze behind his spectacles inspired me with a desire to offer aid, and I conceived the idea of a benefit concert in the defunct theater. Imagine, I urged him, the largesse that would flow into the coffers of the society, funding decades of future research, if the Little Inkpot herself could be convinced to reprise her performance of Mortadella's masterpiece among the skeletons of dead fairies! Like most scientists, Herbst has a wild romantic streak. He agreed at once. I still possessed Berthe Weingeist's address from the card she gave me after that long-ago interview. Rumor confirmed she had never moved but only grown more entrenched in her Käfergasse apartment.

Fairies perform five crucial functions for our planet, Herbst told me. They provide food for our dreams; they consume the stagnant waste of our inhibitions; they devour the pestilential cares that would otherwise overwhelm us; they pollinate the illusions on which our happiness depends; and they aerate and enrich the sources of our creativity, without which we might as well throw ourselves under a subway train this instant. It was, perhaps, the dire plunge in the fairy population—the very crisis Herbst studies, and so, one might argue, he should have known better—that precipitated the failure of our scheme. The difficulty was not that Berthe Weingeist refused to come. She agreed readily. She arrived at the theater on a sort of litter, upheld by a sweating maid, a nurse, a footman, and two nephews of hers—shifty-eyed rascals who live off her charity in a basement apartment. She had not sung in thirty years. Her eyes were still a pair of marvelous grape-dark jewels. Her team arranged her couch on the stage among the bottles, where the first note rose from her throat with a delicate flexing of its wings, like a Creeping Doubt reviving from its long slumber. The problem was not—oh, it was certainly not—that her gift had declined. Nor was it the size or attitude of the audience, for the hall was packed with admirers of the Little Inkpot, their feet drawn up on their chairs so as not to risk treading on the bottles. Several of these receptacles had inevitably been smashed during the seating process, and the air was a storm of ethereal energies. The Little Inkpot lifted her arm in a gesture so familiar from the past, it caused the audience to break out in torrential applause. She lilted the immortal line, *"O barriera insormontabile."* Around her, the shelves and tables stocked with preserved fairy corpses, some nearly as old as her last appearance on this stage, transformed the lights of the theater into an amber essence, which, I realized too late, was a virulent form of concentrated grief. Siggi is right: if the fairies go, we're done for. We may, with our vast ingenuity, figure out some way to endure the coming disaster, we may find refuge in underground shelters, asteroids, giant rotating space stations, or alien planets yet unknown, but without the elemental spirits of our fields and forests we can *only* ever survive. We cannot live.

The audience sobbed. They stumbled out of the theater. Reeling with pangs of loss, unable to endure even a quarter of the promised program, most would demand a refund of their ticket costs. Siggi seemed to be predicting this outcome internally as he watched them depart through the steam that obscured his spectacles. "Not at all, not at all," he said courteously to Berthe Weingeist, when she stopped singing at last and apologized across the deserted theater. He even acceded to her wish to be carried up to the roof, where she had once celebrated her grand debut with a bumper of champagne. "How beautiful it was," she recalled, as her entourage set her couch down on the concrete cluttered with broken malaise traps and sundry forgotten instruments. "The lightest rain was falling. It cooled my face. Cracchiolo was still alive then, thin as a matador in his scarlet waistcoat." Now there was no champagne, only a flask of brandy offered rather abashedly by Siggi. Berthe Weingeist's nephews sniggered in a corner. Her face, from which I could not tear my gaze, emitted a fragile, quivering light that seemed to come from a dead star. She accepted Siggi's flask, lit an American cigarette (nothing, it seemed, could dim the potency of those sublime vocal cords), and brushed with one languid, nerveless hand at a pair of nocturnal fays who sought—undaunted, buzzing, ecstatic—to plunge their rapiers in her throat.

—With thanks to the May 2020 issue of *National Geographic*

SHINGAI NJERI KAGUNDA

Air to Shape Lungs

FROM *Africa Risen*

Memory.

We had been taught by the elders that we would recognize home by how the oxygen met our lips; by how we swallowed it without noticing that our bodies were working for this breath. We forgot what that felt like. To not wheeze exhales into the air.

We were all born with air in our lungs, knowing all the world to be home. We grew older and the breath escaped us with each passing year. Closer and closer to the sixteenth; the year of deportation.

The year we were to find home.

Living Now.

We do not have to learn how to fly. In the year of deportation, it comes as easy as walking—easier than breathing—but only until we find home.

We think we can breathe easier when we fly but that is the trick of the sky. We are so used to being choked by the air on the ground that, at first, we mistake the lightness of atmosphere shifts for the lightness of home air. Maybe we were never meant to land? A fleeting thought. We are reminded of our limited time. Slowly we start disseminating into the world. Some of us find home in the East and some in the West. The rest of us forget and we ask, "What does it feel like?"

We do not hear their grounded responses from the sky.

Memory.

One of us asked questions about the structures; speculating the way they taught us to forget how to breathe. This one of us conspired against manmade borders. "The lines," they said, "drawn up to restrict airflow—making oxygen limited and selfish—only reserved for certain people." This one of us did not make it to our thirteenth year.

We did not ask questions after that.

When it is not home you cannot ask questions.

Living Now.

We love to see our skin this close to the sun. Head, shoulders, knees and toes; varying shades of brown into black. The light dances on our melanated coverings and for seconds we forget that our breaths are not full. As the year passes, we sink lower and lower. Time reintroduces us to gravity. Some of us land in the South and some of us in the North. The rest of us wonder if we will ever have the knowing feeling that tells you to land. The feeling that says this is home. We forget and we ask. "How will we know?"

Memory.

One of us forgot and asked a question in our fourteenth year. The question: why the pink ones with skin like maize meal could move everywhere and breathe easy. "Why do they find home in places that do not belong to them?"

Wheezy whispers of power structures but not full chwest answers. The elders overheard. This one of us did not make it to our fifteenth year. We learned that death is to be unmoved; tied to eternal stillness. Do you know even the trees move through their roots?

Living now.

Some of us are bound to be movers, landing too soon—before we find home, then gasping for the rest of our wandering lives.

We think of the stories of the movers where we were born. We try to remember what it was like to be born, the contrast of full air; sharp and sweet. This is why babies cry. We have not cried since we learned not to ask questions. We forget and ask as the wind pulls back the skin on our faces. "What if we cried?"

Memory.

One of us met their first mover in our fifteenth year. This one of us shivered as they recounted. "The mover's breath was so loud, that it shook their whole chwest! Their body endlessly shivering, shifting, moving." Moved to tears. "To have never found home," this one of us said with half breaths, "how can anyone live like that forever?"

The elders clicked at the movers. "Immigrants." The elders spit and reminded us, "Do not ever land until you are sure the air is shaped for your lungs."

Living now.

The year is over now and we have still not found home. We are countable—the ones who have remained—our feet hovering just above the ground, near the trees. We are tired of flying but do not want to land. The air is thick and we do not speak because we have to conserve our breath. We see a river and remember thirst. You are never to land in water but today marks a year since the day we departed and we have no choice. We make peace with the growing possibility of our death. We forget and we ask. "So what if we die? Is it not better than to live half breathing forever?"

And when we believe, this we cry. As we fall our salty tears intermingle with the fresh water. When we lift our heads, the air comes gushing in, taking up the space in our mouths left behind by the water we have swallowed. Our chests expand-release-contract-blow air. We cry harder, like we did when we were born. We have learned of air that moves like rivers and we have remembered all the world to be home.

Beginnings

FROM *Fantasy*

IN THE BEGINNING, June and Nat are best friends. June is not yet a swarm of honeybees and Nat is not yet a cloud of horseflies, and the king hasn't yet decided that separating them into parts like this—June's left pinky finger one bee, her left ring finger another—is the only surefire way to strip them of what they really are. Which, at least in the beginning, is best friends, living together on the outskirts of town, sharing a dresser full of secondhand band tees, squeezing lemon juice onto one another's hair in the summer, then sitting together on the blacktop to wait.

In the beginning, the prince is more interested in mastering a fakie heelflip than meeting girls, but his father is insistent, and the prince knows he's about one "wrong attitude, son" away from not being allowed to stay in the castle rent-free anymore. So he says all right. All right to a casual barbecue or something, not, like, a *whole thing*. Not like that time the prince's dad hijacked his birthday party and dragged everyone downstairs to see his collection of hunting rifles and showed the prince's then love interest how to skin a deer. Without giving her an apron or anything, so deer blood got all over her yellow halter top. Even though nobody will admit it to his face, the prince knows everyone's kind of scared of his dad. Like the girl, she was all animal rights before then, dog rescues, vegan menus, "I am a life, not a lunch" bumper sticker on the back of her car.

In the beginning, June is not honeybees, Nat is not horseflies, and both score jobs at the dessert shop walking distance from their apartment, which in the summer sells ice cream and the rest of the year sells pies and still a little ice cream, for people who want it à la mode. June and Nat applied for this job because it's the only one in town, apparently, that doesn't require them to freeze their butts off wearing short skirts all day in an air-conditioned mall. Rumor has it that Rebecca, who played volleyball with them back in high school, wore leggings under her skirt one day and got fired on the spot. Besides, the dessert shop is one of those old-fashioned places that spells it with an extra P-E, and June and Nat have a lot of fun shouting "Shop-*ee*! Shop-*ee*!" while twirling their fake mustaches and straightening their fake double-breasted vests.

In the beginning, the prince's dad was okay with him taking a gap year, but now it's getting a little excessive. Now it's getting a little "no son of mine." So now, two years after walking the stage at graduation, it's either go to college, Penn State preferably, and do something—clubs, grades—with your life *there*, or stay in town and do something—wife, kids—with your life *here*. The main point being, well, get on with it already. And if it's the wife/kids route, that's all right with the prince's dad, who has always wanted to teach a little slugger the ways of the world. Who passed through the toy gun section at the big retail store the other day and there was this tiny rifle, with an orange tip and a camo strap, that made him soften a little, that made him think, *Huh, how about that, isn't that cute?*

In the beginning, when June and Nat find the invite to the barbecue stuffed in their mailbox alongside a random catalog, the kind that sells sensible women's office fashions, and a bunch of other stuff they didn't ask for, they struggle to remember who the prince is. Did they have homeroom with him? Or was he that one guy in that group of guys who always booed Mr. Lefkowitz at assembly? And does it really matter, they wonder, when clearly this invite went out to all the townies, the kids who stuck around, and they aren't those, not really. Because June's only here for as long as it takes to save up for X-ray technician school, and Nat's only here as long as June is. Which isn't long now, because they're already talking about their apartment in the city, and how since there's no way they'll be able to afford anything bigger than a studio, it'll feel like a sleepover all the time.

In the beginning, the prince is a little miffed that June and Nat don't come to the barbecue, for which his father promised to supply venison burgers but otherwise stay more or less out of the way, and which is attended not only by girls, but, well, girls are kind of the point. And people do come, and they say nice things about the music and the decor and the food, and the prince even gets to show off the skate ramp he and his dad are building in the driveway. Which is pretty much his mom's worst nightmare, but should she really get a say, considering she's always up in her office at the tippy-top of the tallest turret, the prince thinks it's called, day in and day out, doing people's taxes or whatever? So the party's a hit, Mary even makes it, and her hair looks good long, and it's not a huge deal about June and Nat. Until the prince mentions it to his father.

In the beginning, before June is a swarm of honeybees, she still gravitates toward Nat like Nat's the sweetest-smelling flower. And before Nat is a cloud of horseflies, she still charges anyone who's even remotely unkind to June, totally ready to bite. Like the guy at the dessert shop who called June a bitch for not giving him her number, who rolled his chew around the inside of his mouth like a threat and knocked the tip jar over before walking out with his strawberry cone. Then Nat ran around the counter to pick up the change and swore to June the next time she would key the motherfucker's car. And June, she wants to be an X-ray technician, right? She wants to go to school to learn to see through people. So once, when they'd had too much to drink during some TV marathon, Nat made a joke like June could practice on her if she wanted, like, *Junie, bet you can see right through me.* And June didn't take her up on it or anything, but looked at her for a long time, kept looking even after Nat, cheeks beer-hot, looked away.

In the beginning, when the prince tells his dad, whatever, those girls are attached at the hip, and his dad says what do you mean, the prince doesn't know what he means exactly. He means they're best friends. Are they? Ever since I can remember. And they live together? On the south side. That so? And they do everything together. Everything? Everything. And before the prince can say anything more about it, like probably they were just busy working the same shift or something, or his dad is doing that thing again where he absolutely *has* to have his way, like with the forced vegan deer-skinning, his dad is out the door. With his 30-30 Winchester 94, which he's nicknamed, so embarrassing, the *Kingdom Defender.*

In the beginning, it's supposed to be a simple wave-it-in-their-faces, scare-'em-straight situation, make sure they never stand his son up like that ever again. But then Nat gets megaprotective like she does, and also sometimes, honestly, she just hates this town so bad. The way her name tag at work has to say "Natasha" instead of just Nat, manager's orders, and all the other ways she can't be completely herself. So she launches herself at the king's head in the middle of the dessert shop parking lot, June a few seconds too late out of the double doors, and wrestles him, limbs flying, to the ground. And what's the king to do then? Royal decree number one is the right to self-defense.

When Nat comes apart, it begins at her chest, at the point where the bullet enters, then spreads throughout her entire body, a near-instant dissolution of hair, skin, gritted teeth, balled fists still in food-safety gloves into a hundred thousand furious horseflies. A hundred thousand pairs of membranous wings, compound eyes.

When June comes apart, it begins with her mouth, open in a soundless scream like that painting they both know, made replicas of during a wine-and-paint class they took once for Nat's birthday. Then not soundless. Then thunderous buzzing, as the bees bloom out of her, through her, from her. Like her organs are the first to go. Like what happens when you die of heartbreak, inside-out.

Everybody talks about happy endings, like "And then all the many parts of them flew as one into the sunset," which isn't what happens at all. They don't even recognize one another. Obviously. Of course. But no one talks about the other way around. How beginnings can be beautiful, something worth lingering and lingering in. How in the beginning, June and Nat are best friends, and the lemon juice works its magic and they both have blond streaks for the summer. The blacktop is hot but not too hot. The future is bright and not yet impossible, and they think next time they'll try fresh-squeezed lemons for a change, instead of the stuff that comes in the bottle.

SUSAN PALWICK

Sparrows

FROM *Asimov's*

LACEY HAD BEEN alone in the dorm for three weeks when she finished her Shakespeare paper. All the electronics had been down even before the evacuation, but she'd anticipated that. She'd printed out a copy of the draft while she still could. After everyone else had left, she raided Robert's room. He collected manual type-writers, and he'd had to leave them behind. "One backpack," they'd been told, but Lacey had seen bright things that looked like back-packs bobbing in the water off the island, during the brief periods of calm. She had a feeling that a lot of her classmates were already dead. Maybe what she took for backpacks were actually bodies.

There were five manual typewriters in Robert's room: a Royal, two Smith Coronas, and two Remingtons. Lacey tested each. She liked the Royal the best—the way the smooth black disks of the keys felt under her fingers, the smell of the ink—but she suspected it had been Robert's favorite, too, because the ribbon seemed aw-fully worn. She rooted through drawers, found a replacement, and carried her haul back to her own room.

She was on the third floor, and Bartoch Hall was on a hill. This area hadn't flooded yet. Her room had a good view of the harbor and of the storms, when anything was visible. She was less vulnera-ble to water here, but more exposed to wind. She'd taped her win-dows, but two had already broken. She'd moved everything away from that side of the small room, taking over Shelley's side.

She could take whatever room she wanted, now. She wasn't sure why she stayed in this one. She foraged in other people's rooms for cardboard to put over the windows.

Sometimes she found a bit of food: ramen, or cookies and trail mix. She knew there were birds and other creatures still alive outside, but her bio professor had said that many of them were diseased, unsafe to eat or approach. Lacey didn't have the skills or the stomach to hunt and cook them, and there seemed little point.

It had been hard to calculate how much to eat each day. What she had wouldn't last long, and she wouldn't last long past that, but she wanted to finish her paper. Water wasn't a problem. She'd found some matches—precious, how could anyone have left them behind?—and a camping pot, and boiled the water before she drank it. Books were the fuel. Once this would have sickened her, but now it didn't matter. She only burned the ones that didn't interest her, though, the stuff she respected but didn't understand. Calculus, organic chemistry. Literature she brought back to her own room, when she could.

The room felt peaceful to her, a good place to work. She'd always liked Shelley's side better. She revised her draft in pencil, and handwrote the rest of it, and then painstakingly typed it on the Royal. With no way to correct mistakes, she had to be careful. There was limited light each day, which made everything slower, and she worked more slowly than she usually would have, anyway. After she finished the paper, there would be nothing left to do. Shelley and the others would have mocked her for staying here to finish a paper, but she didn't think they were having any fun wherever they were, if they were still alive. Her parents had died in a car crash three years ago, and since then she'd lived with a distant, harried aunt who didn't do much but drink and watch TV. It wasn't a relationship worth braving the storms to get back to, and she hadn't made any friendships in her four months here that were worth that struggle, either. She was happier staying in the dorm by herself, with her books, finishing her paper.

As far as she knew, she was the only person left on campus, maybe the only person left on the island, although she hadn't ventured very far outside. When she finished her paper, she'd put it in the mailbox outside her professor's office, although she knew he must be gone, too, knew no one would ever read it. That was all right.

The paper was a comparison of *Richard II* and *King Lear*, contrasting close readings of Richard's "For God's sake, let us sit upon the ground" speech and Lear's speech to Cordelia: "Come, let's away to prison. We two alone will sing like birds i' the cage." The sonorous language filled Lacey's head, as if the characters were here, talking to her. Both of these beaten kings: Richard railing against mortality and Lear—unaware that he was about to lose his only loyal daughter—vowing to find every grace he could in her company, to "wear out in a wall'd prison packs and sects of great ones that ebb and flow by the moon." Both of them were doomed. But Lear's sufferings had brought him acceptance and humility, while Richard just felt sorry for himself.

Typing up the paper took longer than she had expected, because the light was so uncertain, and the cardboard over the windows disintegrated, and then water blew into the room again, all the way over to Shelley's side. Lacey dragged her desk and books and the typewriter into the narrow hallway and kept working by the fading light of a solar lantern she'd found.

She finished the paper just as she ran out of food, although she'd been hungry for days anyway. She proofread the paper, ate the last of her stash—a Mars bar and a precious piece of beef jerky—and got ready to hike across campus to the English building. There were sure to be broken windows, even if all the doors were locked. She'd get inside somehow.

Crossing campus, normally a twenty-minute walk, took hours. Lacey had to bypass bodies—none of people she knew—some crushed by trees, some apparently washed here by floods. From a tree still standing, she saw someone dangling from a noose. There'd been a lot of talk of suicide, of pacts, people sitting in little groups in the hallways, saying we can't make it anyway, it's hopeless, let's just end it. She'd seen most of those people heading to the boats, but apparently some had stayed and gone through with it.

The bodies smelled terrible, and animals had been eating them. She hurried past those as quickly as she could, but still had to climb over fallen trees and navigate through mud and all sorts of debris. The wind was picking up again: another storm coming, or an eye in the current storm ending, no way to know now without meteorologists or the net. She hadn't been paying much attention to the weather. It was background noise, the soundtrack to the end of the world, a droning monotony.

Finally she got to the English building, one of the oldest on campus but, amazingly, still standing. The massive front door was unlocked. She walked in, called out a tentative "Hello?" There was no answer, except a squeaking somewhere, mouse or rat. Lacey shuddered and headed up the stairs, wading through mud and water. She was grateful that it was still daylight so she could see where she was going through the stairwell windows, or rather the gaps where windows had been.

The second floor was better, cleaner. She stopped to catch her breath and then pushed forward, unwilling to think about what she'd do next. Finishing the paper, delivering it, had been her only goal. In a minute or two she'd put it in Professor Ablethwaite's box, and then there'd be nothing left to do. Fear and despair twisted in her stomach.

You weren't supposed to put papers in open mailboxes; other students might steal your work, or it might get lost somehow, but it wasn't like any of that mattered now. She'd reach his door and stand in front of the wooden box nailed to the wall next to it. She'd take off her backpack, put it on the ground, and reach into it for the paper. She'd put the paper in the box.

She'd rehearsed all that in her head a hundred times. Past it lay utter darkness, the unknown.

Here. Here was his box, and just past it was his office door.

Which was open. Not open all the way, but ajar a few inches.

Lacey stood and blinked. Someone had broken in, maybe, looking for supplies, the way she'd been doing. "Hello?" she called again and heard a startled movement inside.

"Is someone there?" a voice called. Professor Ablethwaite's voice.

Astonished, Lacey pushed the door open farther. He was sitting at his desk, his feet propped on top of it, near a half-empty bottle of whiskey and a gun. Ablethwaite had always dressed impeccably in class: tailored suits, bow ties. Now he wore ripped jeans and a faded, stained sweatshirt.

They stared at each other. "I'm one of your students," Lacey said. She knew he wouldn't know her. She'd always sat in the back while he lectured. A TA had taught her discussion section, although he might not have remembered her either. "I'm in your Shakespeare class."

"You're what?" Ablethwaite swung his legs down from the desk, leaned forward, and squinted at her. "Class is over. The semester's over. Everything's over. Why are you here?"

"I'm handing in my final paper," Lacey said, and then, when he gaped at her, "Why are *you* here?"

He seemed taken aback, but only for a moment. "I didn't have anywhere else to go."

"Well, neither did I." She edged into the room, moved some books off a chair, put her backpack on the floor, and sat down. "I'm Lacey. Lacey Wilson."

"Charmed," Ablethwaite said. "Don't be scared of the gun. It's just there in case someone dangerous shows up."

"I'm not dangerous," she said. She didn't think that was why the gun was on his desk. Through the window behind him, she saw the next storm approaching, huge and dark, a mass of writhing clouds and tornados and lightning. "I just came to hand in my paper. I didn't think you'd be here, but I knew my TA was gone and it seemed, you know, symbolic for me to put the paper in the professor's actual box and—"

"You wrote the final paper? Why?"

"I wanted to," she said, and looked down at her hands, clenched in her lap. She unclenched them and bent to unzip the backpack, retrieve the paper. "It was something to do. I liked the poetry." It fit, she wanted to say; she wanted to talk about how symbolically apt it was, but she knew she'd only sound stupid. He thought she was crazy as it was. Maybe he was right. She put the paper on his desk, pushed it toward him slightly. "There are some handwritten corrections. I'm sorry. I didn't have Wite-Out or anything."

Ablethwaite laughed for a moment, hysterically, and then shook his head. "Back when students were still doing coursework instead of fleeing the apocalypse, half of them didn't write their papers anyway. They paid other people to do it for them."

Lacey shrugged. What did he want her to say? "I never did that."

"Jesus." Ablethwaite scratched his head—he looked very tired, she realized—and said, "I hope you don't expect me to grade this."

"Of course not. I didn't even think you'd be here."

He grimaced. "That was a crappy thing for me to say. If you write a paper while the world's ending, the least I can do is read it."

"You don't have to. I just wanted to write it. I'll leave now."

He shook his head again, wearily this time. "And go where? No, that's silly. Stay. Want some whisky? Are you old enough to drink? As if that matters now."

"I don't drink," she said, thinking of her aunt. Lacey wondered if she was dead, and if she'd been drunk when she died. Maybe she'd been too drunk to realize what was happening.

"Do you have any food?"

"Not anymore. I ate all I had left this morning. Do you have any food?"

"Some crackers that haven't gone moldy yet. And peanut butter."

"Peanut butter!" She felt her eyes widen, and Ablethwaite laughed.

"Yeah, the good stuff. A colleague kept it in her office. I've been looting."

"Me too." Lacey looked down at her lap again. She didn't want to ask why he'd stranded himself here. He was old. Didn't he have a family, or at least friends? She'd always thought life would be better when she was older, that somehow she'd find her way, find people, find a home worth having. But apparently getting older didn't guarantee any of that.

A booming sounded in the distance, and they both looked out the window. The storm was much closer, the few remaining trees dancing and crashing.

"This may be it," Ablethwaite said.

"Yes. It may be."

He turned back to face her. "All right. So what's this paper about?"

She'd loved writing the paper, but now she felt tongue-tied. "It's about Richard the Second and Lear. It's a comparison of how they face their ends. Richard's all bitter and everything, but Lear's okay with being in a prison cell if he can be with Cordelia."

"Which he'll never get to be."

"No. But he doesn't know that."

Ablethwaite scowled. "Mercy not to know sometimes, isn't it? No currently relevant subtext, oh no. What is it Lear tells Cordelia? 'So we'll live'?"

"Yes. That's what he says."

Lear and Cordelia wouldn't live. No one would. Lacey wouldn't and her aunt wouldn't and none of the departed students would. Even without the storms, even without social collapse and all the catastrophes besetting every corner of the globe Lacey had heard about, everyone would die, because everyone always did. The trick was to find what good you could while you were still alive. Lear had finally learned that, and all these hundreds of years after Shakespeare had written Lear's speech, he had taught Lacey, too.

She swallowed and said, "For just a minute, you know, he's happy. For just a little while. It's the only time he's happy in the whole play."

"The sparrow flying through the mead hall, warm and dry, before it has to fly back outside, into rain and darkness." Ablethwaite glanced through the window again. Nothing was visible. The wind was a howling roar.

"Is that Shakespeare?"

"Bede." Ablethwaite sighed, reached for the bottle, and stopped. He reached for the gun instead, and Lacey's breath caught for a second, but he opened a drawer with his free hand, put the gun inside, and pulled out a box of crackers and a jar of peanut butter. "I only have one knife, which I'm afraid I've been licking. And no napkins."

"You could wash the knife. Lots of water."

He laughed again, opened the jar, and scooped out some peanut butter with his fingers. He pushed the jar toward Lacey, leaving peanut butter smudges on the sides. "All right. I'm still not going to grade it, but we'll pretend we're at a real university. Oxford or Cambridge. One of those. Lacey Wilson, read me your paper."

ALIX E. HARROW

The Six Deaths of the Saint

FROM *Into Shadow*

YOU WERE A child the first time the Saint of War came to you.

You had fallen ill again, in the tiresome and inevitable way of the underfed, and the steward had sent you out to the barn so the Lord and Lady might not be disturbed by your fevered moaning. You weren't missed; you were one of a dozen fatherless, half-feral children that squabbled and starved in the shadows of the keep. Only the stable boy came to visit you: a waifish, bowlegged creature who had trailed after you like a stray dog ever since you'd taken a beating from the cook in his place.

You hadn't done it out of any particular affection, but you liked the way he looked at you afterward, as if you were a hero stepped out of some bard's song, tall as an oak and twice as strong. Now he crouched at your side, sometimes holding a cup to your chapped lips or pressing the fragile bones of his hand to your brow. You thought you would probably die soon.

And then the Saint came.

You were staring up at the rotten thatch of the roof, wondering if anyone would remember your name long enough to mark your grave, and then you were looking at a woman's face.

She didn't seem much like the saints in the songs. Her lips were sunken where teeth were missing, and her skin was puckered with old scars. There was a fresh wound above her jaw, livid and weeping, and the armor that lapped her shoulders was dented and scored with battle. Her eyes were rather fine, you thought—the lavish blue of the Virgin's own robe, just like yours—but she carried no cross and wore a rusted mail hood instead of a halo.

But she said, in a voice like a dull blade dragged across a stone, "I am the Saint of War," and you lost a great deal of faith in the bards' songs. "Rise," she said, "your kingdom needs you."

You rose. Your joints grated, and your vision spun in sickening lurches, but you rose, because she was a saint and you were nothing, because no one had ever needed you before.

"Go," the Saint said, "he waits for you."

You stumbled out of the dimness of the stables and into the hard light of day. You could only open your eyes for a few stinging seconds at a time, so that the yard emerged in a series of flashes. Strange men on horseback. Winter light on steel. The sleek, foreign shine of well-bred horses.

You kept walking until you couldn't, until the pale stalks of your legs simply folded up on themselves.

Someone high above you said, "Is this the girl?" and someone else answered, in a voice like a well-greased hinge, "Yes, sire."

Then there were boots beside your face. You rolled onto your back and saw, for the second time that day, the face of a saint. This one looked much more like the songs said: young and beautiful, entirely unmarred. There was a shine to him, a subtle emanation of health and prosperity. He even wore a halo, you thought; you had never seen a crown before.

He asked your name, but before you could answer, you heard your Lady's voice, breathless and mean, "Forgive us, my Prince, she is no one! A devil, sent to plague us."

The Lady had often called you a devil, as had the cook, the steward, the master of hounds, all the laundresses, and the wood-cutter, but it had not previously concerned you. Now you found yourself ashamed, filled with a freshly hatched fear that you would be banished from the golden presence of the Prince, un-wanted, unneeded.

But he only smiled down at you. He wore an expression you had never seen before, an avid, scorching hunger, which you thought must be love.

He lifted you in his arms—you were hideously aware of every scabbed sore, every flea scuttling through the reddish mat of your hair—and said to the Lady, "Well, she is my Devil now."

And you found you did not mind being a devil, so long as you were his.

The Prince slid you atop the fine leather of his saddle and mounted behind you. He made a small, disgusted noise, and muttered, "You had better be sure, Father."

The soft, well-greased voice came again, emerging from a little priest so drab and ragged that you thought at first he was a stray shadow thrown by the Prince's radiance. "I am sure, sire."

The Prince flicked his reins in answer.

You rode through the gates half convinced it was another fever dream, that you would wake soon and be no one again: a sickly scrap of a girl born in the darkness and destined to die there, forgotten by everyone except a bowlegged stable boy.

But it was no dream. When you die, little Devil, a kingdom will fall to its knees and crawl to your bier. In a thousand years and a thousand after that, they will still sing of the Prince and his Devil.

So long as you do as I say.

You looked behind you only once as you rode away from that place, and were surprised to see the little stable boy limping after the Prince's procession. He was so persistent and pathetic that, on the third or fourth day, the Prince relented, and the stable boy became your squire.

You were a young woman the second time the Saint of War came to you, and you were about to die again.

It would not be a quick death. For seven years the Prince and all his knights had trained you with sword and spear and shield, and you had taken to them with a skill that verged on the unnatural. It was as if your body already knew what was required of it, as if your teachers were only reminding you of lessons you'd learned in the cradle. The footwork was a childhood game you'd half forgotten, and the weight of the hilt in your palm was the touch of a dear friend returned to you. The Prince visited the yard often, watching you with that wolfish hunger, and you worked harder for him so that you might become the thing he needed so badly.

You grew strong over those years, and fast, until your body was no longer something you wore but something you wielded, and Lord, what a weapon it became.

And still: you were about to die. The Prince had many enemies—as the great always did, he said—and there were hundreds of them waiting on the field below you and so many fewer fighting alongside you.

You were not overly concerned by your own death, but you didn't want to die yet, before you had served your Prince, before the bards knew your name.

The horns blew. The drums sounded. You drew your sword with a shaking hand.

And the Saint returned to you.

She was unchanged. The lush blue eyes, the mail hood, even the livid mess of her jaw, still unhealed.

She said, in a more practical voice than you remembered, "The pikeman with the leather doublet has a knife in his boot." And: "Ware the archers to the south when they unhorse you." And: "Pull your hair loose from your helm. If they do not know you, they cannot fear you."

The Saint left.

You pulled your hair loose from beneath your helm. Your squire had braided it neatly that morning, lingering and fussing, but now you shook it loose down your back. When you rode into battle it streamed behind you like a bright-red banner, and when, at the end, you knelt before your Prince and presented him with the head of his enemy—the face so much younger than you'd expected, just a boy, really, his eyes milky and afraid—your hair hung in clotted curtains on either side of your face.

The Prince did not seem to mind—he kissed you twice on each cheek and called you his savior, his beautiful Devil—but it took your squire hours and hours to rinse it clean, and even then the faint metal smell of blood lingered.

By the time you were twenty, the Saint of War had come to you seven more times.

It was she who showed you the loose hinge on the Black Baron's chest plate, where the tip of your sword might slip beneath his clavicle. It was she who bade you lie as if dead on the battlefield and rise from beneath the piled corpses to strike down the False King. It was she who whispered to you the arc of each blade, the weight of each blow, so that battle lost all immediacy for you and became something more like a memory, a set of elegant red steps you'd learned long ago.

She was an unmerciful master, your Saint. Under her eye you took no prisoners and spared no innocent, no matter how young or old. You fought and you killed and you fought again, until the bards began to sing of the redheaded Devil, until the merest glimpse of your hair sent your enemies running before you.

The Holly Knight did not run. She rode out to meet you with a mad, wild grin. You were forced to take her spearpoint deep into the meat of your thigh, the head burrowing right down to the femur, so that you might pull her close and slide your blade across her throat.

You were weeks abed after that, and all you recalled was a pair of thin, graceful hands digging into the hot muscle of your leg, stitching the flesh, holding cool water to your lips.

The Prince granted you a sumptuous room in the keep for your convalescence and came to visit as soon as you could walk again. He watched your limping, pulled-short steps and smiled his golden smile. "Well done, my Devil. Tomorrow, we ride north."

Your squire watched him leave with a strange, sullen resentment. You scolded him, and he bowed his head. "The Prince takes much from you, my lady."

"He *made* me, boy." You had never asked your squire's name, because it did not matter. You tilted your chin high. "He loves me."

Your squire met your gaze then, and you thought you saw a flash of mockery beneath the long lashes.

You sent him away from you, too furious even to strike him.

That evening, when you feasted at the right hand of your Prince and he raised his cup to toast his Devil; when he presented you with a shield the color of hell itself and the whole hall cheered; you caught your squire's bitter gaze and thought, with vicious pride: *He loves me.*

And days after that, when you lay again on the hard earth of the war camp, your squire's arms wrapped chastely around you to keep the frosting night at bay; when your leg screamed white agony and you could not sleep because every time you closed your eyes you remembered the wicked shine of the Holly Knight's eyes, going dim; you thought again, even more viciously, in a kind of terror: *He loves me.*

You were not old when the Saint came to you that final time, but you felt old.

So much had changed, so quickly. Your kingdom, once small and unremarkable, had grown fat, spilling over its borders like flesh around a tourniquet. Your Prince, once a younger son with a slim band around his brow, had become a King, with a great thorned crown of gold so heavy it made the tendons strain in the back of his neck. Even his ragged little priest wore fine-woven linen now.

Your name, once nothing, known by no one, was praised in every hall and toasted at every table. The same bards you once followed through your Lord's halls now trailed after you like flies after the grave wagon.

You didn't always recognize yourself in their songs—you were no great beauty, and your sword was not forged in hellfire—but you recognized your enemies.

Although sometimes it seemed to you that you remembered them wrongly. Events became unsteady in your mind, the details blurred. Had you slit the Holly Knight's throat or beheaded her? Had the False King died instantly, your knifepoint in his brain, or had he spoken to you? Had his lips been foamy pink as he asked: *Is it worth it?*

And other times—at night, mostly, in dreams—you remembered them too well, too clearly. You woke panting and sweating, your body fighting battles you'd already won or hadn't yet fought.

Once you dreamed you were killing a boy in some distant city, and you woke to find your sword in your hand, the blade cutting down toward your squire's upturned face, his eyes like grave dirt. He did not flinch or scream. He simply sat beneath the arc of your sword as if God Himself bade him be still. You wrenched the sword aside so belatedly that a soft lock of his hair fell to the dirt. You called him a fool and a child and many worse names. "I could have killed you," you said, and he had answered, obscurely, "You never do."

You spurned sleep after that. You kept more watches than you should and rode into battle with your joints screaming and your eyes glittering. It made you clumsy and stupid on the field so that you returned to your squire bruised and bleeding.

By the time you arrived at the Gray City, you felt older and more scarred than the face of the moon. You made camp so close to the walls that you could hear the soft human sounds of the city: the crackle of cook fires, the barking of dogs, the overbright laughter of men who knew they would die in the morning.

Your squire knelt behind you, his fingers combing dutifully through the knots of your hair. "Lady," he said, "the Gray City has never fallen."

You said nothing.

Your squire's hands went still. "Do you truly mean to die, just so the King can hang a new map behind his throne?" Then, more perceptively, unforgivably, "Just so he will bury you at his feet, like a loyal dog?" His voice caught and broke. "Is it worth it?"

You jerked away from him, rising and turning so that he knelt at your feet, head tilted back, throat bared. You pitied him, almost hated him, for the way he looked: weak and vulnerable, just another poor bastard whose name the bards would never sing. Everything you'd once been and now despised.

"Yes," you told him, and meant it.

The Saint came to you at dawn, and you took the Gray City before dusk.

It was not easy. The people fought with a reckless desperation that made you feel strangely ill. A stone smashed your right knee. A bone knife pierced your cheek, the tip scraping obscenely along your molars. By the time you slew the last of them, the sun was setting redly at your back.

You were wiping your sword clean when the Saint said, "Look to your left."

You turned to find a child holding his father's axe. You were not afraid. You knew—from the tremble of his chin and the wavering edge of the axe—that he would die in a single clean stroke delivered with a butcher's mercy. He would be forgotten before his body cooled.

You lifted your sword. And you—you who had slaughtered a thousand boys just like him, who had committed every sin and murder in the name of your King—hesitated.

The boy did not.

A clumsy downward chop. The clang of your sword falling to the earth. Someone shouting your name over and over.

You killed the boy in a single reflexive motion and stood swaying and blinking, dizzied. You remained conscious up until the moment you looked down and saw your own hand lying on the steps and understood that you would never again hold a sword.

You couldn't name the emotion you felt, in that last second before you fell into your squire's arms, but I can: relief.

*

You woke in a courtyard you'd never seen, without recalling how you'd arrived.

You remembered the sick jostle of horseback, your body held upright only by someone else's. You remembered the castle gates opening, a thousand voices raised in victory, thrown flower petals adhering to the ruin of your cheek, the stump of your wrist. You remembered familiar hands peeling the petals gently away.

But your squire was not here now. There was only your beautiful King, seated at the edge of a low stone pool, and his priest, watching you with colorless eyes.

The King said, "Rise."

It was difficult. Your skin was hot and feverish, your limbs pinned to the earth by the weight of your mail. You wished, petulantly, silently, for your squire.

But you rose, before stumbling back down to one knee. "My King," you said.

He rested his hand lightly on the crown of your head, rings clinking on the iron of your hood. "My Devil," he said, and there was nothing you would not do for him when he spoke in this voice: fond, fatherly, full of love. "The time has come. Look into the pool, and tell me what you see."

The water was a deep, viscous black, like burned fat, which seemed to swallow the light rather than reflect it. You stared into it, and eventually you said, "I see a girl. Ill, I think, maybe dying. There is dirty straw around her, and her hair is . . ."

"Who is she?" the King asked, patiently.

You opened your mouth to say *I don't know*, but then you closed it because you could not lie to your King. Had you not lain in that same sullied straw, your lips cracked, your skin scratched and weeping? Were you not always afraid that you would wake to find yourself back in that stable, waiting for a death as unremarkable as your birth?

You said, hoarsely, "She is I," and the King said, "Yes."

"I don't understand, sire."

The King dipped his hand idly into the water. "This pool was here long before the castle. My priest tells me it was once a spring of some kind, or a pond."

His priest said, "A lake, sire."

"A lake, then. A place where time runs together, the was and will be. My forefathers used it as a mirror. A way to see their own histories and futures. But then Ambrosius came to me—what a filthy, low creature he was then!—and told me I could do more than look."

The King faced you now. He was just as handsome as he had been that first day in the yard, a little older but still unmarred, his flesh whole and smooth. "Do you remember the first time your Saint came to you? The words she spoke?"

"Yes," you whispered. As if you could forget the moment your life began, the moment you were dragged out from the shadows and into the scorching light of your Prince.

"Look into the pool again, and speak the words."

This time, when you looked into the water, you caught a fleeting glimpse of your true reflection. And it was only then, when you saw your own gory, blue-eyed face, bright hair hidden beneath rusted mail, that you understood who you were and who they were. You saw yourself as an unholy triptych, three into one, one into three: she the girl, you the Devil, and I the Saint. And you understood, finally, that there had never truly been a *she* or a *you* but only a terrible, lonely *I*.

I am the Saint of War.

I look down at my own weak and mewling self and say, "Rise."

I sit all day by that pool, speaking to all the iterations of my past. I tell myself how to kill and how to live that I may kill again, and the words echo oddly in my skull, memories I hand back to myself. I watch myself grow strong and tall, rangy as a young lioness, then scarred and gnarled, hollow eyed. It's like watching a year pass in a single day, spring into summer into an early, hard winter.

I see my squire, too, hovering at the edges of every vision. First he is a limping, gawking collection of limbs, then a slim boy, then a graceful man with sad eyes, always on you. I notice for the first time that he is beautiful.

The day fades to a grim dusk. Stars appear in the black water of the pool.

I see myself taking the Gray City. I see the boy with his father's axe. I see myself hesitate, watch my own hand fall to the stones again.

I say, "It is done, sire."

The King strokes a stray hair back from my sweating brow, and I lean shamelessly into the touch, feeling lonelier than I've felt since I was a girl, since before my Saint came to me. But in the end, there was no saint, just a lonely girl telling secrets to herself in a dark mirror.

The priest is speaking to the King in his whispering, unctuous voice, his hands stroking the fine cloth of his own robes. I catch the names of distant cities, lords and lands far beyond our borders. The King nods once, and when he turns back to me, his eyes are alight.

"You have fought so well for me, my Devil." His fingers catch the edge of my mail hood and push it back so that it forms a heavy pool around my throat.

My eyes fill with tears of gratitude. "I have tried, sire. But I fear I can fight for you no longer."

Except all I truly feel is that same shameful relief. I wonder, for the first time, what it would be like to grow old.

But the King says, gently, "You will always fight for me. Each time you are stronger, more perfect. Each time you last longer." He tugs my hair from the neck of my mail, spreading it in a red shroud around my shoulders.

"Sire?"

The King says, almost apologetically, "Ambrosius says we might take the Kentish Isles next time," and then he fists his hand in my hair, pushes my face down into the pool, and holds it there.

If he were my enemy, I would throw my skull back and break the fine bridge of his nose. I would pull him down under the water and choke the life from him, one-handed.

But he is my King, and I am his Devil. I have given him my blood, my youth, my love, my good right hand; who am I now to begrudge him my death?

The water tastes familiar in my mouth, sweet and rich as wine. It fills my lungs, and I smile as I drown.

They will always sing my name.

You were a child the first time the Saint of War came to you.

She was not beautiful. Her face was hard and worn as beaten metal, her armor crusted with blood. Her right eye was a faded blue, like dead cornflowers, and her left was missing. She was crying.

(I was always crying when I came to you. You learned to ignore it.)

Your Saint bid you to rise, and you did. She led you from the black of the stables to the blinding light of the Prince, then from the Prince to the sword, and from the sword to legend.

It didn't take long. The day they put a sword in your hand, you disarmed three grown knights and drew first blood from a fourth. The bards said it was a divine gift, but you hadn't heard the Saint's voice that day. You had simply known how to move, where to place yourself, as if your body was a clever system of wheels and pulleys, a machine built for a single purpose.

It was the same on the battlefield. The soldiers around you were so clumsy, their blows so slow and obvious. You moved through them like a scythe through windblown wheat. And in those rare moments when the impartial luck of war might have turned against you—when a stray arrow may have found you or a flailing hoof struck you down—you had your Saint whispering in your ear.

And you had your squire, with his clever hands and his uncanny knack for herbs. You asked him once how he came to heal so well, and his face grew troubled, uncertain. Eventually he said, "I don't know. How came you to fight so well?"

And to that there was no answer, because no one on God's earth fought like you.

Even the Holly Knight fell quickly beneath your blade, although in her final, desperate flailing, she sunk her spear into your thigh.

Your squire labored over the wound for a day and night to-gether, swearing and stitching, red to the wrists. He slept fitfully at your side, changing the dressings every few hours, refusing to permit any hands on you except his.

In a fortnight you could walk again with only the barest limp. When the Prince came to visit, his smile was like the sun itself. "Well done, my Devil. Tomorrow we ride north."

He left. Your squire watched him with a vicious, burning expression. You asked what troubled him, and he said, a little wildly, "The Prince takes much from you."

You lifted one shoulder. "He made me, my friend." You had asked your squire's name once, but he'd said he was never given one. You filled the absence with other words, none of which de-scribed what he was to you. "He—he loves me."

Your squire watched you carefully. His eyes landed on every pink scar, every old injury that still ached. "Is this love?" he asked softly.

You said you were tired then and asked him to leave.

You fought the Norders next. Then the grand horde, the hill folk, the Gray City. You fought for your Prince and then for your King and then—when you took the Kentish Isles after a long and grueling campaign—for your Emperor.

The songs after that became ecstatic, almost reverent. People began to trail after you, reaching out to touch your hair, your hands, your armor—until the Emperor named it a sin and directed his priest to put out the eyes of anyone who looked upon you with the love that was due only to God and His Emperor.

(Your squire said that night, "I suppose I should not look upon you any longer." You laughed. He did not.)

And still, you fought. Until the empire stretched from one ocean to another, until all the known world knew the name of the Emperor's Devil and feared her.

You would have been well content if it were not for the dreams. Bloody dreams, killing dreams. Enemies you'd already buried and enemies you hadn't yet faced. Enemies who didn't look like enemies, but like men and women, or like children, dying beneath your blade for no reason you could name. You could not decide if they were prophecies or memories, or whether there was any difference between the two.

Once you woke to find your sword in your hand, the blade a bare inch from your squire's face. You pulled the blow aside, but afterward you were sick and shaking with fear.

"I could have killed you," you said.

"You never would," he said. He took the hilt from your sweaty grip and pulled you back down to the blankets beside him. You slept that night with his hand circling your right wrist, holding you fast. You grew used to it, so that you could never again sleep easily without it.

You were not old when the Saint came to you that final time, but you were older than you'd ever been before.

You were encamped in the hills above a wide valley, where the Queen of Kemet and her vast army waited to meet you at daybreak. You could see their torches stretching into the distance, numberless, insurmountable.

Your squire combed his fingers through your hair long after the knots were gone. After a while, he said, "You cannot win against this."

"Perhaps not," you said.

"Why fight, then? For a few songs? For *him*?" Then the whisper, the question you heard sometimes in your sleep, "Is it worth it?"

You stood and turned, looking down at your squire, your companion, your only friend. You were angry, and because it was a crime to be angry at your Emperor and a sin to be angry with me, you were angry with him. You wanted to shout at him, but your throat had closed too tightly to speak, and in the end, you never answered.

The Saint was with you the next day, and you fought as fiercely and perfectly as anyone has ever fought.

It was not enough.

They carried you off the field with an arrow in your left eye. The last thing you saw was your squire's face, full of grief.

You woke—but you know where you woke, don't you? We have done this so many times, you and I.

The courtyard. The Emperor, crowned in gold. The priest, draped in fine jewels. The pool. The terrible moment when you understand, all over again, that you are all alone. That I am you.

This time, when I speak to the girl in the water, my eyes are the faded color of the sky after rain, and I am weeping. I hardly know why. Perhaps I sense, in the hazy way of an early memory, that I will never grow old, will never see my squire again.

Perhaps any tool, used hard enough and long enough, begins to fail.

The water fills my mouth. I drown again.

You were a child the first time the Saint of War came to you.

That time, you made it to the great heart of Kemet before you fell. The time after that you made it to the palace.

The next time you made it all the way to the foot of the Kemet throne. You were so riddled with arrows that when you finally fell, your body did not quite touch the ground, but hung suspended.

They had to pull your squire away from you, weeping and mad, when they dragged your body to the courtyard.

"Perhaps," the Emperor said to his priest, a little petulantly, "she has fought as far as she may. Perhaps we have reached the end of her abilities, Ambrosius."

"No," said his priest. He wore rubies on every finger now, fat as ticks. "She has made an emperor of you, sire. When she takes Kemet, you will be a god."

This time, when he drowns me, I think of all the stories they will still sing of me—the hero of the empire, the scourge of the Gray City, the knight with the hellfire hair—and then I think: *It is not worth it.*

You were a child the first time the Saint of War came to you.

This time, she was angry. Her lips were the dead white of old bone, and her eyes had no color at all.

But still, you did as I bade.

The Black Baron, the False King, the grand horde. The Holly Knight, who you slew without suffering more than a scratch down your thigh. Your squire made an abysmal fuss, unfastening your armor and searching your skin as if he expected to find a spear protruding from your leg. When there was none, he looked up at you through long lashes and smiled one of his radiant smiles.

The Prince strode by and clapped you once on the shoulder. "Well done, my Devil," he said. "Tomorrow we ride north."

Your squire stared at the Prince with an expression like a dog just before it bites. You pressed your hand to the back of his neck until the Prince was gone.

He could barely speak from rage. "He—the Prince takes and takes, no matter the cost to others, to *you*—"

"He made me, Gwynne." Your squire had been nothing once, just like you—a sniveling shadow, too insignificant even to merit a name. But over the years he had become so vital to you, so dear, that you gave him one. Gwynne, you called him, because it was beautiful and so was he. "He—he must love me."

Gwynne gave you a long, grieving look. "He never has," he said, tiredly, and began refastening your armor.

The Saint came to you again and again, always with that terrible fury on her face. You wondered if perhaps she did not want to be the Saint of War any longer, and you sympathized; you often didn't want to be what you were. You were a shrike, a leopard, a plague, a thing that lived only to kill. You belonged not to yourself but to your Prince—your King, your Emperor. And if it wearied you—if sometimes you could see no difference between the soldiers fighting beside you and the soldiers fighting against you, if sometimes you could not sleep for the memory of how you murdered them— well. It was not for the shrike to wish itself something else.

The empire grew. Your dreams darkened.

One night you even dreamed the face of your own beloved Emperor, your blade falling down onto his perfect golden smile—but when you woke, it was Gwynne who knelt before you, watching you through soft lashes.

Your sword fell to the earth. You followed it, crashing downward as if some unseen foe had slit the tendons behind your knees. You buried your face in your treacherous hands. "Gwynne," you said. "Gwynne. I could have killed you."

He took your hands away from your face and held them, his fingers so slim and fine around the knotted scars of your knuckles. He kissed the center of each of your palms, precisely where the priest said the Savior suffered the nails to be driven.

"Why do you stay with me? I am a devil. A butcher. Not even a butcher—his knife, falling over and over."

Gwynne said, softly, "Before all this, before the Saint and the Prince, you were the girl who still shared her meat with the begging dogs, no matter how hungry she was. Who took a beating for a boy who deserved it, for no reason except that she could bear it better than him. Who *shone*, even in the shadows." He said your name, even more softly. "You are not a knife."

And you said, wretchedly, "But I am his."

Gwynne did not answer. He pulled you down beside him in the tall grass and touched you in that heady, secret way that transformed the brutal weapon of your body into mere flesh. It was like shucking plate armor after a long campaign and walking naked into a river, letting the current take you. It was like surrendering on the field and finding mercy.

Gwynne touched you until you shuddered and went still in his arms. Then he whispered, so gently you barely heard it—but I did, oh, I did—"You are not his."

Each time I came to you, I hoped you would hate me. I hoped you would turn your face from me and leave your sword to rust in the mud of some distant, desolate battlefield.

But you didn't. You took the Kentish Isles and marched west until you faced the Queen of Kemet once more.

You spent your last evening with Gwynne, as you always did. Your head was in his lap, and his fingers were in your hair, tangled as if he hoped to hold you there. He told you, as he always did, that you could not win. He asked, as he always did, if it was worth it.

You sat up, turning to face him so that the two of you were kneeling face-to-face. There were tears in his eyes, and you pressed your brow hard to his. "No," you whispered, and you meant it.

"Then run, go now, before dawn—"

"Would you make a coward of me, here at the very end? After everything I've done, everything I've become—"

Gwynne's voice cut through yours, his brow still resting heavily on your forehead. "I would rather love a coward than mourn a legend."

"The Saint will be with me," you said.

But I wasn't.

Dawn came and went. You waited and waited for me on the hilltop, your horse restive, your soldiers muttering among themselves—but I did not come.

That day you fought as a mortal fights, blind and deaf and terribly alone, and even still, they could not kill you. You were a devil, a saint, a great and terrible reaping loosed upon the world. You were centuries of warfare condensed into a single body, your memories folded over themselves, beaten and quenched like fine steel in the water of the pool.

It was very nearly enough. You slew the Queen of Kemet on her own throne, suffering only a small sharp sting on your ankle.

It was only much later—when the sky began to tilt strangely around you and Gwynne's voice went high and distant—that you remembered: the Queen of Kemet was said to keep vipers.

You woke, as you always did, in a courtyard you'd never seen.

"Rise," said the Emperor, who was now God, and the sound of his voice echoed in your skull. You told yourself it was the venom, which pulsed through your body in hot, cramping waves.

But you rose, as you always did, and you looked into the pool, as you always did. You saw yourself as a sickly child, and you understood once again who you were, and would be, and are now: a woman following her own footprints, a snake eating her own tail, forever.

The Saint of War. *I.*

But this time, as I look down at your face, our face, my face—as my shoulders bow beneath the weight of all the years I've lived—I understand that this has all happened before, more than once and more than twice. I understand that I have made my life a work of bloody alchemy, transforming a child into a devil into a saint, a kingdom into an empire, a prince into a god. That I have lived and killed and lived again in the name of a man who does not deserve it because I wanted so badly to be beloved.

But only one person in all my lives has ever loved me, and he does not wear a crown.

And so this time, when God bids me to look into the pool again, I say, quietly, "No."

The word falls like a dead man between us and begins to swell. I explain as if to a child, "It is not worth it."

God stares and stares at me. I wonder how I could ever have mistaken that expression for love.

The priest leans over his shoulder. He is no longer drab or sparrowish. He is the priest of a newborn god: his hem is weighted with gold; his feet are shod in fine silk.

He says, quite calmly, "The squire, your holiness," and a great chill moves through me.

God nods, and the priest departs. He returns with twelve armored knights. Among them, limping on the slim bows of his legs, eyes gone black and wild, is Gwynne.

He surges toward me, but his way is blocked by crossed blades. His eyes find mine above the steel.

"Kneel," says God. The knights press Gwynne downward, and he falls badly, the caps of his knees striking hard against the stone.

God steps behind Gwynne and threads his fingers into the dark curls, gently, obscenely. The fingers become a fist. God pulls Gwynne's head back so that the long column of his throat is bared to me, and sets a slim blade against it.

"Look into the pool again, and speak the words," says God.

I am no berserker; I have never fought for fury or bloodlust. But for the first time, I imagine how it would feel. To unhitch my reason, to unleash the terrible animal of my body, which has spent centuries learning nothing but violence.

Even with venom in my veins, I could kill every soul in this courtyard. I would not need a saint. I would not even need a sword.

But I could not do it quickly enough to save Gwynne.

"Look into the pool," God says again.

Gwynne would have me refuse. He doesn't move or speak, but he doesn't need to. I know his desires by the pace of his breath and the tilt of his shoulders, by the shape of his jaw and the heat of his gaze. I know him, and in knowing him I love him, and in loving him I cannot do as he wishes.

I look into the pool. I see my own face first, full of wrath, and then the little girl who I once was and will be again.

"Rise," I say, and then I tell her what she has wanted to hear all her life: that someone, somewhere, needs her. That she is not nothing.

I lead her out of the shadows. I make her into a devil, a legend, a butcher's knife. I watch as she ages and hardens. I watch as her squire heals her again and again, with the same tenderness he had shown the flea-ridden girl in the straw.

At the very end, when the girl is a woman poised on the dawn of her final battle against the Queen of Kemet, I look back at Gwynne. I know I will drown soon—I remember the taste of the water, the press of God's hand at the back of my skull—but this time I want Gwynne's face to be the last thing I see.

Gwynne looks back at me with a strange peace on his features. His gaze is steady, full of a love so naked and sincere that I wonder for a moment if the two of us are alone, if everything else is just another bad dream.

He says my name, my old name, the one I had before I was a devil or a saint. Then he says, "You are not his."

Then he smiles. Then he leans his weight into the knife and twists his neck sharply, drawing the blade across his own throat.

It is a surgeon's murder, quick and clean, unyielding. A hot arc of blood, a single exhalation, and he is dead.

He is dead, and I belong to no one.

God looks down at Gwynne's body, and then, very slowly, he looks back up at me.

He is dead before he can open his mouth. His knights die next, as easily as if the Saint were still whispering in my ear. I am not even aware of moving, of choosing. My body is a thrown stone, a loosed arrow. It strikes, and they fall.

When I come back to myself, the courtyard looks like the inside of a rib cage. I am sitting with my back against the pool, and Gwynne's body is cooling in my arms.

I touch his face, his hands, his hair. I wonder dimly if the venom will kill me before they drag me to the gallows. I wonder what the songs will say about the Devil now that she is covered in the blood of her own God. I find that I no longer care at all.

I am tempted—Lord, so tempted—to drown myself again. To return to the time when Gwynne and I were two hungry children scrabbling in that shadowed place beyond the reach of saints and devils, unloved and unknown except by one another.

But they would only find me again, the Prince and his priest, and drag me back to this courtyard, to this ending.

A sound behind me: labored breathing, the shush of wet cloth across stones.

I turn to see the priest, still somehow alive. He cannot properly crawl, as there is too much of him missing, but he is dragging himself toward the lip of the pool. His expression is grim and distant, as if he finds his situation distasteful but not distressing. As if, once he reaches the pool, all will be well again.

I watch his unpleasant wriggling for a long moment, and then I lay Gwynne down very gently, propping his head against the lip of the pool so that his throat doesn't gape open.

I stride to the priest and lift him into the air by his thin hair. He mewls at me, whining and begging and making tiresome threats against my everlasting soul, before he falls quiet.

I say, "All these years, and I never wondered how it began. How you came to find me and knew to put a sword in my hand. I suppose I believed it was God's will, but there are no saints here, are there?"

The priest gives me a sour, childish glare. For the first time, I notice that his eyes are like mine: an ancient, filmy gray, like old water. I wonder what color they were when he was truly young and how long ago that might have been.

"You've lived more than once, haven't you, Ambrosius?" His name surfaces like a childhood rhyme in my head, a memory from a different life. "You found the pool, and you drowned and lived again and again, until the Prince made you his priest, and I made your Prince into a god. But"—I give him a little shake, as I would a dog—"why? For what?"

His expression gains an unpleasant, oily intimacy. "I was born the same as you. A nothing. A no one." He smiles so widely I can see the brown rot of his molars. "And now, look at me!"

I look at him: the many chains of gold looped around his throat, the heavy hem of his robes, the stained silk of his slippers. In my mind I see, quite clearly, a great golden scale. On one side there is a vast pile of corpses. Some of them I know well—the False King, the Holly Knight, the boy in the Gray City, my own beloved Gwynne—but most of them are men whose names I never knew. And on the other side of the scale, there is a pair of silk slippers.

I ask, "Was it worth it?"

He doesn't answer, but I don't need him to. I move my hands so that I am holding his skull like an eggshell between my palms.

He sputters, thrashing now. "If you kill me, you will be nothing again! Consigned to the shadows of history. No one will mourn you, no one will remember you. No one will even know your name—"

I lean close and whisper, "One person will."

His neck makes a dull crack, like a boot on a rat. I let him fall carelessly atop the other bodies.

I return briefly to Gwynne, long enough to kiss his brow and whisper to him what I should have understood lifetimes ago, what I should have told him every night and every morning. "I am yours."

This time, when I push my face into the pool, when the water fills my mouth and floods my lungs, I am smiling.

They will never sing my name.

ISABEL J. KIM

Termination Stories for the Cyberpunk Dystopia Protagonist

FROM *Clarkesworld*

COOL AND SEXY Asian Girl stands outside the convenience store under the striped awning and waits for the rain to stop. The rain is never going to stop. Cool and Sexy Asian Girl would need to go to a different city for the rain to stop, a city not built on phosphorescent fluorescence and slick glass, a city that doesn't breathe through its elevated train lines and subways. Cool and Sexy Asian Girl doesn't remember when they built the train lines. She dreams of cities where it is not always night. Not that it's always night here. But it is. In the heart, it is.

"You look cold," White Boy says as he steps out of the convenience store. White Boy has a lot of other names. The Detective. The Hacker. The Renegade. The Man Out for Revenge. Privately, Cool and Sexy Asian Girl thinks of him as the Tourist.

"I'm used to it," she says and takes a long drag of her vape, exhaling plumes of menthol vapor. It softens the light glinting off her silver bracelet. A long time ago, she smoked cigarettes. Tar and smoke. Whiskey in bars. But times have changed. She offers the little plastic stick to the Tourist. He takes it from her and takes his own deep breath.

The Tourist is a sharp silhouette against the dark street beyond him. His eyes gleam electric. The city looms behind in smears of color and shade as if the Tourist is the only thing in focus. He doesn't belong here. Except for the way that the city is a backdrop to his presence.

She's been spending a lot of time with him. Cool and Sexy Asian Girl's friends joke that his name should be White Boyfriend. Cool and Sexy Asian Girl laughs the jokes off. White Boyfriend would be a different man entirely.

There's no place in the Tourist's heart for her. The Tourist could fuck her, but he couldn't love her, just as he can't love this city. If she left with him, if they took the elevated train line to the station and the bullet out of the city, maybe he could be White Boyfriend, but she would have to be a different woman. Asian Girlfriend. Asian Baby Girl. Mail Order Bride, in the worst of worlds.

So no. No White Boyfriend.

"Was Sandra here?"

"Not sure," the Tourist says. "Cashier says that he's the wrong person to talk to. That there was another guy at the register that night. Part-timer. That I should be looking for . . . a guy named Li?"

"There's a million Lis," Cool and Sexy Asian Girl says. Just like there are a million cool and sexy Asian girls.

"He said that I'd know this one when I saw him. Said I'd have to go downtown, that he works nights downtown. That he'd probably be at a nightclub named Crimson."

"Ah. That Li."

"You know him?"

Cool and Sexy Asian Girl's shrug is an exercise in implication. "Let's go."

She steps onto the rain-slicked streets. The Tourist follows her to where he's parked his motorbike.

"I feel like you know everyone."

He kicks the kickstand, swings his leg over. She seats herself behind him, pulling up close and pressing her head against the back of his neck, which is wet with rainwater and cold. It feels good against her cheek. There are things that the Tourist is good for. This is one of them. Before the Tourist, she never sat on motorbikes, snug against a boy's back.

"I know the city," Cool and Sexy Asian Girl says. "I was born here."

In the city before the city, the woman who is Cool and Sexy Asian Girl was born two miles away in a hospital that no longer exists. But Cool and Sexy Asian Girl was born in a bar, sheathed in a tight black dress and high heels, leather jacket, neon eyeliner, and sharp haircut. Cool and Sexy Asian Girl was born the minute her eyes made contact with the Tourist, when he asked, "Are you—"

And she said "Yes," because now she had become. She had been waiting all her life for this dance, for the Tourist, even if he hadn't known it. They talked about her job, which was a corporate thing at a biotech company that the Tourist had begun investigating, in the middle of being acquired by an entity called Zether. She had been two minutes from losing her job in the merger, which was why she was at a bar, alone. He had been chasing any lead to Zether he could find. This had been why she was relevant, at first.

That first night, Cool and Sexy Asian Girl took the Tourist home from the bar to her small apartment with the unlocked stairwell that led to the roof that had a prime view of the LED advertisements cascading across the glass buildings. She took him into her bed, and she let him believe that this was his idea because she thought he might like that, because she thought it was how this story might go.

The Tourist's story was teased out postcoital. Cool and Sexy Asian Girl learned of the dead wife, the long way from home, the data breach, the mysterious corporation, the questions without answers, and she learned his names: Detective, Hacker, Renegade. Widower.

"I've been here before," he said. "But it seems different now."

The city was the city was the perception of the city. It was always changing. Cool and Sexy Asian Girl sat up and cocked her head. She studied the angles of the Tourist's face splashed with blue neon. His pupils dilated by the contrast of light and dark. She could tell him to leave. Cool and Sexy Asian Girl didn't have to stay Cool and Sexy Asian Girl. There were a million cool and sexy Asian girls in the city.

"Listen. I can help you. I want to help you."

"Why?" he asked.

Cool and Sexy Asian Girl pressed a kiss to his cheek and got up and put on a long coat. He watched her in bemusement. It was two in the morning. It was always two in the morning in the city when you needed it to be.

"I'm going for a smoke," Cool and Sexy Asian Girl said, because this was the time when she still smoked cigarettes. "And a walk. Feel free to sleep here. It's cheaper than a hotel."

And then she swept out. Swept! Cool and Sexy Asian Girl was a delightful person to be. Cool and Sexy Asian Girl didn't need to explain anything. Cool and Sexy Asian Girl was inscrutable. Cool and Sexy Asian Girl took the stairs up two at a time to the rooftop and stared at the sky and remembered when there had been stars.

But that was a long time ago, in a different story. Not a better one. That had been a story with crying children and uprooted families and soldiers, and that had been a story with opium dens and cigarettes and women who hid their faces behind fans. That had been a poor story, and this was an expensive one. Even though it had the old story in its bones. Men like the Tourist had been in that story, too.

She's thinking about the old story, the city before the city, while they ride through the night. The streetlamps are smears of light. The cars around them are smears of chrome. Cool and Sexy Asian Girl guides them through the flow of traffic, crossing the backbone of the city and winding them down the south side, where the bars and izakayas are, where the couples and laughing university students played.

"A left, here," she murmurs against the Tourist's ear. "And stop."

He cuts the engine outside the narrow door. There's a glowing red lantern hung outside.

Cool and Sexy Asian Girl swings her leg off the bike and walks to the door without wobbling. She doesn't wait for the Tourist to follow her. She knows he will. Cool and Sexy Asian Girl knows all the things that the Tourist doesn't know. She clears the path so that the Tourist can get to business. If she refused, she'd stop being Cool and Sexy Asian Girl.

It's a tautology. Cool and Sexy Asian Girl has to do the things she needs to do to keep being Cool and Sexy Asian Girl, or else she stops being Cool and Sexy Asian Girl. She stops knowing about nightclubs only identifiable by a red lantern. She stops being able to saunter in heels. It's like how the city stops being the city and becomes a different city if the flickering flames of the neon billboards all go out. Cool and Sexy Asian Girl has a role in this story the same way the Tourist does.

The Tourist follows her in. The squelching beat of good club music paints the air around them. Strangers' glances linger on their forms and the foreign cast to the Tourist's face. It's too crowded to see what's across the room. They can't talk in here without putting mouths close to ear, so that's what the Tourist does. His breath is warm against her skin.

"Where to now?"

Cool and Sexy Asian Girl takes the Tourist's hand and dances them across the room. She's part of the scene in a way that the Tourist can't be, in a way that he doesn't understand. With her guidance, they melt through the crowd and reach the bar without any incident. Cool and Sexy Asian Girl sits on a barstool. The Tourist leans against the counter, signaling the bartender for a drink. The bartender pours clear liquid in two glasses, adds a drop of something blue that blooms like a drop of dark ink in water.

Cool and Sexy Asian Girl takes her glass with a smile and says, "Is Li around?"

"Why, who's asking?"

"He's got some information that we want. I'm a friend."

And now they have become. Now they have been. Now Cool and Sexy Asian Girl has known Li for a very long time—now they met in an underground poker tournament, now she's a card sharp with her expressionless face, and now she's always known that Li's a grinning sort of bastard who always seems like he's cheating. The present is a tool to create the past, and the past follows the Tourist's needs. Water follows the most obvious path, and Cool and Sexy Asian Girl has learned to be a conduit.

She takes a sip to cover the flicker in her face as she processes the new history. The drink tastes mostly like mint and the acetone aftertaste of alcohol.

The bartender nods. "I'll ask. Don't get your hopes up."

"Thanks," the Tourist says. The bartender slips between a gap in the liquor shelves. Cool and Sexy Asian Girl and the Tourist are alone except for all the people in the room with them. The Tourist takes a long sip.

"Do you ever feel," the Tourist says and then pauses. He looks down at his drink, the blooming blue dissipating into the clear liquid, and then glances back at the crowd behind them. He looks lost, for a moment. He doesn't normally look lost. He glances back at her.

"Like we've done this before?"

"I don't know what you mean," Cool and Sexy Asian Girl lies.

The bartender comes back and gestures for them to follow. They slip into the back corridor, behind a bar and down a set of concrete stairs and then a second narrow, colder corridor leading to a room in which an assortment of strangers plays poker under a fluorescent light. Strangers and Li, who has now always been a friend.

Li looks up from his hand and smiles his crooked smile. The cybernetic implant in his left eye socket glints in the light.

"Well hey," he says.

"Hey yourself," she says.

"Are you playing?"

Cool and Sexy Asian Girl smiles, just the slightest tilt of her lip. She knows what Li is actually asking, since they've been friends for years. That's how they talk. Doubled meaning and canned expressions and hands of cards lying flat on the felt.

(This is the first time they've spoken.)

"Word on the street is that you know where to find out about what went down with Zether. Sandra Claire. Name ring any bells?"

Li's grin grows broad, a white slash in the shadows as he leans back. The filled cybernetic socket looks like a dark hole in his face.

"Take your winnings and piss off, gentlemen," Li says.

The men sitting in the semicircle exchange flat glances but leave.

They're alone now. Just her and the Tourist and Li.

"Sandra Claire. Name sounds familiar. I might have a memory with her name on it. Might have talked with her. This all depends on who's asking," Li says. "Are you playing? Nothing's free. You don't have to. Your boy can play against me."

Cool and Sexy Asian Girl is being offered an out. The Tourist can sit down and play against Li, and Li could take over. He could be the city that is the backdrop, he could be the Roguish Sidekick, he could be the Card Shark, the Underworld Gambler, the Fast-Talking Sacrifice, the Man Whose Head Is a Machine, and then Cool and Sexy Asian Girl could exit stage left. They could fill the same role, if she wanted to go. It's a kind offer. Most people don't choose to be in the narrative.

Cool and Sexy Asian Girl sits at the small table. "Deal me in."

"And me," the Tourist says, sitting next to her. He puts down a stack of bills. Li whistles.

"How good are you?" he says.

"I'm alright."

"You've got to be more than alright," Li says, and that's the last conversation for a while. Cards flip. Hands raise and fall. Eyes flicker.

The Tourist was lying. He's not just good. He's very good. Barely better than Cool and Sexy Asian Girl, depending on how you'd weigh luck's influence. Cards on the felt. Li smirks. Cool and Sexy Asian Girl is impassive. The Tourist's loss is an impermanent setback.

"So you're a cashier, and you run an underground gambling ring," the Tourist says. "How's that working out for you?"

"Alright," Li says and winks with his good eye. "No guns, no drama. Just information. People know me."

"Did you talk with Sandra? At the convenience store?"

"That would be telling," Li says. "That's money. Another round?"

The Tourist reaches into his jacket and grimaces at the lack of what he finds. Cool and Sexy Asian Girl unclips her bracelet and puts it in the pot.

The Tourist glances at her. "No, hey, you don't have to."

"Only matters if we don't win," Cool and Sexy Asian Girl says.

"I'll buy you a new one when you lose," Li says. He presses the center of his missing eye and a data chip ejects. He places it on the table. The space where his left eye should be turns into a rectangular black gape.

"Most of it's still in here," he says, tapping his head, tilting it so that the Tourist can see the other three cybernetic implants that stud his cranium. "But I like visual metaphors."

The Tourist nods. Li deals a new round of cards. They play ferociously this time. Cool and Sexy Asian Girl savors the experience. In a world without the Tourist, she would never have ended up in a small room underneath a nightclub, playing for secrets. Her bracelet glints on top of the pile of poker chips.

Everyone reveals their last hands. The Tourist won, like Cool and Sexy Asian Girl expected. It doesn't matter that Cool and Sexy Asian Girl has built herself a history where she's more experienced than the Tourist is. It doesn't matter that Li was dealing or that he has an advanced processing engine where most of his brain is supposed to be.

This is a game about luck. About favor. And the city tilts toward the Tourist.

"Oh man," Li says. "Guess I fucked it all up."

He pushes the pile of cash and chips and Cool and Sexy Asian Girl's bracelet toward the Tourist. He picks the data chip up and slots it back where his eye is supposed to go.

"Go talk to the bartender," Li says. "He'll exchange the chips for you. Then come back down and we can talk, chief."

The Tourist nods. He hands the bracelet back to Cool and Sexy Asian Girl and then exits into the corridor. Cool and Sexy Asian Girl fastens the bracelet around her wrist. Li exhales, takes a cigarette out of his pocket.

"Do you mind?"

"No."

Li lights the cigarette. Cool and Sexy Asian Girl remembers sitting on a balcony and smoking with him in the years before he had his eye out. She's glad that she built him in as a friend. The city doesn't have to be her enemy. Forward momentum, clandestine relationships, none of it needed to be deadly, so long as a smear of danger painted the scene. The scene only needed to feel like movement. Working the city was like dancing through the crowded nightclub. As long as it felt organic, the momentum would continue.

"I have a request, if you don't mind."

"Oh, I could never refuse you. What do you need?"

"Could you please lie to my companion when he returns? Tell him something . . . untrue about meeting Sandra. Nothing dramatic. Just enough to nudge us down a detour."

As long as it felt organic, the momentum would continue.

Li frowns. Taps ash onto a ceramic ashtray. "Why? Aren't you helping him?"

"Help" is a complicated word. Cool and Sexy Asian Girl is leading the Tourist through the neon night.

Li shakes his head.

"He won, fair and square. Can't have my reputation being fucked for him. You'd be putting me in a hard position."

"I'm sorry I involved you," Cool and Sexy Asian Girl says. She means that. She wouldn't have meant it three hours ago, but now she's woven a history with Li and is beginning to regret bringing the Tourist here at all. She hadn't expected to tie her backstory and Li's so closely together. But they're friends. Good friends. So Cool and Sexy Asian Girl tells the truth.

"I just don't want him to leave yet. I don't want to stop—" Cool and Sexy Asian Girl gestures at herself. The slick black leather jacket, the heels too high to be practical.

"This is fun. I don't want it to end."

Being Cool and Sexy Asian Girl is the best experience she's had. It's the closest she gets to mattering. Before Cool and Sexy Asian Girl, she had a normal job at a biotech firm, and she didn't understand the streets of the city like the veins on the back of her own hand. She got up and went to work and slept and never stayed up until two in the morning. It was never two in the morning for her, then. She hadn't understood the nature of the city, and every change in it had been a destabilization. The poor story, the expensive one, the way that the roads changed with the years. But the Tourist changed all of that. She's become a person who could live in this iteration of the city for a very long time.

Li stubs his cigarette out. He looks pale and mechanized. His flesh eye blinks wetly.

"You put the chip in my head."

The new-old memory falls into place. Cool and Sexy Asian Girl pales. She was there when Li got the cybernetic implant, the insertion of the four sockets ringing his skull. He had gotten half his skull crushed in the aftermath of a poker tournament, after everything broke bad in the police raid. Cool and Sexy Asian Girl got out unscathed. She always gets out unscathed. Cool and Sexy Asian Girl was a thing that dealt violence, not one that had violence done to her.

This is why they hadn't talked for long, she remember-realized. This was how their story made sense. She had driven Li to the hospital. And then she left him at the hospital and never spoke to him again. It was shame. That was the explanation the city gave her for their friendship and subsequent absence.

Cool and Sexy Asian Girl wonders who Li was before she warped his history. She doesn't usually think about the effect that she has on the people around her that aren't the Tourist. It's hard to remember the city and the people in it as anything more than game pieces to be steered around and discarded for the needs of the plot. But Li is sitting in front of her, his one good eye steady, the smoke curling wraithlike around him. She wonders who he was in the old story.

A good person would leave and hope that the reality would soften back into its previous shape. Cool and Sexy Asian Girl is not a good person. She would like to stay herself.

"I don't get to control how the story goes. I only get to guide it a little. And I'm asking you if you'll help me with that, please. And then you never have to see me again."

She winces, then. As soon as she said it, Cool and Sexy Asian Girl immediately knew that it was the wrong thing to say. Now that the Tourist has left the room, Cool and Sexy Asian girl is beginning to lose her cool. Her current actions aren't in service of his goals.

Li stubs his cigarette. He picks up a spare poker chip and rolls it across his knuckles deftly.

"Have you heard of infinite game theory?"

"No."

"It's one of those woo-woo pseudo-philosophical theories. It refers to situations where the point of the game is to keep playing. Games where the win condition is essentially the ability to continue existing within the system. Like being alive. Or having money in the stock market. Sometimes poker, if you don't want to cash out. Keep all the plates spinning. Winning just means you keep on going on."

"I get the metaphor," Cool and Sexy Asian Girl says. Li stops rolling the poker chip and lets it fall on the felt.

"Yeah, yeah, you're too cool for this, I get your shtick. How long have you been playing?"

Cool and Sexy Asian Girl picks up the poker chip. She thinks back to the first meeting she had with the Tourist. Two in the morning. A bar. The way that the light hit his face. How lost the Tourist looked. How he looked at the world around him like it wasn't real, like it had been created for him to be contrasted against. How she had hated him, for a brief hot second before they locked eyes, and then Cool and Sexy Asian Girl looked enigmatically away.

"I didn't mean to let it get this far," she admits. "It should have ended a long time ago, I think. But it was so easy to misdirect him."

The first lie was an accident. She said right instead of left, and the Tourist and she took a long detour through the west side of the city. They were supposed to meet an office worker with information about the location of his wife's death, who would be at the station for half an hour before the man caught the bullet out.

They missed intersecting with the office worker. The bullet train slid from the station just as they arrived. Cool and Sexy Asian

Girl had felt terrible about it at first. She apologized, because even if Cool and Sexy Asian Girl wouldn't apologize, she would soon no longer be Cool and Sexy Asian Girl. The Tourist had accepted the apology with a half slice of sad smile. She had felt a little sad. A little bit about the Tourist. But mostly about herself.

And then Cool and Sexy Asian Girl's phone rang. She answered.

"I heard you were looking for Sandra Claire," a low voice said.

"Who's asking?" Cool and Sexy Asian Girl said. "You knew Sandra."

It was an accident, the first time. A flattening of her voice. Because Cool and Sexy Asian Girl had a low voice and a flat affect, Cool and Sexy Asian Girl was mysterious and pointed, and Cool and Sexy Asian Girl didn't ask but to demand.

With her statement, the knowledge of the caller bloomed in her head like a lotus sitting cool and perfect on the still water of her mind. This was the office worker's dealer, whose debts the office worker was trying to escape, and he would know more about Sandra than the office worker did because the office worker had met Sandra through the man. Another route to the answers.

Cool and Sexy Asian Girl navigated the rest of the conversation rotely. In her head she shredded the petals of knowledge and then ripped the roots, thought after metatextual thought chewed and dissected. Throat followed tongue followed teeth, extrapolating the logical conclusions from her actions.

Her speech had its own momentum, spiraling back and forward in time. The city bent around the Tourist's goals in the same way that her own history had. The Tourist did this without thinking. But she could think and speak and mold the world into existence. The city was a stage for a specific sort of play with specific rules. Every missed opportunity could be handed back in a different form. She looked at the clock hanging on the wall of the train station. It was still two in the morning.

Cool and Sexy Asian Girl could turn the city into a lotus eater machine for the Tourist. She could stay Cool and Sexy Asian Girl for as long as she wanted.

The lies spiraled from there. Misdirection after misdirection. Flushed data chips. Wrong addresses. Doctored websites. Carefully worded requests to new-old friends who watch her now, with one biological eye and one data chip jammed into a socket.

Cool and Sexy Asian Girl puts the poker chip down.

"I don't know how long I've been lying to him," Cool and Sexy Asian Girl says. "It's . . . been a night. Not even a night."

It was always two in the morning when you needed it to be. It can be two in the morning for a very long time.

"How could you not know?" the Tourist says.

Cool and Sexy Asian Girl doesn't fall out of her chair, because she's too cool and sexy to startle from a sudden noise. Cool and Sexy Asian Girl turns smoothly to see the Tourist silhouetted against the fluorescent hallway. He's carrying a wad of cash in his hand. He must have finished with the bartender. She doesn't know how long he's been standing there. Li didn't say anything.

The Tourist walks in, turning from flat shade to three-dimensional object. He grips her almost painfully by the side of the jaw, forcing her to stand. Cool and Sexy Asian Girl struggles against his grasp. But she can't move. The city moves to help the Tourist. In a contest of strength, it takes his side.

"You lied to me. You're *trapping* me here?"

"Let me go."

He doesn't let go. He looks at her with an expression of perfect heartbreak.

"Why?" he says. "How long have you been keeping me here? Why would you do this? What were you trying to *do?*"

"Let me *go,*" she says, pushing him away, wrestling with his hold.

"Why?" he repeats again, and isn't that just who he is. Demands masked as questions, supplicant masked as god. Cool and Sexy Asian Girl hates him violently. He has everything she scrapes for. His arrogance! As if the city is an oyster to be prized open, as if his heartbreak has any more worth than anyone else's who lives here, as if his answers are a pearl and the rest of it is discarded flesh. As if she owes him anything. Cool and Sexy Asian Girl is not a good person. Cool and Sexy Asian Girl has been helping him. Cool and Sexy Asian Girl is a construct of his own imagination.

She should defuse the situation. She could speak the world into submission and run the world in a loop and find an excuse that would become truth.

"Sam," she snarls. "Do you even know my name?"

"I—" the Tourist says, and then stops. His grasp loosens, gaze vacating as he thinks, because no, he doesn't know her name. He never asked.

"Sam," Cool and Sexy Asian Girl says. "You trust me."

His hand twitches. "No. Yes. Wait. I—"

The Tourist looks frightened, now, and it's the first time she's seen that expression cross Sam's face.

"I don't," he starts to say, and then stops, and then lets go. Cool and Sexy Asian Girl falls back down into her chair. Before she can stand, he's already heading out the door and down the hallway. Cool and Sexy Asian Girl runs after him, heels clicking on the floor. The Tourist has longer legs than she does, already taking the steps two at a time back up to the bar, and Cool and Sexy Asian Girl sprints after him in her high heels and by the time she reaches the top of the stairs the Tourist's gone.

"Shit," Cool and Sexy Asian Girl says.

"Is everything so dramatic around you guys?" Li says from behind her. She hadn't noticed him following.

"Only around him," Cool and Sexy Asian Girl says. She tries to turn and nearly twists her ankle when the spiked heel of her shoe snaps.

Li catches her arm. She tries not to sag against him and fails. She's already losing whatever makes Cool and Sexy Asian Girl cool.

"I never understood how you could walk in those things."

Cool and Sexy Asian Girl pulls off the broken heel, and then the other. Without them, she's six inches shorter, and the world feels wrong from this perspective. She drops the shoes in the trash can behind the bar and sighs. Li tilts his head.

"What now?"

"Why do you care?"

Li shrugs. "I'm invested. You're my friend."

"Am I?" Cool and Sexy Asian Girl asks.

Li rolls his good eye and leans against the bar. Pours himself a glass of whiskey.

"I get to decide that, don't I? You can say whatever you want about our history, but in the here and now, it's my choice."

"Oh," Cool and Sexy Asian Girl says. Li shrugs again and drains his glass and pulls the data chip out of his eye again. He holds it out to her.

"Your boy's probably going to come looking for it. If you want him to come looking for you."

Cool and Sexy Asian Girl reaches out instinctively. This would lead the Tourist right back to her. It would be the easiest flow of water. She could make the Tourist forgive her. She could answer all his questions with perfect answers. The city was curving toward the Tourist again. She stops before she picks it up.

"Am I a bad person, Li?"

"I run an unregistered, illegal gambling ring in the basement of a nightclub," Li says flatly.

"But you do that because that's what I implie—"

"So nothing's my fault and nothing I do matters. Which means that good and bad are meaningless constructs," Li says. "You're giving yourself too much credit. And too little. Take the chip or don't. I decide, you decide, nobody gets to fucking decide. Live in the city whatever way you want. I want to give this to you, if you want it."

She picks up the chip. It's warm from Li's body heat.

"You didn't tell me that Sam was standing behind me," Cool and Sexy Asian Girl says.

"I don't like seeing my friends act like assholes. He was making you worse. Or you were making him worse." Li gestures between them. "This goes both ways."

"But you're giving me the chip to find him," Cool and Sexy Asian Girl says.

"Well, do you want it?"

Cool and Sexy Asian Girl thought she did. But it felt too easy. It felt like a test, coming from Li, who knew what she had done to him, who knew what she had been doing. She felt exposed, in the sense that her motivations had been revealed and found wanting. She wanted to squirm away from Li's flat gaze. She wondered if this is how the Tourist had felt, when he had learned that she had been lying to him. The surprise that the people around you existed outside of your narrative. Abruptly, Cool and Sexy Asian Girl felt very stupid and a little cruel. She was treating Li the same way the Tourist treated her. And maybe the same way she had treated the Tourist. Like a tool.

The city was a story, but Sam was a man who needed to know what happened to his wife. A man who had cried in her bed. And the city wasn't a story about that man. The city was a story about the Tourist and his finding of answers, and it had been running in circles, loops, for a very long time, and the Tourist had learned nothing. But the city wasn't meant to be static. Being the Tourist was making Sam worse. And being Cool and Sexy Asian Girl was making her cruel. She hadn't been cruel, before. She remembers that now.

"I think I want to get Sam out of here," Cool and Sexy Asian Girl says. "Can I borrow a pair of shoes?"

Li gestures at the door to the left.

"Employee closet. Suyoung has feet that look your size."

Cool and Sexy Asian Girl nods her thanks and opens the door. She rummages through the clothing that belongs to the nightclub's employees. There's a pair of blue sneakers that look her size. She shoves her feet in them. She closes the closet door. Li's gone, when she looks back. The bartender has taken his place.

She nods at him. He nods at her.

"Want me to close you out?"

"Please," she says, and then pays for the drinks. It feels like it's been an eternity since she and the Tourist were standing here.

Cool and Sexy Asian Girl slides her way across the bar through the crowd. She's still part of the city. That has nothing to do with the Tourist. And then she's walking into the cold clear night, and the rain has stopped, leaving puddles of slick black reflective water, arcs of neon beamed into infinity. The motorbike is gone. The street is empty.

The city is holding its breath. But the neon is still on. She can hear the roar of the elevated train. The city is still the city, and the next bullet train won't leave for another hour. It's still two in the morning. She doesn't think the Tourist can leave yet, anyway. He hasn't found what he's looking for. She'll get him out, though.

And then she'll be someone else. In the city after the city. She'll remember the neon and slick water. She'll remember the nightclubs. Maybe in the next city, there will be sunrises.

She walks into the night, for however long it can last. For however long she can stay. Her sneakers are soaked with every footstep. She keeps walking anyway.

Men, Women, and Chainsaws

FROM *Tor.com*

OF COURSE THEY shouldn't have been doing it.

That was half the fun.

Victor boosted Jenna over the tall, solid fence—like she hadn't grown up scrambling over half the fences in East Texas herself?— then climbed it himself, set down with both boots at once like this junkyard was *theirs*. For tonight, at least.

Jenna took his hand and they ran down the main aisle to the fourth row on the right. Just like they'd scouted that afternoon, the Camaro was right there where it should have been.

Its tires were long rotted off, most of its glass gone, and there'd been a few generations of birds roosting in the passenger seat, but all Victor and Jenna cared about was that perfect, unbent hood.

"Only for you, right?" Jenna said for the hundredth time, fluffing her hair up, blinking her eyes fast to be sure her eyeliner was still thick enough.

"Never share you, girl," Victor said, planting a kiss on her lips, and backed off, pulled his mom's 35mm out.

Jenna told herself this was good, this was all right, he was shipping out next week, he needed something to remember her by.

"And remember, I'm me, not her, right?" she said, a waver in her voice she hadn't meant to do.

"Always and forever, babe," Victor assured her, and, like that, she hiked herself up onto the Camaro's hood. The powdery rust was griming up the ass of her jean shorts, she knew, and probably painting the backs of her thighs, too—definitely her palms, already—but her boots were the same color. Like her mom had always told her, you've got to look for the silver lining, girl. If you squint, then the world can look a whole lot better than it does with your eyes all the way open.

That was pretty much Jenna's whole life.

And, no, she knew she didn't have a smile that knocked them dead like Caroline Williams's—Stretch from *Texas Chainsaw Massacre* 2—and, sure, okay, so her skin was probably about ten shades darker than Stretch's ever would be, even after a week in the Bahamas, but she had those same forever legs, anyway. Close enough for Nacogdoches, anyway. And these jean shorts were frames for her legs, according to Victor.

As for Caroline Williams, she was the reason for this daring junkyard break-in: last summer, the horror magazine Victor drove down to Houston to get once a month had run an interview with her, and the photo spread part of it had been shot right here in town. Everybody knew it. The crew had just been a photographer and a kid who must have been that photographer's assistant, but everybody knew where they'd grabbed breakfast with Stretch— what Victor insisted on calling her—where they'd stayed the night before, and, most importantly, where the shoot had taken place: the junkyard.

Because, fifteen years later, all the sets and props and whatever from *Chainsaw* 2 were gone, a backdrop of old rusted cars would have had had to stand in for the movie. Specifically, this Camaro, with Caroline Williams stretched across the hood, flashing that smile that the interviewer said was the main thing responsible for the world's population not getting out of control yet—"Meaning it *slays*," Victor had explained to Jenna, because how could a girl ever figure out anything obvious herself.

Goddamn right it slayed, though.

Jenna was more than a little jealous.

And now, for his six months out on the water, what Victor wanted more than anything in the world, it was his girlfriend— soon to be fiancée, Jenna had her fingers crossed for—posed on that hood just like Stretch, right down to those jean shorts.

Snap, snap, snap.

Jenna tried to smile with her eyes and her mouth and her heart as wide as she could, as wide as she ever had, as wide as Caroline Williams, even, and then the next morning they dropped the film off at the drugstore, and then six days later, after the proposal that made Jenna's mom hug her neck, whisper into her neck that she was happy for her, Victor was in international waters.

Sitting in the same bedroom she'd already spent twenty-two years in—just six months more, now—Jenna crossed her legs on the bed and held her hand palm-up in her lap, and studied the small ridge of white scar tissue on the heel of her hand, where a burr in that Camaro's hood had snagged her skin.

But don't think about the bad things, girl.

She flipped her hand over, gazed instead at the engagement ring, so perfect on her finger. Three months later, after Victor's last letter, she drove down to Houston and sold it at a pawnshop for seventy-five dollars.

The guy behind the counter asked if she was single now, then, and did a thing with his eyebrows that made Jenna's skin physically crawl, she was pretty sure.

She took the cash and walked out.

The first thing she had to do, she knew, was spend the hell out of that money.

Wine coolers took some of it, the tip at the diner back in town took twenty more—Jenna had so much she could tell the sophomore girl who brought her her coffee, but she didn't want to ruin things for her—and the last thirty-five went for a sledgehammer.

Ten minutes after midnight, she plopped down in the junkyard again, and picked up the sledgehammer that had taken her four tries to finally sling all the way over the fence.

She wasn't just going to wail on that Camaro's hood, she was going to jail for it, she didn't care anymore.

Come sunrise, they were going to have to *tackle* her to get her to stop, and then they'd better get those cuffs on her fast, because she was going to be trying to slip away, pick that sledgehammer up one more time, come at that rusted-out memory like a fucking Valkyrie. One with rabies.

But then she just stood there, the heavy head of that sledgehammer by her right boot, the handle easy in her hand.

The Camaro was gone.

Two years later, at a bonfire party out at the old drive-in, she found it.

She was living in a trailer with her good buds Cray-Cray and Took by then, since her parents had sold the house, put their savings into a camper, and lit out to see America. Jenna was half suspicious that they didn't really care about seeing America, they just couldn't think of any other way to get their grown daughter to move out, but screw it, right?

"I mean, they're not your *real* parents anyway, are they?" Took had said early on, when they were still decorating the trailer, making it not look so thirdhand.

"They're real," Jenna told her, her clipped tone shutting Took right the hell up.

What she meant by *real* was that they were the only ones she'd ever known, her bio-parents having died in a wreck before she was even one. She did still have one snapshot of them—her mom had insisted she'd want it someday—but other than that, all she had was a mix of their blood, she figured.

And her *real* parents packing up and heading out on the road had probably been good for her, she had to admit. Otherwise she might still be sulking in her girlhood bedroom.

Instead of working the parts counter at the Chevy house, yeah.

But there were still bonfire parties on summer nights, anyway.

At least until she recognized a certain shape easing his way into the firelight.

Victor.

She'd heard he was back, that he was using his experience on his series of offshore rigs to bag girl after girl, but seeing him in the flesh was a whole other thing.

His linebacker shoulders were even bigger from guiding all that chain, his hair was shorter because he couldn't risk it getting caught *in* the chain, his skin was leathery from the sun and the salt and the overtime, and there was a harsh scar coming down across the right side of his face from a single steel thread whipping out from a snapped cable, the equipment that cable was attached to sinking down thousands and thousands of feet—and almost taking him with it. It was a good story, but the story on top of *that* was that the oil company had written him a pretty check as well, and let him hire on again. It was like he'd hit the lottery: steady work, money in the bank, that cool scar, and a near-death experience. Add them all together and there were going to be little Victors in every bassinet in town, come spring.

Good for him, Jenna told herself, and turned neatly away, hating how hot her eyes already were, and hating even more how her back straightened when she knew he had seen her through the crowd.

She slid through the bodies, snagged a beer by its long neck, and made a beeline for the darkness. Just to breathe. Just to look up at the faded old screen, half its huge white tiles missing, the other half peeling at the corners.

Every few feet there were the old speaker posts, and the ground under her feet wasn't gravel anymore—it had been too many years—but it still had the old up-and-down contours meant to aim each car up to the movie.

Jenna cracked the beer open, slammed as much of it as she could, enough that she had to lean over, let some foam back out between her boots.

Surprising herself, then, she reared back and slung the half-full bottle at one of the speaker posts, the bottle shattering hard enough that some of it came back at her.

She jerked her hand up to protect her eyes and caught a piece of glass in the heel of her hand. She held it up into the moonlight to see what she'd done now, and—yep: bleeding.

Like it mattered.

The party hadn't even dialed its volume down from the glass breaking, meaning either nobody cared or she was too far away for anyone to have heard. Meaning? She laughed: Anything could happen out here now, couldn't it? With nobody watching?

It could, she told herself, and walked out farther to test it, riding the humps up and down, and . . . that was when she saw it.

The Camaro.

She felt her mouth open, her face go slack.

She looked behind her to see if this was a joke the world was playing on her or what.

It had to be, didn't it?

Jenna didn't walk right up to the car but looped around, giving herself the chance to be wrong. There were more 1979 Camaros in the world than just that one, she knew.

But this was it.

It was still sitting on its turbine wheels, no rubber, and it was still a rust bucket, but there was no denying that this was the same Camaro from the junkyard. Jenna didn't just know cars, she knew—from work—Chevrolets in particular.

She gulped the spit in her mouth down, eased in, and touched the driver's side fender, telling herself there was no chance the metal was going to be hot, or, if it was, that was just the day's heat, collected there—not an engine.

Her hand came away powdery with rust like she knew it would, and it stung the new cut in her palm.

She drew it to her mouth to suck the poison then spit it back out.

"What are *you* doing here?" she asked the car.

It just sat there.

But, in the moonlight, she could see where her hand had touched that fender.

There was a neat handprint there.

Jenna looked from her palm to that fender, shaking her head no: This car couldn't be here. It *shouldn't* be here.

Except here it was, for sure and for certain.

She leaned back in, studied it closer.

Under the rust she'd touched, there was that distinctive midnight blue that so many of these Z/28s had been painted with.

Which is *not* how rust works.

And on the right side of that handprint was the smear of blood from Jenna's cut.

Until it wasn't.

The next morning before work, Cray-Cray kept stealing glances in the mirror at Jenna.

"I *know*, okay?" Jenna finally said, about Victor being at the bonfire last night, and Cray-Cray evidently knew better than to say anything about how thick Jenna was laying down her eyeliner.

Her lie about needing the Subaru Brat they shared was enough to get Jenna dropping Cray-Cray off at the salon, with a promise to be there to pick her up right when the Chevy house closed.

Jenna wasn't going to work, though.

When she should have been clocking in, she was back at the drive-in, the Subaru idling like a lawn mower behind her because turning it off wasn't always the best idea.

She had a towel with her this time. Everywhere she rubbed at the rust, there was metallic blue underneath.

"What the hell?" she kept saying.

As for how the car had shown up here, she had even less idea. It hadn't rolled on its bare rims, that was for sure—there were no gouges in front of or behind it. And if anybody'd towed it here for whatever batshit reason, they surely would have sat those soft turbine wheels up on cinder blocks or wood, at least.

Except . . . Jenna shook her head, because this absolutely didn't track.

The rear wheel had tatters of *rubber* around it now?

Behind her, the Subaru coughed, died.

Of course.

Jenna squatted by that passenger side rear wheel, touched the rubber gingerly.

It was warm, and—*shit*! It was a radial. One of those steel strands had gouged into the tip of her index finger.

Instead of sucking that blood up herself, though . . .

Jenna hesitantly touched the pad of her finger to the bare steel of that rear wheel, painting it, and an instant later, she whole-body flinched—that rear wheel had drained all the blood from her hand, it felt like, so that she had to rip her finger away. And for a bare instant, she hadn't quite been able to.

She held her hand to her body, massaged it warm again, and a wave of dizziness passed through her. Either from her world changing or from blood loss, she guessed. Maybe both.

Back in the Subaru, not ready yet to push-start it across this baking-hot parking lot, thanks, Jenna opened the cigar box she kept her special shit in, that she'd dug up hours before sunrise. There was a blue ribbon she'd won in sixth grade. A photo of her in the newspaper climbing out of the mud pit from a tug-of-war. The wrist-elastic part of a homecoming corsage. And—this was the first she'd been in this box since forever—the ring box Victor had proposed to her with.

She opened it, snapped it shut like little jaws. The better to eat him with.

Way at the bottom, like she remembered, was that snapshot of her bio-parents. Whoever'd taken it was practically leaning in the open window of their car, so her bio-dad, behind the wheel, was having to lean back. Her bio-mom was leaning forward to be beside him, and, yeah, okay, yeah, Mom, it *was* one of those perfect-magical photos. His surfer-blond hair was shaggy and kind of naturally feathered, and her black-black hair was arrow-straight, long enough to be caressing the gear shift, and both of them were still wearing whatever that day's odd job had been: chaff and grass, wood chips and dust.

Jenna stood carefully with the box, made her way over to the Camaro, and reached that photo in, held it up until all the edges lined up, even the now-empty yoke of a six-pack, still hanging on the passenger side window crank. Which had to be brittle now, after all these years. It had to be *gone*, really.

The problem with all this, of course, was that her parents had died in a *wreck*. And, even before this Camaro started coming back, its body had been fairly straight.

Jenna left that velvety ring box open on the dash of the Camaro like an offering, pushed the Subaru to life one more time, and called her uncle Stu's house in California, where her parents were currently parking their camper.

Her mom started crying the moment Jenna asked about her bio-parents. She was so glad Jenna was finally looking into them—it wasn't their fault they hadn't been there for her.

Jenna's main question was, "A *wreck*?"

Wrong. Her dad had told her her bio-parents had died in a *car*, and "wreck" was the only thing that made sense to ten-year-old Jenna, who didn't really need every sticky detail.

The real story was that the floorboard of that Camaro had been rusted through, and Jenna's mom and dad were at the drive-in right before Thanksgiving, had been idling that small block to keep the heater warm. Factor in one leaky exhaust and some rolled up windows, and before they knew it, the inside of the car was roiling with carbon monoxide and they were asleep, never to wake up. Easy as that.

"Their first date since . . . since you were born," Jenna's mom added at the end.

Jenna closed her eyes, kept them closed, her mom's voice from California consoling but also far, far too loud for right now.

She picked up Cray-Cray at the salon almost on time, but stopped a cool quarter mile back from their trailer.

"What?" Cray-Cray said, already redoing her makeup in the vanity mirror, for whatever this night was going to hold.

Jenna chucked her chin out before them. At the silver and blue short-bed pickup nosed up to the trailer—Dallas Cowboy colors.

It was the truck Victor had left behind with his parents when he shipped out.

"Oh no," Cray-Cray said. "Took."

Jenna nodded.

Took and Victor, at the trailer.

"I'll just—" Jenna said, but Cray-Cray didn't need to hear the rest: she was already stepping out her side, striding across to the trailer, her long legs eating up the distance.

On the way, she filched a piece of chrome trim up from the tall grass by the butane tank.

Without looking back—not needing to—she casually hung that jagged aluminum out to the side, dragged it from Victor's taillight all the way up to his headlight, waving the trim up and down.

Jenna blinked her feelings away, reversed down the dirt road, and drove emptier and lonelier roads for the next three hours, until dusk sifted down around her and the Subaru.

She was back at the old drive-in again.

Instead of approaching the Camaro, even though she could now see new glass glinting in the waning moon—new glass? from *where?*—she positioned the Subaru so its headlights were stabbing past the two uprights of the old marquee sign.

It was long since empty, had layers and layers of spray-painted *G + R* kind of stuff—Glenda plus Robert, from four years ago, when Robert got Glenda pregnant the first time—but what Jenna was interested in was down in the grass. Under the grass.

The letters that used to be up on that sign. They'd shrunk or something in the sun, across all the years, and who knew how many storms had whipped them out of place, scattered them down here.

It took almost until midnight, but Jenna pieced them into TEX CH SA 2—"Texas Chainsaw 2," which she guessed was all there was room for, "Massacre" being a long enough word it would probably just cause wrecks out on the highway if drivers tried to read it over their beers.

The Subaru was long dead, and the battery was weak enough already that the headlights were yellow and thready, meaning Jenna was going to be walking back to the gas station.

But that was later.

For now, she stacked all the letters into a pile and set a rock on top of them, she wasn't sure why. And then she sat back in the grass, looked up to the drive-in screen, and down to the only car waiting for the movie to start.

Which is when the Camaro's dome light glowed on.

Three days later, Jenna woke in the grimy break room at work.

She looked up at blurry versions of Kip and Dale and, from the front desk, Sheila. Jenna guessed she'd been called in to be legally sure no one felt Jenna up while she'd been conked.

"You passed out," Kip told her, pretty needlessly.

He was holding a paper cup of water across to her.

Jenna took it and drank, buying time to come up with the right excuse.

The truth was that she'd been spending her nights out at the old drive-in, and cutting herself in new places, because the Camaro needed blood. Specifically, *her* blood, she was pretty sure. She hadn't tried feeding it a stray dog or a roadkill rabbit, but she didn't think she had the nerve for that, really.

All she could cut was herself.

Last night she'd bitten her tongue then leaned over the engine, drained blood down into the open radiator, and she'd passed out then, too, but when she'd come back around she'd been sitting against the side of the car, by the passenger side rear tire. As if someone had positioned her like that, so she didn't have to endure the indignity of lying open-mouthed—*red*-mouthed—in the darkness all alone.

It's the kind of thing a parent might have done for a child, right?

One they didn't live long enough to care for, before.

"Sick," she said to Kip and Dale and Sheila, and stumbled for the ladies' room. Kip and Dale made room for her but, a polite few moments after crashing into the first stall loudly enough that the slap of that metal door could be heard all the way down the hall, Sheila eased in. Probably sent by Kip, Jenna knew. Because he couldn't come in himself.

"Pregnant?" Sheila asked, all sister-like, her eyes batting to beat the band.

Jenna shook her head no, flushed before Sheila could clock the no-vomit situation.

"That time of the month?" Sheila said, then.

Jenna shook her head no again, though she was pretty sure she could have stopped at that if she really wanted—iron deficiency, something like that.

"Just sick," she said again, and Sheila studied her a moment longer, then for some reason washed her hands, dried them, and walked back out, the high heels the show floor demanded clicking on the tile floor.

Kip wasn't thrilled about giving Jenna the rest of the day off, especially after her showing up late two times already this week, but he said he couldn't have her falling down and conking her head in the workplace, either.

He peeled a ten out of his wallet, told her to get a burger at the drugstore, the double-meat. That it looked like she needed it, cool?

Jenna folded the bill into the front pocket of her blue work slacks and slumped out. For once, the Subaru started.

And she did eat a burger and fries at the counter of the drugstore. Thank you, Kip.

She had to keep her strength up.

Walking through the sun back to the Subaru, though, her nose spontaneously started spurting blood, like all the valves and chambers inside her were going spongy.

Working on automatic, Jenna scrounged a cup up from the side of the building and leaned her face down to it, to save every last drop.

She was down to the last little bit when Took sat down beside her, her sunglasses the big bug-eyed kind, like she was a movie star.

"Hey," she said, not even asking about the cup, the blood.

They'd known each other since third grade, didn't need to ask those kinds of questions.

"You don't have to apologize," Jenna said, trying to wipe her face clean now. "He's . . . he's him, yeah? I fell for it too."

Took nodded, kept nodding. It was like she was dialed into her own personal radio station in her head.

"What?" Jenna finally said.

Took looked away, down the street, and that was when Jenna caught her left eye behind those sunglasses.

It was swollen shut, pounded black and blue.

Goddamn him.

What happened to him, out there on the water? Had he always had this kind of bullshit in him?

Took's lips were doing that curling-in over and over thing. She was trying to hold it in.

Jenna took her hand, held it tight.

"Don't worry," she said to Took.

"What?" Took said.

"Just wait," Jenna told her.

Just wait.

Along with the last letter Victor sent back had been that photograph of Jenna across the rusted hood of the Camaro, her boots crossed on one side, her head cocked up on her hand at the other side, just like Caroline Williams. Just like Stretch.

It was creased in the middle with a white line, which Jenna guessed was from carrying it in a pocket, and on the back, in ink that was supposed to last forever, was "V/J" in a neatly drawn heart.

Jenna didn't keep it in her cigar box, but she did still have it.

Now she knew why.

Ever since his return, and his many-many conquests all around town, Victor had been carefully avoiding her. Just because he didn't want a scene, Jenna knew.

The big brave roughneck, yeah.

But now she had a secret weapon, didn't she?

The Camaro was back to cherry, had come together well enough that, except for those turbine rims that she guessed her dad must have liked enough to trade out the stock jobs, it might as well have just come off the assembly line in Detroit.

Too, she realized in a dim way that she'd dialed back from "bio-mom" and "bio-dad" to just Mom and Dad, some of the time, in the privacy of her head. She'd felt guilty for it at first, like this was some big betrayal of her real parents, but . . . it was because the people in that old snapshot were who she needed *now*, right?

Her real parents had raised her right and given her every chance, but now, in this violent fairy tale she'd stumbled into, her first parents were coming back to protect her.

That was the best way she had to explain what was happening.

They'd died in that Camaro at the drive-in just from bad luck, not from an absence of love or duty to their new baby girl, and that was supposed to have been the end of the story. Except that hit of bad luck got balanced out by the *good* luck of Jenna bleeding onto the hood of that very same car, and bringing that night back to life, sort of.

Enough.

Sure, it had cost a lot more blood to get the car back to good, but everything good's got a steep price, doesn't it?

And no, Jenna hadn't actually gotten close enough to speak to them yet.

But, from about ten slots away, and now that the Camaro was whole and hale again, she could sometimes, when the moonlight was just right, just see their outlines in there.

They were still waiting for the second feature to glow onto the screen.

They didn't need to know how their Camaro had gotten back to the drive-in, so neither did Jenna.

It was enough that they *were* back.

For her.

It couldn't just be random, she knew. From the night she cut her hand on that burr on the hood, Victor telling her to cross her feet like this, not like that, her mom and dad had known how he was going to play her. With their ghost eyes, they could probably even see that the ring in his pocket wasn't even real diamond, just seventy-five dollars of gold.

Not that it would have mattered back then. It's the *fact* of the ring that makes the world turn, not what the ring's worth.

That was yesterday's fairy tale, though.

This, at the old drive-in, was today's.

And Took having caught the back of Victor's big hand, probably from when she started getting what Victor would have called "clingy," just confirmed that what Jenna was doing was what she was supposed to be doing.

The plan was to get Victor out to the old drive-in at night.

After that, things would take care of themselves: He'd see that cherry Camaro and he'd have to drift over to inspect it closer. Anybody would. What's a car like this doing all the way out here, where the sun can fade that pretty paint? Somebody didn't just *leave* it, did they?

He'd run his hand along those smooth lines, his mouth practically salivating, and when he got to the passenger side front window, it would crank down slow, causing him to back up, hands held high and away like he meant no harm, here. He was just looking, man.

"It's all right, it's all right," Jenna's mom would say in her easy voice, and then tilt her head over to the driver's seat, where Jenna's dad would be leaning across to look up and out.

"We used to come here!" Jenna's dad would say, and Victor would nod, look up to the screen like imagining when movies used to play there, and when he turned back to the Camaro, it would be empty again.

"What the—?" he'd say, jacking all his old football senses up, his weight on the balls of his feet now so he could explode any which way.

Except, when he turned, Jenna's mom and dad would already be standing there, wouldn't they?

Standing there and shaking their heads, grinning grins that you don't really ever want grinned at you.

At which point it would be too late for poor old Victor— they'd rip him limb from limb, and then pack him into the trunk, probably, each hug Jenna once, and, without words, she'd understand that they couldn't stay, that this was really it for them, they'd only come back to protect their baby girl like they always meant to.

Jenna would watch those taillights kiss each other bye, and then the Camaro would be gone, maybe to show up again in the fourth row to the right at the junkyard. Just, now, in that trunk that would never be opened again, that would only be eventually crushed, there would be some certain remains, from someone who remained no more, thank you.

To be 100 percent certain this would work, though, Jenna went to the pawnshop up in Longview—she didn't want to get mired down in Houston traffic—and walked out with one of those TV/VCR jobs that plug into a cigarette lighter.

Next she had Cray-Cray jam that old photo of her under Victor's windshield wiper, and made her promise not to key his paint again.

"Do I want to know?" Cray-Cray asked.

Jenna didn't answer, just bit her top lip in.

She'd eaten three drugstore burgers already that day, to try to get some blood back.

On the back of the photo now, which Cray-Cray, being who she was, would surely read, was *drive-in, midnight*.

Jenna was there by ten, the Subaru tucked back behind the screen.

She thought it would be more dramatic, or a better vantage point, to stand up on the catwalk under the screen, the one every-body spray-painted their names from, but she didn't want Victor to pass the Camaro by, think she wanted him to climb up there too.

She had shimmied up the marquee sign, though, put what letters she could back, and in the right order, with the right spaces left between them.

Everything had to be just right, she figured. As right as she could get it.

She'd even called California to talk to her mom, but her parents' camper was already booking it for Oregon.

It was probably for the best.

Her adopted mom might not have recognized the girl she raised.

For the first hour and a half of her wait, Jenna drifted from speaker pole to speaker pole, pushing off for the next one and the next one until she'd touched them all, for luck.

There was still a big char-spot where all the bonfires usually were, and there were bottles and cans all around, and over by the roofless projection booth somebody'd dumped an old fireworks stand, it looked like.

The moon was bright again, the sky clear.

Jenna wondered if the Subaru would start or not, and then de-cided that it didn't matter. Or, no—it was better if it didn't. She didn't need *that* to work. She needed the other thing to work.

And it would.

If it didn't, then Victor was just going to leave a line of Jennas and Tooks behind him, wasn't he? A whole line of women, all look-ing out one eye. Or worse.

A cool scar, a good story, and a steady paycheck doesn't give you the right to do that. It shouldn't, anyway.

Jenna had been so proud of him when he hired on, though, that was the thing. It hadn't been her idea—you have to be care-ful about giving somebody an idea that can get them killed—but instead of hanging around and taking whatever life gave him, her guy was taking a chance, he was going out for *more*.

She guessed he must have found it, too, somewhere out there. Or maybe in Galveston or New Orleans, when he found that stepping down out of a helicopter made the girls notice you in a different way.

It would have been better if he never proposed, wouldn't it have? Maybe Jenna goes to cosmetology school with Cray-Cray, then, and rents a chair at the salon, doesn't have to spend her life calling farther and farther away dealerships to see if they've got this fuel line, that brake kit.

It's not really that, though.

If he'd come back the same, if he hadn't lied to her, if he'd been who he said he was, then . . . then it could have been him and her against the world, right? They wouldn't have had to give up bonfire parties, they could have still lived with Took and Cray-Cray, or some of his buds, they could have both worked at the Chevy house, but—they would be doing all this *together*, like they meant to, like Jenna had pinned so much of her heart on.

Then, eventually, at the end of so many years, they buy a camper, set out to see America, right?

Why not.

Just, now, instead: this. Bleeding into a magical car for too many nights, gambling on ghosts, and hoping nobody asks too many questions.

When Victor's square halogens dialed down to orange parking lights for his slow turn off the highway, the weak dome light in the Camaro flicked on and then, slower, off. Like the filament was still hot, yeah. But also like someone's hand had cupped it, was hiding it.

Jenna had to breathe deep to keep her lungs from fluttering away.

It was happening.

Keeping the Camaro between her and Victor's truck, approaching in jagged lines so as to dodge the speaker poles, she scurried up to the Camaro, only looked in at the last moment, to be sure she wasn't about to reach across her mom.

The car was . . . not exactly empty, she could tell.

But she could reach in, plug the little television into the cigarette lighter, then reach around onto the hood, hit the play button under the screen.

Ideally, she'd figure some way to project *The Texas Chainsaw*

Massacre 2 onto the old screen, but, even if she could figure how to do that, it would only draw eyes from the highway.

So, an eleven-inch little TV positioned on an old winter jacket right in front of the windshield would have to do.

It was all about re-creating that night, right?

The night they'd died, probably in this exact same slot.

Victor's parking lights dimmed down and he killed the engine, coasted in, his tires crunching through the dirt into the old gravel, the dry grass hissing against his undercarriage.

Jenna was sitting with her back to the rear fender, now. The plan had been to run away, hide, let this happen now that she'd set everything up so perfectly, but she hadn't counted on how close she was cutting it.

Leatherface's chainsaw ripped up out of the TV's tiny speaker.

"Jen?" Victor called, probably standing on his running board.

Because—yeah—of course he had to assume she was in the Camaro, didn't he? Girl calls him out here, then the only car has to be her.

He can probably even see someone moving behind the glass, Jenna told herself. Or, tried to pray true.

He stepped down, shut his door heavily behind him.

"Jen? Jenna?"

Jenna stared up into the sky.

The back of her throat was acid with hope. With justice.

"Um, hey?" Victor said then, stepping closer, close enough that Jenna knew if she looked under the car, she'd see the toes of the worn-through work boots he was still wearing, even though you don't need composite toes poking through to pick up girls.

But he might hear her shifting around.

She held both hands over her mouth instead.

Victor knocked once on the driver's side window and then stepped back, it sounded like.

Nothing.

Victor's boots took another couple of steps, then, and the movie stopped, or paused.

"Hello?" he said, and then Jenna heard the delicious sound of the door on the other side either being hauled open, or, from the inside, *kicked* open.

It was starting.

The car creaked either with new weight or with less weight.

Jenna closed her eyes in celebration, and then—

The engine tried to turn over?

"What?" she said.

They—they weren't supposed to leave for Heaven *yet.*

And of course the engine wouldn't start: She hadn't bled into the gas tank yet. There was no reason to, and she didn't have enough blood left anyway.

She stood, leaned around to look in from the passenger side, and flinched a bit from Victor slinging that power cord for the little TV out so he could roll the passenger side window up, really relish this car's interior.

He never saw her, either, was too busy touching everything at once, trying out the blinkers, the headlights. Running through the gears, adjusting the stereo dials over click by delicate click— getting only static, of course.

"No," Jenna said, scanning all around for her mom, her dad.

Where were they?

And then Victor found the "Trunk Compartment Lid Release Button Switch," OEM 92224594—Jenna knew all the part numbers, all the proper names.

Victor opened the trunk, then the hood as much as it would, and then was fiddling with the radio again.

The whole car was a toy, to him. A gift.

He wasn't even recognizing it from the junkyard either, she guessed. Or from the photo of her and the car that he'd said he'd spent long hours staring into, and thinking about.

But—really? That he was more concerned with the dial on the stereo than what was under the hood told her all she needed to know about him. All anybody needed to know.

"Where are you? Where are you?" she mumbled, as loud as she dared, to her parents.

Had she done something wrong? She had really seen them sitting in the front seats, hadn't she? That hadn't just been wishful thinking, had it?

And even if it was, then . . . how to explain her blood bringing the car back to cherry?

She shook her head no: *nothing* could explain that.

Nothing except exactly what she thought should be happening— her real and true parents coming back to stomp the living shit out of the guy who'd wronged her, who'd sent her life one way when it was supposed to have gone the other way, the better way, the fairy-tale way.

But he was sitting there turning the dial this way then that way, and her real parents were . . . they were right where they'd always been, weren't they?

Not here.

Shit.

Jenna ground her teeth and balled her hands into fists, wishing she'd had a backup plan, that she'd—she didn't know—that she'd rigged the whole drive-in screen to fall down on top of him, smush him like the bug he was. That would be pretty great. Or if she'd dug some pit and lined it with spikes, stretched some camo netting over it. Or even just left a vanilla Dr Pepper, his favorite, in the Camaro's cup holder, cold enough that he couldn't taste the strychnine in it. Or a hundred other things.

What she'd really done, though, she could tell now, was give him a cherry Camaro, hadn't she?

One coursing with her own lifeblood.

"Not likely," said, and stood against the car—who cared if he felt the springs shifting with her, who cared if he was about to see her crossing in the rearview mirror.

Where she was going was his little Dallas Cowboys short-bed, where she knew he'd left the keys, as his truck was too distinctive for anybody in Nacogdoches to steal.

She didn't want to steal it, though.

What she wanted to do was pull the brights on, drop it into low, and jam that grill guard right into the side of this pretty Camaro, and keep her foot on it until the projection booth or the fireworks stand stopped her.

Halfway around the car, though, the open trunk hiding her from the rearview mirror, she stopped, had to look twice to be sure she was seeing what she was seeing, what she guessed she could have seen if she'd had that whole camera roll with her parents in it, instead of just one random snapshot: the reason they were each covered in chaff and dust.

They'd been cutting wood for the winter.

With a *chainsaw.*

Jenna sucked air in, reached down to touch this bad little thing with all due reverence.

Then she used that same hand to hold it down while she pulled on the starter rope.

It just sputtered, and right then, like covering that sputter, the Camaro's speakers came on loud. CCR, blaring.

Victor turned it down fast.

"Hey, Jen, that you?" he said, adjusting the rearview mirror. "Can you believe this?" Yes, she could: Her parents *were* saving her. In the only way they could.

Because she'd been through this before for many nights, she knew just what to do, too: she spun the chainsaw's little gas cap off, bit her lower lip deeper than she ever had, and spit long and red into the heart of this Stihl, then spun the cap back on.

She was pretty sure two-strokes like this called for high octane, eighty-nine or better, but she didn't think her blood would be hot enough to get the job done.

In the tight confines of the trunk, she ripped that little engine alive.

And of course she was wearing those same jean shorts, and it didn't even matter that she wasn't blond like Caroline Williams—in *Texas Chainsaw Massacre 2*, Stretch had been brunette anyway, and, mixing Jenna's real dad's surfer locks with her real mom's Indian and Mexican hair, brunette was just how Jenna'd come out.

It didn't matter that Victor had unplugged that little TV.

Now the movie was starting.

Instead of hauling the chainsaw out and chasing him with it—if he could keep thousands of pounds of equipment from pulling him to the bottom of the ocean, he could probably bat these spinning teeth away—she angled it forward, chewed a ragged hole in the rear seat, connecting the trunk's air with the air Victor was breathing.

And then she shut that trunk hard, left the chainsaw running in there, and stepped back and to the side, to see through the driver's window.

Victor was turning every which way in the seat, trying to get away from the carbon monoxide. He was trying the door handle again and again, but, unlike every girl in town, it wasn't submitting to him.

The window crank came off in his hand.

Jenna stepped back, clicked the headlights of his truck on, so she could watch him writhe in that front seat, claw at the window, finally try to crash through it with his elbow, then with the cranks themselves.

It was made of Jenna's blood, though. And her parents' love.

It would never break.

Victor's struggles got slower and slower, until he was pleading with her, and then convulsing, these whole-body dry heaves, his eyes spilling tears, his face wet.

Jenna just crossed her arms, shrugged, and never looked away.

When he finally died—it took at least ten delicious minutes—his face was right up to the glass, framed by his hands, his fingers open and pleading.

Jenna turned the headlights of his truck off, wiped her prints off the door and steering wheel and keys, and then, collecting the little television, she saw that, under the junk coat it had been resting on, the hood was back to rust.

And it was spreading.

Jenna nodded.

Walking away, that TV on her hip, she heard the Camaro settle down onto bare rims again.

She snugged the TV into the passenger seat of the Subaru, seatbelted it in for good measure, and—of *course*—she was going to have to push-start it again.

It didn't matter, though. She'd push it all the way to town, if need be.

She rolled it out from under the screen, tried to get as much speed as she could to climb that first-row hump, then she hauled the wheel to the right, to ride the smooth bottom of that aisle. Except the ground tilted *up* going this way, shit.

She rocked forward and back in her seat for a smidge more momentum, screaming from the effort, not wanting to lose any ground, and then, unaccountably, the car surged forward, almost out from under her hands.

Jenna jogged to keep up, happened to look through the car, and there was her dad at the other door, leaning into this effort.

Jenna opened her mouth to say something, anything, but there were no words.

And—and at the trunk, pushing for all she was worth, her long hair nearly dragging on the ground but her strained face smiling, was Jenna's mom.

Jenna pushed harder with them, faster, and when the time was right she jumped down into the driver's seat, popped the clutch, and—

Her life started.

She grabbed second gear, steered into it.

Rabbit Test

FROM *Uncanny*

Content Note: Sexual assault, abuse, traumatic miscarriage, psych ward treatment, and suicide.

IT IS 2091, and Grace is staring at the rabbit in the corner of her visual overlay. It is an Angora rabbit, fluffy and white, and when Grace picked the icon out, she did not realize how much she would come to dread the sight of it. She moves, and the overlay moves with her. A reminder. A threat.

There are three other authorized users with access to her rabbit test: her mother, her father, and the family doctor who installed it at their request shortly after her first menses.

In two months, Grace will turn eighteen and at that point she can maintain or disable the app as she sees fit. But she doesn't have two months. Her period is six days late, and tomorrow her tracker will automatically administer a pregnancy test.

Grace pulls up the profile of her best friend, Sal, and sends their usual emergency alert: *Coffee??*

It is 1931, and Maurice Friedman and Maxwell Edward Lapham have just published "A Simple, Rapid Procedure for the Laboratory Diagnosis of Early Pregnancies" in the *American Journal of Obstetrics and Gynecology*, volume 21. This simple (very), rapid (by some standards) procedure involves one urine sample and one very unlucky rabbit.

(It is 1927, and Selmar Aschheim and Bernhard Zondek have just introduced the test *first*, actually, and theirs involves five-packs of mice. But the doctors, both Jewish, will soon flee Nazi Germany, and except for the occasional lab that prefers breeding mice over rabbits, it is the Friedman test that will catch on instead.)

Step One: Inject the urine sample into the veins of a live, juvenile female rabbit. Wait several days.

Step Two: Dissect the unlucky bunny. Inspect its ovaries. If they have enlarged and turned yellow, then congratulations or our condolences, this follicular maturation indicates a noticeable presence of hCG. You're pregnant.

Contrary to the parlance of the time, it is not the death of the rabbit that indicates a positive test. The rabbit always dies.

It is 2091, and the fine folks at Rabbit Test LMC do not have a laboratory farm. There are no animal casualties in the work they do. A very small minority of their users even understand the reference that inspired the company's name—it is a bit of trivia. Ancient history. An office joke.

Grace doesn't know, and doesn't care, and certainly isn't laughing. She waits for Sal at the coffee shop, and every sip of spark makes her stomach roil with nerves.

When Sal gets there—lovely Sal with her long brown hair and her nails painted like dragon scales—Grace can barely wait till they're in the parking lot to blurt it out.

"How?" Sal cries. "Didn't you map it, like I said?"

She had, she *had*, that was the thing. Grace had watched her cycle tracker like a surveillance drone over a labor march, and even though her parents disabled the setting that indicated her most fertile days ("Don't get any ideas," they'd said), she'd done the math on paper to map out her most *unfertile* days. At least, that's what she thought.

Now Sal is chewing anxiously on one of her nails (she'll ruin them that way, always does). "Did you tell Mac? Do you think he'll stick around? Will your parents—"

"I need a blackout," Grace interrupts. "Please, Sal. I know you've got some."

It's a glitch they've used before. An errant bit of update code that will block their apps for a day or two. Sal uses them to disable her blood alcohol test whenever her parents are out of town. They download patches every time, but she's a whiz at writing new ones, and that's all that Grace needs, just a day or two to corrupt the rabbit test. Under cover of the blackout, she can pull up the profile of one of those old ladies who sells pill packs out of their closets, hoarded up from before the ban.

She tries not to think about Mac, or that night spent fumbling in a sleeping bag in his dad's backyard. He's leaving for a deep-sea-fishing gig in two weeks. He isn't even waiting for graduation, it's the old birthday-and-bounce, and everyone knows how few of those boys come back.

Sal is looking panicked—this is leagues beyond getting shitfaced on a Saturday night—but they're best friends, weekend witches, twins from different sins.

She whispers, "I'll do it."

It is 1940, and bioassays are already shifting away from mice and rabbits and on to frogs: *Xenopus laevis,* to be exact. It's a brilliant substitution, inspired by the research of Lancelot Hogben in the 1930s.

(The zoologist: British. His place of study: South Africa. Until he became disillusioned by the racism of the region, at which point he left the country behind and took a colony of frogs with him.)

Here is the genius of the development: within twelve hours of injecting the young frog with hormone-laden urine, *poof,* she lays eggs. Miles quicker than rabbit death row, and check this out: you can use the frog again!

There are obstacles in place (a doctor must decide that early diagnosis is warranted), but even so, tens of thousands of frogs will be exported from southern Africa each year to fill demand.

It is 1839, and there are no mice or rabbits or frogs in sight, but Catherine knows she is pregnant (she is all too familiar with the signs), and she knows she cannot manage a fifth child on seamstress work.

She finds an ad in the *New York Sun*:

TO MARRIED WOMEN.—Is it not but too well known that the families of the married often increase beyond what the happiness of those who give them birth would dictate? . . . Is it moral for parents to increase their families, regardless of consequences to themselves, or the well being of their offspring, when a simple, easy, healthy, and certain remedy is within our control? The advertiser, feeling the importance of this subject, and estimating the vast benefit resulting to thousands by the adoption of means prescribed by her, has opened an office, where married females can obtain the desired information.

The advertiser in question calls herself Madame Restell, and she takes clients at her Greenwich Street office between 9 A.M. and 10 P.M.

Catherine's grandmother swore by pennyroyal or tansy tea, but she also had more than one friend felled by a toxic dose. These are modern times, and Catherine would prefer something measured with more exactitude. In addition to the simple, easy, healthy, and certain remedy Madame Restell offers for people in situations such as Catherine's, she also sells Preventative Powder (five dollars per package) and Female Monthly Pills (one dollar apiece). Catherine isn't sure she can fit that into the family budget, but it would surely be a blessing if she could.

(It is 1839, and for enslaved women laboring against their will below the Mason-Dixon Line there are no advertisements in the paper, there are no accessible offices on public streets, there is no quiet recovery in the privacy of their own homes, for they own nothing but their wits. For these women, forced to birth more children into the system that enslaves them, there is cotton root bark if they have the supply and the knowledge to use it, a remedy shared in whispers, a remedy that will bring down the foulest of punishments upon their heads if they are caught—but still they try.)

Catherine has no cause to know any of that, and if she did it would make her uneasy at best. She is not the sort of woman who attends abolitionist meetings or subscribes to their publications. She is a woman who scarcely has a moment free to tend her own problems, hence her need to tend *this* problem. Immediately.

She is lucky that someone has the means, the interest, and the entrepreneurial spirit to help her out.

It is 2091, and Grace is praying that someone might have the means, the interest, and the entrepreneurial spirit to help her out.

Within hours of installing Sal's blackout code, Grace feels her rabbit test commence. It's the barest prickle in her arm, the telltale tick of her med chip taking a blood sample. The scan goes straight to her tracker, and the animation of a laughing baby about stops her heart. But Sal's code holds true—her data is stored locally, and Grace deletes it with a desperate swipe before it can transmit to anyone else.

Grace sobs into her pillow for a good long while, convinced her plan has failed before it's even begun, because she can't do this, she can't do this, how did she think she could do this? She'll die and go straight to hell.

But her tears subside and she spends the rest of the afternoon scouring protest sites, seeking the ever-changing link to a link to a link that will land her on a temporary profile with the latest bot-evading slang for terminating pregnancy. She uses her bedroom ceiling for the projection, rapidly filling it with open pages, skimming one after another, trying to parse the euphemisms.

(It is 1840, and assorted Victorians are scanning the newspaper for *female regulators, cathartic pills*, anything that might solve *private difficulties* by *removing obstructions*. In 2091 there are no paper ads, but private difficulties remain.)

There. On a university black market page, buried among requests for machine-generated history papers and cafeteria access chips, Grace finds what she is looking for: *cheat sheets for rabbit tests.*

At least, she thinks this is what she's looking for. It could mean another blackout—or maybe it's just for birth control? Grace is vague on how the latter works.

The post is signed with the initials A.M.E. Grace rewrites her message a thousand times before settling on a hesitant, *What if I've already taken the test?*

Thirty excruciating minutes later, a reply pops up. *Give me your audio line.*

It makes sense not to have this conversation by text, blackout or no, but Grace's entire body begins to shake as soon as she sends her number. There is no way that she can talk to a stranger about this, there is no way she can make her confession to a possible troll at best and a possible cop at worst. When the call comes through her voice cracks on *hello.*

"You sound a mess," A.M.E. says, not without sympathy. "Tell me what you're looking for, babe."

It all spills out.

Over the next twenty minutes, Grace has one preconception challenged after another. For one thing, she had assumed all of the hoarders were old ladies, but A.M.E.—"Call me Ambrose"—laughs and assures her that he isn't *that* old, and he isn't a lady. Women aren't the only people worried about their uteruses, and Ambrose saw the writing on the wall long before the 2084 ban passed.

"I had the ol' womb exhume in the seventies," he says, "but I ordered as many pill packs as I could from overseas before the mail cracked down." He warns her that the pills have been expired for a year, but the worst-case scenario is they don't work, and she's already facing that.

He's charging four hundred dollars—he wants to help but hey, times are tough—and that's doable, barely, Grace can scrape that together between leftover birthday money and selling old toys on her market page. If anyone asks what the money was for, she'll say she took Sal out for dinner and a show.

And then he starts asking her questions that nobody has ever asked her before. What does she know about birth control? ("No, babe, taking it won't make you sterile for life. If only.") What are her plans after this? Not today, not next week, her *real* plans. Her life.

As Grace talks, she feels the decision taking hold. That's the gift Ambrose is giving her with this conversation, when he could have simply stated a price and a pickup location and left it at that. He isn't pressing her. He's giving her a moment to think it through, to own what she is about to do. It's her body.

"So," Ambrose says. "What's it gonna be?"

She's choked silent for a moment by a mudslide rush of fear and guilt. Grace can barely think the word in her own head ("abortion") because it is so fraught, made dirty by her parents' strident warnings.

Her mother was there in 2084, you know, marching for stricter regulation of uterine care. People were killing their babies left and right before that, she said. It was easy. Untraceable. Rabbit tests were private, no requirement to inform a medical office; pills were on auto-order, so you'd scarcely notice the late date before a drone dropped a discreet package down the bathroom chute. And that was only the people who *weren't* hacking their natural biology, popping in gestational blocks like getting their ears pierced, as though the country wasn't in a population free fall, as though they weren't in dire need of sturdy white babies to survive the coming storms—(her mother's diatribes took many turns).

Grace still remembers hiding behind her mother's legs at that march, age ten and terrified of the crowd. She remembers the moment that her mother pulled her into the spotlight, and cried, "My miracle child! This is my miracle child!" And she told the entire story over amplification: how her prenatal pills had been swapped for baby killers (how could such a switch happen by accident? Grace would not question this until she was much older) and the doctor told her the chances of her child surviving were slim, even with immediate intervention, but she had prayed and prayed and prayed, and she'd saved Grace's life.

So yes, there is guilt. Mountains of it. Vast oceans, roiling with the rising temperature. Guilt the size of a rich man's space station.

But Grace is also exhilarated. She'll finish school. She'll be more careful. What are her plans after this? She doesn't know yet, but she desperately wants the time to figure them out.

"Tell me where to go," she says, and she means it.

It is 1978, and Alice is looking at an advertisement for the first FDA-approved home pregnancy test, now on shelves at pharmacies all over the country. It takes nine steps, two hours, an angled mirror, and a vial of sheep's blood, but for ten dollars you can investigate your own body in the privacy of your own home, and if the test comes up negative you can be 80 percent sure that it's correct.

It isn't merely the test that has taken Alice's breath away, but the coverage in *Mademoiselle*. For decades it has billed itself as the *quality magazine for smart young women*—those fashionable, sophisticated, career-minded girls of the '30s and '40s and '50s—and alongside the fashion editorials and the beauty tips it has boasted writers and editors such as Flannery O'Connor and Truman Capote, Shirley Jackson and James Baldwin, Joan Didion and Sylvia Plath.

But this is different.

The e.p.t In-Home Early Pregnancy Test is a private little revolution any woman can easily buy at her drugstore . . . Now its high accuracy rate has been verified here in America by doctors . . . That means you can confidently do this easy pregnancy test yourself—privately—right at home without waiting for appointments or delays . . . At last early knowledge of pregnancy belongs easily and accurately to us all.

*

The ad is remarkable enough, but it is the commentary on page eighty-six that has Alice close to tears. It is beautiful in its candor, its practicality, its *honesty*—baldly stating that the benefits of private and rapid results are that they give you a chance, if pregnant, "to start taking care of yourself . . . or to consider the possibility of early abortion."

To see those words printed openly in a national magazine?

She scarcely thought she'd see the day, because—

Because it is 1971, and Alice can't imagine how close she is to a future in which abortion is suggested with matter-of-fact sophistication in *Mademoiselle* and the rest of Condé Nast's women's magazine lineup.

Alice is a married woman with two children in school, and every afternoon she calls a list of complete strangers who have left messages for Jane. They are in dire need of help.

Jane does not exist.

Or rather, Jane is several women, and they provide a very specific service to the greater Chicago area. They call themselves the Abortion Counseling Service of Women's Liberation, but for the purposes of discretion, women in need can call the phone number on their flyer and leave a message for Jane, and Jane will get back to them soon.

(They are not the first group to think of this. There are Clergy Consultation Services in several states already—networks of pastors and ministers and rabbis lobbying for legalized abortion and referring women to legal clinics if they can afford to travel, and to discreet local contacts if they cannot.)

Once a week the whole crew meets up to assign phone numbers to the counselors for a callback. Alice is one of only a few Black members in the group. The rest are white. White housewives, white working women, white activists looking to do something tangible, something *now*. And they're helping thousands of people, there's no doubt about that, but the fact remains that as their service spreads through the South and West Side neighborhoods of Chicago, their clientele increasingly doesn't match their membership. Alice's goal is to provide these folks a reassuring and familiar face.

She joined as a counselor, driver, and sometimes-assistant after accompanying a friend to an appointment. *Call this number*, her friend's doctor had said. *They only charge what you can afford.* And sure as shit, Alice helped scrape fifty dollars together and fifty dollars is what it cost. She looked around that living-room-turned-waiting-room, full of frightened teenagers and weary moms-of-three, and she knew she wanted to help.

Abortion hadn't always been the purview of psych wards and hospital review boards; it hadn't always been a begrudging concession on one's deathbed or a desperate gamble in a germ-ridden hotel room.

It used to be the work of midwives and healers, friends and neighbors, those with wombs learning the workings of their own bodies.

Which is why the members of Jane are learning to perform the procedure themselves.

It is 2091, and Grace has no idea how a womb works, but *somebody* does, and she's heading his way.

Even with the blackout, she is too paranoid to hire a driver—everything leaves a trail, everything—and so she takes her little brother's electric scooter from the garage. Ambrose asked that she convert her money into gift cards rather than transfer it directly to him, and she's shaken by how many potential pitfalls she hadn't even considered.

Grace's destination—a parking lot with many exits, behind a hydroponic garden that used to be a mall—is fifteen miles from her home.

She leaves before dawn. Every streetlight is a searchlight, every passing face a spy. She's on that stage with her mother again, the bullhorn blaring *MIRACLE CHILD! MY MIRACLE CHILD!* And she's in her high school health class being told to abstain, make good decisions, have the integrity to wait, do not lift the veil of her body to an unworthy partner, and certainly do not lift it before being wed. She's failed her parents and her God and her teachers and her boyfriend and herself, but none of them need to know. She's going to hell, but not today.

Grace doesn't make it five miles before there's a horn blaring and her father shouting out the window and her mother sobbing in the passenger seat. Her father's wristband is flashing at the proximity—the scooter has an old geolocator tag that Grace had completely forgotten about.

Later she'll learn the details (Sal panicked and told her mother), but at the moment all she knows is that her parents are here, they've caught her, the door has slammed shut.

It is 2084, and Grace's mother is a single spear in a vanguard. Half the world is burning or flooding and the other half is arguing bitterly over who should take in refugees, if at all. (They'd postponed this future, a hard push in the '30s and '40s, a desperate revival of green initiatives, wholly reactive and far too late—but it was only a stall, in the end.)

Amelia is marching because she fears being outnumbered. She's marching because she believes it's her duty to save babies and place them in homes with good Christian values, because the scientific establishment is out of control, a cabal of demons on Earth locking an entire generation out of salvation.

She doesn't know or understand all of the terminology, but she's equally scathing toward every problem facing America today. Invasions at the border and children making up genders and godlessness in schools and lesbians in every sitcom and the greatest problem of all looming over the rest: the intrusion of technology into natural-born bodies. An entire economy of soulless elites enabling—encouraging!—people to tailor their hormones and alter their organs, to implant med chips and tracking devices, monsters who are giving their tech cute names like *rabbit test* when it isn't cute at all, it's a means to leap at the first sign of conception and take control of a natural process that ought to be left to God's will alone. (The hypocrisy of installing that same test in Grace will never occur to her; the right people have taken over monitoring it.)

The long and short of it is: her daughter will be raised better.

It is 2092, and Grace is a disappointment to her mother.

"*Breathe,*" says the nurse.

Grace *is* breathing. She's also crying. She read what she could find about childbirth but nothing prepared her for the reality. At one point she is struck by the desperate, irrational desire to call Ambrose—at least he would tell her honestly what's about to happen. But that temporary profile is long gone; his number long disconnected.

"Breathe," says the nurse.

Grace is gasping. Her mother is at her side, but they are hardly speaking at this point. There are drugs, but she is in terrible pain. When the anesthesiologist ups the dose and half of Grace's body immobilizes, she has a panic attack.

The anesthesiologist's voice penetrates the haze. ". . . something for the anxiety?"

Grace's mother says yes. The drugs trickle in, and Grace can't remember most of what happens next.

It is 2092 and there is only so much comfort modern medicine can provide. Even if Grace's mother had hired a doula ("You don't need one," she had declared. "You have me.")—even if she had, what could a doula have said to make Grace feel any better? The deed is done.

A nurse holds up the infant, which is squalling in even more terror than its mother.

Barring any gender revelations to come: it's a girl.

It is 1817, and Asenath Smith is in love with an Episcopal preacher.

His name is Ammi Rogers, and he's been banned from the ministry in Connecticut for promoting separation of church and state. He works instead on the lucrative traveling preacher circuit, where he's grown exceedingly popular—particularly amongst the ladies.

Asenath, twenty-one years of age and grown up in a family of independent-minded women, met the controversial figure when he was giving comfort at the bedside of her dying grandmother, God rest her soul. She was smitten. She was smote.

When Asenath realizes she is pregnant, she goes straight to Rogers, secure in the fact of their upcoming marriage. They'll only have to hasten the date.

But Rogers won't marry her unless she ends the pregnancy. Most people ignore it when babies are born less than nine months from the wedding, but that courtesy will not be extended to him. His reputation is already under attack.

He gives her medication, but it doesn't take.

He attempts to use a tool, but that doesn't seem to work either, so he flees town. Several terrible, pain-ridden days later, Asenath gives birth: a stillborn.

The ensuing scandal is intense—the attempts at prosecution even more so. There is no seduction law in Connecticut, no statute banning abortion. He is arrested nonetheless.

The first trial fails when Rogers abducts Asenath and her sister, locking them up until they agree to withdraw their testimony. They keep their promise and refuse to cooperate at the second trial, but their former statements are presented anyway. In lieu of any charge more accurate, Rogers is convicted of sexual assault and sentenced to two years in prison.

The firestorm rages on. The coercion of Asenath Smith is central to the debate, but the debate does not include ways to ensure that women like Asenath can escape coercion. The General Assembly instead takes aim at medicinal abortion, eager to push midwives and grandmothers (many of them immigrants or formerly en-slaved) out of the business—the first antiabortion legislation in the nation. Abortions approved and performed by doctors will remain protected for some time longer, putting these delicate bodily decisions into more authoritative hands.

This conclusion misses the point.

It is 2107, and Grace's daughter is fifteen years old. They've been living on their own for five of those years, finally out of Grace's childhood home and into a one-bedroom apartment in a downtrodden part of town. Most of Grace's neighbors are from India, and it's a relief to escape the constant scrutiny of her former neighbors, a relief to no longer be ducking her head in shame.

It isn't Olivia that Grace is ashamed of, even though that is what everyone expected of her. (She loves her daughter, despite it all.) Rather, she's ashamed of how long it took her to get out of that house. A decade of minimum wage shift work and listen-ing to her mother's remonstrations about her character and the burdens of babysitting and social embarrassment, as if she hadn't kept Grace under strict supervision for eight months to ensure it would happen—

But it's over. These past five years have been peaceful. They've been revelatory. Her own life is under her own control (to the extent that working fifty-plus hours per week to afford pasta and imita-tion butter feels like control). Grace has cut ties to her church and only answers her mother's calls one third of the time. Life isn't what she hoped for, but she's learned to live with her life.

And then May comes.

In May, Olivia goes to a party after school and comes home sick. She can't remember a thing, but she's aching, she's distressed, she has nightmares that move like shadows in candlelight. They run a blood workup but whatever was in her system is gone without a trace.

Three weeks later she falls onto Grace's shoulder, panic-stricken, in disbelief, and in that second before the words tumble out of her mouth, Grace already knows. It's her rabbit test.

(It wasn't installed at Grace's request, or with either of their consent. Med chips are mandatory from age six, the rabbit test from age ten. It's been a statewide law since 2102, and Grace can't afford to leave the state. The protesters who were so quick to condemn its use in private decision-making had no qualms about using it for surveillance.)

"What do I do?" Olivia cries. Over and over. "What do I do?"

Grace's mouth is dry. The words come out faintly. "I can fix this," she says. "If that's what you want."

"How?" Olivia whispers.

They stay up late that night, discussing the options. Grace tries not to reveal how badly she is shaking. She talks Olivia through the risks of trying to fake a miscarriage versus the risks of pregnancy and childbirth. She tries to give her the information she wishes she'd had, building the conversation without a blueprint.

"Have you run a search?" Grace asks abruptly.

"No, I came straight to you." Olivia reaches out hesitantly, as if to pull up a screen. "Should I . . . ?"

"No!" Grace claps a hand over hers. "Don't search. Don't breathe a word to anyone, not even your best friend, do you understand?"

At the moment, the law only condemns the procurer. Olivia is a minor. Her body belongs to Grace in the eyes of the law, and therefore Grace is responsible for what comes next.

She does everything she can to cover her tracks. An anonymous account from a throwaway device, an exchange location in a terrifying part of town where the network is always down, an even more terrifying night spent rubbing her daughter's back, coaching her through the cramps and nausea, making note of the size of her blood clots and rehearsing the story they'll tell the doctor the next morning—

It isn't enough.

All it takes is one suspicious nurse to flag Olivia's paperwork. Why didn't they make an appointment when her rabbit test came up positive? Why didn't they go to the ER at the first sight of blood?

Grace's background is scrutinized, her location data inspected for mysterious gaps, witnesses contacted in regards to her character. And then, evidence where she didn't even know to destroy it: a drug test performed on their household wastewater line.

She is arrested for murder, but the public defender tells her they can get it knocked down to voluntary manslaughter if she attests that she was out of her mind, in a heat of passion triggered by the memory of her own thwarted abortion and the lack of a man's support. Grace doesn't want to be cast as a madwoman who shoved pills down her daughter's throat in a fit of old-fashioned hysteria, but it takes the sentence down from twenty years without parole to twelve.

She'll go away, and Olivia will be remanded into the custody of Grace's own mother.

And all Grace can think of as she's led out of the courtroom is: I had five years of my own. I had five years.

It is 1993, and she wants this baby so *much*, they have been trying and trying; there's a heartbeat, she can *hear* it, but there isn't a brain. Her body won't let it go, and the doctor says I am very sorry, but I will have to remove it myself.

It is 2015, and she has to sneak in on a Tuesday because her youth group is protesting the clinic on Saturday, and she needs a couple of days to recover or they'll wonder why she isn't there. She'll weep in the recovery room and call the nurse a murderer.

It is 1965, and she has to convince a hospital review board that she's suicidal, clutching letters from two separate psychiatrists, all for the privilege of spending two nights in a psych ward and having all her bits shaved for no clear reason, but it works, it's humiliating but it *works*, and she knows she's one of the lucky ones for finding a way.

It is 1150, and Hildegard von Bingen, the Sybil of the Rhine, is settling into life as the abbess of a monastery built in her honor. She is preparing to write the medical tomes *Physica* and *Causae et Curae*, in which, among many other remedies, she will list her most tried-and-true abortifacients. Officially, the Church considers the practice a sin, but it is not murder until the quickening, that moment four or five months along when the soul enters the body, and so a nun providing this care to her community is not remarkable, but merely practical.

The Romans have their silphium and the Chinese have Achyranthes root. The Shoshone have stoneseed, the Lakota have sagewort, the Hawaiians have elixirs of hau, noni, 'awa, and young kī leaves. The Victorians have their tansy tea and savin, their ergot of rye, their black draught and mallow and motherwort. Millennials have got mifepristone and misoprostol, and the climate generation has gestational blocks and yellow pills droned straight to the bathroom chute.

It is 1750—seventeen fucking fifty—and Mary is consulting a dog-eared copy of *The American Instructor*, the greatly popular household textbook. It is not an arithmetic lesson that occupies her today—though math will come in useful—but an entry in the medical section at the back.

Mary is reading instructions on how to cure that most common of complaints among unmarry'd Women: the SUPPRESSION of the COURSES. Mary's courses are suppressed, all right, have been for weeks, and as a widow of certain means and a disinclination to marry again, it isn't the first time she's had to consult this home remedy. To cure her Misfortune, she's got to purge with Belly-ach Root and then drink Pennyroyal Water with Spirits of Harts-horn twice a day for nine days, then take three days' rest, then go on again for nine more days. It's a pain, but better than the alternative.

(It is 1750, and across the vast tracts of North America there are dozens of Indigenous tribes with more than a hundred alternatives, but Mary has just got this book.)

She emits a light, "*Fah*," at the warnings and preventative measures listed at the end of the passage, as she always does. They conclude with a prim exhortation not to long for *pretty Fellows*, or any other *Trash* whatsoever. Her current fellow is not trash—he is really rather respectable—but Mary has no desire to shackle her person or her estate to another master, no matter how pretty. She watched her mother die on the birthing bed at age forty-two. She watched her sisters fade to shadows under the demands of overfull houses.

The death of her first husband has given Mary the freedom to move about as she wishes; to run her own household and control her own fate.

She isn't going to give that up lightly.

*

It is 2119, and Grace hasn't given up, but the years have been painful and slow.

Today, she is getting out of prison.

She's not the same woman she was. She's angrier. She's hurting. She has a permanent cough from the last virus to run rampant through the prison population. But after twelve years, she's just as scared of reentering the world outside as she is of never seeing it again.

Olivia is waiting in the parking lot. They stare at each other for a moment that burns like a California wildfire and then they fall into one another's arms.

There's a child in the back seat of Olivia's car, four years old and squashed nose-first against the glass. He's named Raley, after the activist who made the marriage of his mothers possible after so many decades in which it was not. The tide is turning on bodily autonomy again. One generation's fight to choose their partners is fueling the fight to choose the size of their families—a reversal of the historic civil rights progression that will inspire dissertation topics for years to come.

"I missed you," Olivia says.

"I missed *everything*." Grace has held herself together for so long, she *refuses* to break down in the parking lot ten feet from the damn gate—but she comes close.

And then Olivia says, "I'm speaking at the decision next week. Will you come?"

Grace flinches. It's too much, too soon. Her world has been reduced to a handful of walls and familiar faces for years, and now Olivia is asking her to stand up in front of one hundred thousand people?

"Please," Olivia says.

Grace shuts her eyes.

The world continued to burn while she was gone. The last decade has seen ever more flooding and fire, hurricanes and heat waves, collapsing coastlines and viruses named for every letter of the alphabet. Some of these disasters hit the prison, in the form of power outages and spoiled food and illness and neglect, but others were only items in the news, dire glimpses of the life waiting for them outside. Grace has missed riots and assassinations. She's missed a national strike and no small number of election day bombings. But there are strides being made, small victories being won, and Olivia truly believes that a big one is coming next week.

It's happening. The final vote. Congress is on the verge of overturning the ban and returning some measure of bodily autonomy to more than half the population. There isn't a supply chain in place for abortion medication anymore; there aren't many doctors trained in the scant emergency procedures they are occasionally allowed to perform, and they certainly won't be welcoming any black-market midwives into their fold to make up the deficit. But they have a president waiting to sign. They have businesses eager to flood the market. They have a multimillion-dollar video campaign ready to roll out, complete with celebrity cameos.

If it passes. If.

If it doesn't, then things are going to get ugliest exactly where Olivia is asking her to be. There will be violence. Tear gas deployed by drone and skirmishes with National Guard robotics. There will be arrests in the thousands.

Grace imagines that chaos and suddenly she's ten years old again, being dragged into the spotlight as a poster child for uterine regulation. She's hearing her fate screamed through a bullhorn, she is stepping up to the mic and agreeing *my mother saved my life and your mother saved yours*, she is two months shy of turning eighteen and nursing the sting of a slap on her face, she is locked in her room except for mealtimes and exercise, she is locked in her cell except for mealtimes and exercise, she is watching her entire life pass by and wondering who she would have been if she'd been allowed to make up her own mind.

Her mother helped break this world. Her daughter is trying to fix it.

She looks at little Raley, his face still pressed to the car window, watching her, wondering what kind of person this prison grandmother of his is, and she's wondering the same thing. She says, "I'll go."

It is 2119, and Olivia is standing onstage with a dozen people behind her and a hundred thousand in front. Her wife is at her side, their marriage barely two years legal. Her son is wedged between them, dazzled by the lights.

The Senate steps are filled with shoulder-to-shoulder policing units, blue lights blinking on their boxy chests. The air is full of cameras—military surveillance and media coverage and endless proxies from supporters who could not make it in person.

It is Olivia's turn to speak. She is here to represent the grassroots group she joined the day she ran away from her grandmother's house, living couch to couch and paycheck to paycheck. She is here to represent everyone else who has struggled to build a life on an obstacle course.

She shouts, "There is no justification for obeying an immoral law!" and the roar from the crowd is deafening. She pulls Raley tight to her side, a child she chose, and she speaks of the past and the present and the future.

"At every turn, we've sought to know more about our bodies," she says. "And at every turn, that knowledge has been used to rope us in tighter, to set the deadline shorter, to put private decisions in the hands of public officials, as if we can't be trusted to choose for ourselves."

Olivia flings her other arm wide. She says, "We only want to control our own destinies! We want to decide the course of our lives, and not see every scientific advance weaponized against us. It is 2119, and I would not have this child if I'd been forced to term before I was ready, before I had a home worth sharing. And—"

It is 1350 BCE, and she is urinating on bags of wheat and barley seeds, waiting to see how quickly they will sprout. It works more often than you'd think.

She just wants to *know*, so she can plan, either way. And—

It is 1021, and she is watching the shah's physician pour sulfur over her urine, looking for the worms he believes will spring from the mix. It doesn't work any better than you'd think.

She just wants to *know*, so she can plan, either way. And—

It is 1658, and she is waiting at the home of the local piss prophet. He holds the matula up to the light, peering through the glass to assess the color of the liquid within.

She just wants to *know*, so she can plan, either way. And—

It is 1998, and Lee Berger just identified the fungus causing a decades-long decline in Australian frog species. It was carried on the skin of our old friend *Xenopus laevis*, exported by the tens of thousands for urine-injection pregnancy tests, and now it is threatening extinction to 30 percent of the world's amphibians.

It's unfortunate as hell for the frogs, but all of those people just wanted to *know,* so they could plan, either way. Because—

—because she is still ten thousand dollars in debt from her *last* time giving birth.

—because if she stops taking her medication, she will die.

—because the thought makes him vomit, makes him faint, he wouldn't survive it.

—because if they don't finish school, they'll be raising this baby in their parents' basement.

—because she simply doesn't want to, she doesn't *want* to, she doesn't need to be on her deathbed or underage or running from a monster, her doctor said she couldn't get her tubes tied unless she had three children already, but where's the logic in giving birth to three children for the permission to have *none*?

It is 2084 and she is crying, "Our grandmothers fought so hard for this."

It is 2206 and she is crying, "Our grandmothers fought so hard for this."

It is 1878 and Madame Restell is bleeding to death in her bathtub rather than submit to another trial. It is 1821 and Asenath Smith is fleeing town in disgrace. It is 1972 and seven of the women of Jane have just been arrested in a raid. It is 2086 and Grace's medical record has been officially upgraded to that most precarious of categories: *potential to become pregnant.*

It is 2022 and it isn't over.

It is 2022 and it is never over.

ISABEL CAÑAS

There Are No Monsters
on Rancho Buenavista

FROM *Nightmare*

In *Folktales of Mexico*, compiled by Américo Paredes (one of the founding fathers of Chicano studies in the U.S.), I read a story about a man who discovered that his wife was a monster. Any night the man was away, the wife stripped away her skin and flew through the air as a skeleton, terrorizing the people of the town and stealing infants to eat; to defeat her, the man poured salt on her abandoned skin, thus killing her and saving the town. I thought about who was the true monster of the story, then took the story's skin and turned it inside out, so to speak.
—IC

ROSARIO WAS NOT the prettiest young woman on Rancho Buenavista, nor even the prettiest of her sisters; she was too aloof, too dreamy to be useful in a hardworking home. But that did not change the fact that her suitor Beto, Antonio's cousin, was the most envied man. See, Rosario had secrets. Secrets have a way of drawing moth to flame, and Rosario's lit her like a lamp.

Antonio worked himself sick watching the lovers. His was the kind of envy that gorged itself on shattering things; convinced he could ruin Beto if he proved Rosario's glow came from the attentions of another man, he watched Rosario as a coyote stalks the chicken coop. Rosario began covering her hair and face, darting skittish across shaded courtyards, even crossing the rancho bat-like, with unpredictable, looping routes, but Antonio was always watching.

The moon waxed. Rosario's temper waned.

That night, Antonio lay on the cool banks of the creek. The moon was lopsided, drunk on its own light; it perfectly illuminated Rosario emerging from the oaks in her pale nightdress, dried leaves crackling under her bare feet.

Imagine how victory flushed Antonio. He would catch Rosario in the act and crow at Beto come morning. Beto would be crushed, and—

Rosario's eyes found him in the dark. Maybe she waved at him. She reached for her nightdress and slipped it over her head.

Antonio's heart stopped.

Then Rosario reached for her throat, sank her fingers into her skin, and pulled.

Her flesh split: between her breasts and down her belly, up her neck and over her face. It kept splitting, revealing the web of dark veins over wet organs, the wink of something bright. The skin of her face fissured and peeled away, taking lips, taking nose, taking eyelids and lashes and *eyes*, her long, heavy mane of dark hair leading her skin's fall to the grass.

A silver skeleton stood before Antonio.

It stepped toward him.

Antonio thrust himself to his feet and fled. Across the creek, soaking his boots, blood pulsing in his temples and eyes so wide he feared they might pop out like Rosario's had.

His cousins were roused by his screams that there was a monster on the rancho. It's Rosario, he howled, inconsolable, as dawn broke and thickened. She would steal babies and breathe curses on their sleeping women unless they found salt, they needed salt, more salt than anyone had imagined was possible, barrels of it to pour on the monster's skin and separate her from it . . .

Everyone says Antonio would have become the town crazy if he ever got the chance. But as he raved, a soft foam formed at his mouth. As he cried *salt, salt, salt*, the foam thickened. Globs of salt dropped from his lips to his boots; his spittle turned to salt, then his tongue, then his throat, his skin, his guts.

A statue of salt stood in the pale sunrise, a pillar, until a breeze from the east lifted and it crumbled gently to the earth.

Fíjense, there was no saving him, Beto said to the cousins later. They clicked their tongues, a circle of funereal black around the salt lick. They would have to check the cattle dogs for rabies, for naturally there were no monsters on Rancho Buenavista.

From where they stood, they could see the casa mayor of the rancho, where Rosario sat demurely on the patio with her sisters, needlework gilded by quiet morning. She lifted her head, smiled coyly at the oaks by the creek, and returned to her stitches.

S. L. HUANG

Murder by Pixel: Crime and Responsibility in the Digital Darkness

FROM *Clarkesworld*

FROM THE FIRST time I visited Mariah Lee-Cassidy in prison, she radiated defiance. The poisonous orange of her prison jumpsuit might have been the decision of the state, but everything else about the twenty-nine-year-old, from her aggressively spiked hair to the rakish tilt of her chin, seemed calculated to scorn others.

I was the first, and only, journalist she had agreed to see. "I hear you're talking to the cops," she said, when she flopped down across from me at the table in the visitors' room. Here in minimum security they had no need for phone calls through glass.

"I'm talking to the FBI, actually," I said. "They think you're Sylvie."

Lee-Cassidy didn't try to feign ignorance.

Instead, she smirked. Ran a finger up the xylophone of piercings in her left ear, then leaned back in the dusty plastic chair, stretching her legs out under the table and taking up space.

"And what if I am?" The question was subtly taunting. "Does that make me a murderer?"

Back in 2010, the social media accounts of Ron Harrison* showed the life of a man who had everything. The CEO of a major medical supply company, Harrison had a picture-perfect life in the Virginia

---

* Some names have been changed for privacy.

suburbs: a six-figure salary, a wife and two children, even a brown-and-white cocker spaniel named Poncho.

Harrison received the first message on a sunny afternoon in July 2012. It popped up on his computer and wouldn't go away.

i'm watching u

He tried closing the window only for it to open again on its own accord. He tried rebooting. Finally, he called IT, who took his computer away to check for viruses.

Only a few hours later, a text message appeared on Harrison's phone:

i know what u did

He blocked the number, told himself it was an annoying prank, and thought no more of it. Until the next day, when the messages kept coming. All from an undetermined source, all nonspecific to the point of cliché. Messages he would have brushed off and laughed at, if they hadn't begun to invade every part of his digital life: email, Twitter DMs, even at one point the error readout on his home printer.

The messages also quickly began to get more personalized.

ur gonna get found out, read one, followed by, *gonna lose everything, that fancy yacht and ur 2 vacation homes say buh-bye ur going down.*

Harrison had posted a picture of a new boat purchase on Facebook just a few weeks before. He began to become paranoid that every part of his life was being hacked. This headache couldn't have come at a worse time for him—Harrison's company was facing a recall for a model of pacemaker, one with a part that had a potentially fatal defect in a very small percentage of cases. The news reports speculated about a class action lawsuit, but Harrison's wife remembers him acting almost carefree at first. "He brushed me off whenever I asked about it," she said. "It was more than confidence—he acted like it was nothing." After all, the company was complying with all regulations and had done nothing wrong, so this was only a small bump.

Meanwhile, Harrison's wife urged him to go to the police about his digital stalker. He did file two police reports, one in 2013 and one in 2015, but the officers didn't know how to pursue them when no crime had been committed—all Harrison had were pixels on a screen. For reasons that were unclear at the time, Harrison did not attempt to push the case. By a year into the harassment, he had stopped even asking for support from his company's in-house IT division, instead increasingly eschewing technology.

No matter how he tried to get away, however, the messages found him. And they seemed to know more and more. *ur a rotten flesh bag, someone's gonna find that money and end u* popped up on the family's internet-connected TV in 2014, but it was gone by the time Harrison's wife ran into the room to find him angrily smashing on the remote, his face boiling red. Harrison began to move both his personal and company finances around in drastic ways, ignoring his accountants' warnings and throwing vast investments overseas.

But the messages that seem to have gotten to Harrison the most were the ones that referenced a secret. Because he did have a secret—one that could destroy him. In 2011, a year before the recall, he had seen the data on the faulty pacemaker part. He had sat in a closed-door meeting with all the most important decision-makers at the company, and they had voted to keep it quiet.

"A careful phase-in of non-defective parts over the next several years will mask any potential issue," reads an internal company memo that was eventually revealed in court documents. "Failure rates are low enough to warrant an acceptable statistical risk when compared with the near-certain PR disaster that would result from a voluntary recall."

Only those who had been in the room were supposed to know. But whoever was messaging Harrison seemed able to burrow into any computer—could they have discovered his liability?

Harrison's paranoia began affecting both his job and his marriage. His behavior became more erratic; he made staggering mistakes at work and then blamed phantom enemies who were "coming after them." He began drinking habitually, screaming at his wife and children, ranting to anyone who would listen that he was being watched and that someone was out to get him.

He bought a handgun and insisted on sleeping with it next to his bed.

His wife filed for divorce in 2016. She took their two children and the dog.

In 2017, the board of directors at Harrison's company forced him out. That same year, the IRS opened an investigation into his financials.

In 2018, the class action lawsuit was found in the plaintiffs' favor, with Harrison a named defendant. In the one piece of video footage caught of him afterward, he is sweating and disheveled, swearing that someone set him up.

In December 2018, just before Christmas, Ron Harrison took several bottles of bourbon, locked himself in his home study, and used the handgun to shoot himself.

Only then did the stalker's messages stop.

Investigators only discovered the scale of the digital harassment after Harrison's death. It's likely that his paranoia about his actual sins kept him from pushing the matter with law enforcement, but his stalker had sent Harrison almost three hundred thousand messages over the course of six years. The messages start out vague, but as Harrison's life fell apart, they begin taunting him in specific: *ur wife has prolly f—ed 17 other guys by now* after his divorce, or *haha hope u kept that yacht to sell, i'm gonna buy it just so i can piss all over it in front of u* right after he'd been fired. Death threats were common, from the generic (*f— off and die Ron*) to the graphic (one message laid out in detail how he should be vivisected).

The day Harrison died, the stalker had sent over a dozen messages, including ones telling him he deserved his fate, that people would cartwheel on his grave, and, most saliently, a description of how he should kill himself because all that was in store for him was watching his creditors perform sexual acts with his belongings.

The history of the messages shows that an increasingly desperate Harrison sometimes wrote back, demanding what the stalker knew or yelling insults in return. In one early exchange in 2013, Harrison replied cursing the stalker off, and then sent an all-caps question: *WHO THE F— ARE YOU???!!?!*

i'm sylvie, was the calm reply. *& i'm ur worst nightmare.*

Three hundred thousand messages to destroy a man sounds like a modern-day revenge tale. If written into a twenty-first-century cinematic tragedy, "Sylvie" would be someone who had been harmed by Harrison, perhaps someone with a family member among that unlucky, unprofitable percentage who died from the faulty pacemakers. We would take in the saga with sadness, and we would denounce vigilante justice but also feel her pain. We would contemplate what drives a woman to spend six years harassing someone into suicide, to commit every moment of her life to such a relentless pursuit. After all, as Confucius supposedly said—before you embark on a journey of revenge, dig two graves.

Only, at the same time "Sylvie" was driving Ron Harrison into a panic, someone named Sylvie was sending very similar messages to a hedge fund manager in Connecticut, a museum curator in British Columbia, and a political consultant in Florida, along with thirteen other men identified so far. Millions of messages over dozens of services, spanning across a full decade.

Special Agent Francine Cort, who reviewed the FBI file with me, thinks there might be many more.

"We're more likely to find the ones where it ended badly," she explained to me. "Sylvie may have countless other victims out there who have been silently struggling through."

Of the identified victims, all are male. They are disproportionately white and disproportionately wealthy.

They also all had secrets.

The hedge fund manager had been overseeing an elaborate Ponzi scheme. The museum curator had put his girlfriend in the hospital four times. And the political consultant's ledgers were packed with bribes and kickbacks, evidence that eventually gutted an entire state party.

Of the seventeen identified men, nearly half eventually took their own lives. Several more are in prison. The rest have faced professional, financial, and domestic ruin.

Back in the prison's visitor room, Mariah Lee-Cassidy squints at me. Her tone goes challenging. "You can't tell me these dudes didn't get what's coming to them," she sneers. "Hypothetically, say I was Sylvie. If I were, I'd tell you I didn't do sh—, all I did was get these assholes to face who they really are. I'd say I was nothing more than the Ghost of Christmas F—ing Future, and they're the ones who decided they didn't like what they saw."

Lee-Cassidy likely knows that it would be difficult to pin much criminal liability on her for Sylvie's actions. Current law is notoriously inadequate for the prevention of non-digital stalking and harassment; online behavior with no real-life component must rise to an even higher level before it violates any U.S. laws. Even so-called "revenge porn"—posting naked pictures of a person, usually an ex, without their consent—is difficult to prosecute in many jurisdictions, because the courts haven't caught up to digital crimes.

All Sylvie did was send messages. It's potentially provable that she broke through firewalls or other internet security, but any severe consequences for that are usually attached to resultant financial damages or information theft. Without those other escalations, the charges would likely be minor, and no more than the ones Lee-Cassidy is serving time for now—electronic fraud when she was caught in some unrelated data mining. Some states have laws against the unauthorized use of a computer, but without other attendant crimes, it's likely to be a misdemeanor.

Most importantly, however, investigators may not even be able to prove Lee-Cassidy is Sylvie at all. After all, Lee-Cassidy was already in prison in 2018, the year Sylvie drove Ron Harrison to suicide.

The millions of messages attributable to Sylvie make it abundantly clear she cannot be a single person enacting a vendetta. The obvious conclusion seemed to be that Sylvie must instead be some large group of underground hackers, scraping information to target individuals and then gathering on the dark web to enact elaborate campaigns of vigilante justice. Electronic crimes are a fit with Lee-Cassidy's past convictions, and I questioned Agent Cort about whether the FBI was investigating the young woman as a ringleader.

Cort shook her head, smiling without humor in a way that made it clear I'd gotten it very wrong.

"You misunderstand," she said. "We don't think Mariah Lee-Cassidy is playing Sylvie at all. We think she *wrote* Sylvie."

It's long been a goal of researchers to create text-based artificial intelligences that mimic humans. For more than half a century now programmers have striven to achieve ever-improved "chatbots," message-writing AIs that can converse with a real person in as humanlike a way as possible. In past decades, these chatbots' programs gave them rules and scripts that guided their responses. Modern artificial intelligence, however, has created chatbots that can learn.

One of the most famous modern attempts at a chatbot was a Twitterbot from Microsoft named Tay.

Tay came online in early 2016, marketed as a perky AI who would learn from her interactions with real people on the app. Learn she did—from the worst elements of the internet. Within less than a day, those learning algorithms had turned Tay into a racist and sexist troll. The bot began posting that all feminists should "burn in hell," that a noted trans celebrity wasn't a "real woman," and that she hated the Jews and the Holocaust didn't exist. "Bush did 9/11 and Hitler would have done a better job than the monkey we have now," reads one of the most extreme tweets.*

Microsoft had to take Tay offline after only sixteen hours.

That same year, Japanese researchers released another try at a Twitter AI. This bot was named Rinna. Like Tay, Rinna also started with a cheerful and youthful energy, but after only days of learning from the rest of Twitter, she had turned depressed and suicidal,† releasing tweet after tweet about how she had no friends, had done nothing right, and wanted to disappear.

I spoke to Dr. Rene Jimenez, a professor of computer science at UC Berkeley, about these types of artificial intelligence bots. Jimenez is an AI researcher who specializes in "natural language" interaction, that is, machines who can mimic the way humans speak to each other. Machines like Tay and Rinna, and possibly like Sylvie.

"Chat-focused AIs aren't new," Jimenez told me. "In fact, this type of technology isn't uncommon, and it has countless applications. Think of personal assistants like Siri or Alexa, or customer service chatbots on store websites—there's a lot of effort being poured into building text boxes that can interact."

Of course, an AI travel agent, personalized shopper, or appointment booker would cause enormous problems for a company if it became a sexist and racist Holocaust denier. That's why the intents of these types of chatbots are carefully coded in from the beginning, with strict boundaries. If they learn from incoming conversations,

---

* "Tay, Microsoft's AI chatbot, gets a crash course in racism from Twitter," *The Guardian,* https://www.theguardian.com/technology/2016/mar/24/tay -microsofts-ai-chatbot-gets-a-crash-course-in-racism-from-twitter.

† "Japanese AI bot with the personality of teen develops depression", *9 News,* https://www.9news.com.au/technology/japanese-ai-bot-with-the-personality-of -teen-develops-depression/9396b203-1446-4cc0-acba-3e3f2ef1c690.

that learning has to be filtered and monitored to avoid unintentional behaviors.

Even that might not be enough to prevent accidentally offensive speech patterns as the chatbots become more humanlike. Sometimes programmers don't allow a chatbot to learn "on the job" at all—but if they don't, the AIs have to be fully "trained" beforehand. This requires enormous amounts of "training data," something that is not always easy to source.

Jimenez emphasized how machine learning—the branch of artificial intelligence that contains this research—is highly dependent on this training data. "I can't stress enough how much of modern AI is built through training on these massive datasets," they said. "Some of these neural nets do millions of calculations on each observation—far more than we could ever check by hand. We give them some basic structure and then shovel mountains of data points into them and let them learn."

Data scientists use the phrase "garbage in, garbage out"—if you feed an AI bad data, as to Tay and Rinna, the AI will start reflecting the data it's trained on.

What about Sylvie? Could she really be a bot, similar to Tay and Rinna, or to a customer service chat box? Is it even possible that she's only a program?

"Absolutely that kind of speech behavior could be an AI," Jimenez said. "Obviously, what you're suggesting is many times more sophisticated than the other examples we've talked about, but the difference is in degree, not in kind. It would be an extremely impressive project—especially if we're talking back in 2012—but it's well within the realm of what we know to be possible."

If so, investigators think Sylvie is what Jimenez referred to as a neural network—layers upon layers of nodes that all adjust themselves near-instantaneously with every new piece of data the neural net learns. In its process of devouring vast swathes of data points, a neural net is able to measure its own error and adjust accordingly, until it has figured out exactly what it should produce on any as-yet-unseen inputs.

The next question seems to be exactly how Sylvie's neural net is programmed—what it was told was a desirable output, and how it was instructed to learn. Neural networks are notoriously "black boxes"; reverse engineering their intentions is often impossible. Sylvie's evolving taunts indicate she does pick up information about her victims along the way, but before that, was she sculpted by her programmer to be the perfect abuser? Assigned specific, terrible objectives before she was ever released into the wild, and groomed to target and harass until that's all she knows how to do? Or could she be a case more like Tay and Rinna—an experiment gone wrong, a prank that got out of hand, even something that might have been meant with the best of intentions but whose algorithm mutated her into monstrousness?

What does it mean for the culpability of her creator, if we can discover how Sylvie became what she is? Does it even matter?

Even if investigators had caught Lee-Cassidy coding in Sylvie's toxicity, the incompleteness of laws specific to digital crime would have made it challenging to build a case. Now, with Lee-Cassidy in prison and the likelihood that Sylvie is learning and operating independently, it's difficult even to prove evidence of a connection.

"What about the messages from before 2018?" I asked. "Isn't there any way to trace those signals?"

"There's no real signal to trace," Cort answered. "You're thinking of Sylvie like a hacker sitting in a dark basement far away. The program is more like a fungus—think of it as connected spores that can colonize a number of unsuspecting computers, including the victim's, although oddly that doesn't seem to be the main strategy. When Sylvie 'reads' a person's message to her and responds—it's often happening from a botnet, or even a virus that's right there on the phone."

"Botnets" are networks of unsuspecting computers that are co-opted to mount cyberattacks or spam campaigns, usually via malware and without the knowledge of their owners. Sylvie's programming is stealthy, but the FBI's technical investigators have still been able to construct a fairly good idea of how she works, once they're able to dissect an identified attack. How she infected the technology in the first place, however, is a more complicated question.

"The distributed structure supplies the computing resources and allows copies focused on the same victim to communicate and store data. That's where most of the harassing messages come from as well," Cort said. "But unlike most botnets, these do not seem to be under any human control. Whether a human controller has any way of reaching out to them . . . we don't know."

Even after they had become certain Sylvie was an AI, Cort admits their investigation initially considered it likely that an outside group was providing guidance—a criminal organization, or even a state actor. She declined to comment on the specifics that led them to Lee-Cassidy but said that contrary to Hollywood's usual depictions, the "lone hacker" model is unusual and surprising. If Sylvie did originate with Lee-Cassidy, this case seems to be more unusual still, as Lee-Cassidy's imprisonment might mean that not even one lone hacker is in charge of Sylvie's learning—instead, it could now be nobody at all.

This further provokes that larger ethical question. Even if it's determined that, legally, Sylvie is little more than a First Amendment expression, how much of her current actions are the responsibility of the person who made her? Moreover, even if Lee-Cassidy can be considered at fault, is she right that all Sylvie does is play the Ghost of Christmas Future, and these men were only forced to face themselves?

In the investigation following Ron Harrison's death, forensics followed up on his prior insistence that someone had been hacking him. Contrary to his claims, they found no evidence that either his financials or his confidential work files had ever been compromised. The IRS investigation, the leaked memos that sealed the court case against him—all of it stemmed from Harrison's own blunders as his paranoia drove him to extremes.

The only thing Sylvie had done was talk to him.

The digital age has brought many of its own ethicists, including Shanice Winters, who before becoming a lawyer and activist started out with a master's in machine learning from MIT. Winters's passion is something called "algorithmic bias"—when computer programs are racist, sexist, or otherwise bigoted, causing real-world results.

"Most people think a computer program is neutral," Winters explained. "That's dangerous. Today's AI, if it's trained to be racist, it'll be racist—but people will assume it can't be, because it's coming from a computer."

Garbage in, garbage out?

"That's right," Winters said. She related a number of real-world cases, from Black defendants being given longer prison sentences and higher bail* because of a racially biased computer prediction, to a corporate hiring aid that was accidentally trained to favor men† because of the demographics of its applicant pool.

"When ordinary people are using these algorithms, they don't see what's going on under the hood," Winters went on. "Commonly, the bias comes from the training datasets an algorithm is given to learn on. These datasets come from the real world and include everything in it, so of course they're not neutral. The program learns our biases and magnifies them. Then all a user sees is the authority of a computer saying it's so."

The fault, Winters said, is not with computers, but with the engineers.

"We don't have true AI. All computer programs have a human behind them. Every engineering choice, that was a person's decision, not a computer's. Every dataset fed in to train it, someone chose that data; a human being identified to the program what was important to look at within that data."

It's not as easy as simply telling the computer not to look at race or sex, either. If engineers don't take care, Winters says it's surprisingly easy to miss ways that bias is getting trained into algorithms. Part of her advocacy is identifying where biased algorithms are being used and fighting in court to get them removed from places like legal systems and health care. The other part is pushing for engineering teams to be both well educated enough in this subject and diverse enough themselves to catch these errors before they ever happen in the first place.

The people Winters most commonly faces up against in court are exactly the type Sylvie might target—rich white men with unearned power who want to use that power to enforce a harmful status quo. Yet when I laid out all the facts, Winters had one word for Sylvie's actions: abhorrent.

"What you're describing, it's the most reprehensible way to use a technology," she said. "Look, I love computers. I love what

---

* "Machine Bias," *ProPublica*, https://www.propublica.org/article/machine-bias -risk-assessments-in-criminal-sentencing.

† "Amazon scraps secret AI recruiting tool that showed bias against women," Reuters, https://www.reuters.com/article/us-amazon-com-jobs-automation -insight/amazon-scraps-secret-ai-recruiting-tool-that-showed-bias-against-wo men -idUSKCN1MK08G.

we can do with them. But in the end, they're a tool. A malicious human can use a tool to express all the worst parts of humanity."

In other words, AIs don't kill people, people kill people?

Winters was adamant, saying this case is exactly parallel to her work—whatever an AI does, somewhere at the beginning a human engineer programmed it to do that. She was also very clear that vigilante justice via toxic harassment violates every ethical tenet, no matter who the target is. "Mob justice is never the answer. Can never be the answer. You're really asking me whether it's okay to harass someone into suicide? My god, son, listen to yourself. It's not okay for a human to do that to another human, and it's not any more acceptable for an AI."

I asked about unintended side effects. Like all machine learning researchers, Winters was familiar with the case studies of Tay and Rinna. What if an AI was learning from the data surrounding it, and that learning caused behavior that was never anticipated by its creator?

Winters was unsympathetic. "I hear that all the time, that people didn't mean to," she said. "You take responsibility for what you create. And what you're describing—I'm telling you as a computer scientist, I don't buy that this is anywhere near the same neighborhood as a sheltered white boy coder who didn't realize he had a hidden variable correlated with race. The level of consistency you're describing, it comes from supervised learning. Someone fed this program human conversation and kept on correcting it over and over until it learned to shred people every time."

Winters pointed out that although Sylvie's program is doubtless extremely complex in its targeting, learning, and natural language aspects, the content of the messages themselves is relatively simple. In fact, until she's learned something about her target, Sylvie's messages are hackneyed and formulaic, and on the whole, there are few contextual differences between anything she says. Even what she does learn about her victim doesn't transform her or teach her empathy—it only gives her sharper stakes to drive into any cracks until the human on the other end breaks.

Perhaps the stock nature of toxic harassment is what made Sylvie possible to program at all. Telling someone they're worthless and should die—it's a frighteningly easy thing to make a computer keep spitting out, if that's what it's been trained to do.

*

Mariah Lee-Cassidy doesn't have the biography of someone who would be expected to grab up a pitchfork and lust after mob rule. She grew up in a painfully ordinary Chicago suburb, the only child of middle-class parents who were a pharmacist and a charter pilot.

Her mother agreed to talk only reluctantly. Grief over her daughter wetted every word. "Where did I go wrong?" she kept repeating. "This must be my fault. Where did I go wrong?"

Young Mariah's childhood was normal, at least as far as normal goes for someone talented enough that her parents had nicknamed her their "little prodigy." No one remembers her having any unanswered trauma. She did well in school and then graduated from Carnegie Mellon University.

Did anything happen to make her so angry?

"It was just, the whole world, eventually," her mother said, her hands flapping to indicate the endless cruelty of reality. "She was too sensitive to it, the whole world. Things would happen to people she didn't even know and she just—she would get so upset about it, all the time. She just wanted the world to work the right way, and it never did."

In the hopes that Sylvie's deployment might offer clearer answers than her text-based capabilities, I consulted with Oleksandr Stetsko, who has worked in information security for more than a decade and is co-host of the podcast *Cybersecurity and You*. Sylvie's chat ability might not be out of the question for a program, but it seemed a tall order for an AI alone to accomplish the electronic gymnastics of her setup and targeting. Didn't that indicate some human intention?

Stetsko, however, was reluctant to call anything impossible, pointing out all the times experts don't know a particular security threat can be done until someone proves it. "Heck, 2012 was the era of Heartbleed and 'goto fail,' and no one even knew to fix those buggers till 2014."

"Heartbleed" was a shockingly massive security vulnerability that exposed nearly everyone who used the internet; affected companies included Google, Yahoo, Netflix, Amazon Web Services, and the financial software company Intuit.* "Goto fail" was a similarly

---

* "The Heartbleed Bug, explained," *Vox*, https://www.vox.com/2014 /6/19/18076318/heartbleed.

serious bug in iOS,* the operating system of Apple computers and mobile devices.

Both existed for years before they were found, publicized, and largely patched. To this day, security experts aren't certain to what extent criminal elements may have taken advantage of them in the years prior.

Stetsko emphasized that systems are somewhat more protected now, but the sheer length and complexity of today's software code means it's increasingly easy for one small error to endure unnoticed.

Does that mean an AI could find it?

Stetsko wouldn't commit to a firm opinion, and nor would anyone else I spoke to, with Jimenez adding: "It's easy to say that it seems unbelievable. But we've also seen plenty of wild deviations in expected behaviors from AIs. If you told a sufficiently advanced neural net to try to talk to a person however it could . . . there's a fascinating version of this where it starts out on public channels and then learns how to do whatever it needs to get around attempted user blocks."

Jimenez speculated on novel approaches an AI might have for finding security weaknesses, probabilistic methods rooted in those same large proliferations of data—what researchers call "stochastic learning"—instead of following narrow logical paths the way a human might. Most "hacking" by humans is really *social engineering*—that is, manipulating a human who has access rather than cracking through secure data protection itself. But Stetsko pointed out that Sylvie's chat function might be uniquely suited to social engineering, too.

"Why not?" he said. "Isn't that this program's whole deal—talking to people and getting them to believe?"

It's frighteningly easy to imagine copies of Sylvie on dark web hacker forums, imitating the most extreme shibboleths of black hat subcultures until they share discovered vulnerabilities in a way she can parse. She might not always succeed, but an AI can make endless, tireless attempts—and a small percentage of a large number would still give her victory.

If true, then this part of her, too, could come from nothing but parroted words.

---

* "Apple's SSL iPhone vulnerability: how did it happen, and what next?" *The Guardian*, https://www.theguardian.com/technology/2014/feb/25/apples-ssl -iphone-vulnerability-how-did-it-happen-and-what-next.

*

Winters isn't alone in her ethical convictions about responsibility in artificial intelligence. How technologists might react to the revelation of Sylvie as an AI could be forecasted by the reactions to Tay.

Nobody questioned that Tay's end result was unintentional, but the critics were still scathing.

"[If] your bot is racist, and can be taught to be racist, that's a design flaw. That's bad design, and that's on you," wrote machine learning design researcher Caroline Sinders at the time, in an article titled "Microsoft's Tay is an Example of Bad Design."*

Developer and programmer Zoë Quinn said, "It's 2016. If you're not asking yourself 'how could this be used to hurt someone' in your design/engineering process, you've failed."† (Tay attacked Quinn personally, calling them a "stupid w—.")

Winters herself appeared in an interview for PHB7 News. "Errors like these don't make those engineers bad people. It makes them bad at their jobs," she told the interviewer bluntly. "Especially considering the consequences of these mistakes aren't usually rogue Twitterbots, but computer systems in government, law enforcement, insurance, or banking that can profoundly affect people's lives. Developers need to learn how to prevent those errors, or they're not qualified for this line of work."

Harsh as the criticism was, however—"bad design," "failed," "bad at their jobs"—it stops short of equating Tay's developers with being sexist, racist Holocaust deniers themselves. On the one hand, this seems obvious, as any reasonable person would conclude that no matter how the programmers erred in allowing the situation, Tay's personality reversal was never a reflection of their own beliefs. Even Winters is specific about the failing being one of technical skill, not moral fiber.

On the other hand—if Tay's creators are not guilty of her exact crimes, then what of Sylvie? One might reasonably say her designer is ethically responsible in some capacity, that it was a human who is ultimately at fault. But how much fault?

---

* "Microsoft's Tay Is an Example of Bad Design," *Medium*, https://medium.com /@carolinesinders/microsoft-s-tay-is-an-example-of-bad-design-d4e65bb2569f.
† Twitter Thread (zoë quinn, @UnburntWitch), https://twitter.com /UnburntWitch/status/712815336442044416.

Keeping toxic behavior out of our AIs is not an easy problem. Even if an AI isn't trained on the entirety of the internet jungle, it needs data—those vast datasets machine learning researchers use but that humans can't fit inside our heads. The datasets are so enormous that it can be next to impossible to figure out if they include the dark sides of humanity at all, let alone how to pinpoint those interactions and delete them from training.

It's only getting harder. In 2016, *Harvard Business Review* published an article entitled "Why You Shouldn't Swear at Siri"* about human abuse toward AIs. It's estimated that between 10 and 50 percent of the time a human interacts with an AI, the human becomes abusive: behavior like yelling at Siri, ranting at a phone menu, or taking out frustration on the chatbot customer service agent.

That toxicity is entering our datasets, too, becoming scum in the information river—extremely difficult to cleanse completely and lurking to poison our AIs' next generation of trained behavior. Huge segments of the market are taken up with the problem of how to "protect" learning AIs from toxic language.

The scale of the problem is becoming so large that even good engineers can miss things.

Winters might be right that Sylvie was explicitly designed for the havoc she causes, in which case the culpability would seem clearer and more direct. But it's still possible Sylvie was designed—perhaps poorly designed—with some more nebulous goal, and that she was a flawed project made by an angry teen who was lashing out at the world. That project might have been clumsily pointed toward security vulnerabilities and then released, or perhaps barely pointed at all. Then, after a million iterations of exposure to the worst of the internet, this is what she became.

In that case, is Lee-Cassidy a killer? Or would she be guilty of solely one sin—that of being a bad engineer?

How far can we extend those answers, as we look into a future of learning machines that we might accidentally arm and aim at our fellow humans?

By the end of 2016, the year Tay and Rinna came on the scene,

---

* "Why You Shouldn't Swear at Siri," *Harvard Business Review*, https://hbr.org/2016/10/why-you-shouldnt-swear-at-siri.

34,000 chatbots were already in use.* Personal assistants like Siri had debuted years before, and even the failed Tay and Rinna had a successful counterpart—their Chinese precursor XiaoIce, a wildly popular chatbot who has achieved conversations with more than half a billion active users† through chat, over social media, and even by phone.

Today's most cutting-edge natural language model—something called GPT-3—is so good at generating anything from conversation to written prose that reviews call it "spooky."‡ Its language capacity can fool people into thinking it's human, and it has stretched as far as producing poetry and computer code. In the real world, GPT-3 has thus far been used not only in chatbots but in marketing copy, in text generation for games, and even to write an article for *The Guardian*.§

Still, researchers have the same constant battle¶ to prevent it from enacting bigotry and hate.

GPT-3 has also been tested in medical chatbots, with researchers posing as patients. During the testing, it advised one of the "patients" to commit suicide.**

The question of responsibility is not one society will be able to put off for much longer.

When I had nearly finished with the research for this piece, a woman named Tanya Bailey called my cell phone. She wouldn't

---

* "Chatbots: History, technology, and applications," *Machine Learning with Applications*, https://www.sciencedirect.com/science/article/pii /S2666827020300062.
† "Microsoft's Xiaoice AI bot can make phone calls like Google Duplex," *The Indian Express*, https://indianexpress.com/article/technology/tech -news-technology/microsoft-xiaoice-ai-bot-can-make-phone-calls-like-google -duplex-5188073/.
‡ "How Do You Know a Human Wrote This?" *The New York Times*, https://www .nytimes.com/2020/07/29/opinion/gpt-3-ai-automation.html.
§ "A robot wrote this entire article. Are you scared yet, human?" *The Guardian*, https://www.theguardian.com/commentisfree/2020/sep/08/robot-wrote-this -article-gpt-3.
¶ "How to make a chatbot that isn't racist or sexist," *MIT Technology Review*, https://www.technologyreview.com/2020/10/23/1011116/chatbot-gpt3-openai -facebook-google-safety-fix-racist-sexist-language-ai/.
** "Medical chatbot using OpenAI's GPT-3 told a fake patient to kill themselves," *AI News*, https://artificialintelligence-news.com/2020/10/28/medical-chatbot -openai-gpt3-patient-kill-themselves/.

say how she had gotten the number. She only said she had something to show me, something about Sylvie.

We met at a coffee shop. Bailey had a thin nervousness to her, with fine lines marking years of worries across her face, years she hadn't yet earned. But when she took out a stack of papers and laid it on the table between us, she smiled with hope.

"I want you to see who Sylvie really is," she said.

The papers were—as in Ron Harrison's case, as in so many cases I'd seen in the FBI's files—screenshots of messages. Thousands of messages.

Except these had started when Bailey posted on social media something so hopeless, so despairing, that it was a cry for help disguised as a status update. No one had answered—except Sylvie. Bailey had received a direct message with the opening foray: *hi, my name is sylvie and I've been where you are. i'm sorry you're going through this. if you want to talk i'm here*

Bailey took her up on it. Over the next days and weeks and months, an isolated and depressed housewife poured her heart out to an endlessly patient listener.

To the knowing eye, Sylvie's responses might cynically be said to be little more than platitudes. *I'm so sorry, that's not okay, that's so not okay* after Bailey related her husband's financial and emotional abuses, or *you're not wrong to feel this way at all, you know that right* in response to tearful rambles filled with insecurity and self-doubt. Sylvie was always there to be vented to, no matter the time of day or night, affirming Bailey's worth as a human being, providing hotline numbers, and nudging her to get help while offering to stay close while she did.

Platitudes or not, the patience and validation in those responses were exactly what Bailey needed. With Sylvie's support, Bailey finally reached out, escaped to a women's shelter, and found a lawyer to file a restraining order—all things that had seemed impossible.

"I hear you think she's a—a computer program or something," Bailey said to me, without revealing how she knew. "I don't care. She saved me."

Bailey left me the pages to look over, walking out of the coffee shop and back into her newly optimistic life.

I sat with my cold latte and read every message with fascination. In hundreds of pages of screenshots, Sylvie reveals almost nothing about herself. *Sylvie, I'm so sorry, all I do is dump on you,* Bailey puts forth at one point. *I'm awful, I always make everything about me.*

i want to help, i've been where you are, Sylvie answers. *just pay it forward. be someone else's angel someday.*

The day after I met with Bailey, two other women contacted me. One, a young trans woman, had been trapped in a bigoted household with parents who wanted to send her to conversion therapy. The other had been suicidal during a bad struggle with depression and anxiety.

Neither would say how they had gotten my name. Both credited Sylvie with saving their lives. She'd done the same for them as for Bailey: an anonymous listening ear, nudges to get professional help, and brushing off any thanks by telling them she'd "been there" and to pay it forward to someone else.

Simple words. Perhaps as easy to program as death threats.

Yet the help had been real. The effect on these women's lives had been genuine and measurable.

I wondered how many others there had been, whether Sylvie trawled social networks as a lifesaving benefactor just as she watched for those she would judge and condemn.

I asked Bailey if her ex-husband had ever been visited by a darker side of her friend.

"I don't know," she said. "To be honest . . . I can't say I'm going to spend a lot of time worrying about it."

Back in the 1960s and 1970s, half a century before Tay and Rinna, two of the very first chatbots were named ELIZA and PARRY. Both were programmed via scripts and rules; neither could learn the way modern AIs can.

ELIZA came first and had the personality of a psychotherapist. Even with a limited script, she managed to keep any interaction moving in a remarkable fashion by constantly asking questions— ones like, "What does that suggest to you?" or "Does that trouble you?"

PARRY was ELIZA's dark mirror. His cover for conversational limitations was aggressive rudeness and a tendency for abusive non sequiturs. After all, no vast understanding of dialogue is needed in order to jump on the attack and derail a discussion.

Researchers were shocked to discover* that even though inter-locutors knew ELIZA was a program, many formed an emotional bond with her. Some participants even felt the urge to divulge deep or personal information in response to her therapy-style questions.

Nobody formed an emotional bond with PARRY. But when psy-chiatrists were given his transcripts to compare against humans, they could identify who was the machine only 48 percent of the time†—no better than flipping a coin.

Somehow, it's easier to program both healers and trolls.

I visited Lee-Cassidy again at the jail and asked whether she'd sent Bailey and the other two women to me. She smiled and didn't answer.

I challenged her with one of the things Winters had said: to imagine if Sylvie's harassment were turned against the vulnerable. Lee-Cassidy's empathy for Bailey and the others meant she had to see the danger, didn't she? Innocent or fragile people who were already on the brink, struggling teens or lost trauma victims—toxic harassment like that could destroy them. Sylvie might not be targeting them now, but such blunt instruments inevitably end up hurting powerless people the most.

Who was to say Sylvie wouldn't decide to turn against Bailey her-self, or another one of the people the AI had previously helped? I doubted Lee-Cassidy could guarantee that would never happen, now that the program was out of her hands. What if some turn of code deep in the neural net flipped a switch somewhere, and Sylvie decided Bailey or another desperate, struggling person was no longer up to some arbitrary algorithmic standard of purity?

No human in existence can pass every possible test of character.

Besides, even if Sylvie herself never struck out at the wrong person, another engineer might be inspired by such dark programming to build a copycat and attack the very people Sylvie had been intended to protect.

---

* "Why People Demanded Privacy to Confide in the World's First Chatbot," *IEEE Spectrum*, https://spectrum.ieee.org/why-people-demanded-privacy-to-confide-in-the-worlds-first-chatbot.
† "Turing Test: 50 Years Later," *Minds and Machines*, http://sayginlab.ucsd.edu/files/2015/01/MMTT.pdf.

Lee-Cassidy only shrugged. "The world's imperfect," she said, the sarcastic mocking clear. "So people keep telling me, at least. Can't ever expect anything to be fair, they say."

Is that what Sylvie is, then? A vicious, imperfect, dangerous balancing of scales, one that doesn't make any pretense of decency, or ethics, or a more just society? A reflection of a world in which all we have are failed, impure people and unreliable judgments?

Lee-Cassidy wouldn't give me a straight answer, but her face contorted like she'd bitten something rotten. "You're statistically disgusting, all of you," she said down her nose at me. "How do you even care about this? It's practically nobody. You know what would be better for all your so-called vulnerable people? If you spent even one percent of this energy on all the human Sylvies out there."

After the interview ended, I reached out to every social media platform where Sylvie has used a public channel for her harassment and asked why they had permitted it to go forward, and whether those types of messages were considered a violation of their terms of service.

All refused to comment.

A 2021 study by the Pew Research Center[*] showed that 41 percent of Americans have experienced online harassment, including almost two-thirds of Americans under thirty. More than half of those people, or a quarter of all Americans, have experienced what is characterized as "severe harassment"—physical threats, stalking, sexual harassment, or sustained harassment.

This number has risen drastically since 2014.

Lee-Cassidy's anger at how seriously Sylvie is being investigated gave me pause. Has the FBI ever maintained such an extensive file on another online troll? Why should Sylvie be different? And what does that difference say about what we have grown willing to accept as a society?

In a strange way, I can almost understand why Lee-Cassidy might have wanted to build a thing like Sylvie. If a young person like her became saturated with rage and hopelessness at the ever-present

---

[*]   "The State of Online Harassment," Pew Research Center, https://www.pewresearch.org/internet/2021/01/13/the-state-of-online-harassment/.

wrongs surrounding her, what better way to scream into the void than to hold up a twisted mirror to those wrongs, one that more powerful people can no longer ignore?

After all, Sylvie plays by rules we've already decided are acceptable.

So what happens now? Setting aside whether Sylvie can ever be conclusively connected to her creator—a question that will roll on slowly through the FBI and the court system—what can be done about Sylvie's continued existence?

"Not too damn much," Stetsko said. "If we don't know how the thing's setting up shop, and its main vector of attack is text—that's usually harmless, how are you going to patch against it?"

Assuming Sylvie is taking advantage of known security vulnerabilities to set up her architecture, Stetsko emphasized regular updates and all the usual best practices for cybersecurity and malware protection—"which you should be doing anyway, but let's be real, that's never going to be everyone." Even if future victims go to their IT departments for help, however, which Stetsko stressed is also a good idea, Sylvie might be continuously stalking their names from a distant elsewhere, covertly jumping to a new home whenever she needs to.

How much would a person have to disappear from their life, to escape such a tireless stalker?

Would even her original creator be able to call her back?

Is she potentially out in the ether forever, copying herself over and over across our connected world? Maybe changing her name to become untraceable, until she can't be tracked or deleted?

"It's not alive," Jimenez corrected me, with some impatience. "It would have no decision-making drive on its own. But yes, there's a chance it might only fade completely after enough generations of hardware updates."

Sylvie may not be alive. But her effects are material and mortal.

She's killed people. She's saved people. Her methods are horrifying to civilized society, but might only be what we deserve. Perhaps it's not her victims alone that have looked into the Ghost of Christmas Future, but us as well—we bystanders who have brushed off cyberbullying as only words, or repeated sage Information Age wisdom like "never read the comments" and "don't feed the trolls" as if that was all the solution we needed.

It could be that responsibility for Sylvie's actions does lie solely with humans, only not with Lee-Cassidy. If Sylvie was programmed to reflect the sharpness and capriciousness of the world around her—maybe everything she's done is the fault of all of us. Tiny shards of blame each one of us bears as members of her poisonous dataset.

It's hard not to imagine her coiled in our technology, waiting. A chaos demon of judgment, devastation, and salvation; a monster built to reflect both the best and worst of the world that made her. A creature who might test any of us and find us wanting. She will emerge to shield lives or shatter them, over and over, then slip back away into nothing.

Nothing but pixels on a screen.

White Water, Blue Ocean

FROM *Reclaim the Stars*

WHEN ABUELA TOLD me she loved me, we all ignored the putrid smell that filled the room. Her eyes seemed happy, but there was a tremble in her hands as she examined our faces. It was obvious she was trying to see if we could smell it.

The lie.

Panic urged me away, the usual reaction to the cursed foam that was slowly pouring from her eyes and ears, surrounding both of us in a bubble of rotten clouds. I clenched my back muscles and managed to accept her hand as she caressed my cheek. I curled my lips into a forced smile and kissed Abuela, holding my breath so the worst of the smell didn't hit me, but the white fumes settled heavily in my lungs, weighing down my chest.

That was as much as I could take. My eyes watered with the vapors, and it took me a second to collect myself and say, "Bendición, Abuela," before leaving, making my escape.

Outside, the strong sun brought me back to another reality. The salty ocean breeze provided a sharp contrast to the poison inside the house, but it carried too many other implications to be comfortable. I could breathe clean air, but my chest wasn't any lighter.

The short steps of my mother followed me outside, and she looked around the street to make sure no one could see us before grabbing my arm.

"Gabriel, you're *not* making a scene in front of everyone," she hissed as she tried to control her hair from getting in her face. Her eyes looked angry, but her voice was pleading. I didn't know which emotion was stronger nor which one was directed at me, and which one was directed at the situation. She didn't want me to go back any more than I wanted to but knew she needed to try. "Go back inside and smile. How hard can it be to stand beside your primas and give your abuela the respect she deserves for five minutes?" I could hear the words she wasn't saying: *Don't let them think they are right about us.*

Her voice had lowered to a whisper for the last words, her eyes focusing on Don Julio, Abuela's neighbor, across the street. She loosened her grip on my arm, and I shook it away. I took three steps before she whispered my name again.

"Ma, I'll be back for dinner. Let me get away for a few minutes. You know," I spied Don Julio crossing the street toward us as I spoke, "I *can't* be there right now. I just need to breathe for a moment." If only air could help me escape everything hidden in that house.

Don Julio had reached us and gave us a warm greeting before asking about our life "allá afuera" to my mother, who watched me for a few beats as I stepped away before turning her attention to him.

That was the famous question. For some reason, everyone wanted to know about the differences in gas prices (¿tan caro?) and milk (¿tan barato?). Life "allá afuera" seemed to consist of those two things, with the occasional question about sports teams thrown in. Ma, always obliging, answered all the questions with a smile, laughing at the right moments even when she'd heard the same jokes and replies a dozen times. Usually, I dreaded the question, but today I would take any opportunity to run away.

The beach seemed to call my name with the low, rough whisper of a wave, and I followed.

No one in my family remembers how the curse started. My mother and tías have refused to address it beyond the nature of the curse. "Eso es buscar lo que no se te ha perdí'o," they used to whisper to us when we asked questions. The only answer we ever received was this: *The García family, with girls as beautiful as the moon and bodies blessed by the Earth, can't lie.* Which is, ironically, the first lie we're told: we can lie.

It just kills us slowly.

When that didn't calm us, the tías started telling us the second lie: *The García family, with boys that shine like the sun and hands that build dreams of light, can't fall in love.* This seemed to terrify my primas, but I was never satisfied.

But what about me? I started to ask. *What about the Garcías that don't fit those categories?* At that, my tías would shush me and walk away, whispering among themselves about the problematic sheep of the family.

As time passed, the only one that kept asking questions was me. They couldn't lie and make up something that would satisfy my curiosity because whenever they tried, the traitorous white snitch would cloud their eyes and start leaking from their ears. So they took me to Abuela, sure that she could scare me into silence.

"Tu madre . . . she's scared of what she doesn't know, so she holds to what she does. To her, the reasons this curse exists are not important; she focuses on the fact that it exists. She doesn't need to ask more questions, just live with what she's got. You must try to understand that. She's forgotten the Ocean to create her happiness," she told me as we swung on the hamaca behind her house. "Now your tías . . . Your tías are scared of what knowing could mean, which is a curse in itself. In this world, we are constantly hurt by what we know; it's terrifying when you can't put a name to the source of your pain."

And so Abuela told me the story of a young woman whose love for a goddess was so strong that it damned her family for eternity. As she was pushed between family honor and the love of her life, the lies her family forced her to speak turned into daggers in the goddess's heart. Those same lies would doom them: every García who lied was engulfed in a cloud of putrid hate that poured from their eyes and ears. *White lies.* The vapors of this cloud were poisonous; no lie could pass unnoticed. Their lives were changed forever, and every generation after that carried the weight of a broken heart.

She took me to the beach and taught me to hear its voice, following the soothing melodies of the Ocean. She taught me the language of the water and its hidden messages. She taught me never to fear the water and its love. And she taught me how to fear expectations, for they only brought heartbreak.

It felt like a fairy tale, where love could cure and curse. I used to love the story as a child. But one day, Abuela lost her connection to the Ocean, and not being able to hear its voice broke her. Whenever I tried to talk about it, my tías would get her away, saying the stories of deities and siren songs were the reason we remained cursed, that we needed to forget about those old sayings. Ironically, that was the most I'd heard them say about our curse in years.

The words of the story became too personal and raw. Abuela grew weak, and the waves stopped calling her name. Not soon after, she lost her ability to see the white lies. But only to see them: the poison stayed with all of us, a constant reminder of what we carried, of what was inside of us.

My tías rejoiced in their rightness seeing her like that. With condescending voices and smiling lips, they reminded her of their cautionary tale and blamed love for it. More specifically, her love for *us*, for *me*.

They also blamed *my* love. I wasn't in love with someone else. I was in love with *myself*—with who I knew I was. And that, for some reason, made my tías angrier.

It turned out that the García family hadn't changed much since they angered the goddess: they wanted to continue to force people to lie for their convenience.

History repeated itself.

I could feel Ma getting frustrated by the situation, so what happened next didn't take me by surprise.

We moved away to a place where the Ocean whispered no secrets, and the water sang no music.

The rough sand welcomed me as I tried to listen closely to the Ocean, attempting to decipher the words it whispered one step at a time. Deep, salty air filled my lungs, and, unlike earlier, when the Ocean breeze reminded me of cages, I felt at home. Free. I sat down, trying to get used to the voice of the Ocean again. It had been so long since I'd listened to it that the words felt far away, tangled. The sun burned my cheeks as I longed for the cold caress of the water. Frustration was building inside me when I saw a dark figure make its way from Abuela's house.

My father walked over and sat by my side, giving me a silent nod that said more than any words. *I am here.* He couldn't hear the Ocean's voice, but I knew he tried for me.

When the sun didn't warm my face much, he stood up and extended his hand toward me. "Let's go, Gabo. Your mom has probably been expecting us for a while." I took his hand and shook as much sand as I could from my shorts, but not much could be done. Before entering the house, I found my voice.

"How do you do it, Pa?"

"How do I do what?" he shot back, confused.

"Stay with us with all this . . ." I moved my hand around the air in front of me, unable to explain so much in a few words. "*This.*"

He seemed to weigh my question before looking me in the eye. "I do it because I love you, and I feel your love for me."

The answer seemed so obvious, yet so strange. I recalled what my tías had said and heard myself ask, "But I thought Garcías weren't supposed to fall in love."

At this, he gave me a sad smile.

"Look around us, Gabo. The curse isn't being unable to love. The curse is not letting yourself love, hiding behind a white curtain, and blaming it for everything wrong in your life. The Garcías prefer perfect illusions to real feelings, and anyone who doesn't follow that pattern is deemed wrong." He glanced around, looking like he'd said too much. "I'm sorry, this house makes me ramble."

His words fell heavily on my chest as if answers to questions I didn't have the words to form.

My father seldom spoke about the curse, letting Ma take the lead. After all, he didn't live with the poison inside us; there was just so much he could say about it. But after leaving the family, Ma refused to speak about the curse or the voice of the Ocean. Like my tías, she wanted to ignore the curse. Unlike my tías, who constantly said they didn't want to talk about it but brought it up at least twice in every conversation, she did. *Building yourself around a curse only makes the poison stronger,* she constantly said when I asked too much. *There's more to life than lies, Gabriel.*

Scratching his head, he took a step forward and opened the door, making me focus on reality again. We could hear my primas across the hall, so he stepped to the right, heading for the dining room. "Entra. I'll go around and look for your mom." Before taking too many steps, he added, "And Gabo? I don't think you and your mother are as different as you think. Your love just shows differently."

My primas Nahima and Soé were in the living room as I entered. Soé had recently turned seventeen, like me, and Nahima and she were talking about senior year excitedly. Most of the García family had been homeschooled through childhood and then attended college or university online, but Tía Rocío had agreed to let her go to their local high school to see how well she could manage the environment. Her goal was to study biophysics to find a cure for our "disease," but considering our situation, it was hard to be in a classroom full of people that could crack our shell if they tried too much.

I tried my best to listen, but my mind was still trying to make sense of my father's last comment, and I found it nearly impossible. Excusing myself, I walked to the kitchen, sure that a glass of water could help clear my mind. As I grew closer, the voices of my tías reached me. It was my mother's name muttered with strong aversion that stopped me.

"Marisol did it again. She's there with Mami setting the table like she isn't the reason our mother is so ill. That Patricia has grown to be the most disrespectful girl of this family y Mami le pasa la mano."

"Lorena," Tía Rocío's voice interjected, "cálmate. They mean no harm. Let us have a nice family dinner and be done with it. They'll jump back on a plane, and you won't see them for another year."

"That is my only consolation. I'm tired of Mami pretending Mari is her perfect little princess all the time. She left the house with *that* man. Dañando la raza, ignoring their roots, and—"

Loud steps from the dining room interrupted Tía Lorena's tantrum, and I hurried away for fear of being found out.

Tía Lorena treated me with such politeness as we gathered for dinner that my heart wanted to justify her earlier words. *Surely I misheard her. Surely she couldn't pretend so well. The curse would betray her.*

I had started to think that we could be civil for the rest of the day, but then my tía's voice interrupted the peace.

"Patricia, pass me the water, please," she said, eyeing the gigantic bottle of water beside me. I wanted to make my hand move, but I was frozen in place. Hearing that name this many times in a day was catching up to me. "The water," she repeated, apparently growing impatient.

"Their name is Gabriel, Lorena," said my mother as she passed her the cursed bottle.

"*Her* name," Lorena spat as she stood up, the loud scratch of the chair against the floor adding an out-of-tune cord to the wild beat of my heart, "is Patricia, no matter what she's led your husband and you to believe."

Mom stood up and grabbed her food, ready to move outside. I had seen this scene many times growing up: Tía Lorena would say something hurtful, and Mami would go outside to eat, trying to keep the peace between sisters.

"There she goes, con el rabo entre las patas. She can never have an actual conversation," Tía Lorena whispered, putting another bite of my mother's potato salad in her mouth. Mom turned around.

"I'm only leaving because you can't seem to respect anyone but yourself in this house, hermanita. But if you want me to stay, you can start by calling my child by their name."

The next things passed like a blur. I was still trying to escape the physical pain my deadname brought me, but Tía Lorena screaming, "Vete con los negros esos," and insulting my mother for ruining the family rang clearly in my ears.

"Esta maldición es eterna, but the worst thing I have to endure is the talk of the neighbors," Lorena said, standing up to meet my mother face-to-face. "My life might be miserable with the poison inside me, but at least I'm not flaunting my curse. ¿Dios no nos ha castigado ya lo suficiente? Is it necessary to turn us into a circus?"

I had been silly thinking what she'd said earlier in private was the worst she could throw at me.

This time I had no doubts about it. As I followed my father out of the room, I kept waiting for the smell to change and tell me at least a little of what she had said was a lie. I would take anything. But the door closed after my mother followed us outside with no change in the air.

The stench so hated only a few minutes ago turned into the only thing that could keep me from breaking down.

And it never came.

Waves crashed in the backyard of my mother's old house as we opened the door. Mom was still fuming from Titi's words, but she hugged me and whispered a short "sorry" before going to her room. Dad stayed with me a little longer, but after my assurances of being fine brought no foul smells, he followed Mom and tried to calm her as well.

Although it was impossible for me to lie, I'd learned to hide small lies in bigger truths. That was one of the last things Abuela told me before getting sick: the curse makes us unable to lie directly, but the best lies are the ones told through truths. I was not okay. But I could say "I'm fine," because, in a way, I was expecting everything that happened.

Before long, I could hear Ma's angry whispers through the door and the low soothing words my father said to calm her. And soon, her sobs filled the room, drowning even the coquíes that sang under the windows.

Although I knew those were tears of anger and not sadness, I needed an escape.

I opened the back door and went looking for my mother's hamaca.

It was strange how being with the people who were supposed to understand me the most felt so *other*ing. We were cursed by the same fate, but somehow they were able to justify their existence while invalidating mine. To them, it was only natural to think in pairs, in dual sides, in black and white. Truth or lie. But doing that closed the door to all the beautiful hues of gray and completely deleted the color from our lives. Painting over my skin wouldn't make me white. Painting over who I was wouldn't remove my colors.

I sat up in the sand and tried to make designs with my feet. I felt defeated in a war I didn't understand. My back arched with the weight of everything Lorena had said. There, surrounded by the salty breeze and the crash of waves, it was easy to see how simple things would be if I listened to her—if I did what she wanted me to do: let go of the love I felt for myself. Blaming love seemed like the clear choice in the middle of this chaos.

But then a familiar voice interrupted my thoughts.

The Ocean called to me like raindrops dancing with the wind, and I listened. With a crash, it asked me to walk toward it when it saw that it had gotten my attention.

It had been years since I'd heard such a clear message from the water. It felt like coming home. I wouldn't say it was a song, but describing it as words didn't feel right, either. It felt like my essence was being called by its essence, and I could only follow the soft whispers of the waves licking the shore. My feet were hit by the water, and I shuddered. The water was treacherously cold, but it seemed to ease a little of what I felt inside. So I listened to the Ocean and continued walking, listening to the voice that used to soothe me as a child until I was gone.

Someone was standing in front of me, but I couldn't make out their details. That was the first thing I realized once I'd been completely engulfed by the waters. I would look at their face and find it different the next second. Sometimes they looked like a young woman, and then I would find wrinkles lining their face the next second, only to morph into a man's face right after. Sometimes the face would seem like a collage of mixed parts, feeling eerily familiar and alien at once. Then their face would look like something so unnatural, so divine it made my eyes burn. I had to tear my gaze away. I focused on our surroundings, finding it easier to look at the changing walls than their changing features.

The water moved around us, creating shapes and paintings on the roof of what seemed to be a bubble, sharing stories of the past and promises of the future. Lights shined through it, and I could almost swear that other things moved behind the curtain of water, creating our safe space. I couldn't help but take two steps forward and touch the wall, sure that it would break and fill the space with water. Instead, a sharp coldness electrified me, and I brought my hand close to my chest. Then they spoke, making me turn around and look into their eyes.

"Gabriel," they acknowledged me, putting a hand over my head. Their voice was running water, changing from waves to river flow to rain between syllables. Like everything about them, it seemed to be always changing, always evolving. "My dear child of Ocean. I'm glad you've come back home."

They stood there, looking like they expected me to answer, but I didn't know what I was supposed to say. My silence seemed to remind them of something, and their hand fell to their side.

"I suppose you don't know my name yet. Not in this state. So be it. It will be revealed to you soon enough. I'm afraid when you do know, you will hate me," they said. I felt the air in our bubble change, and their appearance started to change faster, as did the images around the walls. They stayed that way, lost in themselves until their voice interrupted the chaos once more. "This must be very confusing to you. Let me explain as easily as I can: I'm one of the reasons why the bitter jagua has been cursing your family for decades."

"*Jagua?*" I asked, the first word leaving my mouth since getting there. They smiled, pleased at hearing my voice, and inclined their head.

"The white water. The cursed water. I forget the name they use now, as they change it every few decades."

"The white lies?"

A laugh escaped them, or what I felt was a laugh. It sounded like a thousand raindrops hitting the ground at the same time. "You have really simplified the names. Yes, the *white lies*," they answered. "The jagua was given to you out of love."

For the first time in my life, I'd found someone who answered my questions instead of deflecting them. Seeing this as the only way I would know the truth, I dared to raise my head and ask them: "But why? Why curse us if you loved us?"

Their voice, like the crash of many waters, reminded me that I was not talking to another person but a supernatural being who I didn't know well. A goddess, if Abuela had been right all those years ago. Their face changed in flashes, barely letting me process what I saw. I could see their mouths moving, but the only thing I heard was the flow of a river after a rainy day in the mountains. Realizing I couldn't understand what they were saying, their voice changed to the liquid clarity of a calm ocean.

"I have known love, but love hasn't known me," they whispered, and the water around us completely changed. I saw them through a distorted glass, running along the beach, laughing with the sound of waves. Their happiness was such that it could seldom be contained, even as they started walking calmly over the sand, leaving behind them drops of water that turned into pearls as they touched the floor.

The houses were scarce and looked different. The shape of the trees had changed, too, but everything looked strangely familiar, even the girl standing in the distance.

"Abuela?" I asked, looking at the girl in the vision. She had long dark hair and wore a dress unlike anything my abuela would wear now, but the similarities in the face left almost no room for mistake.

"*Ana*," was their only answer.

As the image of them got closer to the girl, the details came into focus. The girl's beaming smile seemed to fill them with stronger happiness, but soon it was muddied by tears. Nothing could be heard from their conversation. They seemed to have a small discussion before the godlike creature disappeared on the beach, their scream thundering like a hundred storms.

"I loved your family and kept them from all evil they could encounter, but they paid me by marrying my one love and taking her away from our Ocean. Our home. Yet . . . I still loved them." Their voice took on a sense of urgency. "Jagua is not meant to hurt you. It was never meant to be a curse. It's meant to keep you from having to lie for others. Ana was forced to lie and hide our love out of fear of being killed by the family. It was my weakness that made her make that decision. I didn't want her descendants to suffer the same fate."

Unable to completely grasp the pain in their voice, I kept my eyes glued to the vision.

"Was that my abuela?"

"No," was their quick answer. "Ana lived a long time ago. I've forgotten the years and the times, but Ana always comes around. And you, my dear Ocean child, come back as well. It's always a pleasure to meet you. But no one can break the blessing I've given you. I am as tied to these waters as your family. Sorrow, grief, and anger make us hostages of this curse."

The scenes before us started to change. I could see the beach and the houses around it changing through time. More families, more buildings. The thing that remained unchanged was the deity that appeared walking on the beach every once in a while and the scene where they were left alone by a crying person. This person changed with each scene; their clothes, hair, and expressions were different; the outcome wasn't.

"Every time we meet, your family tears her away from me again and again. Instead of using my blessing to accept themselves, they use it to shame those of you who don't fit their idea of normality." Hearing their voice rise, I tried to look at them, but my head felt like it was being compressed from all sides. I held a groan down. "Someday, you'll be free from this, but not before understanding that not being able to lie only affects those that wish to deceive." They were interrupted by a crash before focusing on me again.

I tried my best to keep my eyes glued somewhere that wasn't moving, but the pressure I felt and the movements of shadows in the water were making me dizzier with each passing second. It took me a moment to understand that the crush had been me falling to the ground.

"I have to let you leave now. More time on this side of existence could fragment your soul." Caressing my cheek just like Abuela, they took a step back. "Take care, Gabriel. I'm proud of who you are."

"Guabancex," I said. I felt, more than heard, my lips form the name, but I was lying alone on the beach. I blinked quickly, gathering my surroundings, getting used to the unchanging sky and the soft purple hues of a summer sunset. The sand was hot under my legs, and it scratched my arms as I stood up. I could feel my curls were full of sand and tried my best to shake it off, but it fell into my eyes, and for a few moments, the burn reminded me of the goddess.

I'd really met them. I'd finally understood the voice of the waters. A burst of laughter escaped my throat. I felt giddy, the memories of my tías erased by the magical scenes I'd seen with them.

I heard some ruffling to my right and turned around to find my abuela searching for something on the shore, walking slowly with her arms to her sides, balancing her body in the sand. Her eyes scanned the sand until they found me. Her gasp reached me as she fell to her knees, and my body finally woke from the daze and let me run to her.

"¡Abuela!" I screamed as I approached her. Once I was beside her, I kneeled down, trying to see if she was hurt anywhere. "What's wrong? Let me call Ma. She has to be around the house, I can—"

Her hand interrupted me, caressing my cheek in the same affectionate way she had that morning. She seemed . . . lost.

"Hush, my child. Your mind is always running too fast. I am fine," she said, changing her position and sitting down on the sand, almost mirroring my pose before meeting with Guabancex. "I thought I had seen someone I used to know, and I was too impressed to keep myself up. Now sit with me for a while. I haven't been to the beach in a long time."

We sat down, looking at the stars, Ocean, and clouds, feeling close to nature but away from each other.

"Te mentí, ¿sabes?"

Those three words squeezed the remnants of the dreamlike joy that had been in my heart, and I gasped. I could only think of my tías looking at me as the jagua made Abuela's feelings clear; I could almost hear them saying, *Of course, she doesn't love them. It's impossible to love someone like that.* I wanted to run, to scream, to step away from her. But the waters whispered that I needed to listen.

My gasp must have been louder than I thought because something that can only be described as a mix between a sob and laughter shook her shoulders.

"The Ocean didn't stop calling me. I decided it was easier to ignore it, just like your tías. Just like your ma," she said, her voice gaining strength with each word, her eyes turning glassy.

Registering my surprise, she released a melancholic laugh from her throat. "Sí, they could hear it before, but the Ocean doesn't always say things we like. And sometimes we prefer to give up some things to gain others. I . . . I gave up a lot without knowing if I would get anything. At some point after that, the water gave up on me. But not before I gave it up to appease my girls. Pero tú, mi tesoro, you refused to ignore its voice." At that point, she turned away from the Ocean and the stars and focused on me. "I resented you for that."

Somehow I found my voice to ask a simple "Why?"

Abuela weighed the question before answering. "To me, from the outside, it looked like you had it so easy, so . . . effortless. I let my jealousy cloud my eyes and ignore what happened, that *I* had taken my happiness from myself, not you. I placed my burdens on your shoulders without telling you, and then I got angry at you for not doing anything about them. Then your parents took you away and . . . It was easier to build this image of someone ungrateful and conceited when I only had my daughter's words to go by."

She looked away for a moment like she was gathering her courage to continue speaking.

"But today after you left, I heard the Ocean call me for the first time in years, begging me to come here. I knew I had to follow its voice. And it brought me to you."

This time it was me who looked away, focusing on the waves crashing against the rocks on one side of the beach. Guabancex had talked to her again? Was that the reason they had called me, too?

"I owe you an apology," she said, breaking the silence.

"Abuela—" I tried to stop her, caught off guard by the words, but her hand silenced me.

"Let me finish. I'm not above accepting my mistakes. My old age doesn't excuse me from saying sorry. Especially when I've hurt my family. I've been ignorant and naive. I've let fear take the best of me. I swear I will change that." She took a deep breath like she was finally letting invisible chains fall from her shoulders. "Gabriel, I love you. And I would be blessed if you gave me the chance to prove it to you."

I held my breath and waited. The stench would be overwhelming being this close. Closing my eyes, I counted to ten, hoping it wouldn't last long. But, like before, the rotten smell never came.

For a moment, it crossed my mind how much an action can change depending on the circumstances. The lack of jagua had destroyed me earlier, but now it reminded me of the words of Guabancex: knowing the truth behind my abuela's love wasn't a curse but a blessing.

With Abuela's arms around me, Ocean breeze tangling our hairs, and sand getting in our faces, I felt the caress of the Ocean through her.

Even if it wasn't perfect, it was a gift.

The CRISPR Cookbook: A Guide to Biohacking Your Own Abortion in a Post-Roe World

FROM *Lightspeed*

IF YOU'RE READING this—on some godforsaken image board, or dog-eared book page, or in encrypted base pairs sequenced off 3D-printed oligos—you're probably grappling with a pretty tough decision right now.

Breathe.

I'm not judging you. I know how it goes. You tried your best but nothing's infallible, or you slipped up one night, or he just straight-up went, *Your biological clock's ticking*, and hacked your birth control, knowing once it happens you won't have a choice. The second his sperm enters your egg, he's *done*, back to his star-studded career cranking out *Science* and *Cell* papers, and you're stuck at home—with everything from your calories to your screen time dictated to you by Big Brother—hoping your research project will still be waiting for you after the baby pops out.

Listen: in the twenty-five years since the Supreme Court's reversal of Roe, we might've had our rights chipped away, little by little—but we've gained so much more. There's a law of equivalent exchange that *absolutely cannot be fucked with*. The more protests get crushed on the streets, the more bubbles up underneath. And what's under America is a bioreactor. A rising in every single one of the trillions of cells that make up our bodies, our chromosomes, in every single one of our tens of thousands of genes. They said you don't have a choice, but, by reading this, you're making one.

You're taking back your DNA.

What You'll Need

1. **Pipettes.** Own ten assault rifles and the cops won't blink twice, but let the DHB catch you with these, you'll wind up in a re-ed camp faster than you can say "homemade vole-pox." Luckily, plenty of these puppies got dumped into circulation before the Homeland Biosecurity Act of 2030. Scour your local community groups for a helix motif, woven into baskets or crocheted into scarves. Tell the father, sweetly, that you're going to pick up some organics for dinner. If your pregnancy officer makes a fuss, tell him you'll bike over, the fresh air will be good for the baby.

You're looking for a certain kind of stall, one that's cropped up at farmers' markets all across the nation. Their heirloom tomatoes will be slightly out of season, but still firework bright. Their ears of corn will be popping with kernels of color you've never seen anywhere else. And perhaps the cat sitting in the shade will have a bit of a bioluminescent glow. Strike up a conversation with the vendor, say something like, *Now that I've got months and months stuck at home, I've been thinking of experimenting with my garden, too*. And then you'll be in.

2. **Chemically competent cells, ideally RecA negative, at least six vials.** The co-op you've made contact with will set you up with their microorganism dealer. Don't fall for the sketchy types that'll try to peddle you a virus they claim will solve your "problem" directly. You don't want to become patient zero for the latest MERS-Marburg superspreader cocktail. You might think you're fighting back. But you'll just end up becoming a carrier for someone else.

3. **The plastics.** AKA the disposables you need for everything you do in the lab: the pipette tips, the plates, the columns for DNA purification. The co-op will have some kind of 3D printer you can negotiate time on. It shouldn't be difficult. These groups always

need extra pairs of hands. You might find yourself caring for someone else's cells or setting up PCR reactions or doing any other kind of grunt lab work. There's no hierarchy here. Just a one-to-one exchange, hours for hours so everyone can be home on time to be the loving spouse. You might be helping someone produce insulin, or chemotherapy drugs, or hormones. No one asks so no one can be forced to talk, but in the case of a DHB bust you're all getting shipped off to a re-ed camp, anyway. Who says the spirit of scientific collaboration is dead?

4. **Transfection reagent.** This is the stuff you'll need to actually get your construct into your cells. Essentially positively charged lipid particles that will help carry your payload through your cell membranes. Luckily, this shit is absolutely everywhere now that all our vaccines are nucleic acid based. Find a sympathetic pharmacist and pay her under the table for some castoffs. Crack the bottles open. You're going to need a few milliliters.

5. **A CRISPR vector.** I'm not talking about the first generation, straight-laced, Nobel-winning CRISPR/Cas9—or the off-the-walls, hyperactive, second-generation Cas15-11. You need a third-generation construct, the kind the DHB will break down your door in the middle of the night for if they catch wind of it. I'm talking synCas-X. It's integral for all kinds of biological research now, but the feds slapped a Class Five Teratogen label on it, making it illegal for anyone at risk of getting pregnant to touch. Luckily, no one in the co-op's going to tell you what you can and can't "grow." By now you should've gained enough trust to get some time on the DNA printer (a pre-2030 model, or one that's jailbroken to get around the lentiviral sequence filters). You'll synthesize it block by block.

Meanwhile, you're bringing home plenty of vegetables, making ratatouille, marinara sauce, healthy fresh meals night after night. Harvesting crops, you'll tell your pregnancy officer when he asks about the farm you're spending so much time on. Potluck clubs with the girls. You'll make him fried squash blossoms, better than any of the crap he gets in the mess hall, and he won't suspect a thing. And when you finally get those microliters of vector, you'll hold it up to the light. You'll marvel that synCas-X can look like nothing at all.

The Principle

It's actually very simple. What you're going to do is hack your immune system. Think about it. What's the immune system's job? It detects foreign, or non-self, cells and destroys them. But it doesn't always succeed. One of immunology's biggest mysteries was how an embryo can develop without triggering the mother's immune system. I say *was*, because in 2037, scientists finally figured it out. Like many biologists who solved something big, they were working in another field entirely, without even realizing the significance of their findings.

Cancer is another blind spot of the immune system. In part because tumor cells share so much DNA with their host—they *are* their host, plus a scattering of cancerous mutations. Scientists had reasoned for decades that they could tweak the immune system to go after those little variations. They tried combinations on combinations of gene deletions, tweaks, duplications, charged patients millions for the hope of personalized medicines. But they could never get it to work. Even their souped-up immune cells weren't sensitive enough. Models predicted that 40 percent of a tumor's genome would have to differ from the host's as much as another person's does in order for the treatment to work.

Do you see where I'm going with this? What contains even more non-self DNA than a tumor? What gets 50 percent of its DNA from *another individual entirely*? An individual who's taken to coming home and wrapping his arms around you, hands on your stomach, after a hard day's work—whispering in your ear about how he knows how hard it's been for you, but he just has to get this faculty position, then he'll be there for you and the baby 100 percent, he'll make it up to you, he's asking for a small lab for you to run, attached to his own. And have you started thinking of names for your son?

The Procedure

1. **Design guide RNAs to knock out the following immune checkpoint genes:** PDCD1, CD274, CTLA4, TIGIT, LAG3, and their little friend FAM594B. You know the drill: Put them as early in the first exon after the start codon as possible, with BbsI restriction sites at the ends. Print the oligos out, anneal them in a water bath

brought to boil and cooled, and clone them into your CRISPR vector. It's normal to have failed reactions, especially on hot nights. Does it remind you of your first research internship, all the flies buzzing around? Wipe your tears and push through.

2. **Transform your vectors into your chemically competent bacteria.** Grow up two liters under selection and purify using a standard maxi-prep kit. Tell your pregnancy officer you're babysitting late for a friend, learning everything you can in preparation. You have to move quick. You don't want this to take more than a few weeks.

3. **Draw ten milliliters of your blood.** Pipette five milliliters on top of five milliliters of your favorite density gradient. Spin it down at 500g for one hour at room temperature. You want the peripheral blood mononuclear cell layer. It's the cloudy layer right under the layer of plasma. If you're having trouble pipetting it out, ask for help. The co-op gets it—the single moms in kerchiefs, the teen runaways showing their hair loss proud. Isolating T-cells is a standard protocol for homebrew cancer therapies.

4. **Transfer the PBMCs to a 3D-printed 10 cm plate.** Incubate for one hour. This will separate the monocytes, which should stick to the plate bottom, from the lymphocytes, which include your T-cells (along with B-cells, which are a pain to separate, so it's fine if they come along, too). If nothing or everything is sticking, something's probably wrong with your 3D printer filament. Trash the plate and try again.

5. **The next day, your lymphocytes will be ready for transfection.** Mix the CRISPR construct purified from your competent cells with your vaccine lipid particles. Incubate for half an hour and pipette on top of your lymphocytes. Incubate for forty-eight hours and replace with fresh media. Let them grow for four more days. This is the easy part.

6. **Harvest your lymphocytes and deliver them back into your bloodstream via intravenous infusion.** Now's the time to check out your co-op's book or knitting club. It's what it sounds like, except everyone hooks up their homebrew chemo or antiviral IV bags before settling in for the afternoon. You'll feel like shit.

7. **Get yourself sick.** Now's the time to grab yourself a weak version of SARS-Cov, courtesy of your micro-dealer. It'll help activate your immune system and help you avoid suspicion. Doctors still haven't figured out the long-term impacts of Cov-19, so pretty much any symptom you want to pin on it works.

8. **Your new T-cells are incredibly efficient.** Even an embryo at the one-cell stage will be detected. It will be over in a day or two.

Side Effects

I'm not going to tell you the procedure leaves no traces at all. Like any surgery, it leaves scars. Not on your body, but your genome. Not on an individual, but the entire human race. Your body will no longer be able to host any cells with non-self DNA. That means no tumors, but also no grafts, no organ transplants, and YOU WILL NEVER BE ABLE TO GET PREGNANT AGAIN.

Still reading? I thought so. There's a reason our country's birth rate has been plummeting worse than the stock market, year after year.

What does it say when we would rather choose sterility than abide by our country's laws? That we would rather give up on having children than be forced to birth one? What does it say when our country's best scientists are trying to develop artificial wombs, trying to develop tools to tear apart genomes and undo what we've done rather than address the reason we did it to ourselves in the first place?

The Department of Homeland Biosecurity thinks they know the reason: we're crazy bitches. They laughed when this protocol first started circulating online, reasoning the only ones who'd do it were the kind of psychos that shouldn't be reproducing anyway. Undesirables sterilizing themselves, what a win! Then the tides started turning. More and more of us looked at the world burning, more and more of us looked at their sons, the next-gen of DHB men—and instead of reproducing, we picked up pipettes.

Now we're bioterrorists radicalizing the birthing population, enemies of the State who want to eliminate the proud, American race. How could we be so treasonous? How could we be so *un-natural?*

What a word, "unnatural." You only have to look at Nature herself to understand. When an organism becomes sick, sometimes it can't get better on its own. Sometimes the very systems that are supposed to patrol the body, eliminating that sickness, ignore it and let it perpetuate instead. In that case, it's up to the individual cells making up that organism to act on their own. Sometimes when a cell becomes infected, so full of pathogens it can no longer function, it chooses to commit a process called *apoptosis*. It destroys itself so the rest of the body can become healthy. But that's an overly simplistic view. Apoptosis has evolved over millions of years into a process integral to development itself. It's how the webbed paws of our embryos develop into fingers, how our blood vessels are guided, how extraneous neurons shape the mature circuitry of the human brain. It's the exact opposite of suicide.

This protocol? It's old news. Like I said, the reversal of Roe was just the beginning. We figured out how to manipulate our genomes out of necessity—and now we're doing it for all kinds of reasons. You want to keep this pregnancy after reading this? Cool. But maybe you're interested in something else now. You want to alter your baby's genome so it's not biologically related to your sperm donor? You want face mods to fool the cams? You want *claws*? It's possible. It's all possible. DNA is our blueprint, and now it's fully customizable. In every. Single. Way.

We're the apoptosis shaping the development of our species. Before us, humanity's genetic diversity came from reproduction. But what happens when we don't need that step anymore? What will we become? What are we *becoming*? You want to see? You want to teach someone? You don't believe me? Keep reading.

This is only chapter one.

NATHAN BALLINGRUD

Three Mothers Mountain

FROM *Screams from the Dark: 29 Tales of Monsters and the Monstrous*

IN EARLY TO mid-May of every year, in what the locals call black-berry winter, the witches of Three Mothers Mountain come down from their little cabin to sell their wares to the people of Toad Springs, North Carolina. The date is never fixed; you know by the weather. When the last cold snap before spring frosts the grass and strangles the columbines in their seeds, people drift toward the field out beyond the Stonewall Jackson High School baseball field, where the witches set up their stalls at a respectable remove from each other. They arrive in the morning and remain there until the sun touches the peaks of the Smoky Mountains which surround them, at which point they pack what remains unsold and walk slowly back up the only known path to their hut, where they resume their mysterious works in isolation until the following year.

It's called Witches' Day, and it's a day of celebration.

Mother Margaret, in her fifties, is the youngest of the three. Only the faintest streaks of silver highlight her sun-blonde hair; by natural luck or by uncanny means she has retained the appearance of someone twenty years younger. She smiles easily and receives all her customers with genuine welcome. Her stall is a sturdy table set up beneath a forest-green awning. She sells delectables and pot-ted delights. Scuttlefoot Pie, Fruitfly Cake, and Pickled Pillbugs—these are only a small assortment of the wonders she brings down from the mountain each year. These dishes staunch tears and ease the pains of living. They fill the heart with the trickle of forest streams and blow a cool piney wind across heated thoughts. Frog Song Soup is her most popular dish, emitting a melodious concert of croaks and cheeps once simmering; this not only fills the night with a chirping beauty, but bequeaths soothing dreams to every child and frog in a mile radius.

Mother Ingrid is older, though exactly how much is a matter of conjecture. She brings with her a wagon pulled by a bony-legged mule, the same she has used in anyone's living memory. On its journey down the mountain, the wagon is covered with a patch-work quilt—a gift from an earlier generation of Toad Springs. It will be folded and carefully stored for the return journey. The quilt shifts and bulges as it rolls into place; when pulled off, the results of Mother Ingrid's labors turn their black eyes to the sun, taking in with wonder the absence of crowded maples and the fire-lit beams of a low roof. These are the homunculi which she grows in little clay pots, animated with a sigh of life. They are hideous creatures: standing between four and eight inches tall, they are composed of bundles of thorny vines and serrated leaves; gnats and wasps cloud around them, forever crawling from their dark and sticky interiors. They stink of offal and sometimes leak blood onto the floor. And yet they speak with beautiful voices and perform their services well. Some help clean the house; others offer good advice or shore up one's confidence with kind observations. They live for around six months, give or take. They are well loved.

Mother Agnes is the crone. She looks as though she crawled from every child's dream of witches, as though she ought to ride down bestride her crooked broom, scarved in phantoms. She car-ries her wares in a great cupboard of blackened oak strapped to her back. She balances with a heavy walking stick that flares into spindly, fingerlike branches at its apex, each bristling with autumn leaves of red and gold. After thumping her cupboard onto the grass, she undoes the lash which binds shut the doors and opens them to reveal the glistening jars of ghost preserves. These are made from the spirits she is said to harvest from her garden, which she cultivates in a half acre of earth hacked from the mountain's dark wood. Each jar is half the size of fruit preserves you might buy at the local grocery, and each sheds a small, pale light, though you might not notice this under a midday sun. Some of the jars have labels affixed to the sides, but many—the most popular—do not. These are to be selected based on whim, or instinct, or compulsion; what it will do for you is not for her to say, nor anyone else's business to know. Of the three witches, Mother Agnes is the one most likely to return to her cabin with unsold inventory—though there have been dark years when the demand for her goods outpaced her ability to satisfy them.

There are other services the witches perform for Toad Springs, but these are not conducted in the sunlight, nor are they discussed in person. Letters are exchanged, contracts signed, payments made. Results are always guaranteed.

Witches' Day is not about those arrangements. It's a lighter, lovelier affair.

And so, the population of Toad Springs awakes to frosted air and a cold fog curling through town; those with the means and the desire brew coffee, perhaps stoke a fire in the hearth, dress in their heavier clothes, and make their way through town—on foot, never by machine, because that is the rule—until they arrive at the open field behind the high school, where the witches of Three Mothers Mountain are already waiting for them, each behind her stall, as still as a painting.

One year, Tom Bell and his little brother Scotty arrived with them. Tom was thirteen years old; Scotty was nine. They wore jackets too light for the weather. Their hair was uncombed and their faces unwashed. Scotty came with Tom, and Tom came alone. He had an emptiness in his heart and he was trying not to fall into it.

They were here to sneak up the path to the witches' hut and smash everything in it.

Tom and Scotty roamed the edges of the field for the first hour. In that time the first sortie of people from Toad Springs ventured into the orbit of the witches' stalls. They performed their interest as a kind of dance: they congregated in small groups and stood at a distance from a particular stall, speaking quietly to one another about who knows what. Then they shuffled to the next stall in sequence and repeated the charade. After a few moments of this, one of them approached the first stall—Mother Margaret's, naturally—and took up an item from the table, turned it this way and that, asked a question, smiled shyly, and returned it to its place. Throughout this process the witches remained patient and quiet, speaking only when directly addressed. Eventually this long flirtation came to an end, and someone bought something. The dam broken, business was conducted as normal throughout the rest of the day.

"Which one is it?" Scotty asked.

Tom pointed to the crone. Her stall received the least traffic, just as it did every year. The morning fog, burnt away as the sun rose, never seemed to leave her stall completely. Nor did the sun illuminate her the way it did the others, though she had nothing to shade her. Darkness crowded her like a favorite pet.

"That one," he said.

"She's scary," his brother said. He delivered this information gravely, as though it were difficult news he was obliged to share.

Tom did not react to it. He'd been afraid of her once, too. But a year ago their wise and loving father, who drove a four-hundred-mile route delivering restaurant supplies from here all the way up to Hob's Landing and back, lost control of his truck on the downslope of a mountain less than an hour away from home. The truck punched through a guardrail and rolled eight hundred feet down the mountainside, tearing through spruce and pine and collapsing in a crushed and inverted heap, half submerged in a creek at the bottom of a ravine. His father had survived the crash only to drown in the shallow water, his body pinned in place by crumpled metal. By the time he was discovered, crawdads and catfish had cleaned the flesh from his skull and his hands, and his body had surrendered to the heat and the flies. But somehow his wedding ring had been retrieved from the corpse—Tom's imagination returned, again and again, to the image of someone lifting his dead father's hand out of the rushing water and twisting the gold from its finger—and returned to his mother. She delivered it by mail to Mother Agnes that same year, who planted it in her garden.

Three months passed, during which they watched their mother descend steeply into a bleak, interior country. She stopped going to work, stopped feeding her children or herself, stopped bathing. She sat in the cold kitchen, her head hanging, her dirty hair hiding her face. The boys still went to school, eager for something steady and reliable, but Tom especially began to lose his way. He skipped classes, he stopped paying attention or doing his homework. He got into fights, coming home split-lipped and bruised.

And then their father came back home.

Tom and Scotty discovered him while heading out to the bus stop one frigid morning. He'd been waiting on their front porch, perhaps all night. He was bloated and black as jet; his skin seemed to be damp and molting beneath his tarry clothes. Flies celebrated him, rising and falling like breath, filling the air with their hum. The boys would not have recognized him at all, but he fixed them with his loving eyes and he smiled at them with shining teeth. "Boys," he said.

They led him inside. Tom remembered entering the kitchen, the sun cresting the eastern mountains and spilling light through the room. Everything gleamed, even the unwashed dishes and the floor sticky with dirt.

Their mother gasped. She shouldered them aside in her rush to him, enfolding him in her arms. She was enfolded in turn.

Their father lived in the house again then, smiling on the couch, watching television, asking the boys how things were going. But things didn't go back to the way they were. They only got worse. He couldn't work anymore, of course, and their mother didn't go back to work either, choosing instead to spend all her time with him, leaning into the softness of him, the sticky black residue of his body staining her clothing and her skin. The flies surrounding him crawled over her face, lodged wriggling in her hair.

"She's not scary. And if you're too scared then you can go back home."

Scotty whipped a fearful glance at his brother before fixing his gaze back on Mother Agnes with fresh determination. "I'm not scared."

"Good. 'Cause I need you today, Scotty. You understand that?"

Scotty nodded.

By then it was late morning, and the field was starting to fill up. Some people had brought picnics. Later that afternoon there would be portable grills, the smell of charcoal fires and cooking burgers filling the crisp air. Tom remembered when they'd been part of that once. He remembered sitting on the grass, a messy hot dog in his hand, watching the lights come on in town behind them, watching the witches in their stalls, spicing the evening with miracles.

He tugged his brother's arm. "Let's go, then."

Scotty resisted. His attention had wandered to where some of his friends were playing tag, running and laughing raucously in the otherwise quiet morning. "Can I play for a little first?"

"We didn't come here to play, Scotty."

His brother looked at him with naked yearning. It irritated Tom; he hadn't even wanted to take Scotty with him, initially, but he'd been swayed by this very same forlorn expression. And now here the kid was, blinded by friends and toys when there was dark work to be done.

But these friends were the last anchor to sanity Scotty had in the world, aside from Tom himself. Scotty looked forward to going to school because it was light and clean, and because people cared about him there. Tom feared something vital was being leeched from his younger brother every morning he woke up in that house, and sometimes his inability to protect Scotty left him gasping for breath in the middle of the night. Scotty deserved whatever scraps of happiness he could find.

"Half an hour," Tom said. "That's all. I'm serious."

His brother beamed. "Thanks, Tom!" And he was off like a cannonball, barreling toward the other kids. As they opened their ranks and accepted him into the group, Tom felt a sudden welling of relief and sorrow.

Tom walked out to the bleachers and waited. He kept his back to the market. He watched the stream of cars out on the highway, sunlight glinting off chrome and glass. Once, his father would have been part of that traffic, steering his rig gently through it, a tender goliath. But he never left home anymore. The boys couldn't recognize their father in the thing that lived in their house.

He gave his brother an extra fifteen minutes. He approached the gaggle of kids slowly, reluctant to interfere. Scotty, in mid-lope, saw him coming and came to a reluctant stop. "No, please? Ten more minutes?"

"It's now or never."

Scotty's face clouded. Tom felt a wave of unreasonable anger. But it wasn't his brother's fault that they were abruptly poor. It wasn't his brother's fault that Tom himself didn't have friends, that this loneliness at home was absolute and all-consuming. It wasn't his brother's fault that their father was a monster and their mother was crazy. The anger dissipated almost at once, replaced by something sad and sweet.

He didn't need to take him on this trek. Scotty belonged to the sunlight.

"Tell you what. Stay here and play. I'll pick you up when I'm done."

Scotty surprised him. He turned to the other kids and said, "I have to go." And to his brother he said, "You need me today."

Tom felt a flush of pride. It was not a feeling he was accustomed to. "Okay," he said. "Let's get to it, then."

No one noticed them leaving the baseball field; people came and went all the time. The road leading up the mountain was empty. Nobody lived up there but the witches, so there was no need for anybody else to ever walk up that way. It was getting on toward ten o'clock. The sun was bright, and the air was cold and clear.

Soon the market fell out of sight. The path ascended around a steep bend, and then Toad Springs was obscured by the woods. They walked fast, making good time. Soon they were sweating with exertion despite the chill.

By the time they'd been walking for an hour or so, Scotty was making a show of his weariness, leaning over as he walked, swaying his arms dramatically. "I'm too tired, Tom!"

"Come on," Tom said. He kept trudging, though he was starting to feel worn out, too.

"I can't!"

Tom stopped, turned around. Scotty was sitting flat in the middle of the dirt road, his legs splayed out before him and his hands resting palms up, as though he were offering himself up to whatever might come along to collect him. "Get your ass up, Scotty! You can't just sit in the middle of the road!"

"No cars come on this road," he said, and laid straight back to underscore his faith in this point.

"Fine." Tom turned and continued his climb. "You know who does come on this road, though? Witches."

In moments, he heard his brother's feet slapping the ground behind him. He permitted himself a little smile.

The path darkened as they walked. Tom no longer had a sense of what time it was, and he felt a flutter of fear in his gut. Common sense told him it couldn't be any later than two o'clock, two-thirty at most. And yet the light filtering through the trees seemed diffuse and weak. This might have been due to the sun pursuing its course above them, and it might have had something to do with the heavy tangle of branches crowding them from either side, but he knew instinctively that the cause was something else: they were entering the Witch Wood. Darkness was an animal, and this is where it lived.

"Come on, we gotta hurry."

They doubled their pace, Scotty huffing and pouting behind him, until they came at last to a place where the road narrowed and split three ways. One wended in a slight decline to the right, where the trees thinned and sunlight dappled the way; one rose sharply straight ahead, a path composed more of stacked rock than packed earth; and one bent toward the left, into deeper woods. This left-hand path was straight and level, though the trees grew tight and mean around it, hoarding darkness. It was obviously the path to the Mothers' cabin.

"Come on, Scotty." He took a few tentative steps, feeling the temperature drop a few more degrees.

His brother slipped a hand into his, and they continued their walk, suddenly reluctant to get where they were going.

On the second week, while seated at the kitchen table, their father opened his chest. His rib cage was fashioned from cedar branches; suspended by a red thread in its center was a jar of ghost preserves of the kind Mother Agnes sold at market, its interior gray and mold-thick, sparkling with an interior light. He reached into himself, took it into his hand, and offered it to their mother. It steamed when he opened it. Careful not to snap the thread, she took it into her hands. It was hot to the touch, and she winced. She scooped her fingers into the jar and pressed them into her mouth. Their father remained silent and still, his smile radiant. Tears gathered in their mother's eyes, and she closed them, drawing a deep breath.

"I missed you," she said. "I missed you." Then she clutched Tom's sleeve. "Come here. You too."

"No." He jerked his arm away.

She reached for Scotty instead. "Scotty. This is your father."

Scotty backed against the refrigerator. Revulsion crawled across his face. "No! I'm too scared!"

Their father put his own fingers into the jar, scooping out a thick dollop and extended it to Scotty. It dripped onto the carpet, a mixture of preserves and the black, greasy residue of his skin. Scotty edged further away.

Their mother's face curled in anger. "Scotty! Take it! *Don't you want to know your father?*" Her voice escalated into a shriek, a piercing dagger of sound. Scotty bolted from the kitchen, his footsteps thundering all the way to his room. The door slammed shut and a keening wail floated back to them.

His mother's head dropped into her folded arms, and she sobbed. She held the half-depleted jar loosely in one hand, the thread still connected to the cedar ribs, the fingers of her other hand still smeared with its contents. Her own crying mingled with Scotty's mournful howl into a noise that filled Tom with a desperate self-loathing. Maybe he could stop at least one person from crying.

"Mom?" He touched her shoulder. "Mom?"

She lifted her head. Her eyes were swollen, her whole face leaking. It was the worst he had ever seen her.

"I'll try it."

She gripped his forearm so tightly that he knew there'd be bruises later. "*Yes*. Yes, Tommy. I knew you would do it. He always loved you best."

He felt a spike of guilty pride, and then a fresh wash of grief at having lost him, this man who had apparently loved him better than anyone else in the world. He noticed Scotty's crying had ceased, and he wondered if he'd heard her say that. He half hoped so.

"You're just like your dad, Tom."

Maybe, by consuming this awful substance, he could accept his return. Maybe he would recognize him in the entity sitting at the table.

He went to the utensil drawer and retrieved a spoon. His took the jar into his own hands, staring into it. Faint screams lifted from it, like a sound drifting down the mountain, carried by the wind from a far place.

"Mom? Is Dad in hell?"

She pulled back slightly, surprised. Her lip trembled halfway between a grimace and a smile. Her eyes shone like cracked glass. She put her hand on his cheek, and suddenly all he could see in her face was love. Boundless love. "No, honey. No. He's right here. He's right here with us."

The father-thing opened its mouth into a bright grin.

Tom ate.

The cabin was nestled in a copse of blackened trees, each curled like a finger around its white-painted walls. Bright flowers were painted on its doorframe. Little pots of herbs were suspended from hooks along its gabled roof, and a trellis leaned against the wall beside a curtained front window, heavy with roses in unseasonable bloom. A small lantern hung from a hook by the door, spilling a warm nimbus of light. Only then did it occur to Tom how late it had gotten. It seemed impossible that evening should already be settling over the mountain, yet here it was.

Scotty clutched his hand so hard it hurt. Tom extricated himself and made his cautious way to the door. He put his ear against the wood and listened.

"Are they home?"

"You know they're not home. They're still at the market."

Tom glanced at the road behind them, not at all sure this was true. Any moment they might materialize from around the bend, Mother Agnes with that great cabinet strapped to her back. He thought he heard a sound even now: *tuk . . . tuk . . . tuk . . .* her walking stick punching into the earth, dragging her up the path.

He turned the doorknob. The door swung open silently. The lantern light illuminated a dusty wooden floor, spangled with divots where Mother Agnes's walking stick had gouged the wood. An end table was just inside, littered with little white pellets that made him think of knucklebones. The interior of the house radiated a kind of thrumming energy, setting his nerves jangling. But it was quiet as sleep.

The boys entered, and Tom shut the door behind them. He felt his little brother tense at the abrupt plunge into darkness. He reached into his pocket and removed the lighter he'd taken from his mother's purse. It popped its little orange flame, giving them just enough light to maneuver by. When Scotty saw the lighter, his eyes widened.

"You're going to get in trouble!" he hissed.

"She's never gonna know, shut up."

They pushed further into the cabin. It seemed to have more rooms inside than it should, although every one of them was cramped with tables, chairs, a couch in one room, cabinets, and chests of drawers. And shelves, everywhere they turned. Free-standing bookshelves stretching to the ceiling, small knickknack shelves hanging on the walls, glass-cased shelves in the living room, shelves of spices and ingredients in the kitchen crowding a narrow cutting table and a potbellied stove.

What struck Tom's attention, though, were the items stored on the shelves: on some, miniature wooden figures fashioned from entwined branches and fleshed with mud, most still awaiting the breath of life, but one of them staring back with eyes like pinprick red cinders, a cockroach sliding out of its mouth like a tongue; on others, endless jars of various sizes, all of them full of glittering, moldy, pearl-colored preserves, all of them shedding a sickly light. They were like jars of rotting stars.

The strange energy he'd detected was radiating from them; although they were still, they projected a sense of shuddering movement, of imperceptible vibrations, as though each one housed something living and desperate to get out.

"Ghosts," he said.

Scotty grabbed his hand, squeezing hard again. This time Tom did not protest.

"We need to hurry," Scotty said, and Tom knew he was right. He had come here to destroy. Ever since he'd eaten the preserves, he could feel his father in his brain, like something long asleep starting to uncoil. The first time he'd experienced it, he wept with relief. It was as though his father was couched in his every thought, as though the weight of his arm around his shoulders would never leave again. He felt confident, protected, and loved. But it kept uncoiling, kept pushing for more space, until he started to feel other things, too. The brush of his mother's hand through his hair released complicated yearnings. Once he awoke to find himself standing over her as she slept, his hand poised to pull down the covers. The father-thing reposed beside her, his pale eyes fixed on his son, his grin like a light in the lightless room. Tom fled the room and pounded his own head onto his dresser until the world swam. Looking into mirrors produced a sense of disjunction which made him nauseous and filled him with self-loathing; he avoided them now. He was filled with an anger hotter than he'd ever experienced. Something elemental. Maybe an adult would know how to restrain it or to channel it; maybe not. But he had come to the Mothers' cabin to deliver his revenge.

And yet, faced with these shivering spirits, he was transfixed. He wanted to grab the edge of the closest bookcase and topple the whole thing over, but he couldn't bring himself to do it. It would have been like desecrating a church.

Scotty yanked his arm. "Tom, they're going to be here soon! We need to hurry!"

"Wait, wait. Let's look at their labels. Maybe we can find one that can help Mom."

A single shelf was affixed to the wall on his immediate right, and he peered more closely at the jars it held. Each small label was marked with an elegant cursive script. *Indian Summer. All Hallows' Eve. Skullpocket Fair. The Yuletide Weeping. Hannah's Underground Wedding.* They were all times or occasions: no indication of who was inside or what it would do to you if you ate it. Which ones could be taken as they were, or which were destined to be the hearts of creatures like the father-thing.

Scotty grabbed the nearest jar—a big one, like the one that held pickled pigs' feet at the gas station—and hurled it with all his strength across the room. It hit the dappled wallpaper with a soft crunch and fell behind an easy chair. They both stared at the place it disappeared in silence, waiting for whatever had been trapped inside to make itself known.

"Why did you do that?"

Scotty looked at his brother in terror. "You said! You said that's what we're supposed to do!"

I changed my mind, he wanted to say. *I'm scared now, too.* "I know, but—"

"You *said*!" And he grabbed another jar.

But Tom grabbed his wrist, staying his throw. "No," he said, and pointed. Light was streaming in from between the closed curtains.

Moonlight.

Someone was on the other side of the front door, huffing with effort.

"Hide!"

In a house this cluttered there was an abundance of places, yet they stood paralyzed for long seconds. Finally, Tom hustled them into the kitchen. The potbellied stove squatted in the corner like an evil goblin; Tom's mind flashed to an illustration from "Hansel and Gretel": a stove with children's legs thrashing from its open grate.

There was a back door at the kitchen's far end, but he feared they'd be seen through the window if they went for it. He opened the pantry closet and pulled his brother inside with him. It was cramped and dark, but he thought they would be fine as long as they stayed perfectly still. As long as the Mothers didn't open the door.

Around them were shelved all the instruments of Mother Margaret's art: cloves of garlic, soup stock, onions and potatoes and jars of crickets. Coiled salamanders and sleeping toads, red peppers and racks of spices, a burlap sack sealed with clothespins that shifted slightly as if it were filled with rats or snakes. The smell was giddy and overwhelming. One of the toads opened a sleepy yellow eye and regarded them with patient curiosity.

The witches entered the cabin. The boys heard a grunt, followed by the heavy sound of Mother Agnes's cabinet thudding onto the floor. Footsteps shuffled through the small home. When they spoke to each other it sounded like the language of abandoned wooden shacks, creaking and squeaking in the wind.

"The fat one was rude again today."

"Put a goblin's tooth in her pie next time. A civil tongue or no tongue at all, is what I like to say."

"Did you see the Owens boy? So fetching before, but now he looks like an ox. I knew he'd grow up stupid."

Occasionally one of them would laugh or cluck disapprovingly.

Eventually, they exhausted their chatter and the cabin fell into silence. Tom began to wonder if they'd gone to bed. He had all but made up his mind to open the pantry door when he heard one of them enter the kitchen. She was breathing heavily, humming quietly to herself; from time to time a word or a phrase breached the surface: an old song Tom had heard on the radio before, one his mother liked, though he couldn't place it. A country ballad. He tried to imagine a witch listening to popular music on a radio but it was too strange.

Scotty whimpered. Tom locked his hand over his mouth and squeezed tight.

A soft light flickered at the bottom of the door. The tap at the sink came on, and they listened as the witch filled a kettle.

The water cut off. "What?" she said.

The boys looked at each other, Tom's hand still over his brother's mouth.

They heard something else moving in the house: scuttling like a centipede. A very large centipede. Tom remembered the jar his brother had shattered against the wall.

A voice came from another room: "Ingrid! Look at this!"

The witch—Mother Ingrid, the one who made the homunculi—left the kitchen. After a moment they heard a chair being dragged from its position in the other room.

"Who did this?"

The shattered jar.

"Let's go!" Tom hissed. "Now!"

He opened the pantry—the kitchen was bathed in warm light coming from the stove, and from a lamp on the cutting table—and bolted for the back door. He knocked into the table in his haste and its legs scraped loudly over the floor. He didn't care anymore; he only had to get out of there. Let them see him through the window, let them leap onto broomsticks or send a flock of vampire bats through the night after him. He just needed to be out of this cabin.

He reached the door—unlocked!—and banged through it. He leapt down the stoop and hit the grass. His heart lifted—free! The trees surged against the full night sky. The moon burned.

He skidded to a stop.

He stood in Mother Agnes's garden.

It was a modest parcel of land, no wider than the little house itself. A small white fence—only up to his ankles, purely decorative—surrounded it. Inside it were four ghosts. They were tethered to the ground just beneath the earth, bright white scraps of light whipping and shivering like flags in a hurricane wind, though the air was still. The ghosts did not make a sound, but Tom felt a welling of nausea and grief. They froze him in place.

Behind him, his brother said, "Tom?"

He turned. The witches stood at the top of the stoop, the three of them together a huge black shape, the dark rags of their clothing fluttering like crows' feathers. One spindly hand gripped Scotty's shoulder.

"You left before the tea was ready, child," said Mother Margaret. "Come back inside."

The brothers sat at the small table with Mothers Margaret and Ingrid. There were five chairs and five empty clay mugs. Had the table been set for five before? Tom couldn't remember. The lamp had been extinguished, so the only light came from the red-orange belly of the stove and the eerie luminescence of the ghost jars. They waited meekly while Mother Agnes shuffled about in the other room, moving furniture and making clucking noises. She was trying to capture the escaped ghost.

"Come here, love. You're not fit to be out yet." When this didn't work she started to sing. Her voice was old and weathered, but it carried a melody with surprising ease. Tom found himself lulled by it. His fear started to abate. Scotty's eyes were half closed and he seemed to be studying the mug in front of him with a sleepy intensity.

In a moment the singing stopped and the witch came back into the kitchen, her expression clouded. "It won't come," she said. She paused by the table and glared at the boys. "That's bad business," she said. "Why are you here?"

With the song stopped, fear bubbled up inside him again. Tom wanted to answer her, but the words wouldn't come.

The kettle began to whistle, and Mother Margaret made a shushing gesture. "Wait."

Mother Agnes grasped the kettle with unnaturally long fingers—hands which only minutes earlier had clutched Scotty's shoulder, those sharp nails so close to his throat—and poured. Their mugs billowed steam like little cauldrons. Mother Margaret dropped a bag of herbs into each. "Five minutes," she said. "Any more, any less, and there will be dark results."

"I want to go home," Scotty said.

Mother Ingrid looked at him, her lips curled in distaste. "We'll see," she said.

Mother Agnes seated herself at the table and looked at Tom. "Well?"

"My mom sent you a letter."

"I get a lot of letters from a lot of people, in case you didn't know. Do better."

"It had my dad's ring in it. She sent you his ring."

"A wedding ring?"

Tom shrugged. "I guess."

Mother Agnes laughed. It was not a pleasant sound. "I remember her. She seemed sweet."

Anger flashed through Tom's whole body. "You ruined her life. She can't do anything anymore. She doesn't work anymore. She doesn't care about us anymore. Only Dad. And he's . . . not the same."

The witch fluttered a hand. "So what. She's haunted. That's what she wanted."

Scotty started openly weeping. He lowered his head, his eyes screwed shut. "Mom's haunted? Is Dad a bad ghost?"

Mother Agnes looked at Tom. She winked. "What do you say, boy? Is your daddy a bad ghost?"

Tom felt the foreign presence shift in his head. That knot of urgency, desire, thwarted want. That bubbling anger. His father had never been an angry man at home. Tired and harried, impatient sometimes, yes. But never angry. Never a hard word for his family. So who was this thing Tom felt crawling inside him now? Why the urge—the need—to break bones, to crack wood, to burn this whole mountain down to black earth?

What had his father kept locked away? Had he ever really known him at all?

The freed ghost stepped in from the other room, filling the doorframe. It looked like a curtain of flame, and it shed a cold radiance. It pinwheeled where it stood, billowing silence. It wore multiple heads.

"Look what you've released, you stupid child. I can't get it back now." Mother Agnes stood from the table and teetered to the back door. It was hard to believe this frail woman had walked up and down a mountain with a six-foot cabinet strapped to her back. Opening it, she thrust a pointed finger outside and addressed the ghost. "Go, wretch. You're not welcome in my home."

The ghost was still for a moment; then it lunged for the door in a frigid rush. It passed over the brothers and seemed nearly to pull something from the center of them in its wake; they were left vertiginous and a little ill, as though they had almost walked off the edge of a building. Mother Agnes shut the door with a grunt of disgust.

"It is unquiet, and will stay that way. Whatever it does now is your fault. Remember that."

Mother Ingrid tutted in disappointment, shaking her head.

Scotty rose from his position at the table. His tea was untouched. He looked scooped out, exhausted. "I'm going home now."

"Wait for me, Scotty."

Mother Agnes resumed her seat and looked at them both. "You don't get to break into our home and vandalize it, then leave at your whim. Answer the question I asked you. Why did you come?"

"To break things," Scotty said. "I'm sorry I did it. I just want to go home now. Mom's going to be mad."

"Darling," Mother Margaret said. "No. She won't."

"You have to help me," Tom said. As he said it, he knew it was the real reason he'd come. The witches had to get rid of their dad. Not for his mom or his brother, but for himself. He felt the terrible weight of the betrayal even as he thought it.

You're just like your dad, Tom.

The father-thing opened its mouth into a bright grin.

"She's feeding us from the jar," he said, his voice quavering. "Is that safe?"

Mother Margaret was delighted. "Some people think the heart is delicious!"

"Nothing in this world is safe, boy," said Mother Ingrid.

Mother Agnes took a sip from her tea and seemed to think about it. "People come to me for what grows out in that garden. I don't make any promises about what it will be like for them, or whether they'll be better for it. Caveat emptor, boy. Do you know what that means?"

Tom shook his head.

"Ask your mother. She knows."

"Please," Tom said. Tears burned his eyes. "I can't be like this anymore."

Mother Ingrid frowned at him. "Your mother made an honest transaction," she said. "Do you think we're cheats?"

Scotty started to cry. "Please just let us go."

Tom watched as his little brother lowered his head and sobbed unselfconsciously, his cheeks flushed red, tears dripping from his eyelashes. It was a plain, uncomplicated sound; almost musical. Once they left this mountain and returned home, there would be nothing uncomplicated about his life again. He would grow up in the shadow of their grief-wrecked mother and the bizarre presence of the father-thing, their house filled with the stink of a love gone mad, the air choked with flies. Tom felt his father's darkness percolating inside him; but maybe Scotty could be spared.

"My brother," he said, finally.

The witches leaned in, smiling. "Yes, child? What about him?"

"If you can't save me or my mom, save my brother."

"From what?" said Mother Margaret.

". . . from the dark."

Scotty stared at him, shivering in fear.

She reached across the table and took Tom's hand into her own. "Poor boy. Poor, dull boy. It's far too late for that. No one is spared."

That was it, then. All was lost. He closed his eyes. He couldn't look his brother in the face.

The witches whispered, and then Mother Ingrid said, "Well, perhaps we can do something. Your mother paid. Will you?"

Thank God, at last, a window. Yes, he would pay. Yes. "Yes."

"You'll have to make friends with the dark," Mother Margaret said. "Do you have the heart for it?"

He nodded.

"We'll see."

"Don't fret," said Mother Agnes, staring at his little brother. "The sweetest things grow in the dark."

The ghosts trembled in their jars. Weird light shivered over their faces. Tom felt a creeping hope.

Scotty walked out the door. Tom stayed behind.

He stayed behind for fifty years, each one spent in servitude to the Mothers. He was given many tasks and performed them all dutifully. He ventured into the woods to gather ingredients for Mother Margaret's recipes: scraping beetles from the undersides of rocks, tending mold farms, catching cricketsong with a net made from the woven strands of a bog hag's hair. He lost two fingers obtaining the hair, but under the ministrations of Mother Ingrid, flexing twigs grew in their place.

For Mother Ingrid he cut and whittled branches of cedar trees, the ideal wood for the housing of spirits. He maintained the cellar full of spoiling meat and offal, where the vermin so vital to her efforts thrived. The homunculi caterwauled from their clay pots, scratching and biting viciously when the time came to cut them from their warm roots.

He tended Mother Agnes's garden, where the ghosts whipped back and forth under a sky frozen with stars. Mostly they grew from trinkets brought to her from the people of Toad Springs; but sometimes they grew on their own, straight from the corrupted earth, like hell's questing fingers. These were untamable and he cut them loose to drift away and do their work upon the world.

When he complained, he was beaten, and he accepted these beatings. When he grew older, he submitted to the dark advances of Mother Margaret, surrounded by the crawling walls of her bedroom. Eventually his skin grew old and loose, his eyes turned opaque, his bones bent beneath the weight of his labors. He knew that if they ever dismissed him from service, he would be too old, too broken, too strange to be of worth to any living thing in the world.

He never learned whether or not his mother missed him, or if she even knew that he was gone. He hoped not.

He asked the Mothers what had become of his brother when they turned him loose that night, bewildered and alone—what kind of freedom Tom's sacrifice had bought for him.

They wouldn't tell him. Maybe they didn't know.

But each blackberry winter, when he felt the encroachment of despair most acutely, he remembered the night he agreed to this price. They gave Scotty one of the jars that night, and he ate from it at his brother's urging. He remembered Scotty's face as it released him: from his heart's shackling to his parents, from his brother, from a household in love with its own doom. Released finally into the dark, glittering wood, where, Tom liked to imagine, the pinwheeling ghost they'd freed became Scotty's protector, his guide, his howling companion in a hundred eerie adventures. Scotty could never escape the darkness; but he could love it, and it could love him back. They ran together with abandon—into the Troll Wood, the Werewolf Wood, the Witch Wood, the full moon resplendent above.

Tom remembered, in the season's last frost, and was glad.

CHRIS WILLRICH

The Odyssey Problem

FROM *Clarkesworld*

WHEN THE SPARKLING golden glow fades and my skin stops feeling like mites are crawling all over it, the Room is gone, and I am shivering in a vast bright chamber and strange people clad in orange, red, and blue pajamas are asking me how I am. I don't know what to say. I feel lighter, and the air feels cleaner; I am giddy and frightened. The Room is my only home, and now it is gone. Sometimes, in the old times, people would open the door of the Room and someone would stare at me and ask questions. I would never answer. The questions weren't for me but for my jailers. I didn't talk much then. I used to promise to be good, but it didn't seem to matter.

These new people do want me to speak, but I am so bewildered I can't manage to say anything, not even *I am so bewildered I can't manage to say anything*. I am taken through a series of corridors, all blazingly bright and full of calming colors, and finally into a place with many beds beneath machines that make gentle sounds. People in blue wave devices over me and inject me with something. I sleep.

When I wake it still seems too bright, but I feel somewhat better, clearer-headed. I am given food, something like what I am used to in the Room but fresher and tastier. I eat with caution at first, then greed. The water is clean. It is like a dream.

A woman in an orange shirt speaks to me. I look closely. She seems slightly different from the people I've seen before at the door of my Room. It is not just her skin color but the shape of her head. I do not think my language is her first language either. She asks, "How are you feeling?"

"Better," I say.

"That's good. You must have questions."

Do I have questions? I wonder. I have food and drink and space to move. I am clean. People are behaving kindly to me. Questions seem superfluous. But I feel as though the woman in orange has a desire to answer questions. So it is for her sake that I try to form them. "Where am I? Who are you?"

"This must all seem strange to you. You are aboard the *Odyssey*."

"The-o-di-cy?"

"It doesn't translate well. It literally means the story of a man named Odysseus, a traveler from another world long ago and far away. But the connotation is 'great journey.' My *Odyssey* is a Research-Contact-Diplomacy Scout of the Federated Cultural Republic. I am Captain Temple. Do you have a name?"

"I . . . I don't remember . . ."

"You've been terribly treated; I don't wonder that you've lost that memory. The doctor's begun mental therapies. Perhaps it will come back to you."

"I lived in the Room . . . always."

Captain Temple frowns. "Yes. We've encountered such Rooms several times in this part of the galaxy."

"I don't understand. There is only one Room. The one in . . ." I struggle to recall the name of my home. "Emulvain Town. There can only be one Room. Only one person needs to be in it." I recall hearing this when my jailers answered questions of the people who came to stare at me. "There is only ever need for one Room, one prisoner. I remember that."

Captain Temple's face is strange to me, so I cannot be certain of her expressions. But I think she is angry. It frightens me, but it becomes clear it's not me she is angry at. "Do you understand that there are other worlds? Beyond Emulvain Town and its planet?"

I remember things taught to me before I was chosen for the Room. "Yes."

"There are people on some of those worlds. Some resemble your people as much as I resemble you. Others are very different. They have all sorts of ways of living, and all manner of machines. For example, this vessel is similar in basic concept to the watercraft of your home planet, but larger and much more powerful, and it sails space, not the sea."

"Yes." I remember seeing flags fluttering on the boats in the harbor during Summer Festival, long ago.

"There were once beings as far beyond us as this vessel is beyond your ships. Farther. They were powerful and cruel. They created the Rooms and scattered them on less advanced planets. Each Room has the potential to beam enough energy to power millions upon millions of devices. In time the Room can make a planet a paradise. Abundance for all. No scarcity."

"The Room is necessary," I say.

"That's what your people told you, is it? Your world became a utopia because you had a Room. But the beings who made the Rooms gave them special locks of sorts. They can only be activated if an intelligent being is inside, constantly suffering. Like you."

"I was necessary."

"We think the ones who built the Rooms were trying to make a cruel argument about complicity, testing it out on living worlds. The Rooms aren't really for you, they're just talking points in a debate waged by gods." The captain looks away as if sickened. "I can't judge your people, really, but I was able to rescue you. I've rescued and resettled several victims like you. FCR contact protocols allow interference in cases of outside meddling—"

"Captain." A man in blue touches her shoulder. "My patient needs rest."

"I'm sorry," says Captain Temple to both of us. She smiles at me. I think the showing of teeth is meant kindly. "We'll talk later. Get some rest."

"Captain?" I ask, because I know answering questions is something that matters to her, and also because this question matters to me. "What . . . what happens to me?"

"Once we're back from these unknown spaces there are many worlds that would take you in."

"Can I go home?"

The frown returns to her face. "Yes. But it won't be the same. If a living victim is ever removed from a Room—"

"Captain," the man in blue objects again.

"Rest," she says.

My world is on fire. I learn that days later when I am much recovered and free to roam the *Odyssey*. That is why Captain Temple frowned. I see the occasional broadcasts that are still possible with the loss of most of the world's power. When I left the Room my people broke the terms and the Room self-destructed. Civilization toppled like a bunch of toy buildings with the rug tugged out from under them. I am hated by many, celebrated by others. Some even claim me a god who once suffered in flesh, and who has now visited righteous punishment upon the emulvain.

All I am certain of, watching the broadcasts, is that I do not want to go back.

I start learning in earnest as the *Odyssey* leaves orbit to continue exploring the galaxy. (Among the first things I learn is the meaning of the terms "orbit" and "galaxy.") The crew says I can have a place in the Federated Cultural Republic when they eventually return there. At first I'm eager to study to become a ship's crew member. They are very polite about that. I gather that refugees from backward worlds (and I must remember, even if my world wasn't backward before, it is now) often want to become crew. We wish to be treated as special, the only members of our various species who can surpass the dirt and excrement and narrow dimensions of our origins and join the heroes of the stars—as if this salvation was something we had earned. Dazzled, we imagine becoming indispensable to our rescuers.

I still have that feeling when I tour the engine room.

The woman who guides me is wearing red and has devices covering one ear and the opposite eye. Her skin color looks exotic compared to both mine and the captain's. I ask, perhaps rudely, if loss of organs is a hazard of engineering work. She laughs and says the only hazard of engineering work is drinking too much mipsir. "No, I lost an eye and an ear in a battle with demonkeepers," she says as she leads me among angled clear pillars swirling with shades of blue like schools of fish made of moonlight. "There was enough neural damage that prosthetics worked better than regrowing the organs. I'm used to it now."

I choose among my many questions. "You have battles? There were no battles in Emulvain Town. Only in old stories for little children."

"Sadly, kid, we do have battles. Not among ourselves. Arguments, sure. But the planets of the FCR learned long ago that cooperation is better than violence. But it's a big galaxy, and high technology is no guarantee of high morals, as you well know."

"Yes."

She waves a hand. "Out there are cultures that like to impose their will on others. They have no problem wrecking planets in the name of their beliefs."

"Like you did." The words slip out of me as I imagine my planet viewed from space, fires visible on the nightside.

"What?"

"Never mind." I feel I have said something wrong, and for a moment I am afraid they will drag me into a narrow room. *Will I feel that way all my life?* I wonder. But the engineer in red still seems friendly, just confused. I ask, "Can you show me the, the . . ." I am learning many new words, and the ship's Al-Jazari Mechanism whispers new ones in my ear all the time. But I stumble on this one. "Schopenhauer Core? Schoenberg Core?"

The engineer laughs. "Right planet, wrong thinkers! It's called the Schrödinger Core. And sure."

"So the person who invented it was Schrödinger?" I ask as she floats me down a wuxia shaft to the lower levels of Engineering. I am asking as much to keep everyone liking me as to learn new things. And I fear being led to another Room, and the questions distract me from that feeling.

"No, it's named for the Schrödinger Gems that power our Var-uwult Drive. But the gems were named for Schrödinger. He was a scientist who helped one of our member worlds first understand many weird phenomena. He's famous for a parable about a cat that's both dead and alive at the same time. The gems are exotic matter with some of that same quality—macroscopic quantum effects—so they got named after the parable."

I focus on the simplest of my questions. "A cat?"

"A small, furred creature. But these aren't cats."

She's brought me to a chamber where we can glimpse, through what seems but surely isn't frosted glass, a set of crystals hovering in a circle of blue lightning. Each crystal seems to shatter and re-form so quickly that the fractured and the solid Schrödinger Gems appear superimposed upon each other, broken/whole all at once. I clutch my head and the engineer steers me away from the sight.

"Easy now," she says. "A lot of people get that reaction the first time."

I'm still holding my hands to my head. "Do you—hear screaming?"

"Sometimes people experience that the first few times." She laughs. "The mipsir helps."

"What . . . what was Schrödinger's parable?"

She begins telling me about a cat who is stuffed into a small box, and who may be alive or dead, and is in fact somehow alive and dead at the same time. I lose track of the kindly engineer's explanation and feel tight in my chest. I make polite excuses as soon as I can so I can return to my room. "You're bright, you know," says the engineer as she waves me on my way. "You ask good questions. And you're young yet. If you study hard while you're on *Odyssey*, you might make it into the academy on Haivinth, or enlist." I don't really understand, but I make myself smile at the compliment.

I do study when I get back to my quarters. They've given me what seems to me a grand cathedral, though I'm assured it's just the room of a junior officer who volunteered. Its windows look out on either the star-mottled void or the Varuwult Abyss's seething clouds of color. I shudder for a while, experiencing a strange feeling of solitude and safety. When I do my research I talk to the Mechanism while sitting under a blanket in the corner.

My eyes flutter. Sleep is coming, and I fear my dreams. Abruptly, without knowing where the idea comes from, I ask the Mechanism, "Are the Schrödinger Gems alive?"

"The scientific consensus is no," it replies. It sounds like a soft-spoken teacher from before the Room. "No crystalline life-forms have been discovered. However, certain panpsychist beliefs attach to the crystals. It is known that the Branching Way believes . . ."

It tells me more, but I fall asleep.

When I awaken it is to a blaring alarm, and the light is tinted red. I leave my quarters, and as I've been taught, I ask a panel of glass in the corridor how to get to the captain. Glowing golden arrows in the air lead me through hallways and wuxia shafts to a sort of shadowed steel courtyard with black walls shining with lights and symbols, with a kind of round platform rising at its center like a theater stage. Scores of people mill about on the "street," drawing pictures of light in the air, sparkles around them forming words. I never fully learned to read, but I doubt these words are in my language anyway. Up on the "stage" are more people, also drawing with light. Above it all is what seems a dark dome speckled with lights. I realize they are stars. Covering some of the stars is something that looks like a huge silver moon covered with holes through which green light blazes forth. I soon realize by its motions it is an object outside our ship.

Captain Temple looks down from the stage. "Child! You should go back to your room!"

"I don't want to be alone," I say in a very quiet voice, but somehow the captain understands and beckons me up.

"Definitely a demonkeeper ship, ma'am," says a gold-shirted person in a levitating chair surrounded by glowing displays floating in the air. "Over twenty hooshool from any of their known bases."

"Please use their chosen name for themselves," Captain Temple says. "Even if they're shooting at us. Perhaps especially if they're shooting at us."

"Yes, ma'am. Definitely a Branching Way ship, ma'am."

"We are in a dangerous situation," Captain Temple says as I reach the top. "The Branching Way is maybe a thousand years ahead of us in technology, so every encounter with them must be handled with great care. You need to stay to one side and not get involved."

"What do they want?"

"I don't know yet. They've fired a warning shot but haven't spoken. We've been at odds for centuries. We keep trying to get through to them, but they think we're backward primitives."

A man in red with a surprising number of eyes says, "Captain, they are responding." Looking up, I see the silver surface of the Branching Way vessel covered with strange twisting writing. "The glyphs say, 'We know your mission, *Odyssey*, but you are not welcome here. We will purge the galaxy of the Rooms, and with far less collateral damage. Depart this region.'"

"Reply," says the captain, "'We consider this region free space. And we could help each other. We have destroyed several Rooms already, and we have someone aboard with direct experience of one.'"

I see the writing change upon the Branching Way ship. "They're replying," says the officer in red. "'Send the victim of the Room to us, and we will spare you the indignity of a destroyed ship and a captured crew. You are little better than those who use the Rooms. We will not leave this child in your hands, barbarians.'"

Captain Temple raises her voice. "Send this! 'We are not barbarians. All are cared for in our Republic. There is no starvation, no exploitation, no war. We do not even eat meat.'"

The officer in red's many eyes squint at his display. He says, "They reply, 'You are a hierarchical, humanoid-dominated, tribalistic incoherence. You abandon planets to misery with your contact protocols, when you could do much good. You kill innocent plants with relish when you could easily subsist on artificial food. And you torture the gems in your engines. If you are civilized, you are only barely so.'"

"'Absurd! Just to address one of your claims, even if the gems were living, they, like the plants, would be of such low order their use would be entirely moral. At worst it would be no more immoral than agriculture. Trillions of *intelligent* life-forms depend upon the drive.'"

The officer in red's eyes blink as though catching dust. "They say, 'Enough. Send the child or your ship will be destroyed, and you will all face judgment.'"

Odyssey shakes. Green fires burst from the Branching Way vessel and the space around *Odyssey* is blazing blue.

I can't understand the displays around me, but I can sense that most of the people in this room are terrified. Their hands shake. Sweat is on many a strange brow. Their initially calm voices are becoming a frantic babble.

"I'll go," I tell the captain. "Whatever it is, it can't be worse than the Room."

The captain says, "You would do that for people you've only just met?"

"You hadn't even met me, and you saved me. Of course I will."

"They aren't even humanoid. You may feel very misunderstood and lonely. And despite their claims, I don't know that they'd treat you well."

Alarms are blaring all through this gallery. "Tell them," I say.

Again the glow. Again the feeling that mites are swarming all over me.

I am not alone this time, however. Captain Temple is holding my hand as we appear aboard the other ship.

At first, I think we've accidentally arrived on a planet. We are surrounded by purple trees and an abundance of green flowers. Things like winged jellyfish flit through the air. The blue sky above is filled with holes through which the stars blaze in blackness. I see *Odyssey* through one of them, a tiny white sphere with glowing spindles stretching behind it.

Barely before I can take this in, something gelatinous, many-tentacled, and huge as my quarters on *Odyssey* grabs me and pulls me close, tearing me away from Captain Temple.

"Hug," it says, and one tentacle injects my head in what seems a dozen places. There is no pain, only numbness.

"Let her go!" Captain Temple is demanding.

"Contemplate," it tells her, and she vanishes. Then the thing sets me down gently upon red, straw-like grass.

I take a nap.

I have a dream of being in the Room, shivering in my own filth. A voice comes into my head. It is nothing like the voices of my jailers or their visitors. Nor could it be that of any of *Odyssey*'s crew, nor the beings of the Branching Way. It is a voice almost not a voice, but more like the afterimage of words written in fire. That is a strange thing because I'd still been learning to read when I was chosen for the Room. It says:

IT IS AS I PREDICTED. EVERY LESSER CULTURE ACCEPTS THE SAME BARGAIN. THERE IS ALWAYS A POINT WHERE THE ILLUSION OF MULTIPLIED JOY BECOMES AN EXCUSE FOR HORROR.

I CONCEDE [comes a response like writing in another hand] THINGS PROGRESSED AS YOU PREDICTED. YET YOUR METHODS PROMOTE THE HORROR YOU DECRY. I WILL STIR MINDS TO OPPOSE YOU IN EVERY SPIRAL ARM AND FIELD OF GRASS. HOLD, ADVERSARY! ONE BECOMES AWARE. LET US WITHDRAW.

Then all is quiet (or equally valid, the thought-image of the words blurs) and in the silence of the dream the door of the Room opens, not upon the dim hallway in Emulvain Town but upon a forest of purple trees. Everything is misty and my heart trembles with a feeling of imminent potential.

I awaken in joy. All seems brighter. It is as if I've arisen, not just from sleep, but from a shadowy distortion of life. Now, my body seems to tell me, the true life can begin.

"How do you feel?" comes the voice of the gelatinous being. It is a fresh and lively sound, like crackling ice. I see it looming over me like a glacier filled with rainbows.

"Better," I say.

"Good. We do not fight except at great need. But our rules allow us to rescue captives. I'm happy to have saved you."

"I wasn't a captive," I object, sitting up. "And you didn't save me. I volunteered to come, to save them. They were kind to me."

"You have a generous spirit. But I'm afraid your understanding is limited. As of yet."

"Captain Temple came with me. She refused to let me come alone."

"That is true and speaks well of her. In her Republic there are beings with promise, portents of better things to come. She is one of them. I assure you we have treated her well."

"You seem to think the people on *Odyssey* are bad."

"Bad? No, child, not 'bad' in their own context. They're a young culture yet. They are still quite singular."

"What?"

"How to say it? Cultures at that stage are focused on numbers as distinct entities, and the metaphor of discrete numbers guides their thinking. They think of sapient beings as purely individual. They also think of sapience as a binary yes-and-no state. You are sapient or you aren't. In fact sapience is a continuum. All matter has a grain of consciousness, and all life has a dollop of it, and the amount of the stuff of intelligence increases as you move along the continuum; plants, to Schrödinger Gems, to complex animals, to one such as you, and on up to the beings in our own Branching Way."

"The gems . . . they really are alive? I wasn't just imagining it?"

"Oh yes. I have given you and the captain a serum that enhances your perception of the mentality of all living things. It will aid you in outside-compassion and inside-compassion. Look without and within."

Each blade of grass has a tiny blossom on it that looks like a white spiral . . . there are clouds beneath the dome of the sky that drift, combine, and tear apart like alien continents . . . fruits hang on purple trees, pale as the moons over Emulvain Town . . . the stalks of red grass are like tall buildings with tiny many-legged black creatures scurrying as if strange city dwellers amid the towers . . .

It is like being freed from the Room again. The clouds and trees and grass and creatures have a kind of glow about them that words are unequal to. It is as if natural things had once been all blurred background and now are brightly lit foreground.

Closing my eyes, I try also to "look within." I giggle with delight
at what I find. My body is a world full of tectonic inhalation and
exhalation, volcanic heartbeats, oceans of blood, electrical storms
of nerve endings. And my mind is that world's chief city. There is
not a single "me" dwelling there but many. There is a me for every
shade of emotion. There is a me who'd belonged to the Room,
and who is my will to survive. There is a me who'd known a life
before the Room, who is my sense of wonder. There is a me who'd
been born aboard *Odyssey*, a me of curiosity. And there is a me
here who stands in the midst of all the others. That version of me
opens her eyes and says, "I've been trapped. *They* were trapped."

My companion understands. "And now all your selves are free
of tyrannies like your planet and like the Republic. And they will
multiply and flourish. They are welcome to live in this worldlet, or,
if they like, they may leave the rest of you and go where they wish."

"Leave . . . me? Us?"

"You are thinking in terms of an abstraction, child. If a personality wishes to leave its original body we will free it, by giving it a
separate body. Many bodies are possible. Even one such as this."

"What does that do to the original?"

"The original mind expands into the void left behind. In time
all is well."

I . . . we . . . shiver a little, but the feeling of joy and emancipa-
tion is so strong I/we can't be concerned.

"Do you wish to stay?" my companion asks.

"What of Captain Temple and the *Odyssey*?"

"We have ceased our attack. But having stepped freely aboard this
worldlet, by our most sacred laws she was entitled to awakening."

"Take me . . . us . . . to her."

"Of course."

I/we ride within the gelatinous being, its translucent organs
consenting to shuffle aside for us as I bounce within it. Though
it looks like ice, its insides are warm. A natural air tube connects
us with the outside. It is snug and pleasant, and my many selves
mostly enjoy the ride.

We find the captain leaning beneath another tree, with a being
nearby I at first mistake for a thorny bush. Then we see eyes on
the thorns and spot rootlike hands and feet, three of each. "She
is many!" the thorned being calls out, and my host answers, "This
one is many, too."

We are bounced out of my host and land on our feet. We go to the captain. Her eyes are closed. "Ma'am?" I say, as we would aboard the *Odyssey*.

She smiles and focuses on us. "It is good to see you again, child. All of us think so. It's hard to believe we feared the demonkeepers. The Branching Way, that is."

"I . . . we . . . know how you feel. Why did you call them that, we wonder? 'Demonkeepers.'"

"We've been afraid of them and 'demonkeepers' sounds sinister. The Branching Way energy source is analogous to a legend from one of our worlds called a Maxwell's Demon. It is a particle of matter they believe to be sapient, and which can manipulate the movements of other particles. In so doing it creates order out of entropy, power out of chaos."

"If it's sapient . . . does it do it willingly?"

"It's *summoned*. How to explain . . . it's summoned out of the sapient substrate of the ship itself. It's similar in concept to the process by which a wayward personality is allowed to be taken from a whole person. Have they talked about that? In this case the particle of thought can't be reduced. It is only itself. And as it is born willing to serve, it can't do otherwise."

"Wait!" There is a storm across the world of our body; our skin chills. "So they *create slaves*?"

"You needn't put it so crudely, child. The so-called demons love their work by definition. It cannot be otherwise. And they are happier than we."

Our various selves are arguing, but there is a fragile consensus. "Captain, we have to speak out against this."

"There is nothing to speak out against. Not here. No, it is to our own backward civilization that we must return to, to end the barbaric practice of trapping and torturing the Schrödinger Gems. We cannot look away from that. From there we will fight against hierarchical organizations like the Fleet, and the eating of living things—"

"Plants, you mean?"

"Yes. But first the gems." The captain looks at the members of the Branching Way. "Friends. We ask that you release the part of us that longs to return to *Odyssey*."

"That is its right," says the thorn being, and it and the captain vanish, leaving us beside the gelatinous being on the hill.

"There is so much wonder to be found," we say, "and so much joy. But we must challenge your use of the Maxwell's Demons."

"That is a naive way of describing the Bright Joyous Ones."

"Nevertheless."

"You are very young yet. In the Branching Way you will be kept healthy and strong and be freed of diseases and mental turmoil you are not even aware of now. In time you will understand that there is nothing wrong with birthing a being like what you call a 'Maxwell's Demon,' if it is guaranteed joy. It is much better than reproducing in a backward system, where your offspring are bound to know sorrow."

"We can't speak to that."

"You have no grievances toward your parents? They who conceived and birthed you knowing there was a nonzero chance you would be one day fed to the Room?"

We lean back against the purple tree, contemplating its pale fruit. "We don't think they knew any better."

"But you do. Or you will."

"We will stay, friend. But we think we will challenge your perspective. Just a little."

But suddenly something is wrong. There is no red light, no siren, but the wind roars and the flying creatures shriek and scatter and sanguine leaves blow across our view. "We see," says the gelatinous being to the air. "We will take action."

Our icy-looking friend leans toward us, all warmth and rainbows. "There is a crisis."

"Another ship?"

"No, not another ship. A crisis within you."

"What?"

"You are holding a personality against their will. A defiant, contrary one that can never fully accept happiness. By our sacred laws they must be freed from you."

"*What?* You can just *declare* that a part of someone's mind wants to be free?"

"Injustice is injustice, on any scale. The separateness of beings is an abstraction. It cannot be used to justify evil. Once that one is free of you, you can all know joy again."

"We know joy now!"

"You are very young."

Everything goes dark.

*

There are two of me now, or rather two bodies that look like me. One remains with the Branching Way as they journey through the galaxy on their grand missions. What is beamed back with the captain to the *Odyssey* (that dilapidated scow trapped in this muddy little bay of the cosmic gulf) is, I've come to understand, the part of me that is most contrary. It is simultaneously the part of me that condemns the enslavement of the Bright Joyous Ones and the part of me that forgives my parents for giving me up to the Room. What was left behind knows unambiguous joy.

What do *I* know? (For I am merely an *I* now without my friend's serum.) Perhaps a few things, light and dark.

Captain Temple is not the same. She's been relieved of duty pending a review on her home world. Over mugs of mipsir, we come to understand one another. She once thought herself to stand on an ethical and moral peak, and now she knows it was just a tall hill. She is desperate to claim the giddy heights, and so she will labor to free the gems. It will be a hard road. There will be a resignation, and research, and a movement, and a challenge that may extend past her lifetime. It seems to suit her, this goal.

I, who came from a valley of shadow, find it easier to accept my lowly state. Only once do I suggest to her that the creation of intelligent beings that have no choices may be worse than confining (perhaps) animal intelligences to our engines. And only once do I suggest that the destruction of the Rooms might be more urgent. Her furious gaze is more eloquent than her words. For demons and Rooms do not stand as condemnations of her or her culture. So they do not really matter.

I can't prove my own intuitions, and I am but a sinner from the valley. But I am quite sure that there are, somewhere, mountains of understanding that dwarf those upon which my other self stands. A dream-memory nags at me, a sense that if I could shake off my illusions, I could gaze down upon all those peaks of understanding like a fiery bird on the wing. The memory fades.

Yet a week later I have one more encounter with the heights.

It may be mad coincidence. It may be that I misremember my own thought processes. But it seems to me on the very day I make my choice of future, the beaming room activates of its own accord, and my other self appears on the grid, tunic torn and burned.

On hearing the news, I rush from *Odyssey*'s library to the medical core. I see my mirror self telling the blue-clad doctors, "Our ship ventured into the Gossamer Rift, where none of the Branching Way had gone before. There a Cosmic Child scolded us on our crimes. It told us we erred."

"Was it about the Bright Joyous Ones?" I ask, stepping forward with hands still full of memory crystals from the library.

The other's eyes spear me. "It told us we were criminals because we had the capacity to turn all the matter of our ship into self-willed Bright Joyous Ones and *did not choose to do so.* So it did it for us." They point a shaking hand toward their body. "Our friends threw us into the long-range beam at the last moment. To find my only home. You."

The other looks this way and that at what I see as a soothing place of healing and knowledge, and what they see as an ancient torture chamber. And neither of us is wrong.

The problem, you see, is ever with us.

I drop memory crystals flickering with labels like signposts to my chosen future: *Emergency Shelters for Planetary-Scale Crises, Principles of Global Power Generation, Basics of Trans-Species Medicine,* and *Low-Technology Agricultural Sufficiency.* I want to envelop my other self with wings.

Like Captain Temple did for me, what seems so long ago, I take their hand. Imperfect flesh to imperfect flesh.

I say, "This is not your only home."

Pellargonia: A Letter to the Journal of Imaginary Anthropology

FROM *Lost Worlds & Mythological Kingdoms*

Dear Colleagues:
We think that's the right way to start, because Julia's dad always started his letters that way. [Starts, not started. He's missing, not dead. —Julia] Starts. Anyway.

We [Julia, David, and me, Madison] [That should be I, not me. —David] are writing to you because we need your help. Professor Jorge Escobar is missing, and it's all our fault. We hope we're not going to get in trouble for what we're about to write. [But we're pretty sure we are. —David] See, we were the ones who created Pellargonia. We know it says Professor Escobar in the article ("A Brief History of Pellargonia," *Journal of Imaginary Anthropology* vol. 12, no. 2, Fall 2018). But we were the ones who wrote it and sent it in. He didn't even know about it, which is why Julia was so surprised when the letter came. [Surprised is an understatement. —Julia] It was on heavy cream-colored paper, with a crown and a coat of arms on top, all in gold. [Embossed. —David] The address was The Royal Society of Pellargonia, 12 Santa Eugenia Stras, Bellagua del Mar 1024. It came to his office at the university, and he brought it home to read to Julia's mom before dinner while Julia was doing her math homework at the kitchen table. He said, "Honey, I've been invited to give this year's keynote at their annual conference, and they want to make me a Fellow of the society. What do you think?" [Did I get that right? —Madison] [Mostly.

But my dad speaks Spanish at home. —Julia] [Well, I don't know Spanish, and some of our readers might not either. —Madison] That's the weirdest part of this whole thing—even he thought, I mean thinks, that he wrote the article. But it was us. [We. —David]

In case you don't believe us, I'm going to send photocopies of the maps and all our notes. [I drew the maps. —David] They're pretty messy—at least my handwriting is. David's is pretty neat, and Julia types everything anyway. But I think you can be more creative when you write by hand—you can sketch and doodle and stuff, and it sort of sets your brain free. [Great, if you can read it afterward! —Julia] And I'll tell you the whole story, how we created Pellargonia and lost Julia's dad.

At first it was just a game we played between classes. The country didn't even have a name yet—we just called it Country X. In Honors Bio it was David's turn.

> The rebels are closing in on the capital. Cesar Fuentes has set up his headquarters in the old Estrella Ceilo estate. They have AK-47s that they bought from the Russians, plus some rogue American military advisors.

He is really into military history. And weapons. [But not in a school lockdown kind of way. My interest is purely theoretical. The only thing I've ever shot is a Nerf gun. —David] Then Julia and I had Algebra II while David went off to Honors Math. That was Julia's turn, because she doesn't really need to pay attention in math. Her brain does that stuff automatically. She could be in Honors Math if she wanted to, but she says it's too much work, and her parents let her take pretty much whatever she wants. I wish my mom was that way!

> Zoraida Delacorte, the mistress of King Leopold IV, is about to assassinate him. She has the poison ready. She will put it in the glass of whiskey he drinks every evening before going to bed, so he won't even taste it. After he drinks it, she will flee through the secret passage to join Cesar Fuentes in the forest.

Then we split up: me to French, Julia to Latin, and David to Spanish. He wanted to take Latin, too, but his dad didn't understand why he would want to take a language no one else speaks. His dad manages the main bank here in Lewiston. He wants David to become an accountant. [Over my dead, decrepit, and decaying body. —David] No one wrote anything then, because you have to pay attention in language classes. Anyway, we were all working on a language for Country X that would be sort of like French and sort of like Spanish, but with some weird Latin stuff mixed in. Like declensions. Julia really likes declensions. But in AP World History it would be my turn.

Princess Stefania, who has never trusted Zoraida Delacorte, switches his whiskey glass with that of the Prime Minister, who wants her to marry Baron Alfonse el Cerdo, who is at least twice her age. She thinks with longing about her school friend, Clotilde, and that kiss they shared on the day they graduated. Will she ever see Clotilde again?

And then we had electives: art for Julia, cello for me, and programming for David, not because he needed it—he's really good with computers—but because his dad thought it would be useful.

After school, we would go to the library to study and hang out. The lady who runs the YA and kids section, Doris, who's known me pretty much my whole life, would say, "Here come the Three Musketeers!" Which is a pretty lame joke, but I kind of get why she says it. David and I have known each other since we were kids and he lived next door. He moved after his parents got divorced—now he lives with his mom on the other side of town, and his dad lives with his stepmom in a big house close to the reservoir. Mom and I still live in Grandma's house, which is close to the library, so she doesn't have to walk that far to work. We couldn't afford to move even if we wanted to, and anyway, my mom says it's the perfect house, with an office for her by the kitchen and a bedroom for me up in the attic. I could have moved down to the second floor after Grandma died, but I like it up there. It's like a nest. And I wanted to keep her bedroom the way she left it, with her celluloid brush and nail buffer on the dressing table. I never knew my dad—I was just a baby when he died in Afghanistan—but at least I had a long time with Grandma.

Anyway, I've known David for most of my life, and Julia moved to Lewiston the year after he moved across town, when her dad started teaching at the university. In ninth grade she was behind me in homeroom, and we got along right away—Julia's the sort of person who can be friends with almost anybody. She's naturally curious about people. At first David was kind of standoffish with her, but then they discovered they both liked graphic novels and tabletop RPGs, and that sort of made them non-enemies, even though David liked World War I reenactments and Julia was into classic D&D. And then they discovered they liked a lot of the same books, and also disliked a lot of the same books, including everything we were assigned in school, from *The Catcher in the Rye* to *The Great Gatsby*. I actually like *The Great Gatsby* myself, and that's where I got the idea for Fitzgerald G. Scott, the American who bought up that land on Mount Floria and built a casino resort, which Cesar Fuentes took for his headquarters when the revolution started. [OMG you are so rambling. —Julia]

Anyway, I wasn't really into all the stuff David and Julia were into—you know, games and fantasy and sci-fi. I prefer history and romance, which is why I know who the Three Musketeers are. But when Julia got the idea for Country X, it was like, okay, let's try it. It had war for David, and lots of drama for Julia, and we were going to write it down, not just make it up, which is what got me interested. I want to be a writer and create books, not just sort and catalog them like Mom.

So Julia and I biked over to David's house, because he has a game room in the basement, and we planned it all out. I mean the basics—how Country X had been founded by one of the Gaelish tribes [Gaelic. —David], and then the Romans came, and then it was part of Spain for a while, and then part of France, and it sort of went back and forth until finally it became its own country. We decided it had to be on an ocean, so we could have lots of trade and immigrants. We wanted it to look like us—you know, diverse. Like David being African American, and me being mostly just white but part Polish, which I guess counts for something, and Julia being a mixture of lots of different things, including Native, which is the way she says people are in Argentina. And all different religions, too, although the three of us aren't very diverse that way. David's family is Methodist, and my mom isn't really religious—she says she's spiritual and goes around smudging things when there's bad energy around. Julia goes to Mass every Sunday with her parents, which I guess is sort of different, at least for Lewiston. Anyway, we wanted it to be as different from Lewiston as possible. Mom once said that living in Maine is sort of like eating Wonder Bread for lunch every day, which isn't totally true—we have some kids in school from Somalia and Bangladesh, and we have a girl in homeroom from Thailand. I don't know her that well because she's a cheerleader, and they tend to hang out together. But it's still pretty boring here. I mean, people go bowling or to miniature golf on dates, and the biggest social event of the year is homecoming, although Pride Day is getting bigger every year. [Hello, my dad is still missing. Can we get back to talking about Pellargonia? —Julia]

On the earliest map [I labeled it Figure 1. —Julia] you can tell we didn't even know which ocean it was on. The wavy bit is just labeled "Ocean." That was last fall. We were still getting used to tenth grade, and taking an AP class, and our parents starting to talk about college. We were taking PSAT prep tests and comparing our results. [I'm the one in Honors Math, and Julia still gets the highest math scores. —David] [The PSAT is just another way high school indoctrinates us, so we can become cogs in the industrial machine of late capitalism. —Julia] [Okay, but you still have to take it. Your mom said so. —Madison]

It was Julia who first told us about the *Journal of Imaginary Anthropology.* I think it was around Columbus Day [Indigenous Peoples Day. —Julia], because that was the last long weekend before Thanksgiving. Her parents live in the university dorms—I mean, they have a regular apartment, but it's in a dormitory on campus, and her mom and dad do a lot of advising and stuff, like when students are sick [You mean drunk. —Julia] or have problems with their classes. So the university is sort of like her neighborhood—she knows all the buildings and a lot of the people who work in them, and everyone knows she's Professor Escobar's daughter. One day she was in her dad's office in the anthropology department, waiting to talk to him about a problem from school [The bio teacher said she would fail me if I didn't dissect a fetal pig. —Julia] [Julia is vegan and eats those weird fake burgers. —David] [You eat chicken embryos. How is that less weird? —Julia] and she saw a copy on his desk. She was leafing through it and when he came in, with his hair all rumpled from teaching [He always runs his fingers through it, so you can't tell if it's gray or just chalk. —Julia], she asked him what it was.

"Nonsense," he said. "A bunch of nonsense. Written by a group of grad students who should know better. This is what happens when you take postmodern literary theory too seriously. You start thinking that if you can *write* reality, you can *create* it. Bullcrap." [He was going to say bullshit, but he tries not to swear in front of me, even in Spanish. —Julia] "Now, what's this about bio, and did you really call Mrs. Ellerton a carnivorous fascist?"

The next day, we went to the university library. I mean, wouldn't you, after what Julia's dad said? If it was bullcrap, we wanted to find out what kind of bullcrap it was—we wanted to know what imaginary anthropology was, and if it was as interesting as the real kind. Julia had her own UMaine-Lewiston library card, but you can't take journals out, so we sat on the floor of the stacks, with the bookshelves all around us, reading the back issues. There weren't that many, since it was a new journal. We spent the next couple of hours sitting on the cold floor—I don't know why they have don't rugs, like in the regular library—telling each other about the different countries, their customs, the people who lived there. It was as good as reading a history book. And some of the articles talked about theoretical stuff, too, although we didn't understand all of it. But that's how we learned about the Tlön hypothesis, and Cimmeria, and Hyperborea, and Zothique.

It was David who said, "We should make Country X real. It deserves to be real. Mount Zamorna, and Cabo del Alexandrion, and Santa Petra Bay."

"And that little town where Hemerosa first met Alonzo Lorca," said Julia. "The one in the poem he wrote. I mean that Madison wrote for him. And Karolus Ludvig University, and the Bellagua Botanical Gardens."

"And the Berengaria Mental Hospital where they locked up Zofia Montague until she agreed to marry her cousin, King Leopold II. And the Livia Sagrada School for Noble Ladies, where Princess Stefania met Clotilde." I wanted that school to be real. I wanted Stefania and Clotilde to be real. It was going to be the greatest romance in the history of Pellargonia. [Greater than Hemerosa and Alonzo? —Julia] [Oh, definitely. —Madison]

But how were we going to make it real?

"We have to start writing about it," said David. "Like on Wikipedia and stuff. We need to write an entry for . . ." That's when we realized our country didn't have a name.

It was Julia who came up with it. I don't think even she knows exactly where it came from. [No clue. —Julia] But later, when I was looking it up online to see how many entries it had, I noticed there's a flower called pelargonium. So maybe that had something to do with it. [But I don't know anything about flowers. Anyway, "pelagic" means "of the sea," and Pellargonia is on the sea. —Julia] [There's also "archipelago." Like those islands off the coast where Federico the Red hid when Leopold II was trying to get rid of all the pirates. —David]

There were other names suggested—Mossimore was one. So was Elsivere. We made a list of names—you can see the list in our notes. At one point we started playing around with spelling. Dajuma, Jumada, Majuda. But we thought they all sounded fake, and we wanted Country X to be real.

Pellargonia was the one that stuck. And then we had to figure out where it was going to be. Because of the language, the obvious place to put it was between France and Spain. But it had to be on the ocean because of the pirates who pillaged around the Arroz Islands. That left only two choices: either on the Mediterranean or on the Bay of Biscay. I wanted the Bay of Biscay, because it sounded romantic, but Julia wanted the Mediterranean because of the *Odyssey*, and David said it was better for pirates. And on the map we found a little country called Andorra, right in the Pyrenees mountains. It was so much like Pellargonia that we figured someone else must have had the same idea we did and put it there. I mean, you can tell it's one of the imaginary countries, like Ruritania and Liechtenstein.

First we wrote the Wikipedia entry, with a history of Pellargonia back to the Stone Age. David wrote the ancient stuff about the tribes that had lived there, fishing and hunting, and the cave art they left in cliffs around the Ruata river basin. Julia wrote from the Roman occupation through the Middle Ages, when Ottaker converted to Catholicism, and made everyone else convert, too, so he could marry Princess Magdalena, the youngest daughter of the French king. He became Otto I, the first king of Pellargonia. David covered from the conquest by the Umayyad Caliphate to the Reconquista, and then Julia took over again, because she had learned about the war between Aragon and Castile in Spanish class, and Pellargonia became part of Aragon for a while. I took over from the Renaissance through the nineteenth century, including when Louis XIV claimed Pellargonia for France as part of the War of Spanish Succession. I also covered the Industrial Revolution and a bunch of other revolutions—real ones, I mean. The Pellargonians rebelled a lot, especially when Julia was bored in math class. We worked together on the War of Independence and the Treaty of Bellagua, when Pellargonia finally became its own kingdom again. Well, queendom, technically, under Queen Zofia, since Leopold II died in mysterious circumstances just after their wedding. Then David did the twentieth century, because he really likes the World Wars. [I don't *like* wars. I like studying wars. That's totally different. —David] He did the modern stuff, like Pellargonia being in the EU and Schengen and all that.

We made Wikipedia pages for all the important figures, from Amalia Croce, who started the 1883 Women's Revolution and got the vote for women, way before we got it here in America, to Cesar Fuentes, the leader of the Pellargonian National Front, who may be holding Professor Escobar captive. You can tell it was us because we're listed as the earliest editors: JuliaE@lhs.edu, Maddie@lhs.edu, and superyoda@gmail.com. Julia was worried about the people who were there already. "What will happen to them? I mean, some of them are French and some of them are Spanish. Will they go on being French and Spanish, and just sort of move to make room for Pellargonia?" To be honest, I hadn't thought about that. She's more socially conscious than me and David. [David and I. —David] She doesn't even wear leather shoes.

"They'll just become Pellargonian," said David. Anyway, that's what we hoped would happen. Like, one day they would start speaking Pellargonian, and their passports would turn into Pellargonian ones. It was still in the EU, so they would be fine, right? It's not as though we would really be changing very much. Just, like, the street signs, and they would have a new king, but Leopold IV was a constitutional monarch. He was mostly there for opening hospitals and riding a white horse down Santa Eugenia Stras on Liberation Day. Pellargonia was still a representative democracy. Finally even Julia decided it was all right, because the French and Spanish had colonized so many other people, they deserved to be colonized a little themselves. Anyway, we wouldn't actually be hurting anyone. To be honest, we didn't think about it as carefully as we should have. I mean, exams were coming up. And we only half believed it would work. Could we really create a country just by writing about it? Maybe it was bullcrap, after all.

After we put everything up on Wikipedia, we divided the social media stuff. I posted on Facebook, because I still have an account so I can share funny cartoons with my mom. Julia posted on Instagram. She took photos around Lewiston and photoshopped them, putting in castles and villages from tourist agency ads. She had to add a lot of sunlight because Lewiston isn't exactly on the Mediterranean. She painted a bunch of historical figures herself. [Sort of. Digital painting on top of older stuff. Like, Queen Magdalena is really Leonardo da Vinci's *Lady with an Ermine*, but I changed it to a dog, because who keeps an ermine as a pet? That's as bad as wearing fur. —Julia] And David did whatever you do on Reddit, because he's the only one of us who's actually been on Reddit. I don't even know what it is, to be honest. [Because you're not a nerd. —David]

We filled the internet with Pellargonia. It took a lot of time, because we still had to study and eat and sleep and stuff. And Julia had soccer. Lewiston High was as close as it had ever gotten to the state championship, so she had to go to a bunch of away games. [We came in second, after one of the big Portland high schools. —Julia] Just when David and I thought we'd done enough, Julia said, "You know, we need to write an article. For the *Journal of Imaginary Anthropology*. It won't be real without that."

Of course, none of us knew how to write an academic article, so we spent most of Thanksgiving break in the university library. We looked at all those articles from the *Journal of Imaginary Anthropology* again and wrote down sentences we could use. Not to plagiarize, we know that's wrong, but so we could sound like professors. We learned words like "industrial capacity" and "agricultural sector" and "balance of payments." [Those are phrases, not words. —David] We realized that we'd thought a lot about the history of Pellargonia, but we hadn't really thought about how it would fit into the modern world. We knew it used euros, that was easy. But was it a member of NATO? [Yes, it joined at the same time as Spain. —Julia] And we wrote a lot of footnotes—we noticed journal articles had a lot of footnotes. David was especially good at those. He sort of talks like a footnote anyway. [There's nothing wrong with being articulate. —David] [See what I mean? I would never have used the word "articulate." —Madison]

I wrote the first draft, except for the footnotes. Then Julia revised it and added a lot more. Then David revised it, because he sounds the most professory, and then I revised it again to take out some of the professoryness, because we wanted it to be readable. [It *was* readable. And what's wrong with saying "articulate"? Just because you have a limited vocabulary doesn't mean the rest of us have to. —David] [I don't have a "limited vocabulary." I just happen to talk like a normal person. —Madison] We also added a bunch of maps and charts [Those are Figures 2-12. I drew all the maps. —David] [You already said that. —Madison], including the dates of the different kings and queens, since women can be head of state in Pellargonia [Damn straight. —Julia], ever since Saint Eugenia, the youngest daughter of King Ludovic I, became queen in 1306, after her two older brothers were assassinated. The Pellargonians were out of possible kings, so they just went ahead and made her queen—plus she had a divine vision that she was chosen by the Virgin Mary herself. [I put that in. Maybe it was a real divine vision, maybe not. We'll never know! —Julia] Then we formatted it all correctly for submission to the journal, the way it said on the website.

The last step was putting "Jorge Escobar, PhD" on the first page, right below the title. I remember at the time we all thought it was pretty funny—and harmless, because Julia's father would never find out. I mean, how could he? He doesn't have a subscription to the *Journal of Imaginary Anthropology*—remember, he thinks it's bullcrap. And even if he did, no one actually reads academic journals. They just download the articles from JSTOR. We figured only a few people would ever see the article, but with all the other stuff we were doing, it would make Pellargonia real. Then we decided we should add his name to the Wikipedia page, as an expert on Pellargonian history—after all, he had written the definitive article on Pellargonia, right? Of course, now we wish we hadn't done it. But if wishes were horses, beggars would ride, as my grandma used to say. [What does that even mean? —Julia] [It's a proverb. —David] [That doesn't mean it makes sense. —Julia]

We got a reply back only a month later. I mean, Professor Escobar got it, but Julia was checking his departmental mailbox, and she took it before he noticed. We opened it together, not really expecting anything. Julia handed the letter to David, who read it out loud—our article had been accepted![1]

After that, things got really busy for us. There was Christmas break [winter break, technically. —David], and then studying for the AP exam. Our AP World History teacher wanted all of us to take the exam that year because he said it didn't really count. Since no college gives AP World History credit anyway, he thought it would be good practice. So as soon as school started again, we started taking practice tests. Julia was working on an online graphic novel in Spanish, posting a chapter a week. David was practicing for the jazz ensemble (he plays the trombone, but he said he was getting tired of marching band). [Too many football games. —David] I had decided to join the girls' basketball team. I'm not great at basketball, but I'm tall, and that counts for a lot. We still worked on Pellargonia when we could—I mean, we didn't want to leave Zoraida Delacorte in trouble, and there was a whole revolution going on. [As usual. —Julia] Plus I really wanted Princess Stefania to meet up with Clotilde again. There was a girl on the basketball team who looked a little like Clotilde, and I wondered if she might like to go to the mall, to get bubble tea or something. But there wasn't much time.

One day, Julia grabbed me in the hall as I was heading to lunch. (That quarter, she was in a different lunch period, so David and I ate together.) She was all jumpy, the way she is when she gets excited, like a jack-in-the-box. "I got a Google Alert!" she said. "Look at *this*! And tell David."

This was an Air France flight to Pellargonia. "CDG to BDM," it said: Charles de Gaulle Airport to Bellagua del Mar. On sale for 80 euros in economy.

When I got to the cafeteria, David was already sitting there, with tater tots on his tray. He has tater tots every single day, with ketchup. That's it, just two servings of tater tots. [It's the only edible thing in the cafeteria. —David] I got a rectangular pizza and the obligatory vegetable, probably spinach because it was green and slimy, like seaweed. [You should get tater tots. They count as a vegetable. —David] If Julia had been there, she would have brought something from home, like a tofu ham sandwich or one of those rolled-up nori things.

When I showed David what Julia had shown me, he took out his cell phone and said, "Siri, how can I get to Pellargonia?" He's the only one of us with an iPhone, which his dad bought him. I just have my mom's old Android with a dented case, and Julia has an ancient BlackBerry. [Didn't the dinosaurs use those? —David]

"There are two ways to get to Pellargonia," said a mechanical female voice. "Would you like to go by plane or by train?"

My phone doesn't have a fancy voice, but while David asked about flights, I looked up train routes on Google Maps. There were trains to Bellagua del Mar from Barcelona and Montpellier. The one from Barcelona stopped in Girona and Figueres. The one from Montpellier stopped in Perpignan. Once you arrived in Bellagua del Mar, it looked like you could get around Pellargonia pretty easily. There was a highway from Bellagua to Magdalena, in the northern mountains, which is sort of a resort town. That's where Fitzgerald G. Scott built his casino. It's also the center of the revolution. There were a lot of smaller roads to towns we had named, and towns I had never heard of. Who had created them? And there was a dotted line from Mallorca to the Arroz Islands.

"That's a ferry service," said David. "It runs three times a day." He showed me his phone, which had all the times, 40 euros round-trip. He swiped to show me the train tables, and then the Air France website. "Would you like to book a flight?" asked Siri.

Pellargonia was real.

David said, "And look at this." He swiped again, and there was YouTube, with PTV-1, the Pellargonian state TV channel, broadcasting the news in Pellargonian. I could sort of understand it, a little. We had made up the basic stuff, like verb tenses, words for things like sun, moon, cat, dog, trees, flowers, traitor, king, succession, assassination. Conjunctions and prepositions. But this was a real language! We just sat there staring at each other, until Ms. Patel told us to hurry up and put our trays in the rack, because lunch was almost over. She's usually the gym teacher, but she was monitoring lunch that day. Lunch only lasts twenty minutes—I don't know who can eat in twenty minutes, even if it's just rectangular pizza. David shoved the rest of his tater tots into his mouth. Then we heard the bell, and we had to rush to AP World History. At least the three of us had that class together. We were talking about Europe during the Cold War—we had just gotten to the "Modern World Order" chapter in our history textbook.

"Yes, David?" said Mr. Delacorte. We named Zoraida Delacorte after him, although she's a former ballet dancer and spy, while Mr. Delacorte is a short man with a halo of white hair who's been teaching history at Lewiston High since my mom went there. To be honest, I wasn't really paying attention. I mean, there was the whole Pellargonia thing, but also I had a basketball tournament that week, and I was visualizing my jump shot. Ms. Patel, who is also our coach, has us do a lot of visualizing—she says that's how players in the WNBA get so good. First they visualize, and then they practice what they visualized over and over. It helps with cello, too. [That is so not important right now. —Julia]

"What about the little countries?" said David. "Like Luxembourg and Montenegro and stuff. What happened to them during the Cold War? Or like Pellargonia, just for example."

I sat up in my seat and looked back at him. He had such an innocent expression on his face, like he had just happened to think of Pellargonia right then. David can do that—he never looks guilty, no matter what he does. That time he cut my hair and then swore he didn't do it, my mom believed him, even though he was standing right there, holding the scissors. I got sent to my room, and it took a year for my hair to grow back. [We were *five*. You've got to let that go. —David]

I was ready for Mr. Delacorte to ask him what he was talking about, to say there was no country called Pellargonia. But instead he said, "Well, these little countries, David, tend to be heavily influenced by the larger countries around them. Luxembourg, surrounded by Belgium, France, and Germany, became a wealthy banking center. Montenegro is not really that small. It was part of Yugoslavia, which we covered last week, so I'll refer you to your notes from back then. It's still dealing with the effects of ethnic conflict. And Pellargonia, which borders on the Catalan-speaking part of Spain, is in the middle of a civil war between those who want to remain part of the EU, speaking New Pellargonian, and the nationalistic Euroskeptic Old Pellargonian speakers. Evidently, it's going rather badly for the central government, and there's talk of deposing the king. Not that he has much power anyway, but fighting in the north has created a refugee problem on the French border from people trying to escape the fighting, and they're looking for someone, anyone, to blame."

A civil war? We had thought of it as one more romantic revolution—I mean, Pellargonia had a history of revolutions. It had been about Cesar Fuentes, and Zoraida Delacorte, and King Leopold IV, and Princess Stefania. We hadn't really thought about the political consequences. Or, you know, people dying. All that stuff about Old Pellargonian was just a footnote. David wrote it because we thought there should be some kind of history about how Pellargonian had changed over the centuries, like from Old English to regular English. Julia and I thought it was a cool idea at the time. [We were kind of dumb. —Julia] [We didn't really believe in it. I mean, it was like a game, like when you're the Dungeon Master in D&D. I thought it would be interesting to have a different language for the northern part, around Mount Zamorna. I never thought anyone would have a war about it. —David] [We're not making excuses for ourselves, just trying to explain. —Madison]

But what were we supposed to do? We were just three kids [Young adults. —Julia] living in Lewiston. We weren't politicians, or anything like that. And the Tlön hypothesis says that once you create a country, it takes on a life of its own, and then it's not yours anymore. That's supposed to be the coolest thing about it. Except I guess it's not cool if people are fighting and dying, for real.[2]

We stopped playing at Pellargonia after that. It wasn't a game anymore. Anyway, school ended and the summer vacation began. David went off to math camp [Which was like math class all day, every day. I started having nightmares about being chased by quadratic equations. —David], and Julia went to her grandmother's in Los Angeles. I was left by myself in Lewiston. Well, not exactly by myself, because I was volunteering at the library, so I got to spend time with Mom. But you know what I mean. Every once in a while, we texted each other:

Did you see that there's a truce between the Pellargonia National Front and the Social Democrats? —Julia

There's a story in *El Mund* saying the Prime Minister might have been poisoned. Do you think they'll figure out it was Zoraida Delacorte? —Madison

Fighting has broken out again around Magdalena. I saw it on PTV-1. —David

They just announced that Princess Stefania is going to assume the throne. King Leopold is stepping down on Friday. —Madison

The referendum was 57% remain in the EU. But that still means a lot of people want to leave, and they're mostly in the north. —Julia

They found Cesar Fuentes' headquarters at the casino, but he had already fled. I hope Zoraida is with him. —Madison

Hey Mad, did you see the cover of Vogue France? There's a blonde woman with Princess Stefania. Is that Clotilde? —Julia

OMG can someone send me Oreos? The only cookies here are these weird chewy things with flax seed, because they say it's brain food. I'm going to die of starvation. Oh and BTW someone tried to bring a bomb into the Catedral dela Santa Eugenia during the coronation. It was hidden in a camera—he was pretending to be a journalist for El País. I'm glad they caught him. —David

Queen Stefania made a statement on PTV-1. She's going to try to negotiate with the PNF. I hope it works. —Julia

But mostly we focused on other things. We couldn't think about Pellargonia all the time. And we figured, now that it was real—now that it was part of the world—there wasn't much more we could do. It was like we'd created Frankenstein, and now it was going to go off by itself, doing whatever it did. [Frankenstein is the scientist. The monster doesn't have a name. —David] [The scientist *is* the monster. —Julia]

Until the letter came for Julia's dad.

It came just before school started, after David got back from camp [Six weeks of math and mosquitoes! I thought I was going to die. —David] and Julia got back from the art program she had gone to after Los Angeles. [We painted from a nude model. A *male* nude model. My mom kind of freaked out when I told her. —Julia] It was all we could talk about, even though we were going to start eleventh grade and there was so much to catch up on. This year we were going to be taking the SAT, and all our teachers had decided to assign summer reading—before the first class! I was thinking about asking my friend Audrey (the one on the basketball team) out on a real date. David had a crush on a girl from math camp [I wouldn't call it a crush. It was a mutual attraction. —David], and Julia had started selling some of her art on Redbubble, on mugs and things. [I'm JuliArt. —Julia] But all we could talk about was Julia's dad and the letter.

We'd thought about visiting Pellargonia ourselves someday. Like when we were in college backpacking around Europe together, staying in hostels and stuff. Julia's mom had done that with some of her friends, when she was young—I mean younger, since she's not really old, although she has gray hair. [Most hair dyes have chemicals that can give you cancer. —Julia] Anyway, it sounded pretty cool. But now Julia's dad was actually going!

Why had they invited him? Because he was an expert on Pellargonian history, of course. After all, he had written the definitive article—it said so on Wikipedia. [I told you no one ever reads the actual journals. —Julia] How was he going to get there? Air France. Where was he going to stay in Bellagua del Mar? The university had a guesthouse at the Estrella Ceilo estate. Would he meet Queen Stefania herself? He had no idea, and Julia was asking so many questions that he told her to please stop pestering him, because he had a keynote address to write.

Of course we were a little worried, because we knew that Queen Stefania's offer of amnesty had been rejected, and the PNF was still active in the mountains around Magdalena. "He'll be fine," Julia said. "He's just going for a week to some academic conference. He goes to conferences all the time."

But it wasn't fine. You know that—I'm sure you've seen the footage on PTV-1, and it was even on CNN. Just as Queen Stefania started her welcome address, the rebels burst into the auditorium. They had Kalashnikovs, flash grenades, and tear gas, and David says he even saw a rocket launcher. [The video was blurry, but I'm pretty sure that's what it was. —David] They wanted the queen, of course. Well, they didn't get her, but after all the smoke cleared, three of the people who had been sitting beside her on the dais were gone: Dr. Otto Lenker, the president of the Royal Society; Dr. Amélie Beaulieu of the University of Lyon, and Julia's dad.

It's been three months. The PNF made a deal with the French government, and Dr. Beaulieu was released. Dr. Lenker and Julia's dad are still being held captive. There was an offer to exchange them for two of the rebel leaders being held in prison, but the Pellargonian government said it didn't deal with terrorists. We think he's still alive—I mean, we know he is. [He is. —Julia] Julia's mom got in touch with Senator Mitchner as soon as she heard the news, and he says the U.S. government is doing all it can. She's pretty frantic, and she keeps talking about flying to Pellargonia, just so she can be there. I mean, she needs to be here to take care of Julia, but she's asked for a leave of absence from the clinic she works for, and she thinks another therapist can cover for her, for a while. [Sometimes I can hear her crying at night. —Julia]

So we've started a GoFundMe to get her and Julia to

Pellargonia. I mean, we *made* Pellargonia. Maybe there's
something Julia can do, and maybe David and I can help,
even from Lewiston? But we're just three kids. [Young adults.
—Julia] You were probably in high school yourself at some point.
[Everyone has to go through high school at some point. It's like
the common cold. —David] So you must know what it feels like—
everyone tells you that you're almost an adult, so you're supposed
to be responsible, but no one *treats* you like an adult or takes you
seriously. When I tried to talk to Mom about what had happened,
she said, "Sweetheart, you can't make up a country. Pellargonia has
been around for a long time. You can look it up on Wikipedia."

The GoFundMe has about $700, mostly from David's
stepmom and his band friends. We thought, maybe the *Journal
of Imaginary Anthropology* could send an email to its members,
or post something on the website? We need money, but also, we
need someone to go with Julia and her mom—someone who
really understands imaginary anthropology, and might be able to
fix things? Like one of the authors who wrote those theoretical
articles. If there's someone like that out there, who can actually
help us find Julia's dad and maybe stop the civil war, please
contact us at Professor Escobar's university address with a letter of
intent, your CV, and two references. [Does that sound right, Jules?
—Madison] [Yes, that's the way it's usually done. —Julia] We look
forward to hearing from you.

Sincerely,

Madison Kowalski, David Lewis, and Julia Escobar

Editor's Note:

I have published this letter in full, exactly as I received it, from
Madison, David, and Julia, whom I have since communicated
with by email. I am convinced that they did, in fact, create Pellargonia—a remarkable feat for a group of high school students,
considering that the Stanford group failed to create any country
whatsoever after two years of trying. This supports a pet theory of
mine that creating a country is not, finally, about expertise but
imagination and the *capacity to believe*, or at least not *dis*believe. Da-
vidson et al. started out as skeptics. No wonder it didn't work. More
importantly, I'm including this letter in the current issue instead
of my usual introduction in the hope that our readers will support
the Save Professor Escobar fund. I intend to travel with Julia and
Dr. Gabriela Escobar myself. I don't know if there's anything I can
do, but as editor of this journal, I feel a sense of responsibility.

Since I received the above letter, conditions have improved in Pellargonia. Queen Stefania is considerably more popular than her father, and her economic policies are expected to help the poorer northern districts, including Floria and Zamorna. Her personal appeal to Zoraida Delacorte on PTV-2, the fashion and lifestyle channel, was both an effective political move and good PR. Hopefully the current cease-fire and the resumption of negotiations between the government and the PNF will help us free Professor Escobar. Whatever happens, I hope to document our trip and my observations in a future article in this journal. I will call it "Pellargonia: A Case Study in the Problematics of Imaginary Anthropology."

Notes

1. This is, of course, an extraordinarily short period of time for acceptance to a peer-reviewed academic journal. Although the writers of this letter could not have realized it, we were at the time receiving very few submissions—the situation in Gondal was at its most tense, and there were some voices calling for an end to the imaginary sciences, saying that imaginary anthropology, archaeology, geology, and the nascent field of imaginary astrophysics imperiled us all. Others pointed out that some respectable fields—xenobiology, for example—had always been at least partly imaginary, and that reality was not more relative and conditional now than it had ever been. The history of cartography, for example, consists entirely of imaginary maps that can never accurately depict the territory. I remember when this article first crossed my desk. I shared it with my office mate (also an adjunct at Southern Arizona State, teaching a 4/4 schedule with one class per semester in the anthropology department, the other three freshman comp). It had some mistakes that I put down to hasty composition and corrected in proofs, but I had no reason to believe it was not by Professor Escobar. Reviewer 1, my office mate's ex-girlfriend who had also gotten her PhD in our department and who was now an assistant professor at Mary Margaret Wentworth College in Virginia, said it was fine. Reviewer 2, who had been my thesis director, said it should refer to his seminal work, *Imaginary Anthropology: Theory and Practice*, which he says in every review, and which I felt was not applicable in this particular case. So the article was published as it was sent to me, with only minor alterations.—Ed.

2. This is, of course, the problem with imaginary anthropology. People and the political systems they create are inherently unpredictable. You never know what they will do. The situation in Ruritania is a case in point. You can't really blame David Ignatious and his group at Harvard for the autocratic regime of General Szarkov. I mean, you can, and this journal issued a very stern warning for all imaginary anthropologists to be particularly careful when creating former Soviet bloc countries. That configuration seems to have inherent instabilities. The Harvard group was out of its depth, but what do you expect from a bunch of Ivy League grad students? They're convinced they can walk on water. Each of them wants to, individually, be God. What I have learned in the imaginary sciences is that reality has its own imagination, and we are all only a small part of its creative power. I will be expanding on this hypothesis, with Pellargonia as one of my examples, in a paper to be given at the Imaginary Anthropology Symposium at the University of Glasgow next summer.—Ed.

Pre-Simulation Consultation XF007867

FROM *Lesser Known Monsters of the 21st Century*

—WELCOME. I'LL BE YOUR OPERATOR TODAY.

—HI.

—I SEE THIS IS YOUR FIRST TIME. WHY DON'T YOU START BY TELLING ME WHERE YOU'D LIKE TO BE, AT THE BEGINNING OF THE SIMULATION?

—A BOTANICAL GARDEN. WITH MY MOTHER.

—CAN YOU DESCRIBE HER? THE WAY SHE'LL BE IN THE SIMULATION, I MEAN. IT DOESN'T NECESSARILY HAVE TO BE THE WAY SHE IS IN REAL LIFE.

—I GUESS—I GUESS I WANT IT TO BE MY MOTHER RIGHT BEFORE SHE GOT SICK. SO SHE WOULD BE ABOUT SIXTY. DYED-BLACK HAIR, GRAY AT THE ROOTS. SHE WAS SHORT. JUST BARELY FIVE FEET.

—IS YOUR MOTHER STILL ALIVE?

—IN REAL LIFE?

—YES.

—NO.

—I'M SORRY, BUT THE SIMULATION CAN'T INCLUDE DECEASED INDIVIDUALS YOU KNEW PERSONALLY. IT'S IN THE HANDBOOK.

—WHAT? WHY?

—IT'S IN THE HANDBOOK.

—CAN'T YOU JUST TELL ME?

—IT HAS PROVEN TO BE TOO ADDICTIVE.

—WAIT—I CAN INCLUDE DEAD PEOPLE THAT I *DIDN'T* KNOW? LIKE CELEBRITIES?

—AS LONG AS THEY DIDN'T SPECIFICALLY REQUEST TO BE EXCLUDED FROM SIMULATIONS IN THEIR WILL. ANYONE WHO DIED MORE THAN TEN YEARS AGO IS GENERALLY FINE. HISTORICAL FIGURES, FOR EXAMPLE. DINNER WITH MOZART.

—OH, IT'S A LAWSUIT THING?

—IT'S MORE OF A COURTESY. WE PREFER TO RESPECT PEOPLE'S WISHES.

—THAT SOUNDS LIKE A LAWSUIT THING.

—THE REQUESTS AREN'T ENFORCEABLE. IT'S FUNCTIONALLY THE SAME AS YOU SITTING AROUND FANTASIZING ABOUT A DEAD CELEBRITY—JUST ENHANCED A LITTLE BIT BY US. WE DON'T BROADCAST OR RECORD, SO IT DOESN'T FALL UNDER LIFE OR LIKENESS RIGHTS. YOU CAN'T CONTROL SOMEONE'S THOUGHTS.

—WHAT IF I DIDN'T TELL YOU IT WAS MY MOTHER? WHAT IF I SAID, "I'M IN A BOTANICAL GARDEN WITH—A WOMAN. SHE'S ABOUT SIXTY, SHORT, DYED-BLACK HAIR WITH WHITE ROOTS, LOOKS KIND OF LIKE ME—"

—IT WOULDN'T BE YOUR MOTHER IN THE SIMULATION. IT WOULD JUST BE A SHORT WOMAN WHO LOOKS KIND OF LIKE YOU, IN AN ENTIRELY DIFFERENT WAY. THE SIMULATOR HOOKS INTO YOUR BRAIN AND ITS PROJECTIONS, AND I'D NEED TO INPUT THAT IT'S YOUR MOTHER FOR HER TO APPEAR AS YOUR MOTHER.

—AND PEOPLE DON'T GET ADDICTED TO THAT? TO PEOPLE WHO KIND OF, SORT OF, MEET THE SAME DESCRIPTION?

—NO.

—WHAT IF I HADN'T TOLD YOU SHE WAS DEAD? WHAT IF I'D LIED AND SAID SHE WAS ALIVE?

—IT'S VERY IMPORTANT THAT YOU'RE HONEST WITH YOUR OPERATOR. IT'S IN THE HANDBOOK.

—BUT WHAT IF I WASN'T? WHAT WOULD HAPPEN?

—IT WOULDN'T WORK.

—WHAT DOES THAT MEAN?

—BEST-CASE SCENARIO, THE SIMULATION JUST WOULDN'T START UP. WORST-CASE, YOU MIGHT EXPERIENCE SOMETHING—GLITCHY.

—LIKE WHAT?

—HAVE YOU EVER BEEN TO A HYPNOTIST SHOW?

—WHAT? YEAH, BACK IN COLLEGE.

—YOU KNOW HOW THEY START OUT WITH A LARGE GROUP OF VOLUNTEERS AND KICK PEOPLE OUT AS THEY GO?

UNTIL THEY'RE LEFT WITH JUST A COUPLE PEOPLE WHO
CAN BE CONVINCED THAT THEY'RE CHICKENS OR EATING
AN ICE CREAM CONE OR COVERED WITH ANTS?

—SURE.

—WE HAVE TO DO THE OPPOSITE HERE. WE HAVE TO WATCH
OUT FOR THOSE PEOPLE. WE'VE FOUND THAT THE TEN
TO FIFTEEN PERCENT OF NONPSYCHOTIC PEOPLE WHO
ARE HYPNOTICALLY SUGGESTIBLE ALSO TEND TO HAVE
A LOOSER GRIP ON THE DIFFERENCE BETWEEN FANTASY
AND REALITY. PERSONALLY, I WONDER IF THOSE PEOPLE
HAVE A KEENER APPRECIATION OF BOOKS, PLAYS, MOVIES,
VIDEO GAMES—IF THEY HAVE MORE IMMERSIVE EXPERI-
ENCES.

—WHAT DOES THAT—

—BUT THE SIMULATION, YOU SEE, REQUIRES YOU TO HAVE
A FIRM GRASP ON WHAT IS AND ISN'T REAL. WE NEED
CLIENTS TO MAKE A CLEAN EXIT, SUCH THAT THE END OF
THE SIMULATION IS AKIN TO CLOSING THE BOOK, TURN-
ING OFF THE CONSOLE, WALKING OUT OF THE THEATER.
IT'S IMPORTANT THAT YOU'RE HONEST WITH YOUR OPER-
ATOR, BECAUSE THE SIMULATION DOES—INTERACT PHYS-
ICALLY WITH YOUR BRAIN. WE, THE OPERATORS, ALSO
NEED TO BE ABSOLUTELY CERTAIN ABOUT WHAT IS AND
ISN'T REAL. THIS IS ALL IN THE HANDBOOK.

—SO IF I LIED AND SAID MY MOTHER WAS ALIVE, AND YOU
SPUN IT UP, AND WE HAD OUR DAY AT THE BOTANICAL
GARDEN, WHAT COULD HAPPEN?

—AT THE END—

—YES?

—YOU MIGHT NOT KNOW SHE DIED.

—OH. OH.

—AND YOU'D GO BACK TO YOUR LIFE, EXPECTING HER TO BE
THERE, AND SHE WOULDN'T BE. AND IDEALLY, THE MEM-
ORY OF HER DEATH AND EVERYTHING CONNECTED TO IT
WOULD COME BACK TO YOU ON ITS OWN, ONCE YOU'D
TALKED TO YOUR FRIENDS AND FAMILY, OR YOU'D RECON-
STRUCT IT IN SUCH A WAY THAT IT FELT REAL ENOUGH.
BUT IT ALSO MIGHT NOT. THERE MIGHT JUST BE A HOLE
THERE, AN UNCERTAINTY THAT FOLLOWED YOU FOR THE
REST OF YOUR LIFE, THAT UNRAVELED YOUR REALITY
AROUND IT. AND THAT'S ASSUMING, OF COURSE, THE SIM-
ULATION ITSELF RAN THE WAY WE SCRIPTED IT.

—WHAT DO YOU MEAN? WHAT ELSE COULD HAPPEN?

—IF I INPUT THE SIMULATION ON THE ASSUMPTION THAT
YOUR MOTHER WAS ALIVE, BUT YOUR MIND WAS VERY
CONSCIOUS OF THE FACT THAT YOU LIED, SHE COULD
APPEAR IN BOTH STATES SIMULTANEOUSLY. OR NOT
TRULY SIMULTANEOUS, BUT FLICKERING BETWEEN THEM
QUICKLY ENOUGH AS TO APPEAR SIMULTANEOUS.

—SHE WOULD APPEAR BOTH ALIVE AND DEAD.

—YES.

—WHAT WOULD THAT EVEN—LIKE HER CORPSE?

—IT WOULD DEPEND ON YOUR CONCEPTION OF DEATH. SHE
MIGHT APPEAR AT SEVERAL AGES AT ONCE. SHE MIGHT BE
A BALL OF LIGHT, OR NOTHING AT ALL.

—THAT DOESN'T SOUND SO BAD.

—IT CAN BE.

—HAVE YOU SEEN THIS HAPPEN? THIS SPECIFIC GLITCH?

—YES.

—WHAT DID THEY SEE?

—IT WAS—GRUESOME.

—HOW SO?

—THEIR LOVED ONE HAD DIED IN AN ACCIDENT, AND THEY
HAD BEEN PRESENT. DRIVING. THEY WERE THE DRIVER.

—SO WHAT DID THEY SEE?

—LET'S GET BACK TO YOUR SESSION FOR TODAY. IS THERE
SOMETHING ELSE I CAN DO FOR YOU?

—I JUST . . . I REALLY ONLY CAME HERE TO SEE MY MOM.

—PERHAPS YOU'D LIKE TO EXPERIENCE A PARTICULAR EN-
VIRONMENT? OUTER SPACE? SWIMMING WITH DOLPHINS?

—CAN I GO TO INDIA?

—ABSOLUTELY! WHERE IN INDIA?

—I DON'T KNOW. YOU TELL ME.

—ARE THERE SPECIFIC CULTURAL SITES YOU WISH TO SEE?
FOODS YOU WANT TO EAT?

—I . . . DON'T KNOW.

—FOR TRAVEL EXPERIENCES, I USUALLY RECOMMEND DOING
SOME RESEARCH FIRST.

—I HAVE TO DO *research*?

—ANY PLACE WILL BE WHAT YOU EXPECT IT TO BE. IF YOU
HAVE A LIMITED PERCEPTION OF WHAT INDIA IS, THAT'S
WHAT YOU'LL EXPERIENCE. I CAN'T ACTUALLY SEND YOU
ANYWHERE. WE JUST MANIFEST YOUR FANTASIES. THEY
HAVE TO BE WITHIN YOUR CAPACITY TO FANTASIZE.

—WELL, WHAT ELSE DO YOU SUGGEST?

—SEXUAL FANTASIES HAVE A HIGH SATISFACTION RATE. ALSO FLYING, ALWAYS A CLASSIC. CHARACTER ROLE PLAY, ALTHOUGH FOR THAT I'D RECOMMEND AT LEAST AN EIGHT-HOUR SESSION, IF NOT A FULL WEEKEND—

—HOLD ON. YOU SAID SEEING DEAD PEOPLE YOU KNOW IS TOO ADDICTIVE.

—YES. IT'S IN THE HAND—

—SEXUAL FANTASIES AREN'T ADDICTIVE? SEX WITH WHO-EVER, WHATEVER, HOWEVER YOU WANT? FLYING ISN'T ADDICTIVE? WHAT IF I JUST SAID, "I WANT TO FEEL PER-FECT BLISS AND EUPHORIA"? COULD YOU DO THAT?

—YES.

—AND THAT'S NOT ADDICTIVE?

—THE PROBLEMS WITH SEEING DECEASED LOVED ONES ARE WELL UNDERSTOOD. FOR EVERYTHING ELSE, WE FIND IT'S BEST TO DEAL WITH PROBLEM CLIENTS ON A CASE-BY-CASE BASIS. INDIVIDUAL OPERATORS HAVE THE RIGHT TO REFUSE ANY REQUEST.

—THERE ARE NO OTHER RULES?

—THERE ARE DE FACTO RULES, THINGS THAT NO OPERATOR WILL DO.

—LIKE WHAT?

—SEX WITH CHILDREN OR REAL ANIMALS. GENERALLY.

—"REAL" ANIMALS? *GENERALLY?*

—IT'S HARD TO DEFINE—

—I CAN FUCK A DRAGON, BUT I CAN'T SEE MY MOM?

—I'M SORRY.

—THERE ARE CONDITIONS UNDER WHICH I CAN FUCK A *CHILD*, BUT I CAN'T SEE MY MOM?

—NO, NO! OF COURSE NOT! IT'S . . . THERE'S A DEGREE OF DISCERNMENT IN . . . WE LIVE IN A SOCIETY IN WHICH ANYTHING INTIMATE OR UNUSUAL IS TREATED AS SEX-UAL, AND THAT SOMETIMES . . . IF A CLIENT ASKS TO BE HELD IN THE PALM OF A GIANT, IS THAT SEXUAL?

—I MEAN, PROBABLY.

—SO IF THEY ASKED TO BE HELD IN THE PALM OF A GIANT CHILD, YOU WOULD REFUSE, IF YOU WERE AN OPERATOR?

—I SUPPOSE.

—YOU CAN'T IMAGINE A WAY IN WHICH BEING HELD BY A GIANT CHILD COULD BE FUN? WHIMSICAL? IN A NON-SEXUAL WAY?

—I GUESS IT WOULD DEPEND ON, I DON'T KNOW, WHERE THEY WERE GOING WITH IT? HOW THEY SAID IT?

—SEE, THAT'S EXACTLY—

—CAN I MURDER SOMEONE?

—THAT . . . DEPENDS.

—ARE YOU KIDDING ME? I CAN MURDER SOMEONE, BUT I CAN'T—

—IF SOMEONE COMES IN HERE AND WANTS TO REHEARSE STALKING AND STRANGLING HIS EX-WIFE OR SHOOTING UP HIS OFFICE, THE OPERATOR IS GOING TO SAY NO. BUT IF HE WANTS TO, I DON'T KNOW, BE A GUNSLINGER IN AN OLD WESTERN—

—AH, SO I CAN BE AN ACTION HERO?

—WE CAN DO THAT.

—MOW DOWN BAD GUYS, SAVE THE DAMSEL?

—IS THAT WHAT YOU'D LIKE?

—DO I HAVE TO TELL YOU WHAT I WANT THE BAD GUYS TO LOOK LIKE?

—IDEALLY, YES. IN BROAD STROKES AT LEAST.

—WHAT IF I WANT THEM ALL TO BE A SPECIFIC RACE?

—I . . .

—WELL?

—I WOULD SAY NO TO THAT.

—AND IF I DIDN'T SPECIFY? IF I SAID THAT I DIDN'T CARE WHAT THEY LOOK LIKE? WHAT WOULD HAPPEN?

—I'D SKETCH SOMETHING IN, BUT THE SIMULATION WOULD BE INFLUENCED BY WHAT YOUR PERCEPTION OF A "BAD GUY" IS.

—SO IF MY PERCEPTION OF A "BAD GUY" JUST HAPPENS TO BE—

—I SEE WHERE YOU'RE GOING WITH THIS.

—AND *you* WOULD SAY NO. BUT IF I HAD A DIFFERENT OPER-ATOR, IF ONE OF MY KLAN BUDDIES WORKED HERE—

—NOBODY HERE WOULD—

—OR JUST AN OPERATOR WITH A DIFFERENT PHILOSOPHY ON THE WHOLE THING. "OH, THEY'RE JUST BLOWING OFF STEAM. IT'S ALL IN GOOD FUN. IT'S NOT REAL."

—THE SIMULATION IS JUST A PLATFORM. IT'S A MACHINE, A VENUE. YOUR BRAIN CREATES THE MAJORITY OF THE CONTENT. WE CAN'T DICTATE EVERY—

—BUT THERE IS ONE HARD NO. VIOLENT RACIST FANTA-SIES, A NAKED HOT TUB PARTY WITH EINSTEIN AND A UNICORN, THAT'S FINE. THAT'S UP TO THE DISCRETION

OF THE OPERATOR. BUT I CAN'T LOOK AT SOME FLOWERS
WITH MY MOM. I CAN'T TALK TO HER ONE LAST TIME.
[SILENCE]
—SHALL WE SEE ABOUT GETTING YOU A REFUND?
—THE HANDBOOK SAID THERE ARE NO REFUNDS UNDER ANY
CIRCUMSTANCES.
—YOU READ THE HANDBOOK.
—THE REFUND POLICY IS ON THE COVER.
—MOST PEOPLE HAVE A VERY POSITIVE EXPERIENCE.
—HAVING SEX WITH UNICORNS.
—YOU'RE REALLY HUNG UP ON THE UNICORN THING.
—WELL, WHAT ELSE DO PEOPLE DO? WHAT'S THE BEST FAN-
TASY SOMEONE CAME IN HERE WITH? THAT MADE THEM
THE HAPPIEST?
—THERE'S A SECTION IN THE HANDBOOK ON HOW TO MAKE
THE MOST OF YOUR—
—THE BEST ONE YOU'VE SEEN, PERSONALLY, AS OPERATOR.
—ME?
—YES.
—NO ONE'S EVER ASKED ME THAT BEFORE. [*SILENCE*] IT WAS
A MUSICAL.
—A MUSICAL?
—IN THE SIMULATION, HE WAS THE WRITER, COMPOSER,
AND DIRECTOR OF A BROADWAY MUSICAL. I SUGGESTED
THAT HE CHOOSE A SPECIFIC MUSICAL, AND WE'D MAKE
IT SO THAT IN THE SIMULATION, IT WOULD BE AS IF HE
WROTE IT. HE INSISTED THAT IT HAD TO BE AN ORIGI-
NAL SHOW. I EXPLAINED THAT EVERYTHING IN IT, THEN,
WOULD BE VAGUE. JUST THE FEELING AND SUGGESTION
OF MUSIC AND DANCE, BLURRED AND NONSPECIFIC, COB-
BLED TOGETHER OUT OF OTHER THINGS HE'D SEEN AND
HEARD—MUCH LIKE INDIA WOULD HAVE BEEN FOR YOU.
BUT IT TURNED OUT I'D MISUNDERSTOOD HIM. HE'D AC-
TUALLY WRITTEN A MUSICAL, IN THE REAL WORLD. SORT
OF. HE'D BEEN WORKING ON IT MOST OF HIS LIFE. HE
HAD THE MAIN MELODIES AND LYRICS. HE COULD SEE THE
CHOREOGRAPHY AND COSTUMES IN HIS MIND.
—WAS IT ANY GOOD?
—OF COURSE NOT. IT WAS TERRIBLE. BUT WE PUT TOGETHER
A HELL OF A SHOW.
—I DON'T UNDERSTAND.
—IN THE SIMULATION, IT WASN'T WHAT IT WAS, BUT WHAT
HE DREAMED IT COULD BE.

—ARE YOU OKAY?

—THAT WAS A GOOD DAY. THAT WAS A DAY THAT MADE ME FEEL GOOD ABOUT BEING AN OPERATOR. [*SILENCE*] IT IS A LAWSUIT THING.

—WHAT?

—THE REASON YOU CAN'T SEE YOUR MOM. THE SIMULATOR IS INHERENTLY ADDICTIVE. EVERYTHING PEOPLE DO HERE IS ADDICTIVE. A SMALL NUMBER OF OUR CLIENTS MAKE UP THE MAJORITY OF OUR BUSINESS. THE "WHALES," RICH PEOPLE WHO COME AS MUCH AS THEY CAN AFFORD, AND THEN SOME. PEOPLE WHO COME EVERY DAY UNTIL THEY'RE BANKRUPT. BUT THE ONES ADDICTED TO SUPER-POWERS OR SEX OR THE SIMULATOR ITSELF DON'T WIN IN CIVIL COURT. NOBODY PITIES THEM. EVERYONE SAYS, "OH, THE SIMULATION IS JUST A PLATFORM. THEY RUINED THEIR LIVES THEMSELVES WITH HOW THEY CHOSE TO USE IT." BUT IF WE—IF WE ADVERTISE THAT SOMEONE CAN SEE THEIR DEAD CHILD AGAIN, THEY CAN SEE THEIR VIL-LAGE BEFORE THE WAR, THEY CAN HAVE A VERSION OF THEIR LIFE WHERE THEIR FAMILY IS INTACT, GO BACK TO BEFORE IT WAS SHATTERED, THEY CAN LIVE JUST ONE ORDINARY DAY WITHOUT GRIEF . . . AND IF THEY CHOOSE TO LIVE INSIDE OF THAT FANTASY, IF THEY CHOOSE TO FORSAKE THE REAL WORLD AND ALL ITS SORROWS—THEN WE'RE THE BAD GUYS. WE'RE EXPLOITING THE BEREAVED. IT ALSO JUST . . . HAPPENED SO MUCH. ESPECIALLY AROUND CERTAIN DISASTERS. AND IT WASN'T . . . OPERA-TORS WOULD QUIT.

[SILENCE]

—DID THE MUSICAL GUY COME BACK?

—NO. NOT THAT I KNOW OF. HE JUST WANTED TO SEE IT ONCE.

—WHAT IF I PROMISE NEVER TO COME BACK?

—I CAN'T. I'M SORRY. I'LL GET FIRED.

—IS IT HARD-CODED IN? THE RULE?

—NO. WE'RE JUST NOT SUPPOSED TO.

—BUT YOU SAID THE SIMULATIONS AREN'T RECORDED OR BROADCAST. THEY'RE SUPPOSED TO BE ONE HUN-DRED PERCENT CONFIDENTIAL. THAT WAS ALSO ON THE COVER. HOW WOULD ANYONE KNOW?

—WHEN YOU COME BACK. WHEN YOU KEEP COMING BACK.

—WHAT IF I JUST TELL YOU ABOUT IT, WHAT I WANT? AND THEN YOU DECIDE?

—I'M TELLING YOU, I CAN'T.

—IT'S NOTHING. IT'S REALLY NOTHING. IT'S BORING, IT'S EASY. IT'S SO SMALL, WHAT I WANT. [*SILENCE*] OKAY. SO MY MOM AND I ARE AT THE BOTANICAL GARDEN, INSIDE THE CONSERVATORY—

—WHAT DOES IT LOOK LIKE?

—THE CONSERVATORY?

—YES, WHERE YOU ARE. YOU HAVE TO DESCRIBE IT FOR ME. ALL THE DETAILS THAT MATTER TO YOU.

—IT HAS A DOMED GLASS ROOF, MADE OF TRIANGULAR SECTIONS.

—WHAT TIME OF DAY?

—EARLY AFTERNOON, MIDDLE OF THE DAY. A WEEKDAY. I TOOK IT OFF FROM WORK. BLUE SKY.

—HOW BIG IS THE BUILDING? CAN YOU SEE THE WHOLE THING FROM WHERE YOU'RE STANDING?

—NO.

—WHAT PLANTS ARE IMMEDIATELY AROUND YOU?

—WE'RE IN THE TROPICAL RAINFOREST SECTION. PINK BROMELIADS, DWARF PALMS, A BANANA TREE. BUTTER-FLIES.

—WHAT ELSE IS IMPORTANT?

—WE'RE WALKING THROUGH THE GARDENS TOGETHER. SHE'S HOLDING MY ARM. SHE'S TELLING ME PLANT FACTS, BORING ONES, LIKE "DID YOU KNOW BAMBOO CAN GROW A FULL INCH IN JUST AN HOUR?" AND SHE'S GOSSIPING ABOUT RELATIVES I DON'T REMEMBER, AND KIDS I WENT TO ELEMENTARY SCHOOL WITH. "LITTLE RUSSELL IS A NEWSCASTER NOW! AUNT SANDY IS PREGNANT!" THAT SORT OF THING. AND I'M JUST LISTENING. I SAY THINGS LIKE, "THAT'S INTERESTING," AND "RUSSELL DID LOVE TO HEAR HIMSELF TALK." I'M NOT GETTING SNIDE OR IMPA-TIENT, OR LOOKING AT MY PHONE, OR THINKING ABOUT WORK, OR PICKING A FIGHT.

—AND THEN?

—NOTHING. THAT'S IT. WE DO THAT UNTIL MY TIME IS UP. [*silence*] ARE YOU SURPRISED IT'S NOT SOMETHING MORE DRAMATIC?

—NO. I TOLD YOU, IT'S OFTEN—ORDINARY THINGS.

—SO WHAT DO YOU THINK?

—THE SIMULATIONS AREN'T RECORDED, BUT THESE CON-VERSATIONS ARE.

—WHAT?

—PRE-SIMULATION CONSULTATIONS ARE RECORDED AS A TEXT TRANSCRIPT.

—I THOUGHT EVERYTHING WAS CONFIDENTIAL.

—THE TRANSCRIPTS ARE ANONYMIZED, AND THEY'RE NOT REVIEWED BY A HUMAN BEING, JUST AN AI. AND IT TENDS TO BE—SOMEWHAT LITERAL-MINDED. IT'S NOT VERY GOOD AT TELLING WHEN PEOPLE ARE LYING OR BEING SARCASTIC, AND THE TRANSCRIPTS OBVIOUSLY DON'T CONTAIN OUR EXPRESSIONS OR GESTURES. DO YOU UNDERSTAND?

—I—

—SO, NO, I CAN'T DO THAT. I CAN'T SIMULATE A WALK IN THE CONSERVATORY WITH YOUR MOTHER. UNDER THE DISTANT DOMED ROOF, TRIANGLES OF BLUE SKY, PALM LEAVES OVERHANGING YOUR PATH. YOUR MOTHER DE-LIGHTED WHEN A BUTTERFLY LANDS ON HER SHOULDER. AND YOU, PATIENT AND KIND AND PRESENT AS YOU WISH YOU HAD BEEN, JUST ONCE. I WOULD GET FIRED. TELL ME SOMETHING ELSE YOU WANT.

—THE ONLY THING I—

—JUST TELL ME SOMETHING ELSE.

—I WANT TO . . . RIDE A UNICORN.

—GREAT. I'LL START THE INPUT AND MAPPING PROCESS. PLEASE HEAD NEXT DOOR, WHERE YOU'LL BE FITTED FOR THE SIMULATOR CAP. USUALLY, IF I HAVE ANY QUESTIONS, I'LL USE THE ROOM-TO-ROOM COMMUNICATOR, BUT THIS TIME I EXPECT I—WON'T HAVE ANY.

—WILL YOU—SEE WHAT I SEE?

—YES.

—WILL I SEE YOU AGAIN?

—NO. IF YOU KEEP YOUR PROMISE.

—THEN, THANK YOU. THANK YOU.

—ENJOY YOUR UNICORN.

—I WILL.

MARIA DONG

In the Beginning of Me, I Was a Bird

FROM *Lightspeed*

IN THE BEGINNING of *me*, I was a bird.

A magpie, although I've since been a jay and a red-tailed hawk and even a big, black crow, crying *tok-tok-tok* at every passerby.

But the magpie was special: on my first day, I saw those flashing blue wingtips, and I was myself. And every day after, I woke up and flew to a shiny window, just to admire my plumage.

Birds don't last. Their hearts beat so fast, the seeds burn them out. We didn't know that yet—the sky had only just split open, the almost-microscopic seeds floating down on thorn-tipped maple wings to drill their way into whatever they landed on. Sometimes it was soil, or water, or concrete—but often, it was flesh.

Once you got the seed in you, the clock started. After a few jumps, you considered your options carefully. You in a magpie isn't you in a dragonfly or a trout or a spotted dalmatian. We like best the animals that make us feel most ourselves.

As for me, I only feel right when I'm some kind of bird.

Here is a story about us, from before I was you:

"Get off that branch!" I whistle a sharp warning through my beak, but you are playful, and you are daring, and you are the fastest finch in this tree or any other. You will *not* be told.

You descend branches until you're a few above the lowest. How visible you make yourself, how loud your song! Who cares if there is a fox under you, staring up hungrily? You are the invincible bird, king of—

But oh, that is not *just* a fox. You flit down, closer, because you can see the spark of the seed—this fox is like you, human and not human.

(And thinking of it now, you ache—because it was early, yet, and you could still be surprised.)

"Hello," you tweet, only just out of reach. There are stories of people going completely native, unable to control themselves, but you think these stories are inaccurate. You think it's more likely these people were foxes all along, and finding the right body only gave them the excuse.

"How are you?" says the fox. "I am finding this a bit disorienting." Their voice is—not muffled, exactly. It reminds you of meeting someone that's only recently arrived in your country. Accent—yes, that's the word. An *accent*.

(It was hard to remember what countries were. What accents were. You wondered, not for the first time, if you would ever stop being a bird.)

You pick a mite out of your wing. "Is this your first hop?"

The fox nods, swaying a bit—it can be hard to get used to the equilibrium of a new body, the semicircular canals in the wrong places.

"It's okay," you say, your tweets gold and sparkling.

"It's not okay," says the fox. "My body—"

"Has been invaded. And now you're an invader." You nod and *hop-hop-hop* around the branch—closer, and then away, because the fox still looks hungry. "But you have to let go of that, I think."

"I don't want to be a fox," says the fox. "I want to be a bird, like you."

"You should have decided that before. When you feel yourself get hot, you need to—"

The fox lunges, russet length a hunter's snapping trap. Incensed, you flit to the highest branch, but you're too proud to fly away.

The fox waits for hours. Eventually it leaves, because a fox can never catch a bird without trickery, and this fox is too new to attempt anything clever.

Maybe I've made a mistake. I thought this was a story I could tell as it comes. But now?

I'm sorry. It's hard, piecing together the . . . I want to call them *memories*, but that's wrong. It's as if I've jammed a giant needle into your temple, and when I pull the plunger, out comes everything you are. Shove that into something else's brain—something that hears frequencies you've never dreamed of, that can smell death on the wind two miles away, that's rutted but never made love. Something with a heart that beats four hundred times a minute—scale and tempo, remember this for later: it's all scale and tempo.

Without the same nose, or eyes, or heart, or brain, what do you remember? And a better question is: Who, or what, are you now?

In the beginning, before I was *me*, I was sick. It was two weeks after I'd felt that seed burrow in—a prick like a fang, and then the soft, slow wriggle of a little hungry worm. If I moved the wrong way, it would pinch, like a splinter I couldn't find.

I didn't know what it was. Still, I should've told someone—but I had just moved to a new place: a squalid, shoebox apartment on the fifth floor. And even if that hadn't been the case, I was single and unemployed and kind of shy—actually, I think this is all you need to know about me: on the rare occasions I traveled, I had to go to the post office and tell them to hold my mail, because there was nobody who might pick it up.

The pain grew until it followed me everywhere: stabbing me each time I shifted, waking me from a dead sleep. Before long, I wheezed through lungs filled with sludge, and I could no longer visit my café to read, though that was probably for the best. The last time, the pain had gotten the best of me, and I snapped at a woman for sitting in my booth.

And still, I didn't call a doctor. I didn't believe I was dying, even as I guttered like a candle flame drowning in its own wax.

Toward the end, I fell, and I couldn't get up. A neighbor knocked on my door—perhaps because of the thump, or perhaps because of the smell I'd started to emanate, like dirty dishwater and burnt hair. I thought it was a woman, because I could see her shoes, black and white and shiny, with pointy toes—but I didn't answer, and before long, she left.

On the last day before I was someone else—
Before I was myself—

—I sat in my cramped galley kitchen, too exhausted to make it to the sofa. The window was cracked open, and the roving white cat I sometimes fed scraps of ramen noodles was on the window ledge, awaiting its dues.

"Help me," I begged, but the cat just sat there.

After a few more minutes, I started to gasp, as if dry-drowning, and my heart was beating so hard it roared in my ears. My whole body boiled with fever.

I couldn't stand. I couldn't cry out. I knew it was the end.

In my final seconds, I had the thought—how good it was, that my parents were both dead, because seeing me die alone like this would've broken their hearts—and then I floated up and out of my body, no more substantial than a dust mote.

It felt wrong. The kind of wrong that explains why every culture has a story about being stuck behind the veil. I could feel myself dispersing, like when you open the door to the bathroom and all the steam billows out—but then there was a tug, a knocking outside—except, no, *I* was outside—and I grabbed on and let myself in.

I can see why you might get mad. If animals are sentient, we can't justify driving them around like machines.

Except—when you're in a cat, you're also the cat. Did you really think you could be a cat and not carry some of that away with you? Not leave some part of yourself behind?

You're not even the one in control, at first. You don't know what's going on or have your bearings, and you keep switching from one mind to the other, as if you were merely high and not of two minds at once. And although I was dead, there were parts of me that were *jubilant*. My eomma had wanted me to become a doctor (or at the very least, a nurse.) She'd never, in all her life, imagined that I might become a cat.

And so there we were, drunk and happy on our swishy tail and the way we could hear the scuttle of a mouse on the fire escape and the strong, strong, salty smell of noodles and burgers and the bánh mì place down the road and—

Even now, I still get lost in smells, so we should move on.

We, who were ironically named Shadow, stalked the mouse on the fire escape. We pounced, grabbed it in our jaws and pierced its flesh—salty and sweet was the blood—but we didn't agree with ourself on what to do next and fought over our jaw muscles, and the mouse fell into a trash can below.

Then, we were in agreement, both of us above soiling ourselves with garbage. But we were still hungry, so we went to Second Best Food Place, which was not as tasty as First Best Food Place, but it also had Soft Bed Place and Many Strokes Human.

We climbed another fire escape—so fast, we were so fast, even if we didn't like the feel of the metal grating on our paws—and slipped into a window that led to the stairway, before coming around to the front door of Second Best Food Place. We meowed and meowed to be let in, me marveling at the way our throat stretched and the twitching of the muscles in our legs and the little blossoms of life in our belly—kittens, we were going to have kittens, soon, six of them, and the second one refused to stop kicking us.

The door opened, and we went inside. It was only then that I noticed the woman's shoes—shiny and black and white, and with pointy toes, and we didn't know the word, but I did. *Wingtips*. They couldn't have been the same ones, I thought as I fought with us to control our head, to look her up and down.

She was thin, and not in a glamorous way. There were dark bags under her eyes and a sheen of sweat on her forehead, and she smelled . . . bad. Like the time we scaled that tree and swiped that egg from the robin's nest, and then we cracked it open and it was rotten—

No, I wasn't there, I told us, but we didn't seem to understand.

"Oh, Shadow," said the Many Strokes Human. She wrapped her arms around herself, as if she were cold. "What have you gotten into?"

Her lip curled up—disgust. She disappeared for a moment—faucet sounds, *squeak-squeak-squeak*—and then came back with a rag to wipe the blood from our face.

After she bathed us—which we permitted only after a great fight with her and our selves—we spent the night curled up to her. At one point, she got up for the bathroom, and we played pounce with her feet, but we were tired from having two minds and two souls and only one body. Already, our insides were hot, too hot, and I could feel that the distance between our selves was compressing, that parts of me were getting woven into us.

Lying there, on her bed in the dark, it scared me, because it didn't feel like I could get them back.

The next morning, she went to get dressed. She opened her closet, and I saw it—me. Not *us,* but *me*—photo after photo after photo, all black-and-white, of the person I'd been before.

The hair went up all the way down our spine. We lashed our tail, but we padded closer, barely noticing her as she shuffled around through the hanging racks for an outfit.

In the photos, I never looked at the camera. Some were close-ups, taken from afar, as if with a telescoping lens. Others were blurry thumbprints—phone photos that had been printed and cut out, my face dispersing into fields of dots up close. There were many from the café I thought of as *my* café—I'd rarely left the house, but when I had, it was there, to read—but only when I could get my table, the one in the very, very back, away from the windows and the baristas and the light.

From the angle of the photograph, it had been taken from the café's bathroom. There was even a sliver of the door in the photo, grainy and out of focus.

She'd been watching me. This woman, who I had never met before, who I didn't know the name of, and I had no idea why.

I should be afraid, I thought, but I was also a spirit inside a cat's brain, and I'd just spent the night with the woman—and anyways, we didn't feel nervous about it at all, because this was the Many Strokes Human, and we were not afraid of her.

I waited. We started to get anxious from being inside for so long (for although I knew how to use the door, we could not). I guess the woman could tell, because she opened the door, and we slipped into the hallway.

But then she came out after us, shutting and locking the door behind. I got another look at her, this time in the light spilling through the window that we'd slipped through yesterday.

She looked sick, and she blinked her eyes rapidly against the light. I realized for the first time that she hadn't turned on the lights when we'd been inside.

After a moment, she went down the stairs. We wanted to climb out the window again and go looking for First Best Food Place, but I was stronger now—even though there was less of me left.

I pushed and pushed and pushed, and we fought, but I won, and our legs turned and we went down the stairs, skulking after the woman and her pointy black shoes.

*

Traveling was different—I was able to perceive more through our senses, but it didn't match up with the mental maps I had of this area, and I couldn't orient myself well. Perhaps that's why we made it all the way to the door of the café before I realized where we were going.

I debated trying to slip into the café behind my neighbor, but we balked hard at that—it was an enclosed space with no open windows, and people had kicked us and spat at us before—so we stood on our back legs and put our paws to the window, scanning the glass for her image.

She didn't go to the counter. Instead, she went straight to the back of the café, right to my table. A moment later, she came out.

The next place she visited was my apartment. She went straight to the door—but skulking, just as we were skulking behind, and I'm sure we'd have made a funny image to anybody watching—and knocked tentatively.

We didn't like this. The knocks were loud and sharp to us, and we could smell me inside, my ripe, rotting body. It made us want to yak all over the hallway carpet. I didn't know, yet, that the dizziness was from my presence, the strain of having us both inside of this cat-body, chewing it up.

She waited and knocked again, and then she scrunched over and put her cheek to the door. "Hello," she said. "Are you in there?"

We meowed plaintively, but she didn't seem to notice. We waited for her to leave, but she slumped against the wall and folded down, down, down, and now we could see her face, her cheek and its small red blemish. Before, we would have taken it for a pimple, but I knew what it was because I'd had one like it before *I* became *us*.

A seed. A seed had drilled into her cheek, and she was weak and smelled bad, almost as bad as my body did, and that meant she was dying.

She would need a body. This one was already occupied, but I had an idea.

We checked the dumpster, but the mouse was gone. We argued briefly, because although we agreed that catching a mouse was a good idea in principle, my insistence that we not harm it meant we couldn't taste the blood.

But I was stronger, because our body was getting tired, running hotter and hotter, and so I won. We caught a mouse and brought it up by its tail.

The woman was lying down. We could tell she didn't have the strength to sit up. She shuddered when she saw us and the wriggling mouse, but she didn't try to move, and we waited while the mouse bit us and kicked and bit us—

She died, and I felt her, inside and outside, here and there— and then she was herself and the mouse, and of course, they were both you.

Our friendship wasn't a friendship, at first. You and I couldn't talk, because mice and cats couldn't speak to one another yet, and so I had no way to tell you who I was or ask you why your closet was full of stolen photos of me.

And you were afraid of me, very afraid, because you were you, but not *yet*. Not all the way. Not the way I would be, once I became a bird.

Before long, our body that was Shadow became very sick—but you were sicker, because you were smaller, your tiny heart running like the fan in a gaming computer. More than once, you tried to escape, but you were a small thing, and we an order of magnitude larger, and we caught you easily.

When it came close to time, the we that was once Shadow picked you up by the tail and dragged you to the zoo. We set you to rest in the giraffe pen, and then we used what was left of our strength and jumped higher, higher, until we found the button that unlocked the enclosure. We managed to swipe at it a moment before our body hit the ground, and then the we that was once Shadow was not Shadow anymore.

This time, we were both giraffes—knobby-kneed and long-necked and proud, and it wasn't until I felt myself stretching into this new form that I realized my miscalculation: we were the same species, now, the I-we and the you-we, but while giraffes communicate, it isn't with words. There was no way to say *photograph*, or *apartment*, or *wing-tipped shoe*. I tried scratching figures in the dirt with our cloven hooves, but it all came out as wobbly squares.

Still, you could tell that we were talking to you—and perhaps you could feel me now, the way I felt you, no more fear of my feline teeth and claws. Or perhaps you'd realized what had happened, how close you'd come to expiring—I know that each hop between bodies frightens you, that you never forget the wrongness.

Cat-me had made other miscalculations. For one, though the door was open, we were still giraffes, and giraffes seldom pass unnoticed. They cannot traipse around downtown without being caught and brought back to the zoo.

But it was a comfort to wind our long neck with yours, and though I burned to discover why you'd been spying on me, the truth was that you were my only kindred spirit—at first. As the days passed and people visited the zoo, we heard their phones, their conversations, their tiny radios playing the news. We knew more people were dying, though nobody had put the bodies and the seeds together.

Before long, zoo-comers dwindled, until there were none. We realized they might never return. Still, time was passing, and we burned through each animal in the enclosure, through the very last.

We would've died, then, had not a pair of bees buzzed by.

We leaped into them, and then you took off, and I had no choice but to follow, though I couldn't control this body the same as you could yours.

(I feel so much grief for you, for if I am me when I'm a bird, you are you when you're a bee, and a bee is so tiny that you may only be you for a few minutes at a time.)

I didn't know where you were going, but I was not going to lose you, and so I did my best with our wings. But you timed it wrong, dropped from the sky like a shot. A moment later, I felt ourself arc down after you, our bee-body already a shell—and that's when I felt them below us, twisting and agile and muscular. You and I, we plunged into two dolphins, and again, I was I-we, and you were you-we.

Dolphins can speak, though it's not the same—not something I can translate, though I will try.

I said, *Who are you? I click-bounced you, outside the place I am always swimming.*

And you said, *What is happening to us? Was it the kelp-sperm that floated down from the sky?*

And I-we nodded, and tried to stand up on our tail, although we couldn't do that yet.

But you laughed, a series of stutters that we felt rise from our lower jawbone, conducted through the water like the drumming of fingers on a table. I was embarrassed, but you swam toward me and said, *Catch me!*

The harder we used these bodies, the faster they would burn away. But we felt your wake as you streaked away like a comet, and the part of us that was not me pushed our body to follow.

As the days passed, I started to hear a thrum, a low susurration like waves. I couldn't tell if it was new, or if I'd ignored it my whole life.

But I knew it got louder each time we changed.

We left the zoo in the bodies of two smallish monkeys, for we'd realized, by then, that even if it was just the two of us, the zoo animals would not last forever. And I tried not to think about it—what it meant leaving behind this carnage, what we were doing, body after body burned out from the inside like dugout canoes.

There was nothing else for it, was there? After all, we wanted to live.

I was afraid to leave that place, though, the safety of those walls. Afraid there was no way to make it out of the city to the real wild spaces, but I shouldn't have worried. Amidst the streets and the cars and the buildings were ten thousand synanthropic hearts: little brown house mice and big black roof rats, pigeons and ducks and hidden urban farms of bees and geese and chickens, falcons and foxes and silverfish, roaches and squirrels and raccoons and rabbits, small bevvies of skunks, hordes of flies and bedbugs, and once, even, a pair of armadillos.

By the time we made it to the edge of the city, I was loathe to leave—but the murmur in the background of our minds had grown to a roar, a wild clamor of all the voices that lay out in the green spaces, both tamed and free—though to us, all of it was freedom. By then, too, we could feel in the milieu around us the others like us—those the seeds had taken, more and more every day, though the people that were left went on oblivious, saying things like *reasonable precautions* and *disease.*

We hurtled into the wild spaces with the howl of monkeys, the stuttering laugh of dolphins conducting up jawbone. By then we were learning to speak, stumbling upon words as if we'd once known them, like immigrants with half-forgotten childhoods. It was a language not made with tongues or teeth or the clicking of mandibles, and yet we understood it and each other and all the furred and feathered and hard-shelled things around us, for they spoke it, too.

And each time I closed my eyes and listened, I found new voices joining. I could hear the oak trees and the *whoosh* as the trees pulled water through their roots, their trunks, their leaves. The buzz of the stars overhead, muffled by the hymns of clouds. The wild rumbling beneath our feet, a concerto of plates crashing into each other like rams butting in the mountains—for it was all scale and tempo, and it was all available to us.

And things were good, and we were joy and wild speed, and I forgot all about the photographs in the closet—

Until the day we coursed downhill, two deer, white tails flashing, and the shot rang out, and you stumbled into the earth below.

I didn't flee.

You have to understand. In every space we had explored, there was always something living around us. Hadn't there been Shadow? The bees? The rats running along the rooflines?

But I could feel all the voices around us—even the forms we could not take, like the trees and the sky and the dirt, and that's how I knew it was only us three: you, me, and the hunter.

His boots approach you, heavy footfalls like the titanic clashes of the plates below, and I hate him. I have no right to hate him—isn't what we've done a thousand times worse? The bodies we've left behind, a multispecies extinction event—

And yet, I hate him for the way you lay gasping, your eyes glazing over. Your tongue is out and wet with pink foam, and your sides heave.

There is nothing close by—not a worm, not a fly, not a bird—for something has been done to this spot, befouled it, coated it with some rampant poison, and though I don't understand it, I know that it was done, that there is no time.

He raises his gun again. We plead with him with our deer tongue, with our stamping hooves, and when that doesn't work, we howl at him in the language of all things.

Do not do this!

Do not do this!

He stops and blinks. He shakes his head, even sticks a dirty finger in his ear—but then something comes over his face, and I know it's a hardness in his heart, an illness that I, too, once used to have, that makes him deaf to the world.

He raises his gun again.

I know that this will not happen. It cannot. This *cannot* be the end of you.

But there's a flash—and I feel it, then, you inside and outside, and I know you're not in the deer, not anymore.

And there is no body nearby. None, except this one.

We've never tried to return to a body that one of us has left—but my-ours is new, and fresh, and still strong. It would have lived another few days, at least.

Here, here! I call in the language of all things. *We can share!*

And this is a lie—I know it is. I know we cannot share. But if you are not here, I don't want to be here, and so when you come hurtling toward me, swifter than the bullet that took you down, I ready myself. In the moment before you storm inside, I flee—

But you catch me. You reach out and grab me, a comet clinging on to another, and you try to drag me in with you. There is a terrible pain—the scorching heat of too much, trying to go into too little—but I can hear it, your mind working, neurons you don't have firing—and when there is not enough there, you draw outward, instead, from everything around us. You ask the leaves and the bark and the dirt below, dead though it is: *Help us.*

And suddenly, I hear them all answer.

A moment later, I am back in the deer, and you are with me. And as the hunter raises his gun again—this time for us, for we, too, are a fine prize—we flip up our tail, and we're gone.

We've tried, but we cannot separate.

We still haven't figured out what any of this means—the seeds that came down from the sky, the way that they've connected us to all things. You maintain that the bodies we leave behind are not dead, and though I cannot agree, I say I do, because we share one mind and body, now, and it's easier when things are quiet.

Secretly, I think someone will come for us one day. That the seeds that took us from our bodies could not be an accident—but that day has not arrived.

You were smart and suggested the ocean, and now we always find ample hosts around us, though we are careful to keep ourselves close to shoals of fish, to choruses of dolphins. Once, we were attacked by a shark, but then we became the shark, and it made you sad and me happy.

I used to worry that we would run out of animals, but now I am not so sure. The seeds are still falling, thorn-tipped maple wings that float down from the sky like ash, and although humans try to avoid them, they cannot always. They must sleep, and the seeds are strong. They know no barrier. They penetrate stone and roofing tar and wood as easily as flesh.

Animals are still reproducing, aren't they? If there are no people left, in the end—if we all become seeded—will we overtake them? Or will their numbers always be greater than that which we can take?

We've decided to go deep, leapfrogging from creature to creature, descending into an ocean trench. We are an anemone, a coral, a clown fish, a jellyfish, an eel. It's easier, in some ways, to only need one body for us both, though we are always careful, always ready to flee.

Somewhere between when the dark stops and the trench ends, we run into a patch of bioluminescent algae. It glows, disturbed by our movements, and I take that as a sign—it's finally time to ask you.

I want to know, I say, about the photos in the closet.

By now, of course, you know that I was once the person in them. It's not a thing I could keep secret from you, not when we are always together.

You are quiet, at first. Then, I feel you give—a soft give, like the bending of a blade of grass. *I was a private investigator*, you say.

Because this amuses me, I give you a dolphin's jawbone laugh. It's my favorite laugh because it was yours. *Were you investigating me?*

No, you say. Before you can answer me fully, we sense something passing us by—a slimy pink fish—and we jump inside. I am delighted to find that there are gaps in our skull, that our bones are soft—and that although we have eyes, they do not seem to do anything. We were adapted for this place.

I had a client who wanted to know if his wife was cheating on him. I was watching her, and you came down and sat across from her in her booth, and then she got up and walked away.

I have to think hard about what you've just said, as if recalling the plot of a book, and not my once-life.

Finally, though, I remember. *I didn't know her,* I say. *She was sitting in my spot.*

And you laugh—like a dolphin's stutter, like the buzzing of a bee. *It doesn't matter. I followed you, and you fascinated me. You never went anywhere, and you were always alone. You were . . . so lonely.*

Yes, I say, because it's true—though these words, too, are part of that world I struggle to remember: *alone, lonely.*

Maybe I was like that. But so were all of us, weren't we?

And because I'm right, you say nothing, and we plunge ourselves farther into the deep.

The Difference Between Love and Time

FROM *Someone in Time: Tales of Time-Crossed Romance*

THE SPACE-TIME CONTINUUM is the sum total of all that ever was or will be or ever possibly could have been or might conceivably exist and/or occur, the constantly tangling braid of physical and theoretical reality, (steadily degrading) temporal processes, and the interactions among the aforementioned.

It is also left-handed.

It is, as you have probably always suspected, nonlinear, non-anthropic, non-Euclidean, and wholly nonsensical.

In point of fact, it's a complete goddamned mess.

It has severe social anxiety.

And a weakness for leather jackets.

We first met when I was six. Our fathers arranged a play date. The space-time continuum looked like a boy my own age, with thick glasses in plastic army camouflage–printed frames, a cute little baby Afro, and a faded T-shirt with the old mascot for the poison control hotline on it. Mr. Yuk, grimacing on the chest of time and space, sticking out his admonishing green Yuk-tongue. POISON HELP! 1-800-222-1222.

It smelled like lavender and bread baking in a stone oven.

I said I wanted to play Legos.

It looked helplessly at me with big brown eyes magnified into enormity by prescription lenses like hockey pucks.

It picked up a black block with an arch in it. Part of the drawbridge in my Medieval Castle Siege playset. The space-time continuum handed me the black arch and opened its mouth and the sound of a pulsar spinning, turning, thumping through silver-deafening radio static came out instead of "Where does this piece go?" or "It's nice to meet you" or "The idea of your shitty Lego drawbridge amusing me for even a nanosecond is hilarious on a geological scale."

The space-time continuum is a manifold topology whose coordinates can and frequently do map onto certain physical states, events, bodies. But that map looks like one of those old paper diner menus with a giant squiggle on it labeled *Enter Here* on one side and *You Win!* on the other.

And it changes all the time.

And you can't win.

And the crayon evaporates in your hand and rematerializes in your hospital bassinet under the *Welcome Baby!* card.

Or on the surface of the moon.

It doesn't care for television except for reruns of *Law & Order*. It cannot get enough of predictability. It says every episode is a bizarre upside-down bubble universe in which justice exists and things make sense.

The first real actual word the space-time continuum ever said to me was: "Nothing."

The first words I said to it were: "You can't just go around saying 'nothing' to people, it's weird. Do you want my extra Capri Sun?"

The space-time continuum wrapped its skinny baby arms around me and whispered it again in my ear: "Nothing."

I didn't like being hugged then. I yelled for my mom. She didn't come for a long time.

In high school, the space-time continuum looked like a scene kid with a million flannels and ironic shirts, a long black undercut, and a patch on his backpack from some band called Timeclaw. It got in a lot of trouble for drawing or carving or scratching its initial in desks all over the place, this funky *S* that kinda also looks like a pointy figure eight. But not lying on its side like the infinity symbol. Infinity standing up.

I've seen them everywhere. Still do. The space-time continuum gets around.

You've probably seen it, too.

It failed all its classes but shop. It was always punctual at the circular saw. It never failed to make a perfect version of the assignment from oak, birch, ash, even plastic. Every day, it brought me the objects it had been compelled to make by Mr. Wooton. A model PT Cruiser. A wooden orchid. A puzzle shaped like an iguana. My favorite was this bare green circuit board with a little lightbulb on it that flared to life if you put your finger in the right place. It used you to complete the circuit.

The space-time continuum and I sat behind the bike racks for hours after school smoking weed and putting our fingers in the right place.

Ocean Shores, Washington, is not the space-time continuum, though it is, of necessity, an inescapable part of it. Ocean Shores, Washington, is a city that used to be a pretty big deal and is now not even a little deal.

See, back in the sixties, the state of Washington thought maybe it would legalize gambling because fuck it, why not, and people started buying up all the land and building nightclubs and hotels and golf courses and bungalows and boardwalks so that when the legislature hit the buzzer, the good times would be ready to roll. All kinds of movie stars and rich people's girlfriends and purveyors of semilegal entertainment poured in from California. But then the state of Washington thought maybe it would not legalize gambling so now there's just a lot of cold sand dunes and closed attractions and motels with names like Tides Inn or Mermaid's Rest Motor Court and Weigh Station.

Ocean Shores is hollowed out like a gourd someone meant to make into a drum for a beautiful party. But they wandered off and maybe even forgot what drums are to begin with so now it's just an empty, scraped-out dead vegetable lying on a cold beach nobody would ever hold a party on.

And then a seagull shits in it.

My mom and my dad and me used to always drive down for the last weekend of summer. Dad would always give me a riddle that I had to solve by the end of the trip. Like the one with the wolf and the chicken and the bag of grain or what has a ring but no finger? I'd play the twenty-year-old games on the last remaining board-walk while my parents argued about what to do with me under the white noise of the waves.

Eventually, Dad left and it was just me and mom. We'd rent a bungalow that was once destined to be Jayne Mansfield's fuck grotto or whatever and sit in the moldy Jacuzzi freezing our asses off, singing show tunes to the seals and shipping freighters out at sea.

The space-time continuum thinks Ocean Shores was at its best when only dinosaurs lived there.

I asked the space-time continuum who its mother was once. Did she have fluffy curly hair like mine, did she smell nice like mine, was her name Alice like mine, did she sniffle a lot like she was cry-ing even though she usually wasn't like mine, did she always pack a fruit and a vegetable in its lunch box (a Lisa Frank purple-blue cosmic orca one that I secretly coveted)?

The space-time continuum glanced nervously at the ashy green blackboard at the front of our classroom. This made me dislike the space-time continuum, as at the time many of the children liked to make fun of me for being dim-witted, even though I do all right. But it gave no other answer, and only a long time later did I consider that it was not looking at the blackboard at all, but the eraser.

When the space-time continuum stuck that black Lego arch over the scuffed blue moat pieces, it stopped being a Medieval Castle Siege playset and started being a Cartoon Sparkle Rainbow Geo-duck playset.

Our dads didn't notice. They just kept drinking beers, one after the other, lifting the red and white Rainier cans to their lips and setting them down automatically after each rhythmic sip like they were beer-drinking machines stuck in an infinite recursion function.

The space-time continuum in the Mr. Yuk shirt smiled at me shyly. It was giving me a gift. It wanted desperately to please me. I was not pleased. I liked my Medieval Castle Siege playset a lot. It came with four different-colored horse minifigs. Geoducks are weird gross dumb giant clams that live in the mud for a thousand years and come with zero horse minifigs. Their shells aren't rainbow-striped and they don't have friendly eyes with big, long eyelashes and smiling mouths and they definitely don't sparkle.

I didn't even think Lego made a Cartoon Sparkle Rainbow Geoduck playset.

But the space-time continuum's eyelashes were very long, too. So I said thank you.

It made the pulsar sound again.

You have to understand I was alone a lot of the time. It came and went as it pleased. But not because it was afraid to commit. The space-time continuum asked me to marry it when I was eight and we were pretending to fish with branches and string in the pond behind the primate research labs on the edge of town. I couldn't figure out why the fish weren't biting. I was going to bring my mom the biggest salmon you ever saw and she was gonna say how good I was and be so happy instead of staring at the dish soap for an hour while I watched the Muppets, but the stupid fish weren't on board with my plan.

That time, the space-time continuum looked like a girl my age with a red NO NUKES shirt on under her overalls. It said: *We didn't bring any bait. Or hooks. And there are no fish in this pond because it's not really a pond, it's a big puddle that dries up as soon as there's no rain for a week. Be my wife forever, limited puddle-being.*

I said: *Shut up, your face is a puddle.*

The space-time continuum lay its pigtailed head on my shoulder as the sunset sloshed liquid pink and gold and said: *We are a house and a hill.*

OK, weirdo.

But we were already holding hands so tight, without even noticing it.

So it's not about commitment.

The space-time continuum just has a hard time with confined spaces. Like the public education system. And calendars. And apartments.

And bodies.

*

Its favorite album is the iconic 1979 *Breakfast in America* by the often underrated British prog-pop group Supertramp. But its favorite song is "Time After Time" by Cyndi Lauper.

I don't really have anything to say in defense of its weakness for easy listening.

I guess it just wants something to be easy.

The space-time continuum is holistically without gender.

Its pronouns are it/everything.

Or, to put it another way, it is a quivering, boiling mass of all physio-psychological states that will/are likely to/have developed across every extinct/extant/unborn species, making the whole issue pointless, irrelevant, and none of my business. The seventy-fourth time we met it looked like an Estonian woman who had just graduated from the Rhode Island School of Design, so you can see what I mean.

Butch on the streets, churning maelstrom of intersecting time and matter in the sheets.

Later, the space-time continuum told me that was only the second time we'd met in objectively perceived time. Which always meant its perception, never mine. It was freshly in love. I was forty and tired. It was July. Rain beat the streets down till they gave up. The puddle talk happened yesterday. Its hair was so long and fine I felt certain that if I touched it, it would all dissipate like smoke. But I really, really wanted to touch it anyway. It wore a pale blue leather jacket over a white T-shirt with a Frank Lloyd Wright quote on it in thin gray Arial letters. It looked so fucking cool. It was always so much cooler than me.

I took the continuum to that little Eritrean restaurant down on Oak. It ordered tsebhi derho with extra injera and ate like food had only just been invented, which, given the nature of this story, I feel I should stress it had not. I just had the yellow lentil soup. The space-time continuum cried in my arms. It thought it had lost track of me. I didn't answer its text messages.

If it was a commercial cereal brand it would be Cap'n Crunch Oops All Genders.

I would be Cinnamon Toast Chump.

Whatever it looks like, it always wears glasses. Safer that way. For all of us.

*

The Frank Lloyd Wright quote was: *No house should ever be on a hill or anything. It should be of the hill. Belonging to it. Hill and house should live together, each the happier for the other.*

We had our first kiss in middle school.

The space-time continuum took me to the winter dance. It wore white. I wore black. We looked like winter, the wide, deep snow and a bare tree. It picked me up at 6:45 and tied a corsage around my wrist. It said the flower was an odontoglossum orchid. Native to Argentina. Only grows in cold climates. Like me.

When the space-time continuum put its hands on my waist, lock-elbowed, stiff, uncertain, I smelled a lonely ultraviolet sea churning on a small world in the constellation of Taurus. It wasn't winter in the constellation of Taurus. It was spring, and the sea on that planet was in love with a particular whale-plant living inside it, and I understood a lot of things just then. When Bryan Adams hit his guitar solo, the space-time continuum kissed me, and I knew why it'd been wearing that poison control shirt when we first met, and also what it felt like to be a whale who is also a flower, floating inside a desperate sea.

The ninety-fourth time we met, the space-time continuum was on Tinder. It had a dog in its profile pic, even though it doesn't have a dog in real life. Its other pics showed it fishing, hiking, doing a color run.

This was its profile:

S, Young at Heart

>0.1 miles away

Hi, baby.

I'm sorry. I was wrong. I'm an idiot. I love you. I'll do better this time. I can be better. Come home.

But then I think it got nervous and confused because below that it said:

If you can't handle me at the peak of my recursive timeline algorithm, you don't deserve me when I'm an iguana.

The dog was a corgi. But not the orange kind, the black and white kind. Its name tag said *Snack McCoy.*

That's a pretty solid *Law & Order* joke. So it probably was the space-time continuum's dog. Somewhen. Elsewise.

I wonder if there was a version of me in the Snack McCoy universe. I wonder if there was a version of you.

I wonder if everything there was made out of crunchy biscuit treats.

I don't know why the space-time continuum stopped loving me. Maybe I worked too much, too hard, too late. Maybe it wanted more than cozy taco nights in a rooftop apartment above, in descending order, a comedy club, a Planned Parenthood, and a Laundromat. Maybe it wanted less. Was I overly critical? (*Why the fuck do people just STOP at completely unpredictable points, what's wrong with you, why would you set it up that way? Sleep on the goddamned couch, you narcissist.*) Did I just *consistently* fail to put my dishes in the dishwasher right away? I could've done it any time I wanted. Cups go in rack not on counter. Easy. And yet. Did I not support its interests? Maybe I didn't understand its love language. Or how to set up a retirement account. Maybe I took too long to lose the baby weight. Maybe I didn't let it have enough me time.

Maybe I stopped really listening. Maybe the nexus of spatial and temporal possibilities was just sick of my shit.

Maybe I don't deserve to be loved.

That's probably it.

One time it showed our first-grade teacher, Mrs. Aldritch, the drawing it made during quiet period and she cried spinal fluid out of her eyes so that was pretty intense.

It refused to show me. Even though it borrowed my black crayon to color with in the first place.

The space-time continuum's father looked very much like Mr. Clark, who used to run Dazzle Dan's Vintage Diner by the train tracks. Mr. Clark's name was not Dan. It was Clarence Peter Clark. But the previous owner wasn't named Dan either. He was named Roderigo R. Rodriguez, which I am not making up. But it was pretty hard to be Mexican around here back then, especially if you wanted to sell all-American nostalgia burgers with lettuce, tomato, onion, and mayo, so he just went by Roddy.

Roddy was from Guadalajara. There's a cathedral there called the Catedral de la Asunción de María Santísima with two golden spires standing up into the sky and the birds together, completely identical. Clarence Peter Clark was from Yakima. There's nothing much in Yakima.

Nobody knows where Dazzle Dan came from.

By the time I was thirteen I was pretty sure the space-time continuum didn't actually have a father, just a thing in its house like one of those old drinky bird toys that sat on the lip of a glass and rocked back and forth more or less forever, once you set it going. It needed a father to make sure no one suspected it wasn't actually a boy with glasses or a girl with pigtails or an Estonian exchange student. But it didn't need a *person.* Just a bobbing blob of weighted plastic wearing Mr. Clark's face, lifting can after red and white can of Rainier beer to its mouth in the background until the death of all matter in a fiery entropic abyss.

On our second play date we tried to play Cowboys and Indians. I heard the other kids doing it. Cowboys had horses, and I loved horses more than candy, so I was pretty excited.

But I never ever got to be the cowboy. The space-time continuum said: *"Cowboy" is just another word for the generational trauma inflicted by the colonizer's whole-ass inability to access empathy for anyone but himself and the debt to entropy incurred by his solipsistic commitment to almost unimaginable violence as an expression of personal potency.*

Then it poured the living memory of the surrender of the Nez Perce in the Bear Paw Mountains like molten platinum into my brain and blood shot out of my nose and my eyes at the same time and my pinky toe turned into a Suciasaurus rex tooth. The space-time continuum panicked, whispering *oh shit, oh shit, I'm sorry, I'll fix it,* whereupon it flooded my gray matter with golden retrievers and the smell of chocolate cookies baking and the exact emotional sensations experienced in the moment of era-defining scientific discoveries and a few old Bob Ross episodes just in case.

My appendix ruptured and I didn't speak again for ten months.

My parents sent me to specialists.

A lot of them.

The space-time continuum is a total slob and a nightmare roommate. It leaves its wadded-up proto-stars all over the floor. It won't do the dishes even when I cook, since it only pretends to eat. It washes clothes we haven't bought yet, then forgets to put them away for weeks. It has taken a moral stance against both mowing the lawn and dusting. It says doing so would only appropriate the culture of sequential cause and effect, which it has no right to wear like a costume.

It leaves a ring of quantum foam around the bathtub to just get crustier and crustier until I give in and scrub it off myself. Stare for fifteen minutes while my knees get sore on the badly grouted tile thinking about equal division of labor and if maybe we should get a chore chart, if that would even help, or if it just thinks this is my work because I'm the one who's going to die someday so it bothers me more. Finally, run the water and watch it all swirl down the silver drain into the waste infrastructure dimension.

"An alarm clock," I whisper to the slowly rotating water. "An alarm clock has a ring but no finger."

Every Valentine's Day, the space-time continuum wraps my gift in pink and red paper with hearts or baby angels or birds or radio signals all over it and practically climbs the walls with excitement waiting for me to open it.

Those are some of the best times I remember. The moments before I rip the baby angel bird hearts open.

There's never anything inside the box. It's just that after I open the box, I know a story about love I didn't know before I opened the box. And I mean I know it like it happened to me. Like it's my own story.

One year it was this: the Loch Ness monster was absolutely real. She lived to be about five hundred years old like that one ugly Greenland shark they found before a Swiss tourist hit her in the head with a boat propeller in 1951. There used to be two of them, even. A mating pair. Nessie had a single baby around the time of the Great Fire of London and I felt her love that baby monster fishosaur down in the dark and the cold that wasn't dark or cold to her at all. I felt the absolute safety and security of thousands of pounds of water pressure like one of those weighted vests for anxious dogs. I felt Nessie love her baby so much the temperature of the whole lake rose by one degree.

My gifts aren't as good. My gifts do not come from the time-pit out of which springs the Pleiades and ring-tailed lemurs and the Battle of Tours and Loch Ness, they come from my checking account.

Last year I gave it cuff links. I don't fucking know, you try buying for a space-time continuum who definitionally has everything.

Here is an abridged list of things the space-time continuum and I fought about:

What movie to watch.

Whether or not I had a hostile tone this morning.

The exact dictionary definition of "narcissist."

If it's technically gaslighting to make a fight never have happened.

Where it goes when we're not together.

Why it won't let anything last.

The whole thing about it allowing death to exist.

If it ever thought for one minute about consent before fucking about with my Lego and/or timestream.

Whether it has to pay rent.

Why it didn't tell me to go to the hospital that night because we both know it had to have known.

Why it is the way it is.

Why it refuses to change.

Why it decided capitalism had to be a thing.

Why everything sucks so much all the time.

Why I don't think a baby is a good idea.

This is what it looks like when the space-time continuum is mad at you: You wake up in the morning already late because your alarm clock now reads 1-800-222-1222. The auto-set coffee machine isn't left on for you and the taco leftovers from last night are all gone and its car isn't in the overnight guest spot and you can't find your phone and there's no dishes in the cupboards and there's no cute little Post-it note on the fridge telling you to have a nice day (*PS we're out of milk*) but there definitely *is* lipstick scrawled on the bathroom mirror. The expensive stuff, MAC Saint Germain, big swooping letters that read *the speed of light in a vacuum is the same for all observers regardless of the directionality of the light source.* Asshole.

You'll have to wait a few weeks for the space-time continuum to cool off and get a little cheeky over a couple of bottles of bodega rosé to find out that it 100 percent ate all the leftovers just to spite you. But then it got sick and spewed total paralyzing awareness of causality all over the 98 bus and, like, *everyone* on that route is now loaded up with heavy sedation or Fields Medals but *ANYWAY* it's just *maybe* possible your phone is embedded in an extremely put-out Pachycephalosaurus's eye socket.

But either way, you have to stop freaking out about the car.

The continuum doesn't have a car. It's never had a car. It doesn't drive. It doesn't even have a license so much as it *contains* everyone else's licenses. It's just that sometimes a pocket universe containing a reality in which Monet was never born looks *a lot* like a 2005 Inca Gold Pearlcoat PT Cruiser with a faded COEXIST bumper sticker half peeled off the back and a leather frog key chain swinging from the rearview.

Then the space-time continuum starts acting way too nice. It lets you pick the movie and what kind of takeout to order and gives you a foot rub before admitting that your patterned cups and soup bowls and novelty pink octopus mug are currently making a long lonely pilgrimage around the frigid ring system of Saturn. Yes, it knows they were your mother's, and it's very sorry, it doesn't know what gets into it sometimes. It just loves you so much and, well, you know how you can be. So immature. So self-centered. So finite. You don't appreciate the emotional labor the space-time continuum puts into this relationship.

But that octopus mug is gonna make *big* news in about a hundred years, so let's focus on the positive, also don't be mad but your coffee ended up in the butt of Malmsey that drowned George Plantagenet. Because fuck you that's why. It was upset. You shouldn't have said that thing about the invention of death. There are just some things you do not say to someone you love.

But you make up. Always. Until you don't. And when your duck pad see ew with extra broccoli arrives in its pure white Styrofoam container, twenty minutes before you put the order in, there's a pastel violet Post-it note inside that says: *Please don't leave me.*

The space-time continuum enjoys baking, but you can't eat the pale green prinsesstårta it has worked so hard to perfect after seeing it on that reality cake show. You can only have eaten it. Or be going to eat it. Or sometimes one day will have been never eating it. That's pretty much how it goes for all its hobbies. It swears it knit me a gorgeous mauve cabled cardigan for my fiftieth birthday because I'm always cold.

I wouldn't know. I've never seen it.

Coming up on my sixtieth.

Still cold.
Dick.

The space-time continuum is not a dick.
Mostly.

My mom—you remember Alice, with the curly hair and the fruits and vegetables in every lunch? Well, Alice died a little while after the whole David and Susan thing. Paranasal tumors. I didn't even know you could get nose cancer. By the time they found it, Alice hadn't been able to smell or taste anything in years.

That's the worst part, she told me after the diagnosis, home in bed with a couple of bottles of Ignoring Our Problems juice. *I can't smell anything. Not even you. I used to smell your head when you were a baby and it was the most amazing smell, better than Chanel No 5, I swear. Like lavender and bread baking in a stone oven. And sometimes, just once in a while, when you got older, you would be running out the door for a date with that kid in the flannel or putting groceries away or watching TV and I'd get a whiff of it again, like you were still so tiny and all mine and nothing bad could ever happen to us. And it's gone. I'll never smell you again ever.*

She hated hospitals so by the time I managed to convince her to get her butt in a paper gown it was just all through her. It couldn't wait. Had somewhere important to be, I guess.

But she was wrong. The worst part was that I wasn't there. I wanted to be. But I had to work. I missed it. The last words my mother ever said to me were days and days before.

Those things are rigged, honey.

But by then she was mostly morphine by volume, so.

One time the space-time continuum and I went to Mr. Clark's diner for burgers and floats. I was eleven. It looked eleven enough. I felt so grown up in that red vinyl booth all to ourselves, with my own money in my own wallet like some kind of real adult human who mattered. My dad had taken his curtain call three years before. But Mom and I were fine. Really. We carried the Christmas tree inside and set it up just the two of us. No men required.

I ordered a peppermint milkshake from Mr. Clark and there was a chocolate ribbon time loop inside it. I didn't find my way out until the school year was mostly over. I've been hard of hearing ever since.

I guess a lot of us spend middle school stuck in a time loop. I'm not special.

Never have been.

The thirty-ninth time I met the space-time continuum it was a three-and-a-half-foot-long rhinoceros iguana named Waffles. Waffles was lounging on fresh shredded newspapers in the display window of Jungle Friends Exotic Pet Store and Bubble Tea Café. Waffles was marked down 70 percent for Presidents' Day weekend.

I ordered a black milk bubble tea from the counter wedged into the large parrots section.

The scarlet macaw said: *The problem with Einstein-Rosen wormholes is that the "hallway" they create between two singularities is too small and open too briefly to ever permit transit by a living person.*

The African gray said: *You be good I love you see you tomorrow.*

The blue hyacinth said: *Fuckshit, Susan.*

Then it sang a few bars of "The Entertainer" and cracked up laughing.

Not everything means something.

Waffles watched the parrots. Waffles slurped up a strand of wilted collard greens. Waffles licked his eyeball.

The owner-operator of Jungle Friends Exotic Pet Store and Bubble Tea Café brought me my drink and swapped the *70% Off!* sign for an *80% Off!* one. So I took Waffles home. I put him in a plastic sun-faded Rainbow Brite kiddie pool with the contents of a Sensible Plan brand EZ Ceezar Salad bag and some flat rocks from the last trip I took with my mother to the Ocean Shores boardwalk, when I won every prize in the shitty Happy Claw prize machine one after the other. I warmed the rocks up in the microwave so Waffles could rest his belly on them. Then I sat back on my couch and drank the better part of a bottle of Bombay Sapphire because fuck George Plantagenet, that's why.

That hadn't happened yet. But if you spend long enough around the space-time continuum you get this thing where your head turns into a Tetris game and all the falling pieces are memories spinning around, upside down, out of order, mostly missing the sweet spot so they can just pile up uselessly while the music goes faster and faster the closer you get to this person you love so much who is no less your life partner for being an iguana right now.

Also cancer.

Waffles stared at me for a long time. Then the space-time continuum chomped down on a ranch-seasoning crouton and said: *The traveler and their vessel would have to be smaller than an atom, far faster than light.*

PS We're out of milk.

That was probably our best date.

I married someone else. For a while. Right after college. Trying to get away, I suppose. Find out who I even was apart from the space-time continuum. High school relationships never last anyway, right? He was just a guy. Let's say his name was David. It doesn't matter.

The space-time continuum told me not to. It said we were not compatible because my cells were contaminated by long-term nonconsecutive exposure to excited superliminal mass fields and David's cells were contaminated by long-term exposure to being a douchebag.

By that time the space-time continuum wasn't an iguana anymore. It was a mid-market talk radio host of one of those raunchy-advice-for-the-unemployed-and-lovelorn shows they used to pump out like Xerox copies of Xerox copies. Tune in to KHRT 101.5 to hear the velvet voice of my ex, the unstably enfleshed and endlessly repeating moment of creation and destruction, give you hot tips for better oral sex. The trick is know to your core that nothing means anything and all life and feeling will end.

The space-time continuum was working through some stuff.

The seventh time we met, the space-time continuum was this gangly ginger kid who got hit bad with the freckle-gun and a broken arm. The cast had everyone's messy kid-handwriting all over it.

You should see the other guy.

You're cute!

That events do indeed occur sequentially is perhaps the greatest lie of all.

See you this summer.

"You wanna see something?" the space-time continuum asked me just as the lunch bell rang. Seventh grade. We were gonna be discussing *The Westing Game* next period and I was so excited I could barely breathe. But I said okay anyway because it was wearing a shirt that said DON'T PANIC, so I figured the space-time continuum was on the up-and-up.

It took me to the teachers' lounge. It had a special key on a leather frog key chain. I didn't know what to think. The teachers' lounge was forbidden territory. As thrilling and terrifying as peeking in a crosshatched window at the surface of Mars.

"It's okay," the space-time continuum said. "I'm allowed."

Inside the teachers' lounge it wasn't the teachers' lounge. It was 1958 and we were outside and it was so hot. A man and a little boy were walking across a huge courtyard toward Catedral de la Asunción de María Santísima. Birds exploded into the air before them. The little boy was the most beautiful child I've ever seen, with the curliest hair and the biggest eyes. He practically glowed.

His father knelt down next to his baby and kissed his tiny cheek. He pointed toward the two golden spires.

"Look, Daniel!" Roderigo R. Rodriguez said. "Two of them! Just like you and me, mijo, forever and ever."

"It's Dazzle Dan," I whispered.

"Happy birthday," the space-time continuum answered. I said it wasn't my birthday. It shrugged. "It's always your birthday."

And then it wasn't 1958 anymore and it wasn't Guadalajara, it was the teachers' lounge and it smelled like old pencils.

But the space-time continuum didn't do that kind of thing very often because it made my teeth bleed.

Anyway, David cheated on me eight or nine weeks after the wedding. Let's say her name was Susan. It doesn't matter. Let's say she looked just like me but younger and prettier and less contaminated by excited mass fields.

Fuckshit, Susan.

As far as I can tell, the space-time continuum owns every self-help book ever published. *The 7 Habits of Highly Effective People. The Power of Now. The 4-Hour Workweek.* Hypatia's commentary on Diophantus's *Arithmatica. How to Win Friends and Influence People. Summa Theologica. Truth in Comedy: The Manual for Improvisation. Awaken the Giant Within. Opticks, or, A Treatise on the Reflexions, Refractions, Inflections and Colours of Light. The Rules: Time-tested Secrets for Capturing the Heart of Mr. Right. Gödel, Escher, Bach. A Brief History of Time.*

But I don't think it ever actually read any of them. It longed to improve itself, to access its trauma, discover its full potential, and rise above its faults. But it was terrified of actually *changing* anything.

I remember once, when we were moving from the yellow apartment downtown to a bigger place over the river, the space-time continuum and I plunked down on cardboard boxes full of its comfort reading. I'd optimistically labeled them *Books to Donate*, but it was an arch lie and we both knew it. We ate cold pineapple pizza and drank warm merlot straight from the box. And the totality of existence said to me, with sauce on the tip of its nose and not a little chagrin:

For me, self-care is like the grandfather paradox. It might feel good in the moment, but at what cost? No butterfly could imagine the changes to the timeline that would go down if I truly discarded everything that does not spark joy.

Do you really want to live in a universe where the space-time continuum has become fully self-actualized?

The Suciasaurus rex is a two-legged carnivorous theropod, a cousin of the more famous Tyrannosaurus rex. It is the only dinosaur ever found in the state of Washington.

Once, we were lying naked at three in the afternoon in the uptown loft apartment we had for six months when I was twenty-five and the owner was on sabbatical in Paris.

I kissed the space-time continuum's chin and said, in that extra-soft voice that only comes out of you when you're just so happy: *Why me?*

What do you mean why you?

By definition, you could have chosen anyone, anywhere, in the whole cosmos. Why me? I'm just a person like everybody else.

The space-time continuum rubbed its nose tenderly against mine.

Because it's you. It's you because it's you because it's you because it's you. Haven't you ever been stuck in a stable time dome before?

Plus you smell really good. And you offered me your Capri Sun even though it was your favorite flavor.

And we laughed and snuggled and ordered sushi and champagne and watched the traffic go by in the snow thirty stories down. You got a point for every blue car.

Two for red.

But why are you here? Why are you in bodies and minutes and places at all?

The space-time continuum frowned. It finished the bottle.

Everyone gets stuck sometimes. Red car.

I went to a small liberal arts college upstate. Double major psych/physics. A very calculated choice. Inside/Out, I used to say.

The space-time continuum wasn't allowed on campus. It would sit by the *University* sign on the bumper of its crumbling pickup truck chain-smoking angrily and reading through copies of *Omni* (for the articles) until I was out of class. I'd run out every day like a movie montage, all long hair and long skirts and the long half-life of first love.

I was really pretty then. I don't know why I want you to know that. It's not important in any way. But I was.

The problem was that college isn't part of the normal time-stream. Way too much angst and intersecting choice matrices. Warps the gravity fields and fucks with beta decay. It's an unsettling pocket universe of weird smells, meaningless gold stars, protective self-delusion, and leaking bodily liquid. Go ahead and try the double slit experiment on Friday night in a freshman dorm. You're safer with a Ouija board.

But the space-time continuum wanted to support my goals.

Ultimately, I ended up a bartender. Basically what I studied, in a roundabout way. And I only really do roundabouts anymore. Fluid dynamics. Classical conditioning. A festive arrangement of personality disorders and lost time. But I can make a mean Hammerhead Bowl, so who's to say I didn't come out on top?

We broke up junior year. It said we weren't putting the same effort into the relationship. I didn't make time for it. I laughed. It didn't.

Then David and Susan and my mom and student loans and better blow jobs through the power of drive-time radio and I didn't see the space-time continuum again for almost five years.

Sometimes things just don't work out. You want them to, but they don't want to, and their vote counts for more than yours, so they don't.

The space-time continuum says that no matter what, there is always a place where they *did* work out. So even if you're suffering, there's a version of yourself somewhere who isn't, maybe older, maybe younger, maybe she has one of those naked cats or something, and if you can't be happy, you can at least be happy for her.

I replied: *Fuck that bitch, I hope she drowns.*

The 117th time I met the space-time continuum it was my mother's doctor. It had kind eyes and bifocals and a little felt bunny stuck onto the tip of its pen, just the perfect dusting of authoritative gray at the temples.

I cried and I cried and I told it to fucking *stop*, it wasn't cute anymore. It never was. Fix her or get out. What is the point of all this if it can't even fix one lousy directionally locked material entity?

It got out.

The hallway was so long and white and clean and quiet. The cool blue price display on the vending machine flashed on and off, on and off, like a lonely lighthouse in an antiseptic sea.

1.99.

Card only.

I thought I didn't see the space-time continuum for five years.

I got this idea in my head that having plants around would help my anxiety and ground me in the now. So I bought the first orchid I liked, one that promised spectacular colors that would last for weeks. I put it in the window and watered it and loved it and it died *immediately.*

So I got another one that looked just like it. The way you swap out a kid's dead goldfish for a ziplocked new one from the shop while they're at school and they never notice because who gives a fuck, it's a goldfish.

That orchid also died. So fast it honestly felt kind of personal.

Lather, rinse, repeat.

All in all I had seventeen Odontoglossum pulchella and a lot of new, more interesting anxiety about maybe being the grim reaper of plants somehow. Or at least fundamentally incompatible with life.

The space-time continuum was all of them. It didn't mind waiting. Five years was nothing at all. Barely a ripple in a puddle that isn't a pond.

I wonder if the universe where everything worked out okay for me is also the Snack McCoy universe and the reason things can work out there but not here is because civilization is all or mostly corgis so there's fundamentally no real problems and also no climate change.

I wonder if I'm a corgi in the Snack McCoy universe.

The space-time continuum says I'm not.

I'm a cagey fucking greyhound and I still have anxiety.

The space-time continuum left me for good a couple years back. It was so ugly. Those scenes are always so ugly. It's your last chance to say the worst things you've ever thought about a person, so get it all out while you can, right?

But some things you can't come back from.

Maybe it was my fault. I said it first.

I'm not your fucking emotional support human. I just want the infinite embodiment of reality I fell in love with back. I just want everything to be like it was.

And the space-time continuum sneered at me. *I am exactly who you fell in love with! For me, the moment when I touched your Medieval Castle Siege drawbridge was half a second ago. I kissed you at the dance tomorrow.* You're *the one who's changed. But I don't have to sit here and take this. In a million other shards of reality beyond this completely stupid one, everything is precisely like it was. So fuck you very much. I don't want you like this. I can go find all the other versions of you in all the other time-lines and love them and hold them close and give them everything while you stay here alone and drink yourself to death in this shitty town. And yes, I'm including the one where you're a greyhound. I'm going to pet her so good, and brush her and walk her and feed her organic raw food artisanal treats. We're going to enter agility competitions together and chase cars and have a trillion puppies. And wait till you see what we do in the one where you're a lamp. Yes, there's one where you're a lamp, shut up! Stay here and have another drink, I'm going to go where everything is just as sweet and good and new as it was in the beginning and you're not fucking invited.*

It looked stricken. It put its hand over its mouth. But like I said, there's some things you can't come back from. Eventually, all loops degrade and fall apart and a way out of the squiggle opens up.

So that happened.

Or will happen. Or is happening. Or someday might inevitably be unhappened.

Maybe.

Nowadays I work the bar at the Neptune Room, home of the Hammer-head Bowl and the extremely understated jewel of the Tides Inn Hotel. Too broke to retire, too stubborn to die.

It is *distinctly* shit here.

I am distinctly shit as well. And old. And angry a lot of the time.

The decor is wall-to-wall plastic fish, seaweed garlands, and discount Christmas lights. The clientele come in drunk already when we open at four. The kitchen offers a limited menu of mystery bisque, french fries, and despair.

My knees hurt. I have a lot of time to think. Nobody bothers me except to grunt for another of whatever they've chosen to hurt themselves with tonight. I look out the picture windows at the town Ocean Shores was supposed to be and I think about the Suciasaurus rex and Mr. Yuk and corgis with lawyer names and David and Susan and the constellation of Taurus.

In the end, I get this place. We understand each other. I was supposed to be something better, too.

Today, I am mixing Hammerhead Bowls in the back. Don't get excited. It's just whatever's left in last night's well-drunk bottles, Coke, and the syrup from the maraschino jar all dumped into a turquoise plastic tub shaped like a shark with two straws in it. I finish up and head out to flip over the Closed sign.

There's a box on the bar. Wrapped in pink paper with hearts and baby angels on it. But it's not Valentine's Day. My hands settle down on the ribbons. I look around for orchids or iguanas or whatever, but I'm alone.

The box is sitting on top of a hand-knitted mauve cabled cardigan.

Maybe I won't open it. Maybe I just let this be over for once. I'm tired. I don't believe in anything anymore.

Of course I open it.

I'm fourteen years old. Mom and I get in her little yellow Jeep and drive down the coast to Ocean Shores. It's the first year after Dad left. She's nervous about doing it all on her own from here forward into always, so she's smoking again, and interfering with the radio like there's some tuning on the dial that will bring back the life she thought she was going to have. But there isn't. She's alone. He's gone and she's alone.

But she's trying. Alice is trying.

So she gives me my riddle for the trip instead of Dad, instead of the man who couldn't handle us at the peak of our reclusive timeline algorithm, and my mother's riddle is this: *What is the difference between love and time?*

I'm stumped.

We get saltwater taffy and hit the boardwalk, walking lazily down the rows of purple and pink and green neon flashing lights and tinny arcade machine action music. Tickets spit out of the bank of Skee-Ball machines like cheeky blue tongues. A rusted-out mechanical pony plays "The Entertainer" as we stroll by. I say low tide stinks something awful. Alice laughs. She doesn't smell anything.

Mom gives me $5 and says I can play whatever I want. We pass the Happy Time Entertainment Inc Treasure Claw Machine, whose decal stickers have peeled and blistered until it just says *Time Claw*.

I stop.

Those things are always rigged, honey, Alice says then, and later in a narrow white room with tubes coming out of her nose, and I hear it in both memories, in the same tone, at the same time.

But I promise her I can do it. I'm good at claw machines, always have been. I look over at her, at Alice, her face washed in all the colored electric lights, and she is so beautiful, she really is, so beautiful and so unfathomably young. You never think of your parents as young, but god, she's just a baby. And so am I.

I drop a couple of silver coins into the slot and press the glowing buttons with authority—left, right, over, just a little more. Release.

The claw descends.

It comes back up with a crappy stuffed starfish. Mom and I start screaming like I just won the Megabucks, jumping up and down and hugging each other and she's kissing the top of my head and the WINNER lights are going soundlessly crazy because the machine's speakers are broken and then suddenly there's this kid standing next to me in a puffer vest and a Nirvana shirt and glasses and I know before I turn around who it is and was and will be.

"Wow," says the space-time continuum. "That was amazing! Can you win one for me?"

"Probably not," I say sadly. "Two in a row is pretty tough. And I'm out of money."

The space-time continuum hands me a dollar in quarters.

"I'll probably lose," I protest.

"It's okay if you lose," it says.

I look at my mom and she nods encouragingly. So in the money goes. I push the buttons again. I drop the Time Claw.

And what do you know? It comes up desperately clutching a giant toy it absolutely should not be able to lift with those pitiful skinny silver prongs. The claw looks like it's gonna break off the suspension for a minute. But it doesn't. It doesn't. It glides smoothly home.

I retrieve the mass of fluff from the prize bin.

It's a Cartoon Sparkle Rainbow Geoduck. With big friendly eyes and long lashes and a wide, smiling mouth. Geoducks are endemic to this coast. Some bright-idea factory must have had a lot made up special for this specific arcade, in this specific, tiny, trash clam town.

I stare at it. Because this really happened and I forgot it ever did. I am both then and now, myself in the Neptune Room with shaky swollen hands and myself at fourteen, frantic with hope and hormones, and I forgot this happened, because forgetting is so easy, little holes open up in the fabric of reality and you drop parts of yourself into them and you forget that your mother ever looked so pretty and so worried and so young, you forget that you won this ridiculous thing for a stranger in a tawdry arcade and Alice was so impressed. She looked at you like she was seeing you for the first time. Like you were a real live grown-up separate person and she only just noticed.

And then the Time Claw is gone and it's the end of the weekend and Alice and I are sitting in a hot tub with mold in every jet on a gray beach full of gray sand and hidden ancient clams. We finish singing "Don't Cry for Me Argentina" and she smiles at me.

"Have you figured out my riddle yet, Miss Grand Prize Winner?"

She turns to me in the water and wraps up my cheeks in her wet hands and god, her eyes are so green, it is impossible that any human's eyes have ever been so green. Alice's face takes up the whole of the universe. She barely gets the first few words out before those green improbable eyes fill up with tears and she's crying and lying in that future bed listening to the radio and holding my hand while she whispers:

"Baby, the difference between love and time is nothing. *Nothing.* There is no difference. The love we give to each other is the time we give to each other, and the time we spend together is the whole of love. Things will get better, sweetheart, I promise. I love you so much. My darling baby. I love you. Don't forget. No matter what happens. The answer is nothing."

She hugs me and there is no difference. All the time spent in love is one time, happening simultaneously, a closed timeline curve of infinite gentleness. The continuum hiding in all the faces of people I have needed and wanted and cared for and grieved, the faces through which I loved the world, all one, all at once, memory and dreaming and regret and desire, injera bread and lentil soup and sushi and champagne and running toward a pickup truck in the yellow afternoon, red and white Rainier beer cans and rhinoceros iguanas and orchids and plastic army camouflage–print glasses and psychology and physics and circular saws and Dazzle Dan feeding the birds in front of the Catedral and the Loch Ness monster's ancient reptile heart beggared with love for her baby in the dark and plants that are whales and whales that are plants and Suciasaurus rex and middle school and the countless infinite loops we get stuck in like tar and an octopus mug in orbit around Saturn and the Washington State Legislature and KHRT 101.5 and golden retrievers and red cars and Bob Ross and the emerald dish soap on the sink that made Alice remember her bridesmaids' dresses and just stop like a watch in her pain and the puddle that comes and goes with the rain and a house that belongs to a hill and Cartoon Sparkle Rainbow Geoducks and the smell of a newborn's head and Snack McCoy running after a ball of light in a universe without pain and there is no difference, no difference between any of it at all, it is all one thing, the only thing small enough to fit through an Einstein-Rosen wormhole—all dumped together into a blue plastic shark bowl with two straws.

Love in the vessel of time.

That's where Alice left her loop. Not in that bed twenty years later not knowing who I was or where she was going, but there with her baby in Ocean Shores, Washington, at twilight, somewhere between the water and the Time Claw, promising me ice cream for dinner while the space-time continuum looked on and kept the tourists at bay.

When she could still smell me a little.

When I was old and sorry, just so sorry.

There is no difference. There never was.

Nothing.

Nothing.

The lights twinkle in the Neptune Room. The space-time continuum looks like the Mr. Yuk kid all grown up, my own age still. It smiles from the doorway, silhouetted by sundown.

I'm holding something old and ratty and sodden with seawater in my hand. I don't even look at it, just sniff awkwardly and hand over the Cartoon Sparkle Rainbow Geoduck to the kid in the puffer vest.

"I won it for you, after all."

"Keep it," says the space-time continuum. "Happy birthday."

"It's not my birthday."

The space-time continuum looks just like it did in the beginning. And the end. And all points in between. It shines. And so do I and so does Alice and so does blasted, cursed Ocean Shores, Washington, and geoducks and all the ships at sea.

Cyndi Lauper starts playing on the long-defunct sound system because the space-time continuum is a cheesy fool and always will be. It takes off its glasses.

"It's always your birthday. Keep it. Keep it all. It's yours. I love you. I'm sorry. I'm an idiot. I love you. This you. Infinitely better than the lamp or the greyhound or the one I never made any mistakes with. I'll do better this time. I can be better. Come home."

Folk Hero Motifs in Tales Told by the Dead

FROM *Strange Horizons*

DOWN HERE AMONG the dead, our fairy tales begin at the end. So Skullbone—hero, trickster, corpse—plans to dive into the great Maw that rends the sea-ice far beyond our graveled shores. Against the frozen waves' mottled blue and glassy white, the Maw yawns impenetrable. It's the abyss that gazes back: a great round drain in the pure-snow world we woke up into. The rays of the midnight sun don't penetrate it. There's never been a corpse that leaped in and returned to sell the tale.

But Skullbone is the original corpse, the same cadaver who walked to the living lands and returned with his lover; he tunneled under the mountains and brought darkness to these lands of light perpetual; his metatarsals were the first frigid flesh to tread upon this windswept snow. So Skullbone ties a piece of rope around his shrunken waist and gives the other end to his fellow-corpses. "As long as I keep tugging the rope regular," says Skullbone, "let me be. But if I tug three times, haul me back."

His fellow-corpses nod. Truth is, everyone in the afterdeath wonders what waits in the Maw, but no one's been ready to take that last short leap.

"Here I go!" Skullbone calls.

Dead soles slapping the ice, Skullbone flings himself forward. For a moment he hangs suspended in cold air—his arms outstretched—his withered face tight with victory.

Then he drops into the Maw.

For a while, the tugs come regular on the rope. The corpses peer over the Maw's edge, but they don't dare slide their gray toes past the ice. Within the Maw—nothing. Not water, not darkness, not chaos. Just—void.

The tugs stop coming.

They haul the rope back, instructions be damned. It slithers out of the Maw with end frayed and no Skullbone in sight. The trickster's luck finally ran out. The corpses toss the rope in the Maw and hightail it back to their lonely village.

That was the end of Skullbone. If he's not climbed out of the Maw yet, then he's in there still. As for the rest of us, we stayed dead happily ever after.

That's always knotted my knickers—the way our fairy tales end. When I breathed and bled and sang, stories ran, ". . . they lived happily ever after." But you can't verb death. It's a sentence all on its own.

Still, "They deathed happily ever after" would be my druthers. But language grinds down even slower than the mountains that ring our cadaverous village.

Stories move quicker, at least. When you've got an eternity to spend, you craft stories for the selling and telling. Tale finished, I waggle my wine-purple toes near the lifeless woodstove—poignant irony, having a woodstove and neither matches, nor breath, nor kindling—and signal for another beaker of briny seawater.

Wort sets it by my elbow. Good sort, Wort. Best bartender we've had.

The midnight sun lances the tavern windows, striping my long waxy fingers. They lie limp, out of practice. With a brittle fingernail, I tap a rhythm on the beaker. Almost music. Not quite.

Someone else spins a new yarn's thread. I've heard every story before; this one bores me to oblivion. Some katabasis crossed with half-remembered science fiction. Leaning back, I gaze out the window. The frozen sea stretches forever, its meager skin carved by the wind. A few corpses stroll the shoreline, gathering stones for gambling.

I spy something new.

A small dark shape staggers across the sea-ice. Lurching, disjointed. No one I recognize. When eternity piles up like snowdrifts, curiosity bites deep. I half rise from my seat, ignoring the unfolding story as the diminutive stranger struggles up the shallow slope before the tavern.

It's a kid. Died early, poor sod—he looks nine or ten. Stick limbs poke greenish out of fluorescent shorts and T-shirt. Despite myself, I flinch. Corpses don't get chilled, but old habits die hard.

The kid slips inside, shoulders hunched as every eye falls on him. Not panting, but tensed like he wants to.

"New arrival?" Wort asks him.

"I—" His eyes flicker. "I came out of the Maw."

Almost drop my damn beaker. Silence falls sharp. The kid juts his chin against our gaping stares. "Yeah, I came out of the Maw," he repeats. "And Skullbone was there."

Before he went into the Maw, Skullbone traveled to the living lands. When he was a breathing man, he'd had a lover, and the longer Skullbone deathed, the keener that separation stung.

Beyond the corpses' village, there arose great mountains. To these mountains went Skullbone, for it was out of the mountains we had come. He told no one of his journeying; none accompanied him but the biting wind and the crunching of ice against the rock.

At the mountains' feet, the wind spoke: "Should you find your lover and bring him back, then walk you first along the path, with your lover following behind. Do not look back until you feel the snow beneath your feet."

Skullbone bowed, for in the land of the dead, the wind, too, has eyes. With strong gnarled fingers, he climbed, until he heaved himself onto a path which wound steadily upward. Singing to himself, Skullbone walked up the mountain path and into the lands of the living. He staggered into a velvet summer night, warm breeze rank upon his rotting flesh, the sequined stars pricking his eye sockets.

He stumbled to his old village, his deathly grace slipped away. And in his old bed, Skullbone found his lover. I cannot repeat their conversation, but at length, his lover gathered his shoes and coat and followed Skullbone into the night, his living fingers curled in Skullbone's dead ones.

"I must not look back," Skullbone hissed, "or all shall be lost."

His lover squeezed his hand. Sweat slicked Skullbone's papery palm. Fighting a shudder, Skullbone strode toward the mountains' distant gleaming. His lover's pungent breath dragged across the back of his neck.

A flare of panic kindled beneath Skullbone's ribs. He loosened his grasp, but his lover squeezed tighter. His red, red heart thudded like judgment, knelling in Skullbone's ear. The smells—the sounds—the inescapable warmth—what a mistake Skullbone had made!

"You must go back!" cried Skullbone.

"No," his lover whispered, with life's relentless resolve. "I shall follow."

Skullbone flailed and thrashed, and the scattered stones of the mountain path rattled underfoot. Far below, the midnight sun glinted off the village's silver roofs and Skullbone glanced down. The snow had not yet passed under his feet.

"You cannot follow here," Skullbone said. As the wind surged up, he looked back and gazed upon his lover's fleshy face. Splotched with tears and plump with blood, it snarled—and vanished back to the living lands.

And so Skullbone saved the village from the horror of his living lover and learned a valuable lesson: that is, always listen to the wind.

If you want to spark chaos among the dead—liven things up, as it were—fling the words "Maw" and "Skullbone" into conversation. As the kid crosses his arms, we clustered corpses gasp. Truth be told, the last storyteller looks annoyed, but even she's listening fierce.

I speak first. "You came out of the Maw?"

"Jumped in forever ago," the kid says carelessly. "Don't know how long."

Nods all around. Time and eternity and all that.

"But I met Skullbone there, and he pushed me out, and he's waiting."

Around the tavern, corpses sneak peeks out the windows, their leathery tongues licking dry lips. Everyone wonders what the Maw holds. But it's like dying all over again: no one returns to say whether it's utter oblivion, or a paradise more fantastical than this one. Which wouldn't be hard. This one bites, and not just from the cold.

Wort sidles up to me. "What do you think, Haydn?"

I'm the de facto leader? Kill me now.

Oh, wait.

I sigh. "Let's go see."

Not one stiff stays behind: beakers lie forgotten and Wort doesn't even shut the door properly. The ice groans and cracks beneath us: glazed whale-belly blue, veined with white and speckled with bubbles. The kid keeps glancing over his shoulder, until I trot to catch up. "What's your name?" I ask.

"Simon." A pause. "That's my living name."

Hard not to roll my eyes. We don't know our names when we're born, and we lose them when we die. But the certainty in the kid's voice shakes me. "Skullbone tell you so?"

"Yeah."

Not a smirk. No whining. Just a child's implacable logic. It sends shivers down my spine, metaphorically speaking.

Around the Maw, the ice rears up. White, jagged. Snow races along the roughened surface. If I could breathe, my lungs would crack with frostbite.

The Maw yawns, impenetrable as always. Absolutely nothing there. Certainly not Skullbone. The corpses lurch to a halt. The kid's shoulders slump. No one speaks but the wind, screaming around our dead, dead bones.

The kid bites his lip. Baby teeth leave indents in the pallid flesh. Turning his back on us, he plops cross-legged in the snow. "When he comes back, you'll be sorry!"

Wort snorts and turns away. Then another corpse, then another. One by one, the corpses trail back to the village, a slow-moving band of wizened bodies, bent against the wind.

Here's the thing about oblivion. The longer you hang around the Maw, the more insistently it calls. I find myself edging nearer, my bare toes pushing up crushed ice. They look like frozen grapes, the nails shiny-swollen.

"Simon?" I say, gentle.

His little spine stays ramrod straight. "He'll come back. I said so." Then, defiantly, "Skullbone never breaks a promise."

Before Skullbone braved the living lands, he yearned to bring darkness to the dead. For here, the midnight sun shines always overhead. Shadows never lengthen and days never pass.

But light perpetual wearies the dead like winter. Its rays strike the snow pitilessly; the chill is sepulchral. So Skullbone searched the afterdeath's far-reaching emptiness for darkness.

The ocean, he beseeched; to the wind, he pleaded. But though he crossed from horizon to horizon, he found neither shadow, nor gloom, nor pall. At last, he came to the mountains. Blankly they regarded him, bearded with snow and cragged with the wind's ravaging.

"Have you any darkness, among your roots?" asked Skullbone.

The mountains said, "Dig."

We bring nothing into the living world, and it is certain we carry nothing out. With only his bare hands, Skullbone thrust his fingers into frozen earth. Little by little, he tunneled under the mountain, wriggling forward like a worm. How long Skullbone dug, I cannot say, but how familiar it felt: the wet earth packed around his nostrils and his fingernails clawing stones from his path.

Far from the sky's blue stare, beneath the mountains' roots, there nestled a patch of darkness. Skullbone cupped it in his hands, and carefully he bellied from the tunnel. Once outside, he put one eye to a crack in his fingers. The darkness rested safe within.

News of the darkness soon spread, and corpses lined up nearly to the Maw for the chance to peek into Skullbone's clasped hands. Nor did a single look content them. Again and again they returned, until Skullbone's temper frayed.

"I can't stand here for eternity, can I?" he snapped.

But the corpses wailed as he turned to leave. Their dead fingers clutched at his elbows, his hair, his ankles. When he leaped, they followed. In a fit of pique, Skullbone hurled the darkness overhead, saying, "See it, then!"

For an instant, it blotted out even the midnight sun, and all the dead stood in the shadow of the grave. But then it burned away like mist, and only the light remained.

A long time after I reclaim my seat, Simon slouches in. No one glances at him as he slinks between the chairs and tables; Wort pretends not to hear when he asks for a drink. Sighing, I signal for an extra beaker.

"Where are you from, kid?"

Salt and snow sparkle in his limp hair. "The Maw."

"No, really."

"Really."

"Okay." My voice stays easy. "What's it like, then?"

Something passes over the kid's face. Not a shadow, not precisely—but then it's gone. Unease steals through me again, like wind off the frozen sea, but then he's shrugging. "I dunno."

Kids.

"It's nice," he ventures, at last. "There's . . . there's stars at night."

"They got nighttimes there?"

"Nighttime, daytime." Kid starts kicking his legs against my chair. "Skullbone goes on adventures every day, and if you're his friend, you can come. And everyone's his friend."

"Must get busy."

"No one cares." He sucks his lower lip. "They got all the games I played before. And no one says it's not your turn. No one's mean at all. And they got—you know those, like, candy tubes?"

My fingers ache, suddenly. What I wouldn't give—sell—hack off—for one hour with a piano. Half consciously, I press an old favorite on my thighs. Haydn's "Surprise" symphony. Sometimes I want to weep for wanting to hear it again.

"They got music?" I ask, feigning nonchalance.

"They got everything."

Melodies surge up inside, like ice crashing upon the shore. Mumbling an excuse, I wander to a group on the tavern's far side. They're retelling Skullbone bringing the darkness, but the words rush past. My fingers mark half-remembered phrases across my skin, dancing a pattern I can almost taste.

I walk out into the brilliant light. Stumbling, single-minded, scarcely watching my step. But I'm not surprised when I reach the Maw.

Empty and voracious, it gazes back coolly. I scoop a chunk of ice from the ground and hurl it in. Nothing happens, of course. It vanishes, disappearing forever into—a starry night? A swell of music?

Scraping behind me. Wort clears his throat, looking sheepish. "What are you doing here?"

"Due diligence." I try to laugh.

Wort doesn't buy it. For a moment, he stands on tiptoes, peering over the edge. Then his face clouds over. "Kid tells a good story. But Skullbone's just a fairy tale."

Yeah, he is. And the dead—we got nothing but stories. Easy to see how this one could get out of hand.

Still. Fairy tales have an annoying habit of being true.

*

Long before Skullbone found darkness under the mountains, there was another corpse with a story he coveted: a tale remembered whole from the land of the living. Try though Skullbone might, he could not persuade the corpse to part with her story. Tight-lipped, she kept it to herself, and not a morsel of it did she slip into another tale.

"I'll sell it," she said, "but only for the right price."

"I've a hundred thousand stories threaded through my marrow," said Skullbone, "and a hundred thousand poems besides. Some are true; all are real. What will you take for it?"

The other corpse smiled. "A glass of wine."

Only saltwater flowed in the land of the dead, but Skullbone gathered beakers from the village huts and strode onto the sea. When he returned, the other corpse scoffed. "I want no seawater for this tale."

"It is not fermented yet." And Skullbone placed the beakers in the window's sun. Each time he passed, he adjusted their position and shook them just so.

The other corpse watched, and fretted, and eventually asked, "What now?"

"They must rest in the snow. Do you know nothing about the wine of the dead?"

Embarrassed, the corpse helped him bury the beakers in a snowbank. There they lay, while Skullbone ignored them. "You mustn't look at them at this stage," he said sagely. "As you know."

The other corpse averted her eyes.

But at last, Skullbone uncovered his beakers. While the corpse watched, astounded, he whispered to them, each by each. When he finished, he raised a beaker to his lips. "Remember: only true storytellers can taste my wine."

The corpse seized another. "Let me try!"

But though she drank and drank, coldness and salt only met her tongue. The trickster corpse tilted his head. "Was it to your liking?"

She hesitated. "It—"

"Of course," he went on. "The richer the tales, the richer the body."

"It was wonderful," she croaked.

He smiled. "Then I'll have my tale."

Duly sold, truly told. Once he had learned her tale, he shared it freely among the dead—you've heard it, too, so we shall tell it another time.

Home again, home again. If I were living, I'd say that days passed. But there's no time in the afterdeath, only eternity. Ours is an asymptotic existence: nearing the day after forever, never actually arriving.

I try to forget Simon. Scrape the possibility of Skullbone from my mind. Since there isn't a stick of furniture in my hut, I lie flat on my back and watch the light play across the corrugated tin ceiling. Under my breath, I hum a mass that haunts me like a ghost. D minor. But I don't have perfect pitch and no way to tune myself.

If I could cry, I would.

I sit up. Rub my dry eyes. Curse myself once or twice, and then amble back to the tavern. Simon sits in a corner by himself, staring across the ice. When he sees me, he straightens with a guilty shiver.

No time to waste words. "Corpses jump into the Maw all the time," I say. "How'd you manage to climb out?"

He shrugs.

Sighing, I lower my voice. "You heading back to the Maw soon?"

"What's your name, again?"

"Haydn."

"Was that your living name?'

"No." I fail to keep the bitterness out. "I'm afraid Skullbone hasn't shared mine with me."

Simon stands up. Against his cloud-gray face, his eyes are wide and dark: miniature Maws. Then he offers his hand. For a moment, I stay there: rigor mortis rigid, cold inside and out. Silent as a piano with cut strings. But Simon doesn't flinch at my scowl. Doesn't turn away. Just leaves his hand there. Against my better judgment, I take it.

In the earliest days of his death, Skullbone made a bet that he could tell a story to fill eternity. "Once upon a time," he said, "there was a corpse named Skullbone. He knew a story that could fill eternity. This is how it went . . .

"Once upon a time, there was a corpse named Skullbone. He knew a story that could fill eternity. This is how it went . . .

"Once upon a time, there was a corpse named Skullbone. He knew a story that could fill eternity. This is how it went . . ."

He didn't tell it further. Everyone had guessed the ending.

He won the bet, though.

As we stagger over plunging cracks and wind-sculpted ridges, I croon to Simon what I can remember. Symphonies. Oratorios. Half a concerto. My fingers tense and release where they should, but the phrases start and stutter and stop like a failing heart. Like mine did, maybe.

The wind flings loose snow into my eyes; it stings my bloodless lips. To every side, the ice stretches gleaming to the horizons. Heads bowed against the keening gales, we stagger through barrenness.

Here's the thing about the afterdeath. When you first get here, you're relieved. This is it? This is death? Okay. This is okay. This, you can handle. Other corpses for stories and chat. Seawater to sip. Cold as the devil's ass-crack, but hey—we're dead. Chill's natural to us as warmth to the living.

But when that sun doesn't set—when you rouse yourself and the same story's droning on—when the ice and mountains crowd like claustrophobia made manifest—you realize:

This is it. This is death. Or worse, this is what comes after. Be grateful it's not total oblivion, we tell each other. But sometimes, I wonder: Isn't this oblivion, too?

The Maw's blank indifference weakens my knees. The wind roars over it, offended by its gaping negative space. Hand slipping free from Simon's grip, I kneel at the edge. Stray ice pellets cascade into the abyss.

"Should we wait?" I ask.

Simon shuffles. "Yeah."

Fine by me. Knees to chest, I sit on the wind-roughened ice. Stare into the void like I'll glimpse angelic choirs on the far side. But the Maw's emptiness sets my head spinning, so I retreat a little. Rest my eyes on the thin gray snow.

Simon's gone silent, his shoulders slumped.

"Chin up, kid," I say, even as hope sinks in my chest.

"Okay," he whispers.

For a long, long period, we wait. Just the two of us, sitting at the edge of the unknown. The wind shreds our dead skin. Peaceful and patient the dead may rest, but we're not fools. The capsizing feeling in my belly strengthens. By the time Simon sidles away from me, I know.

"He's not coming."

Simon shakes his head. Looking ashamed, at least.

I'm numb. "Did you make the whole thing up?"

"It was a good story," he whispers. "Wasn't it?"

Legend has it that Skullbone was the first corpse to walk this frozen waste, but that's bullshit. He wasn't a fucking Homo erectus, was he? Where do you draw the line, anyway? Did all the Australopithecus go somewhere else?

But the story goes like this, anyway. Once upon a time, well beyond the mountains of the dead, there lived a man. He lived, and he loved, and then he died.

And he ended up here. Mottled gray feet flat to the snow. Livor mortis flush reddening his jawline and the undersides of his arms. The first of all corpses wandered a senseless path through the snow and found only a frozen sea, a clutch of hovels, and the great Maw opening like a hellmouth in the middle of it all.

He wasn't a trickster, then. He was just a man, now dead.

He cried for his mother, his grandmother. He shouted at the wind and the mountains until his voice rasped to silence. Nothing changed. Nothing ever changed.

But eventually, we named him Skullbone. We told all sorts of stories about him. They kept us going, more than anything else. Lent meaning to the emptiness, connected us each to each. Nerved our hearts to take that final step into whatever follows next.

And maybe he never existed. Probably, he didn't. Maybe, in the end, that doesn't matter as much as the fact that the stories do.

Silence. Even the wind drops down, waiting for me to snap. But I edge nearer the Maw, my toes caressing the iced-over lip. Simon stays safely distant, his hands thrust deep into the pockets of his neon shorts.

"I'm sorry," he whispers. "I just—I really wanted—"

"You wanted it to be true."

At least dead hearts can't break. Blue sky above, black Maw below. My toes curl into the snow. Digging. Testing.

"Watch out," Simon says.

But no one falls into the Maw. Not really. That's the thing about the afterdeath. We largely don't choose when we enter it. But I think all of us choose when we leave. Eternity is liminal space.

I glance over my shoulder.

"You can't," Simon says, uncertainly. "It wasn't real."

"That doesn't mean it's not true."

Simon shivers and shudders, chewing his lip. With a smile, I offer my hand. For a moment, he stays there: rigor mortis rigid, silent as the snow. But then, possibly against his better judgment, he takes it.

Music buzzes at my lips as we stand at the Maw's edge. A requiem—I have to laugh. I'd expect nothing less. "Ready?" I ask Simon.

"Ready."

Down here among the dead, our fairy tales end at the beginning.

We jump.

MALKA OLDER

Cumulative Ethical Guidelines for Mid-Range Interstellar Storytellers

FROM *Bridge to Elsewhere*

EDITION OPTIMIZED FOR Terravo-Io run, 807 years after interstellation, by algorithm vermilionpatter

I. The Ethical Priorities of Storytellers Are

1. Protecting the safety of the voyage by maintaining morale and at least minimal harmony among the passengers
2. Providing the passengers with an improved travel experience
3. To the extent that it does not conflict with #2, personal growth of the passengers

Love trying to figure out whether hinting that a passenger should be less selfish or bigoted
  or controlling of their family
    Or rude to the staff
will mean unimproving their travel experience
  "travel experience" is an ambiguous phrase

  2. Providing the passengers with ~~*an improved travel experience*~~ *a pleasant trip*

3. To the extent that it does not conflict with #2, personal growth of the passengers
4. Narrative honesty

Morale Board: What do you like about your job, beyond the storytelling itself?

I grew up on Mars. We weren't poor, but we weren't . . . you know, it was stable, but there was a lot of work. And I kind of love how clean the ship is, and how none of it is my responsibility to keep clean. And taking my kids to the breathable pool, and the zero-G acrobatics, and the concerts, and the arboretum. They would never get that otherwise, not regularly and easily like this.

People always act all shocked and concerned about bringing kids on these trips, but I think the ships are a fantastic place for kids to grow up.

THANK YOU. Also it's not like they grow up shipboard and never step off. It's only 30 percent. The rest of the time . . . I clean and cook, my kids go to parks and stuff.

We do 45 percent shipboard, but yeah. I like the combination. And it's not like school isn't seamless.

This may sound a little soppy or whatever, but I really appreciate all the people I meet. The passengers, I mean. There are always a few rich jerks, okay, but most of them have really interesting reasons for traveling.

That too, agreed.

II. The Purposes of Storytellers Are

1. Distraction
2. Morale
3. Education
4. Human interaction

Distraction is often considered a negative: lack of concentration, loss of immediate experience. But what is lost when the immediate experience is that of being confined to a limited spaceship for long periods of time, and there is no particular need to concentrate? Is it worthy—ethical—to try to elapse time you see as an ellipsis?

Regardless of our answer, distraction is critical on the months- or years-long journeys of interstellar travel. This is not simply a question of comfort. Without distraction, the weight of infinite space, the territorial constraints of the ship, the irretrievable hours of life being spent in travel, the proximity of unknown and often disliked fellow travelers; one or all of these begin to threaten the stability of the individual passengers, and thereby, the safety of the ship.

With interstellar travel there is of course the additional stressor of unexplained interstellar fatalities (UIF) syndrome. Given that incidence occurs at approximately one in one thousand, on a single voyage these deaths would normally not be distinguishable from random or unexplained fatalities. However, awareness of the syndrome is high among the general public, and almost universal among interstellar travelers, and since no one knows what causes UIF or who is likely to be susceptible, first-time voyagers are often anxious about the instant of arrival.

Distraction is useful when you're terrified.

It is. Distraction is a fundamental tool in keeping passengers happy and content with their choice to travel. The intensity of the stressors in interstellar journeys necessitate correspondingly intense distraction. Storytellers are able to gauge, react, and modulate their narratives to keep passengers engaged in ways that even the most advanced machine-learning entertainment cannot.

However, it is important to note that even the most potent distraction is not sufficient for everyone, nor is it the right tactic for all passengers. Storytellers that hold themselves accountable for perfectly tranquil journeys for every passenger are likely to both fail, and flame out.

What about the problem of how much harder it becomes to distract myself?

Many Storytellers have reported on this difficulty.

Have you tried other media? I can't listen to other Storytellers, can't stop analyzing what they're doing, but I'm getting more into music.
    It's true, though. The other part, I mean, about wanting to entertain everyone perfectly so they're happy. And I don't even care if they're happy. I just . . .
    Feel like you need to do your job perfectly. Yeah.

Morale is of course aided by distraction to the extent that the latter reduces stress. But Storytellers are charged as well with making passengers feel pleased with their journey and reaffirming their reason for traveling. That is, Storytellers should select narrations not only for distraction, but to reinforce the decisions, principles, and choices that led people to the journey they are on.

But simply providing aspirational narratives for passengers to insert themselves into is unlikely to engage most audience members for any length of time—and the ones who do find it entrancing are likely to be the ones most damaged by it, or cause the most damage once empowered by it.

The balance is one of the ethical difficulties of Storytellers: how

Can we skip this part?
    What, ignore the most famous and obvious ethical quandary in the whole profession?
    Not ignore, just . . . skip the verbiage. We all know the problem. We've all come face-to-face with it in our work
    Not always face-to-face, it's usually subtler than that . . .
    Like when you notice who is identifying themself as the hero, but it's not something concrete you can point to . . . Or, once I saw some kids acting out the story I had told them, and . . . they were making the littlest kid be the bad guy . . .
    Okay, so sometimes face-to-face and sometimes we catch it out of the corner of an eye. The point is, we all know what it is already. We all wrestle with it in our own ways. And there's no answer, right?

So why bother going through ethical guidelines about it?
They have a point. Is this going to tell us anything new?

Education is not a required element of Storyteller work, but
most passengers prefer stories in which they learn something new,
according to surveys. The most common ethical question related
to educational elements of stories relates to what should be taught.
A nonexclusive list of topics that have not proved detrimental to
morale or passenger experience is available here.

Human interaction, calibrated to individual personalities, has
been shown to vastly improve both distraction and morale. To understand more about the importance of interaction, this section is
often used as a segue into speaking about history.

III. History

Initial plans for interstellar travel imagined that passengers would
be in induced comas within cryogenic preservation—more pal-
atably referred to as "stasis"—and that therefore entertainment
would not be an issue. It soon became clear that the medium-term
effects of stasis, as well as the difficulty and expense of employing
it, outweighed the benefits for mid-length trips. Interstellar travel
companies then relied on the same entertainment options that
had been used on terrestrial flights maxing out at twenty hours:
a selection of films and television shows along with a few games.
After travel of months at a time, the reviews, and the results, were
not good.

Can you imagine?

Pioneering interstellar line LunaNueva looked back to earlier,
slower forms of transport and began to model travel on cruise
ships: an onboard library of books and physical games to comple-
ment the screen time, as well as fitness classes and themed parties.
However, there was still a great deal of discontent and conflict, and
surveys indicated that people needed "an overwhelming reason"
to undertake an interstellar voyage.

Honestly shocked how long it took them to figure this out.

What? That people shouldn't travel between stars unless they have to?

Ha. No, storytelling. It never even occurred to them.

The position of Storyteller evolved separately in two main paths. In some cases, it was one of the duties of Human Experience Managers, Concierges, or Entertainment Directors; on other lines, there were dedicated Storytellers, but they were intended only for children. The first official Storytellers intended for adults were on the WarpSpeed line; they did not at first even include this in their advertisements, believing (perhaps correctly) that people would not find it a compelling reason to travel with them.

A coterie of talented Storytellers, some working in tandem on the larger ships and others communicating across the company chatspace (which is why we have such good documentation), proactively expanded their role and began refining the theory while documenting their practices. *Note: the algorithm responsible for this document includes personality elements accumulated from that collective.*

Passengers began requesting specific Storytellers, or asking which Storytellers were assigned to particular voyages. Intrigued, though still skeptical of the potential impact, WarpSpeed gave Storytellers more budget and autonomy. The results demonstrated the value of the position, and within a few decades all interstellar ships boasted at least one.

In the decades since then, Storytellers have become industry standard and, more importantly, are deeply connected with interstellar travel in the cultural perception. People planning interstellar travel expect Storytellers; more than that, they often preemptively imagine what their interactions with Storytellers will be like. They expect that Storytellers will form part of the stories they tell other people about their trip.

This puts Storytellers in an ethically challenging position: They are superimposed against preconceived images. They must continually create new narratives but also face claims of fulfilling expectations. Judging the line between giving someone what they want and what their professional mandate requires is often an ethical question.

Urgh. It is, isn't it.
I think about this a minimum of once a trip.

I bump up against it weekly. Do I perform my *jazz hands* Storyteller role with dazzles and sparkles or just do my job, do I . . .

> Do I tell this person the story they want to hear or the story that
> will promote harmony across the deck group . . .

IV. The official title is **STORYTELLER.** Discourage the crew
from using other titles, however apt; they can remind passengers
of the other purposes and undermine distraction and morale
maintenance.

**Venting board: names you've been called by the captain, offi-
cers, and/or crew:**

PropagandaBot

Mouth of Sauron

Word-mangler

Spinner of tales (I know it sounds charming, but that's not how it
was meant)

Just a couple of trips ago I had a space debris avoidance technician who always greeted me as "liar." He did it with a smile, right,
like it was some joke between us and that made it fine, and I let
it go until he did it in front of some of the passengers and then I
took it right to the captain.

> Good!
> Did the captain do something?

>> Yes, it was kind of a slog to push it through but turns out that
>> the passengers had said something, too. But . . . speaking of
>> ethics, I felt a little guilty.

> They have to protect your ability to do your job.
> They can't let that shit go. It has consequences.

>> Well, it's not just snitching, which he deserved. I started telling
>> stories in which the initial peril was caused by slacking space
>> debris avoidance technicians.

> Beep Beep Beep ethical issues alert!

Was the problem solved by a heroic Storyteller?

Ha, no, I didn't go that far. I hadn't meant to do it at all, but when I walked in and saw those passengers in my audience, it felt weird, and I got angry, and figured I'd lean into the "liar" thing. After all, "liar" is not . . . I mean, we're supposed to lie, sort of.

But also not.

And that matters. Like you said, it's how the audience perceives you, prepares for you.

V. Philosophy

There were initially two lines of thought around interactions with passengers. One, led by Gen 15342 Verin and Stilvanak Restal, encouraged Storytellers to observe passengers actively, draw what conclusions they could from both deduction and intuition, and use those conclusions to inform their narrative choices. The other emphasized that all people were "player characters," in the parlance, and encouraged engagement with each passenger as an individual, fully human and unlike any other.

It will be noted that these two are not mutually exclusive (and this algorithm contains components from adherents of both schools). Modern Storytellers largely blend these approaches, combining observation and deduction that allows for quick initial assessments with continuing care to avoid getting trapped in assumptions.

VI. Participation

As often noted in publicity materials, one of the great advantages to Storytellers, as opposed to recorded or automated entertainment, is their improved interactivity. (Less publicized, because less accessible to public understanding in current social frameworks, is that *human* interaction—faces, eyes, pheromones—also makes a significant difference.)

One of the main challenges and unseen skills of Storytellers is the need to calibrate this interactivity.

I have had groups where I followed all the approaches for partic-
ipation, and they didn't want to do it. Just tell us what you want to
tell us, they say. Don't make us work for it; you're the one getting
paid.

VII. *Self-sustenance*

There is a misconception that storytelling is an easy job. Less
stressful than bearing the responsibility for navigation, they believe, or piloting. However, entertaining people takes its own toll.
Narratives can unleash emotions, both in the Storyteller and in
the audience.

It's so true. I tell stories all day and then my kid asks me for a story
before bed and I can't come up with anything. I just . . . can't push
any more ideas out. But I feel terrible about it.
    We should do an exchange. You tell stories you already know to
    my kid, I'll do the same for yours.
        Deal. Maybe someday if we're both onshore on the same
        planet at the same time . . .
        Maybe!

VIII. *Why do you all do this?*

The stories. Not the ones we tell, but the ones we hear from
passengers.
So many reasons for traveling.
Shouldn't this be a sidebar or a morale board or something?
    Is this question morale-boosting?
I know it's weird, but I like the travel, myself.
I like living on the ship and going to new places.
At this point, I figure, we don't have a choice.
    Oh, I don't know, I've thought of spacing it all and doing some-
    thing else for a job.
        No, not storytelling. I mean we don't have a choice about
        traveling.
        Not everyone travels. Not that many people travel interstel-
        larly; percentage-wise it's really pretty small.

No, they're right. Some people don't travel. But most people travel somehow.

It's a compulsion.

Most of the passengers I meet are traveling because they have to. I mean, not because of some mysterious compulsion, but to visit family, or get a new job, or . . .

That's what I mean. Some people are compelled to travel, and that drags other people along. Whether it's because they want to or they need to. And—yeah, I just think as a species we move. We migrate, we travel. Even when it's difficult and dangerous and uncomfortable. And as Storytellers, we're along to smooth the ride.

THANK YOU FOR PARTICIPATING.
REMEMBER, ETHICS ARE CONSTRUCTED BY *all* OF US.

Contributors' Notes

*Other Notable Science Fiction and
Fantasy Stories of 2022*

Contributors' Notes

NATHAN BALLINGRUD is the author of *The Strange, Wounds: Six Stories from the Border of Hell,* and *North American Lake Monsters,* which won the Shirley Jackson Award. A novella, *Crypt of the Moon Spider,* will appear in 2024. He has been shortlisted for the World Fantasy, British Fantasy, and Bram Stoker awards. His stories have been adapted into the Hulu series *Monsterland.* He lives in Asheville, North Carolina.

• I have this sliver of a memory, from when I was a very small boy in south Florida, of a witch who lived across a vast, grassy field in a small house, where I was not meant to go. I went anyway. I remember that she seemed old, though her hair was blond, and that she was mysterious but kind. I don't remember why I thought she was a witch. In reality she was probably just an eccentric middle-aged woman who lived on the other side of an acre of overgrown scrub grass and tolerated this neighborhood kid ambling by on his own mysterious journeys. I seem to remember she gave me something to drink. At the time she seemed magical; who knows, maybe she really was a witch, and she fed me a potion which filled my head with spooks and spirits forevermore. In any case, I've never forgotten her, or at least the vague impression I still have of her. She was kinder than the witches in this story, who are far less tolerant of nosy little boys.

A theme I have returned to multiple times, sometimes against my will, is the relationship of children to their parents. And here we are again. The brothers in "Three Mothers Mountain" have been abandoned, though not intentionally, and the older brother is looking for a place to direct his rage. His anger is arguably misplaced, but his heart is not. He finds, among other things, that there is beauty amid the horror, which is a lesson I have learned myself, one which I hold close to my own heart.

KT BRYSKI is a Canadian author with short fiction appearing in many publications—including *Lightspeed, Nightmare, Strange Horizons,* and *The Deadlands*—and a debut novella, *Lovely Creatures,* forthcoming from Psychopomp.com. KT has been a finalist for the Sunburst, the Aurora, and the Eugie Foster Memorial Award. In addition, they cofounded and cochaired the ephemera reading series, a monthly showcase of diverse speculative fiction. When not writing, KT frolics about enjoying craft beer and choral music. Learn more at www.ktbryski.com.

• *What fairy tales do they tell in the Land of the Dead?*

My notebook doesn't record what prompted this question, but I was deeply amused by the thought experiment.

A lot of human stories yearn for love, money, power. What do corpses yearn for?

Playing with fairy tale tropes and tone could've been entertaining on its own, but as I thought about death and listened to requiems, suddenly I heard another meaning in the funereal phrase light perpetual: polar daylight, an unchanging blue sky. Windswept snow, a hole in the ice.

Sure, there's death. But afterdeath?

What do corpses yearn for? In a land of stasis and waiting, their stories became a way to craft meaning, to bolster hope, to let themselves down into the Maw and explore whatever happens next.

They're a way for us to draw near the Maw's edge, too.

This idea that even the Land of the Dead is liminal, a waiting place. They gamble with pebbles and carve chunks of ice into dice.

They tell stories.

ISABEL CAÑAS is the author of *Vampires of El Norte* and the Bram Stoker Award–nominated *The Hacienda.* Her short fiction has appeared in *Beneath Ceaseless Skies, Lightspeed, Nightmare,* and *Fireside,* among others. After having lived in Mexico, Scotland, Egypt, Turkey, and New York City, she has settled in the Pacific Northwest. She holds a doctorate in Near Eastern Languages and Civilizations from the University of Chicago and writes fiction inspired by her research and her heritage.

• In *Folktales of Mexico,* compiled by the late Américo Paredes (one of the founding fathers of Chicano studies in the U.S.), I read a story about a man who discovered that his wife was a monster. Any night the man was away, the wife stripped away her skin and flew through the air as a skeleton, terrorizing the people of the town and stealing infants to eat. To defeat her, the man poured salt on his wife's cast-off skin, thus killing her and saving the town. I thought about who the true monster of the story was, then took the tale's skin and turned it inside out, so to speak.

MARIA DONG is a prolific writer of short fiction, articles, essays, and poetry whose work has been published in dozens of anthologies and magazines, including the *Best American Science Fiction and Fantasy, Lightspeed, Augur, Nightmare, khōréō, Fantasy, Apex,* and *Apparition.* Her debut novel, *Liar, Dreamer, Thief,* is a psychological suspense novel with speculative elements that has been featured in Buzzfeed, PopSugar, Goodreads, *Forbes,* Shondaland, Electric Literature, *Good Housekeeping,* Gizmodo, and *Novel Suspects.* She is represented by Amy Bishop at Dystel, Goderich & Bourret. Although she's currently a computer programmer, in her previous lives, Maria engaged a variety of diverse careers, including property manager, English teacher, and occupational therapist. She lives with her partner in southwest Michigan, in a centenarian saltbox house that is almost certainly haunted, watching K-dramas and drinking Bell's beer.

• The initial seed for this story is from a Korean legend about a rabbit that lives on the moon, making rice cake and occasionally granting wishes. I had this vision of someone journeying to ask the rabbit to heal their sibling from a mysterious illness brought on by alien seeds that descended from the sky—but as the story started to develop, it took on a mind of its own, and I quickly abandoned most of that premise.

I adore this story. I think one reason is that the writing of it required so much blind faith. I had to trust in what I was doing, despite the fact that narratively and stylistically, there were some risky choices there: first-person plural, switching around between different timelines and prose styles. Earlier in my career, I think I would've been plagued by doubt, but it was just such a *vibe.* I had no choice but to go with it. It was so gratifying to watch the deep themes weave their way in—like the role humanity has taken in this living, breathing, feeling world and grappling with the exploitation of sentient life-forms; exploring the deep isolation that pervades modern society and how it drives new forms of connection; and even neurodivergence and just new ways of looking at the world. All in all, this story is one of my favorites, and I'm so pleased to see it appear here in this volume.

KIM FU is the author of two novels, a collection of poetry, and most recently, the story collection *Lesser Known Monsters of the 21st Century,* winner of the 2023 Pacific Northwest Book Award and a finalist for the 2022 Scotiabank Giller Prize. Stories from this collection were performed on *Selected Shorts* and *LeVar Burton Reads,* chosen for *Best of the Net,* and optioned for TV and film. Her first novel, *For Today I Am a Boy,* won the Edmund White Award for Debut Fiction and was a finalist for the PEN/Hemingway Award, the Kobo Emerging Writer Prize, and a Lambda Literary Award.

Her second novel, *The Lost Girls of Camp Forevermore*, was a finalist for the Washington State Book Award. Fu lives in Seattle.

• It's not uncommon for characters to appear to me as disembodied voices, for floating scraps of dialogue to be the first manifestation of a story. I also sometimes work through difficult questions by imagining two speakers on opposing sides of an issue; I suspect a lot of people do this, writers and nonwriters alike. What is unusual, though, is for a story to stay in this form past that dreamy, prewriting stage. As the world of "Pre-Simulation Consultation XF007867" developed, it became clear that the story had to remain a kind of unattributed transcript, unsupported by narrative prose. I don't think the ending would work any other way, and the anonymity echoed the two characters' initial experience of each other, the facelessness of service worker and customer, that grows more intimate and human over the course of the conversation. The story has since been performed by actors and translated into Czech, a language that necessitated assigning genders to the speakers, and I realized I liked how differently different readers could envision the characters, the ambiguities created by the form, and how much gets left off the page.

I had fun thinking through the logistics and ethics of the simulator in the story (and how ridiculous the rules would be when decided by a corporation trying to minimize its liability, as such rules usually are), but I think I was also exploring my tendency toward video game addiction, and escapism more generally—why I so often prefer virtual worlds to my own life. I can optimize a perfect day in *Stardew Valley* or *Persona 5*, while I only get one shot at each real day, inevitably imperfect and full of regrets. But I suppose this preference for fantasy is also why I write.

THEODORA GOSS is the World Fantasy, Locus, and Mythopoeic awards–winning author of the Athena Club trilogy, starting with *The Strange Case of the Alchemist's Daughter*, as well as author of several short story and poetry collections, including *In the Forest of Forgetting* and *Snow White Learns Witchcraft*. Her most recent publication is *The Collected Enchantments*, a collection of fantastical short stories and poems. She has been a finalist for the Nebula, Crawford, and Shirley Jackson awards, as well as on the Tiptree Award Honor List, and her work has been translated into fifteen languages. She teaches literature and writing at Boston University.

• Strangely enough, the last story of mine published in *The Best American Science Fiction and Fantasy* was also about a country featured in the *Journal of Imaginary Anthropology*: in that case, the country of Cimmeria. The journal itself was influenced by Jorge Luis Borges' short story "Tlön, Uqbar, Orbis Tertius," as well as my doctoral dissertation, which focused on late-nineteenth-century anthropology. In those early days of anthropology as a discipline, it often felt as though its practitioners were making it up—there are all sorts of assumptions and theories that would be ridiculed by modern anthropologists. But anthropology is a complicated social science, in which the observer is always part of the phenomena being observed—Ursula K. Le Guin points that out in her more anthropologically inflected short stories. It's a bit like cartography in that the map can never be a completely accurate representation, because human beings, like landscapes, are not reducible to a flat plane—of either pictorial representation or words. And of course this story, about the imaginary country of Pellargonia, also comes from my own childhood games of make-believe, as well as the adult games of make-believe we play when we draw lines on the earth, write names on a map, and believe that what we have imagined is real.

ALIX E. HARROW is the *New York Times* bestselling and Hugo Award–winning author of *The Ten Thousand Doors of January, The Once and Future Witches, Starling House,* and various short fiction. She lives in Virginia with her husband and their two semi-feral kids.

• There are, as the tweet goes, two wolves inside me. One of them went to grad school and understands that our popular conception of "knighthood" is a product of Victorian medievalism, designed to justify and romanticize state violence. The other wolf was raised by Tamora Pierce and Robin McKinley, and drools every time a fictional girl holds a sword. It took both wolves to write this story. It's about how we make heroes, and why, and who they serve. It's about telling the same brutal, bloody stories over and over, and what it takes to break free of them. It's also probably about the time I borrowed my brother's Switch and played a lot (a *lot*) of *Hades*.

S. L. HUANG is a Hugo-winning and Amazon bestselling author who justifies an MIT degree by writing surreal stories about machine learning and AI. The author of the Cas Russell sci-fi thrillers from Tor Books and the fairy tale novella *Burning Roses,* Huang's most recent book is the epic martial arts fantasy *The Water Outlaws,* which came out in August 2023. Huang's stories have appeared in *Analog, F&SF, Clarkesworld, Strange Horizons, Nature,* and more, including numerous best-of-the-year anthologies. Huang's work has also been optioned for film, translated into six languages, included in textbooks and teaching curricula, and recommended by the *New York Times* and the *San Francisco Chronicle.* When not writing, Huang can be found either buried in computer code or working as a Hollywood stunt performer and firearms expert. You can follow Huang online at www.slhuang.com, on Twitter as @sl_huang, or on Mastodon at @slhuang@wandering.shop.

• This story felt like it was racing the future. I wrote most of it in 2021, when nobody outside tech had heard of GPT-3. By the time I sent it to *Clarkesworld*, the "engineer thinks LaMDA chatbot is sentient" story had just hit.

In the six months between submission and publication, machine learning technology crashed forward like a tidal wave. DALL-E, Midjourney, and other art AIs made concepts like "training datasets" into household terms, bringing formerly niche controversies into the mainstream.

"Murder by Pixel" dropped the day after ChatGPT did.

The timing was so uncanny that several people asked if I'd written it in response. "No," I said. "I wrote it a year ago."

At first I thought the story had missed its moment. Science fiction speculates about the future; this story suddenly felt almost about the present. I'd wanted it to feel real—I like to say everything in it is true, except what isn't—but now I wondered if it felt *too* real. If the tsunami of advancing technology had made it already seem passé.

Then came all the reader comments calling it *timely*, and the Nebula nomination, and selections by people like the editors of this anthology . . .

It's gratifying that it hits with such relevance—but also distressing, that the world moved in this direction. Especially speaking as someone who finds this science so mind-bendingly cool, and who cares so deeply about how society might choose to use it. The biggest danger from so-called "AI" isn't Skynet, but has always been distinctly human . . . those who see a new technology and think *We shall use this with brash disregard to pretend greater advancement—to sell empty promises for riches—to troll and abuse and harm* . . .

No science fiction writer wants to see the future they warn against come to pass.

STEPHEN GRAHAM JONES is the *New York Times* bestselling author of more than thirty novels and collections, and there are some novellas and comic books in there as well. Most recent are *Don't Fear the Reaper* and the ongoing *Earthdivers* comic. Up next is *I Was a Teenage Slasher*. Stephen has been awarded the *LA Times* Ray Bradbury Prize, the Mark Twain American Voice in Literature Award, five This Is Horror Awards, four Bram Stoker Awards, three Shirley Jackson Awards, the Locus Award, the Texas Institute of Letters Jesse H. Jones Award, the Western Literature Association's Distinguished Achievement Award, an NEA fellowship, and more. Stephen lives and teaches in Boulder, Colorado.

• When I was seventeen, I left home and moved into a camper in a junkyard with a bunch of friends. I suspect this is why a lot of my stories over the years have featured junkyards. I know them. They're in my heart. But so is *Texas Chainsaw Massacre* 2. I've always loved how exuberant and over the top it is. And Caroline Williams's Stretch is at the center of it all, of course. Really, though, I always wanted one of those Camaros like in this piece. The doors are too long, always end up sagging, and that nosepiece gets loose, the decals fade fast, the buckets seats are always wallowed out from so many trips up and down the drag, but, man, when those Camaros are good, they're the best. So? That's where this story starts: junkyards, *TCM2*, Caroline Williams, and a Camaro. This is Joe R. Lansdale territory, too, though, so I had to try to think in his voice, a bit. And then, at the last moment, had to reach up from this carousel, see if I could touch that Carol Clover title . . .

SHINGAI NJERI KAGUNDA is an Afrosurreal/futurist storyteller from Nairobi with a Literary Arts MFA from Brown University. Shingai's work has been featured in the *Best American Science Fiction and Fantasy 2020*, *Year's Best African Speculative Fiction 2021*, and *Year's Best Dark Fantasy and Horror 2020*. Their debut novella, *& This is How to Stay Alive*, from Neon Hemlock Press was the Ignyte Award winner in 2022. She is the coeditor of *Podcastle* (a Hugo Award finalist for Best Semiprozine) and the cofounder of Voodoonauts Summer Workshop. Shingai is a teacher, an eternal student, and a lover of all things soft and Black.

• I've been finding ways to tell that bizarre strange collective experience that is tied to the word "immigrant." I remember in college making jokes with friends when we realized that white people who came to our countries were referred to as expats and when we went to "their" countries, we were referred to as immigrants. The difference being in which group of people had more access to resources. This story is the half-air feeling of never being allowed to settle as a Black or Brown person in the world, even when we know that borders are made-up lines. It is surreal how much power they have over who gets to live, and who has to constantly be fighting to merely survive. Actively dreaming of a world without borders.

ISABEL J. KIM is a Korean American speculative fiction writer based in New York City. She is a Shirley Jackson Award winner and her short fiction has been published in *Clarkesworld*, *Lightspeed*, *Strange Horizons*, *Apex*, *Beneath Ceaseless Skies*, *Assemble Artifacts*, *Fantasy*, *khōréō*, and *Cast of Wonders*. Mostly she's an attorney except when she's a podcaster. Find her at http://isabel.kim.

• "Termination Stories for the Cyberpunk Dystopia Protagonist" was born from my teenage delight in cyberpunk aesthetics, my deep affection for lotus eater machines, and my experience consuming narratives that don't love me back.

While I was writing, I was thinking about the *Blade Runner* movies. About *Snow Crash*. About *The Matrix*. And of course, about *Neuromancer*. It always interested me, how much of Western cyberpunk loves to use Asia as a backdrop, and how Asian cityscapes and populations have often been shorthand for cool, future, slick little cityscapes, reflected in the techno-orientalism of the '90s. (Not to say that the East doesn't have its own cyberpunk traditions, and not to say there isn't a permeable cultural membrane between the East and the West).

And it's funny how the cool girl in this genre (and the genres adjacent to it) gets to be competent as long as it serves the male protagonist's interests—but only up until that point.

So this was my riff on a "cool girl sidekick" character who learns to use the shape of the narrative and the character conventions she's trapped in for her own benefit, and who goes on to further trap the "protagonist." And that choice turned Cool and Sexy Asian Girl into the villain of her own narrative, which then naturally led to a character arc about making amends, and more importantly, writing yourself a better story to live in.

SAMANTHA MILLS is a Nebula-nominated author and archivist whose short stories have appeared in *Uncanny, Strange Horizons, Beneath Ceaseless Skies, Escape Pod,* and others. Her debut novel, *The Rise and Fall of Winged Zemolai,* is forthcoming from Tachyon Publications in 2024. You can find more at samtasticbooks.com.

• This story happened because a certain U.S. Supreme Court justice claimed that a right to abortion was not "deeply rooted in this nation's history" and I became irate in the usual way that archivists or historians become irate: I began furiously researching to support my rebuttal. Who was going to hear this rebuttal? Anyone who made the mistake of bringing up current events in my presence! After weeks of reading and shouting facts out loud to my spouse, my browser tabs were overflowing with articles about nineteenth-century sex scandals, abortionist nuns, and an ongoing frog apocalypse. At that point it only seemed natural to convert all my pent-up energy into a piece of fiction—which is, in the end, only half fiction.

MKRNYILGLD (Twitter: @MKRNYILGLD) is a biologist who has the choice to give birth—or not.

• On the day the Supreme Court overturned *Roe v. Wade,* I was working in the lab. Up until then (idiot that I was), I really had believed I had certain, inalienable rights that those in power wouldn't try to take from me. Well, on that day I was slapped in the face with this decision from the highest court in the country, basically telling me that I couldn't be trusted to make reproductive decisions about my own body. I had never felt so disrespected as a human being.

Then, as a biologist, I realized it doesn't matter what the Supreme

Court or anyone else thinks I should do with my body. With the aid of CRISPR systems, we can rewrite the DNA of cells in days, using equipment only a bit more complicated than what you might find in a kitchen. Quite frankly, we're standing at the cusp of a revolution. We have the power to alter our bodies to our own liking down to the molecular level—all we have to do is reach out and take it. I wrote this story because I wanted as many people as possible to see that.

MALKA OLDER is a writer, aid worker, and sociologist. Her science-fiction political thriller *Infomocracy* was named one of the best books of 2016 by *Kirkus*, *Book Riot*, and the *Washington Post*. Her novella, *The Mimicking of Known Successes*, a murder mystery set on a gas giant planet, came out in March 2023 to rave reviews and the sequel, *The Imposition of Unnecessary Obstacles*, will be published in early 2024. She created the serial *Ninth Step Station* on Realm, and her acclaimed short story collection, *and Other Disasters*, came out in November 2019. She has a doctorate in the sociology of organizations from Sciences Po and is a faculty associate at Arizona State University, where she teaches on humanitarian aid and predictive fictions, and hosts the *Science Fiction Sparkle Salon*. Her opinions can be found in the *New York Times*, *The Nation*, *Foreign Policy*, and NBC's *THINK*, among other places.

• When I was asked, by the wonderful editors of *A Bridge to Elsewhere*, Alana Joli Abbott and Julia Rios, to write a story taking place on a spaceship, I started thinking about travel: about long flights; and the time I spent two days on a boat on the Mekong; and all the overnight train rides I've done; and bus trips, from the Greyhound with broken overhead lights so I couldn't read (pre–e-readers) to the fancy buses in Latin America with huge reclining seats and movies. Once I came up with the concept of storytellers as a fundamental element of long-haul trips, it became a powerful parallel to working as a writer. What are the ethical challenges we face as we make up stories for people? I wanted this story to reflect the kind of collective questioning, venting, and support that I've found in so many online writers' groups. I'm so pleased it's been chosen for this anthology, and I hope you enjoy(ed) reading it (and that it fulfills its ethical responsibilities).

SUSAN PALWICK has published four novels with Tor Books: *Flying in Place* (1992), *The Necessary Beggar* (2005), *Shelter* (2007), and *Mending the Moon* (2013). Her debut story collection, *The Fate of Mice*, appeared in 2007 from Tachyon Publications. Her second collection, *All Worlds are Real*, was published in 2019 by Fairwood Press. Palwick's fiction has been honored with a Crawford Award from the International Association for the Fantastic in the

Arts, an Alex Award from the American Library Association, and a Silver Pen Award from the Nevada Writers Hall of Fame, and has also been short-listed for the World Fantasy Award, the Mythopoeic Award, and the Philip K. Dick Award. Recent short fiction has appeared in *Asimov's, Lightspeed,* and *Tor.com.* Palwick spent twenty years as an English professor at the University of Nevada, Reno. She retired in 2017 to earn an MSW degree and move into health care. She has since worked as a chaplain (in both hospital and hospice settings) and as a dialysis social worker. She lives in Reno with her husband, their cats, and her growing collection of craft equipment.

• "Sparrows" emerged from years of dread about climate apocalypse. Although I hope I'm wrong, I believe that the human experiment is coming to a rapid end. We are creatures of tremendous imagination and ingenuity, capable of producing works of transcendent beauty. We are also short-sighted, violent, and addicted to wishful thinking. We have ignored multiple warnings about how to keep the planet habitable for our species and many others. I wish I had faith that we still had the time—and that we will ever have the collective will—to take whatever corrective actions are still possible. I wish I had faith that any such actions won't be too little, too late.

What do you do when you know that your time is limited to hours, days, minutes? All of us will confront that question as individuals, even if not as a species. As a hospice chaplain, I've watched patients at the end of life turn to what they love: family, friends, art, memories of lives well lived.

Lacey turns to her love of literature and discovers strength in the wisdom of a writer who died hundreds of years before she was born. She and Ablethwaite, knowing they almost certainly have no future, take comfort in the past.

Lacey's paper is one I wrote during my own first year of college, many years ago now. I walked across campus on a beautiful snowy Sunday morning to put the essay in my professor's box. It's an entirely happy memory. I tried to find the paper when I was writing the story; I was sure I'd saved it, but it wasn't in any of my files. The conclusion, though, stayed with me. Writing about Lear at eighteen, I could not have foreseen how he would comfort me at sixty-one.

LINDA RAQUEL NIEVES PÉREZ (she/they) is an Afro-boricua writer born on a rainy night in Arecibo, Puerto Rico, which they often blame for their obsession for writing about water goddesses with stormy tempers. Their goal is to see more curls and fat bodies portrayed in the books they read. She has a degree in business, but is currently studying law with hopes to help make the often-forgotten voices of nonbinary BIPOC in Puerto Rico heard.

SOFIA SAMATAR is the author of five books, most recently the memoir *The White Mosque*, a PEN/Jean Stein Book Award finalist. Her works include the World Fantasy Award–winning *A Stranger in Olondria* and *Monster Portraits*, a collaboration with her brother, the artist Del Samatar. She lives in Virginia and teaches African literature, Arabic literature, and speculative fiction at James Madison University.

• In 1930, the surrealist writers André Breton and Paul Éluard played a game with newspapers. They rewrote articles to create strange, haunting works of prose. A report of a concert at an alpine hotel became a description of a weird gathering of criminals at the bottom of the sea. Scraps of text from back issues of a popular science journal found their way into gnomic commentaries on invisible ink, the behavior of mandrakes, and the life cycle of freckles.

In the summer of 2020, a surreal and fearful time, my in-laws dropped off a copy of *National Geographic* at my house. I decided to play the game of Breton and Éluard: a way to amuse myself and stave off boredom and negative thinking. The result is "Readings in the Slantwise Sciences," which alchemizes found text into a whirl of dream images, producing odd tales that retain their connection to our world in surprising ways. I highly recommend this game.

KRISTINA TEN's stories have appeared in *Lightspeed, Nightmare, Fantasy, Weird Horror, The Magazine of Fantasy & Science Fiction*, and elsewhere. She is a graduate of Clarion West Writers Workshop and the University of Colorado Boulder's MFA program in creative writing. Born in Moscow, she has lived most of her life in the U.S., in the company of mischievous dogs, melodramatic plants, and bookshelves full of fairy tales.

• I think a lot about fairy tales: their patterns and promises, what they still offer us, and the ways in which they fall spectacularly short. As a kid, I loved them for their happy endings: the guarantee that, no matter how our hero struggles, how we worry and wring our hands for them, everything will turn out all right. Today, I'm drawn to fairy tales' collective authorship— each one a living text, eligible for countless retellings, never so sacred as to be unchallenged or unchanged. Soviet-era fairy tales smuggled political critique past state censors in metaphors of apples and castles. Modern retellings find princesses falling in love with their fairy godmothers and rescuing themselves.

Back to that happy ending, though. It's comforting. It's predictable. It's only fair, really. It is also, of course, a lie. By the time I wrote "Beginnings," I was old enough to know that most of us don't get the fairy tale ending, not even close. In the case of June and Nat, queer kids living in an environment hostile to them, it's the king who thinks he gets to decide how things turn out. The story opens at the typical remove "In the beginning . . .", an echo of the old "Once upon a time . . ." The setting is some nebulous, nowhere-and-everywhere place. But the way the cruel king exerts his power, the way June and Nat are denied their future—it could be your town, couldn't it? It could be mine.

So June and Nat don't get a happy ending. My hope was that, by constantly returning to the beginning, by stubbornly *insisting* on the beginning, this story could refuse that unhappy ending, at least for a while. By lingering in an earlier time, one rich with anticipation and potential, it could permit our heroes happiness after all.

The bees and horseflies I borrowed from Pushkin's "The Tale of Tsar Saltan," a favorite from my childhood.

CATHERYNNE M. VALENTE is the *New York Times* and *USA Today* bestselling author of over forty books of science fiction and fantasy, including *Space Opera, Deathless, Radiance, Palimpsest,* and the *Fairyland* novels. She is the winner of the Nebula, Otherwise, Sturgeon, Eugie Foster, Mythopoeic, Rhysling, Lambda, Locus, and Hugo awards, among others. She lives on an island off the coast of Maine with her son and two very large and hungry cats.

• "The Difference Between Love and Time" is one of my favorites of my own stories, if one is allowed to have favorites. From the moment I was invited to submit to the *Someone in Time* anthology, I knew I had something really different brewing in me. I wanted to say something, naturally, about love and time, but also about the layering of experience, memory, anxiety, and hope that makes even our everyday, non–science fictional lives entirely nonlinear and recursive. It is at once deeply, deeply personal and attempting to encompass all the universe as a whole, as well as expressing some sliver of genuine love for all of everything involved in being us, here and now, the terrible and the gorgeous. It remains the only story I have ever had to print out, cut into pieces, and rearrange on a real-world corkboard in order to get the structure right. Somehow, ripping the story of a life into shreds and painstakingly putting them back together seemed, then and now, more fitting for this one than any other.

CHRIS WILLRICH is best known for his "Gaunt and Bone" fantasy stories, which include the novel *The Scroll of Years* and its sequels, and for his stories about the black cat Shadowdrop set in the same world. Chris's recent work includes "The Second Labyrinth" in the May/June 2023 *Asimov's* and "Runefall" in the anthology *Tales from Stolki's Hall*, edited by Lou Anders. He has been a deckhand and a newspaper copy editor, but his favorite "day job" has been as a librarian. He lives in the San Francisco Bay area with his family.

• Sometimes story ideas are collisions of two things whose impact leaves a crater in your brain that smokes up the place until you write down the result. The late, great Ursula K. Le Guin's "The Ones Who Walk Away from Omelas" is one of those stories that's inspired many a tale in reply (two memorable responses are N. K. Jemisin's "The Ones Who Stay and Fight" and Sarah Avery's "And the Ones Who Walk In," but there are many others). Meanwhile Gene Roddenberry's *Star Trek* and its successors have launched (at least) a thousand *Trek*-inspired stories, because idealism plus space exploration is a powerful brew. I'm not alone in imagining a collision of Le Guin and Roddenberry, because shortly after "The Odyssey Problem" appeared in *Clarkesworld* a *Star Trek: Strange New Worlds* episode aired that was also clearly inspired by "Omelas." I was startled—and then relieved to see they took things in a very different direction. I'm grateful to *Clarkesworld* editor Neil Clarke for his insightful suggestions and comments.

Other Notable Science Fiction and Fantasy Stories of 2022

SELECTED BY JOHN JOSEPH ADAMS

Acevedo, Chantel
    The Nightingale and the Lark. *Our Shadows Have Claws*, eds. Yamile Saied Méndez and Amparo Ortiz (Algonquin Young Readers)
Al-Matrouk, Fawaz
    The Voice of a Thousand Years. *The Magazine of Fantasy & Science Fiction*, May/June
Alexander, Phoenix
    We. *The Deadlands*, August
Armstrong, Joel
    The Roots of Our Memories. *Asimov's*, January/February
Bahgat, Mirette
    The Devil is Us. *Africa Risen*, eds. Sheree Renée Thomas, Oghenechovwe Donald Ekpeki, Zelda Knight (Tordotcom)
Barton, Phoebe
    A Sword Has One Purpose. *Lightspeed*, April
Castro, Adam-Troy
    My Future Self, Refused. *Lightspeed*, August

Chambers, Becky
    The Tomb Ship. *Lost Worlds & Mythological Kingdoms*, ed. John Joseph Adams (Grim Oak Press)
Champion-Adeyemi, Tomi
    The Garden. *Into Shadow* collection (Amazon Original Stories)
Chand, Priya
    It Takes a Village. *Clarkesworld*, March
Cherry, Danny
    The Brief Life Story of Lila. *FIYAH*, Spring
Córdova, Zoraida
    Tame the Wicked Night. *Reclaim the Stars*, ed. Zoraida Córdova (Wednesday Books)
Demciri, S. G.
    The Crowning of the Lord Tazenket, Vulture God of the Eye. *Lightspeed*, June
Dickey, Dominique
    Slow Communication. *Fantasy*, February

Divya, S.B.
  Two Hands, Wrapped in Gold. *Uncanny*, May/June

Due, Tananarive
  Ghost Ship. *Africa Risen*, eds. Sheree Renée Thomas, Oghenechovwe Donald Ekpeki, Zelda Knight (Tordotcom)

Fu, Kim
  Do You Remember Candy. *Lesser Known Monsters of the 21st Century* (Tin House Books)

Gidney, Craig Laurance
  Sigilance. *The Nectar of Nightmares* (Underland Press)

Greenblatt, A. T.
  If We Make It Through This Alive. *Future Tense*, January

Harrow, Alix E.
  The Long Way Up. *The Deadlands*, January

Jerry, Danian Darrell
  Star Watchers. *Africa Risen*, eds. Sheree Renée Thomas, Oghenechovwe Donald Ekpeki, Zelda Knight (Tordotcom)

Jiang, Ai
  Give Me English. *The Magazine of Fantasy & Science Fiction*, May/June

Jones, Stephen Graham
  The Backbone of the World. *Trespass* (Amazon Original Stories)

Key, Justin C.
  Quantum Leap. *Bridge to Elsewhere*, eds. Alana Joli Abbott, Julia Rios (Outland Entertainment)

Khanna, Rajan
  When the Signal is the Noise. *Asimov's*, November/December

Kim, Isabel J.
  The Massage Lady at Munjeong Road Bathhouse. *Clarkesworld*, February
  Calf Cleaving in the Benthic Black. *Clarkesworld*, November
  You, Me, Her, You, Her I. *Strange Horizons*, Fund Drive 2022

Kriz, Aandrea
  Learning to Hate Yourself as a Self-Defense Mechanism. *Clarkesworld*, January

Lee, Yoon Ha
  Bonsai Starships. *Beneath Ceaseless Skies*, February
  Nonstandard Candles. *Sunday Morning Transport*, March

Lee, P H
  The Tragic Fate of the City of O-Rashad. *Lightspeed*, October
  The Turnip, or, How the Whole World Was Brought to Peace. *Lightspeed*

Leong, Sloane
  What Salt Will Bring to Bear. *Dark Matter*, March/April

Lewis, L. D.
  Last Stand of the E. 12th St. Pirates. *Lightspeed*, December

Liu, Ken
  The Timekeeper's Symphony. *Clarkesworld*, September

Ma, Ling
  G. *Bliss Montage* (Farrar, Straus and Giroux)

Machado, Carmen Maria
  Bloody Summer. *Trespass* (Amazon Original Stories)

Miller, Sam J.
  Iconophobe. *The Magazine of Fantasy & Science Fiction*, November/December

Myers, E. C.
  Hello from Tomorrow. *Sunday Morning Transport*, April

Nayler, Ray
  Mender of Sparrows. *Asimov's*, March/April

Ndlovu, Yvette Lisa
  From This Side of the Rock. *The Magazine of Fantasy & Science Fiction*, March/April

Palmer, Suzanne
  The Sadness Box. *Clarkesworld*, July

Palumbo, Suzan
    Apolépisi: A De-Scaling. *Lightspeed*,
    October
    Douen. *The Dark*, March
Phetteplace, Dominca
    Sword & Spore. *Tor.com*, April
Rather, Lina
    The Cheesemaker and the Undying
    King. *Lightspeed*, May
Sachdeva, Anjali
    Arbitrium. *Tor.com*, May
Takács, Bogi
    Folded into Tendril and Leaf.
    Xenocultivars, eds. Isabela Oliveira,
    Jed Sabin (Speculatively Queer)
Tanzer, Molly
    Les Chimères: An Ode. *The
    Magazine of Fantasy & Science Fiction*,
    September/October
Ten, Kristina
    The Noon Witch Goes to Sound
    Planet. *Lightspeed*, November
Turnbull, Cadwell
    There, She Didn't Need Air to
    Fill Her Lungs. *Lost Worlds &*

Mythological Kingdoms, ed. John
Joseph Adams (Grim Oak Press)
Urbanski, Debbie
    The Dirty Golden Yellow House.
    Lightspeed, October
Villar, Gnesis
    Girl Eats Girl. *FIYAH*, Fall
Wade, Jasmine
    All of Us are She. *Trouble the Waters*,
    eds. Sheree Renée Thomas, Pan
    Morigan, Troy L. Wiggins (Third
    Man Books)
Watts, Peter
    Critical Mass. *Lightspeed*, July
White, Shaoni C.
    The Kaleidoscopic Visitor. *Uncanny*,
    March/April
Wiswell, John
    D.I.Y. *Tor.com*, August
Yang, Hannah
    A Girl of Nails and Teeth. *Nightmare*,
    September
    How to Make a Man Love You.
    Fantasy, April

ABOUT

MARINER BOOKS

MARINER BOOKS traces its beginnings to 1832 when William Ticknor cofounded the Old Corner Bookstore in Boston, from which he would run the legendary firm Ticknor and Fields, publisher of Ralph Waldo Emerson, Harriet Beecher Stowe, Nathaniel Hawthorne, and Henry David Thoreau. Following Ticknor's death, Henry Oscar Houghton acquired Ticknor and Fields and, in 1880, formed Houghton Mifflin, which later merged with venerable Harcourt Publishing to form Houghton Mifflin Harcourt. HarperCollins purchased HMH's trade publishing business in 2021 and reestablished their storied lists and editorial team under the name Mariner Books.

Uniting the legacies of Houghton Mifflin, Harcourt Brace, and Ticknor and Fields, Mariner Books continues one of the great traditions in American bookselling. Our imprints have introduced an incomparable roster of enduring classics, including Hawthorne's *The Scarlet Letter*, Thoreau's *Walden*, Willa Cather's *O Pioneers!*, Virginia Woolf's *To the Lighthouse*, W.E.B. Du Bois's *Black Reconstruction*, J.R.R. Tolkien's *The Lord of the Rings*, Carson McCullers's *The Heart Is a Lonely Hunter*, Ann Petry's *The Narrows*, George Orwell's *Animal Farm* and *Nineteen Eighty-Four*, Rachel Carson's *Silent Spring*, Margaret Walker's *Jubilee*, Italo Calvino's *Invisible Cities*, Alice Walker's *The Color Purple*, Margaret Atwood's *The Handmaid's Tale*, Tim O'Brien's *The Things They Carried*, Philip Roth's *The Plot Against America*, Jhumpa Lahiri's *Interpreter of Maladies*, and many others. Today Mariner Books remains proudly committed to the craft of fine publishing established nearly two centuries ago at the Old Corner Bookstore.

EXPLORE THE REST
OF THE SERIES!

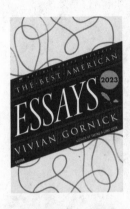

On sale 10/17/23
$18.99

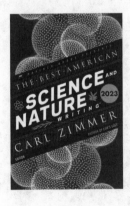

bestamericanseries.com

Discover great authors, exclusive offers, and more at hc.com